DREAD
IN THE
BEAST

Charlee Jacob

CHARLEE JACOB

DREAD IN THE BEAST

CHARLEE JACOB

NECRO PUBLICATIONS
2007

This book is dedicated to my husband, Jim,
who showed me there could be light in the unlikeliest places.

And to Dave Barnett,
who showed me the dark wasn't necessarily all bad.

INTRODUCTION

by Edward Lee

L et me begin this introduction with a review. It's a review I wrote for a long-dead horror magazine called *Midnight Hour*, and I'm reviewing *Dread in the Beast* by Charlee Jacob. Here's the review:

"I've been writing horror and reading horror for almost twenty years. I've had almost two million words of my own work published, and with all the stuff I've read in between, I thought I'd seen it all.

I was wrong.

I'd heard of Charlee Jacob over the past few years, had read a story of hers here, a story of hers there. Always good stuff, but in the every-growing avalanche of small-press and limited-edition horror fiction cropping up, I never paid this name much mind.

I was wrong.

The word "horror," of course, is a bad word now amongst most New York editors. The genre bottomed out in the early-to-mid '90s—a glut, they called it—and broke the field's back. Some of this sensibility is legitimate, some is not. All that aside, the horror genre did not die at all, it merely picked up where it left off in the independent press. Things seem to be turning up lately, though: New York houses such as Tor and Harper, to name a few, are suddenly increasing the number of horror titles they release per year. And after a marketing revamp, Leisure is supporting horror fiction to the absolute mass-market max, releasing two horror paperbacks per month.

To make my point, horror fiction seems to be crawling back from its own grave, and this is good news for the typical horror reader. A mass-market resurgence in the genre is inevitable—in fact, it's already started.

But before horror can get fully back on its feet in the average bookstore, we still have a considerable inventory of excellent material being actively released by the independent press, and one such book that deserves serious attention is *Dread In The Beast* by Charlee Jacob. To slap some tagline on her like "A feminist Clive Barker" or "A startling new voice" would simply be insufficient. Charlee Jacob, instead, is clearly one of the best new writers working in the horror field today. Her work *blows away* so much of the competition it's almost scary, and now a collection of her very best short stories is available in an inexpensive, autographed trade-sized paperback.

A woman with a burning-flesh fetish? A story in which a growing tumor proves as an apt allegory for modern society? Spiritual transcendence via surgical addiction? A deity revered by *human waste?* This ain't the Headless horseman, folks. This ain't the Wizard of Oz. This is, instead, serious, primo, important new horror fiction more daring than anything you've likely read. The only thing missing is a warning sign on the cover. With crystalline prose and images as concise as a piano-wire garrotte, Charlee Jacob takes you on an excursion through hell that might even cause the devil to reconsider the trip. Each of the 16 stories in this collection is unique, shocking, and brilliant, and the title piece is probably the very best horror novella I've ever read in my life.

You got thirteen bucks for some of the best horror fiction you could ever imagine? Then pick up a copy of *Dread In The Beast* before it sells out."

That's the review. Keep in mind the book I was reviewing back then is different from the novel you're holding in your hands, despite identical titles. The former, as mentioned, is an outstanding small-press horror collection released by Necro Publications, and has been sold out for quite a while. The reason for the sell-out can be found simply by reading the above review. Jacob's fiction, in general, exists several rungs higher on the excellence ladder than most of what I'm reading today. But remember, I'm generalizing.

And, back to the review, I was right in my thesis about the ups and downs of mass-market horror. Since those shaky days, things have gotten much better for the field and, conversely, the field has gotten better within itself. Charlee Jacob is proof. She remains not only one of the small-press' most distinctive short-story writers, she is now an actively published mass-market horror novelist.

But remember, I'm generalizing.

I'm also rambling a bit (I'm prone to that; I'm no spring chicken anymore) but I only ramble when I'm excited. You can tell by the above review that I was very excited about the release of Jabob's short-story collection. I'm even more excited now about the novel by the same name.

Look back at the review. I referred to the collection's title piece, "Dread in Beast," as "...probably the very best horror novella I've ever read in my life."

That's no bullshit. And my mind hasn't changed in the four years since I wrote that. Hence, the keystone of my excitement.

I'd love to tell you some of the devastating things that happen in this novel...but then I'd blow it for you. I'd love to describe my most favorite and impacting scenes...but I won't go to the trouble because Jacob does it better in the text. A recant by me would be useless and inferior. But at least let me say this: the book kicks off with what has to be among the most atrocious crimes ever depicted in fiction. It's a brick in the fuckin' face come Chapter One, and that's just the beginning. This novel *doesn't let up. Ever.* What's the book about, in a nutshell?

Folks, there ain't no nutshell that this could be placed in. It's a slot-buster. It's a category-defy-er. It's unlike any horror novel you've read, yet it's not obscure at all, it's not avant-garde or experimental. It's not pseudo-literary drivel or over-intellectualized pap. Jacob wisely harnesses comfortable formulae and then transfigures these elements into a total individuality. We don't feel hoodwinked by a writer whose ego needs to bury readers in self-pretension. This book is wonderfully different while not treading into perimeters of abstraction or experiment. With all the book's oddity, with all its intricate myth, philosophy, and sophistication, Jacob never once lets indulgence seduce her muse and run away with her. Her focus remains resolute on the "job" of any horror novelist: to entertain the readership. How is this accomplished? By delivering a solid story peopled with characters whom we can—however positively or negatively—relate to. I won't lay some clichés on you like "*Dread In The Beast* is a joyride through hell!" Oh, lord, it's no joyride. It is an exercise in the absolute darkness of the human heart. No "joy" here—instead, you're dragged *kicking and screaming* through hell. Wear a raincoat. Bring an umbrella.

In other words, there's no nifty tagline for this book. More antithesis: it's completely different while being exactly what any great horror novel must be. Its merit exists on many levels but chiefly in the manner through which it succeeds as a great read.

But remember, I'm generalizing.

Let's speak with more specificity. What's most unique of all here (and jealously fascinating) are the creative guts of the author. If there's an ultimate dichotomy in the horror genre, it's got to be Jacob. Call her an antipode. Call her an aesthetic contradiction. Imagine Raphael or Claude Monet painting a picture of a demonic rape. Imagine a sleek and flawless supermodel prancing down the runway in designer garb fashioned from human skin. Imagine a poet who writes with the finery of a T.S. Eliot or an Emily Dickinson crafting stanzas about trans-vaginal evisceration. This is Jacob, armed with a talent to write the most beautiful prose yet using that talent to examine the most unspeakable and detestable horror.

Here's an example:

> "This was her own poignant torture and then frenetic release. It filled her with delicious grief, then emptied her out again. Made her buck with her sturdy pelvis until she lifted him right off the mattress. Slung herself upward and across the ceiling like some metaphor for orgasmic levitation, then made all her flesh turn into frosted peach jelly."

Is this not beautiful? It's a young woman losing her virginity, for God's sake. Yet a moment later, here's her next observation:

> "She went blind for an instant, next saw the city's stygian shit straining at the window, matting itself in brown sworl against the panes, trying to desecrate this single pure moment of hers by passing through the glass by means of a feculent osmosis. It did enter the room, overtaking Dorien and Gavin, covering them in suffocating purgation until they froze in mid-thrust, fossilizing as ash-covered victims in Pompeii. It was evil coming in, determined not to let her escape through love, determined to drag them into the underworld which existed on a tide of worldly sewage."

Some "first time," huh?

Dread In The Beast is swollen to the gills with such fine, fine writing—hence, the lucid, gorgeously etched prose unveiling the most primal atrocities ever depicted in fiction. I won't reveal any of those atrocities here. I'd love to but I won't…

You'll know 'em when you come to 'em.

In all, to me, Jacob is what we sometimes call a "Throw in the Towel" writer. I'll read a passage by her and think: "Fuck it. Why do I even bother? In a million years, I could never write this well." She makes me jealous. I could never think of this:

"In the great house, she could see a hole in one stone wall of a bay which surely contained a privy. Refuse was falling from it into a stream which ran below, sluggishly carrying the muck to the heavily polluted river, itself clogged with corpses as if with logs."

Or this:

"What was touching this substance if not touching the proxy of oblivion, coming back to life with its stench in your sinuses and its secret madness yours to flaunt?"

Or this:

"Before tonight Dorien thought she understood what evil consisted of. It was graphic, intentional of blunt force and explicit with gore. It grinned as it turned cities into abattoirs, dancing without subtlety with blood splashed to further inflame already burning loins. Evil was extreme, unspeakable, relentless violence. Its aim was to dismantle you unto your most sacred atoms, rape your soul into uncreation, rip your sanity from asshole to lips, and snort the names of your most sacred beliefs until you were damned forever in the five-second high it enjoyed immediately after."

Nope. Not in a million fuckin' years. I could never come up with that if my life depended on it.

So instead, I'll toss my jealousy aside (all writers, deep-down, are egomanic) and tell you that it was an honor to be able to read this book essentially before anyone else. After all, it's a novelization of my favorite horror novella, and the result of that process is a monumental achievement in the field. It, too, was an honor to write this introduction—I hope it does you some good by at least conveying my admiration and my utter awe. I hope you find the same distress, provocation, and wonder that I found in this work. *Dread In The Beast* is maximum horror via maximum talent. It's one of my all-time favorite novels in the field.

Edward Lee
St. Pete Beach, Florida
August 23, 2003

"One does not...find dread in the beast, precisely for the reason that by nature the beast is not qualified by spirit."

—Kierkegaard

CHAPTER 1

The night was brown when Dorien Warmer lost her virginity. Big city, blanketed with pollution lit to the hilt. Nobody her age had an inkling of what true darkness was. What it had been before smog and neon became permament factors of alteration.

She'd been depressed lately. It wasn't unusual for teenagers to develop antagonistic views of the world. Dorien had decided it was a sewer. It stank the moment she stepped outside her door, air no longer sanitized through filters and temperature controls. She choked, heard corruption clattering in her lungs, wanted to spit—but was too much of a lady to do so. It clung to her skin, clothes, hair. The first thing she did upon getting home every day was to strip and shower, soaping up in fragrant foam, shampooing and repeating until the strands of her beige blond hair squeaked. She'd want to burn whatever she'd worn as contaminated, but that would be too expensive. She even cleaned her shoes nightly, spraying them with disinfectant. She wiped down her purse and used an antibacterial spritz on her jacket.

She wasn't really that fastidious, not obsessed with toxic and germinal contagions. It was the blasphemy she had to wash away, the filth of degra-dation...a logical expression of almost two decades of experiences here. She'd just seen too much of people and cruelty, of the rampant crime at large in any metropolis.

Why, just that morning, after she'd stepped down from the bus, and walked down the street toward the college, there was a gathering around a baby carriage which had been found in the alley behind a submarine sand-wich place that catered to the university crowd. Several had turned away to throw up or gag. This ought to have spurred Dorien into hurrying past without trying to see...but it didn't. This was a reflex in city dwellers that made it necessary for them *to see*. Perhaps it was a shared gene to be wit-ness to calamity, believing deep down that souls couldn't rest until outrages done to them had been solemnly viewed and accorded even the flimsiest or even most apathetic of prayers.

She'd pushed through the little collection of audience. Wished she hadn't—there must be that, right? To tell herself she didn't want to see such a thing, not her idea. She wasn't jaded or voyeuristic.

Her nostrils caught the scent before her eyes registered the image. Of the sight being just the dome of the baby's head and one doll-like fist emerging from under the congealed toilet the interior of the carriage had become during the night.

There was a gang in the city these days calling themselves (or had the media dubbed them this?) The Shit Detail. All their victims had been killed in a variety of ways which employed the excreta of the gang's members. And something was always written on the victim or nearby in shit.

An enterprising reporter had interviewed a professor at a college across town. This man, an archaeologist, had given an interesting background on television the night before.

"Outhouse graffiti," explained Dr. James Singer, "goes back to the Romans. They used public latrines in which a wiping stick was employed by all, unsanitary by modern standards surely, to say the very least. As the next person would wipe the stick clean before they used it themselves, he or she might—out of inspiration or boredom—be moved to use the matter clinging to it, deposited by the last person, to write some comment on the wall with."

Bile washed up Dorien's throat but she swallowed it back down. She felt an almost religious need to get to where she could read what the gang had left this time. Where would it be? Somewhere on the baby carriage? Yes, on its fold-out roof. The print for these messages was usually rather small, seldom easily read, especially depending on where it had been written. The sleek plastic of the carriage top must have been too slippery. So a page from a notebook (with a crinkled edge and three-punch holes, indicating a spiral) had been the canvas used. Then the paper had been fastened to the top with a couple shards from a broken bottle. As they usually did for their epitaphs, they used a bit of poetry or a quoted piece from some philosopher, leading the authorities to theorize that the gang might be made up of students from one of the local colleges.

The coprographic note left with the baby carriage was this:

> Why have all our fruits become rotten and brown?
> What was it fell last night from the evil moon?

—Nietzsche

Dorien heard a man reading it aloud, then cursing. A young couple squeezed each other's hands and prayed fervently. Someone else was punching 911 on a cell phone, babbling frantically into it to call for help that was long past possible. Another woman sobbed.

Dorien realized this last was her. Then, surprised because she'd have thought herself too hardened by now to react so negatively, she fainted.

Someone caught her and eased her to the sidewalk. When she opened her eyes again, she found Gavin Parrish bending over her. She knew him from her English Lit class. A handsome kid, almost inevitably surrounded by admiring females. Where was his gaggle today?

"Are you okay? Dory, isn't it?" he asked, face a mask of concern. "Police are on their way. We could get an ambulance for you if you think you need one."

"Dorien, actually. Thanks. It won't be necessary," she told him as she struggled to sit up. It was spring but early enough in the day that the concrete felt cold under her back. "My god, that poor child."

"Where do you suppose the parents are? I didn't see an Amber Alert on TV this morning," he said, helping her to stand. He shut his eyes for a moment and shook his head. "What sort of monster would you have to be to do that to a kid?"

"I hope I never find out," she replied.

He'd gone with her to class, the same one they both took. They sat together at the back of the lecture hall, almost too quiet, shocked. How was it they made a date to see a movie later? Dorien had been surprised when he'd invited her. She didn't consider herself to be especially attractive, probably why she didn't date much and still hadn't slept with anyone. She wasn't sexy or vivacious or even remotely fashionable. But he'd asked and she'd said yes, counting lucky stars one by one to have (however the ill-favored auspices of their introduction) the attentions of such a gorgeous guy.

Dorien hardly remembered the rest of the day. She'd had one other class in the afternoon, biology. They were studying parasitic flatworms prone to infesting the liver and digestive tract. The textbook showed photographs of invertibrate Cestoda (phylum Platyhelminthes) and the occasional drawing or painting of extinct or at least very rare species like the *aureum incretum*. Her biology prof, Leonard Landa, droned, "Called *'aureum'* because of its bile-yellow color, this pest was quite a problem in the ancient world where it bred in unsanitary conditions in primitive cities that didn't have the benefit of modern sewage management. Similar in appearance to many tapeworm species, it possessed a definite head, followed by a series of identical segments called proglottids. The head, called the scolex, bore suckers and hooks which allowed it to fasten onto its host. The body was covered in tough cuticle through which food was absorbed. It had no mouth or digestive tract and was hermaphroditic. Unlike tapeworms, the *aureum incretum* would live in its host without reproducing until fully grown, reaching a length of up to many meters coiled within the digestive tract. But it was only an eighth of an inch in diameter. Upon reaching this stage, it would then exit the host by swimming down the intestine and the rectum, sometimes killing the host but usually only causing a great deal of discomfort as the bowels were blocked and locked up for a time. Ancient doctors—when a patient was stubbornly constipated—used to quip 'he's raised a champion goldworm.'"

Landa paused in case anyone wanted to laugh. When nobody did, he continued, nasally and upon a single note. "The last time the *aureum incretum* was actually seen much was during the heyday of Victorian patent medicines. Ladies would ingest one to keep them slim enough a man could put his hands all the way around their waists. Then one decided to swim downstream to spawn—as it were—while the lady in question was at a function attended by Queen Victoria, and this was the end of that particular fad."

Dorien felt woozy, leaving biology fifteen minutes early. She went home, showered and sanitized, then stretched out on her couch until it was time to get ready for her date. Maybe it was because she couldn't get the image of that baby out of her head. Or perhaps it was a case of nerves, giddiness at going out with somebody like Gavin, someone clearly out of her league.

Dorien didn't even remember what movie they saw. Some chick flick. Women in fussy clothes talking about their orgasms in high prose, profound pussies yack yack yack. He'd chosen it, perhaps to prove himself sensitive. Dorien always found those dull, preferring action to pretention. *Show me life as I've learned it: blood and guts, violence and sex.* Even if she'd never had sex nor hurt anyone. That wasn't the question anyway; the question was realism. Anything less was a sham, unworthy of anybody who recognized grimmer truths.

The theater was across the park from the university. She lived farther into the city, but Gavin had an apartment just off campus.

"Come back to my place first, Dory?" he offered, not pushy, not acting as if he expected her to screw him for the price of the movie ticket. But the scent of his aftershave was a scented, secret garden. "Sure," she answered, trying not to appear nervous. "And really, I prefer to go by Dorien."

There had been several students at the movie. Dorien and Gavin were hardly alone as they took off across the park. It was about 10:00 p.m. The moon had already climbed halfway up to the top of the sky, where it sat like a round caramel, sullied by the smog. They strolled across a bridge, in a group of at least ten others. When a scream came from the culvert below, everyone ran to the railing to look down.

"Hey!" Gavin cried out. "Don't! Hey!"

It was dark below. There had been lights but the bulbs had been smashed. It was hard to make out the black-clad group as they attacked some hapless, homeless old woman. Their victim managed only the single shriek before something scooped from the ground was thrust down her throat to shut her up. She'd been stripped naked and beaten. No one knew if what had been stuffed into her mouth was her own shit or a gang member's. Dorien heard her choking, strangling. A couple of guys ran to either ends of the bridge to scramble down the slopes to help the woman.

The assailants wore stocking masks, dark-tinted hose stretched to distort and conceal their features. They'd hunched over the woman and relieved themselves, now shaking their naked asses at the people on the bridge. From what she thought she saw, some of the punks were female. One pulled a pistol from a coat pocket and shot a boy coming down to save the woman. He—or she?—then swung about and aimed it at the other would-be-rescuer until that kid started trying to climb the slope again, slipping, sliding down toward the culvert.

They pulled their jeans up slowly-as-you-please, understanding full well there was an indignant audience overhead. They didn't even care that someone had turned a video camera on them, getting their fifteen minutes of fame. Fuck yeah! Well, if that camera lacked night vision, they wouldn't get much. So it was no big deal that this was the first time anybody had witnessed one of The Shit Detail's crimes. How much did they really see? Dorien assumed they were leering and sneering under the stocking masks, but there was no way to know for certain. It was strange how silent they were, not gesturing and shouting obscenities. Yet when they ran off, they howled and yipped for about fifteen seconds, raising the hair along her arms and on her scalp.

She clung to Gavin, frozen with horror but also oddly detached. As if watching a crime as it was committed a long time ago...or somehow witnessing an act destined to come about painfully, atrociously in the future.

Was this the worst thing she'd ever seen? Or had the baby carriage been that? How did you measure atrocity? Was there a point system for grading, so much for each participant and more for every perversion? Did each blow count? Every drop of blood or splinter of bone or inch of greasy coprolith?

Was gang defilement necessarily worse on a scale of one to ten than murder, and ought there to be a greater distinction made if the victim took an especially long time to die? Before tonight Dorien thought she understood what evil consisted of. It was graphic, intentional of blunt force and explicit with gore. It grinned as it turned cities into abattoirs, dancing without subtlety with blood splashed to further inflame already burning loins. Evil was extreme, unspeakable, relentless violence. Its aim was to dismantle you unto your most sacred atoms, rape your soul into uncreation, rip your sanity from asshole to lips, and snort the names of your most sacred beliefs until you were damned forever in the five second high it enjoyed immediately after. She seemed to have eagle eyes, seeing down into the dark so clearly, senses at a crucial peak she wouldn't have thought possible. She saw the bloody mass as it leaked from the old woman's torn rectum where something—a bottle or piece of brick—had been forced. She heard her wheezing the final breath. Smelled rust and uric acid and earthy stool. Tasted from the air the spaghetti the woman had found in the trash outside an Italian restaurant, her last meal. Felt her own sphincter muscle clench. Read the message written on the hard culvert wall, printed in darkness in the dark, in a spot where the lights from the bridge didn't shine. So how could she see that? What? Did she suddenly have super powers?

> A small black angel getting sick
> From eating too much licorice stick.
> He takes a shit, then disappears;
> But as the empty darkness clears,
> Beneath the moon his shit remains
> Like dirty blood in dirty drains.
>
> —Rimbaud

Dorien's vision abruptly spiralled, turning round and round faster, faster, clockwise and completely lightless. Then she was in Gavin's arms, hearing him shout, then whisper her name. "Do you do this often, Dory?" he asked when she finally came around.

"Do what?" she wanted to know. Did he guess she'd just had these sensations, like some smutty savant?

"Faint," he clarified. "You know, you almost tumbled over the railing."

"I never faint," she said. "Twice today is a coincidence."

He managed a subdued chuckle. "Sure you're not pregnant?"

She smiled back, rueful. "That I'm positive I could not be."

And she added in a whisper, "It's Dorien…"

'Dory' had always sounded infantile to her. It was demeaning to be rendered down to the childish component. As if you didn't have even the remotest possibility of survival. Her father had always called her Dory, a growl that drifted down the hallway as he prowled it. Sirens in the distance came nearer, sound gargled in the clotted atmosphere. Several of the witnesses on the bridge had gone down to help the boy the one gang member had shot. From his moans and gasps, it was obvious he still lived, even as he clutched his gut and bent double in the shadows. A couple others checked the old woman but only shook their heads, hands pressed protectively against their noses and mouths, keeping out the stink—and shielding themselves from the invasion of evil.

Gavin and Dorien remained long enough to give statements to the police. She'd started shivering even though the night was warm yet. Gavin took off his shirt and wrapped it around her. It made her feel guilty, noticing how muscular he was, broad-shouldered, narrow-waisted, washboard abs. This was inappropiately arousing, moistening her between the thighs as an emergency crew loaded the old woman's corpse into the back of an ambulance. *Shame on me, shame shame. How can I allow myself to feel steamy? Guess I'm no better than a jungle creature myself.*

They continued their walk to his apartment. She really should have just gone home but she shook too much. He wouldn't hear of it. "I think you need to sit down and rest first. My place is just right over there, quarter of a mile tops."

He kept his arm around her to help hold her up. Then once inside his door, he led her to the sofa and got her a glass of sherry. Could you believe that? In this age of imported beer and flavored wine coolers, he gave her a glass of sherry for chrissakes. Amontillado, pale in the glass. Its flavor was high and dry, no note of sweetness in it. Nothing of the taste of alimentary-processed, garbage can spaghetti.

He gave her this romantic swill, then held her, stroked her wheat hair, studying it with an admiration that said he could tell it was natural—not dyed. She'd wilted from the sheer stress of the day. Coming upon the scenes of two separate murders was extreme even by the standards of their city, which had from time to time been the murder capital of the country. She couldn't just flip it off as simply more random acts in homey hell. She felt unclean and knew that once she reached home, she would indeed be burning this set of clothes."

"Would you like a hot bath, Dory?" he suggested. How had he realized that? Could he be the perfect man? "Of course you would! After something that nasty…"

And this time she didn't bother correcting him on how she preferred her name to be. She was starting to think she liked the way he said it: no growl, no thrum from the jungle.

He ran the bath, pouring in foaming soap which smelled of vanilla. He gently removed her dress, panties, bra. Carried her to the tub like she was a child who'd been pushed down at a river bank. Still naked to the waist so there was no need to roll up his sleeves, he washed her, caressed with strong yet tender hands. Gavin massaged the horror right out of her back, arms, legs.

This is a dream, she thought. *And I've no plans to wake up for a while, thank you.*

Could he be for real? Dorien didn't know, not having anyone to compare him with. But she'd heard other women talk. She'd heard them bitch was more like it. Drunken, selfish dicks, the lot of mankind. Didn't care, didn't call.

No, Gavin was wonderful. If he wasn't, then how come he always had so many females chasing him? He possessed the raw, magical talent to banish evil from the moment, disarming its threat with holy finesse. He anointed her into believing there might be hope yet.

Damn, did that sound like emotional drivel? Right out of a vapid paperback with a couple on horseback, riding across the beach? Fragile lady and Renaissance hunk? Well, so what? It's how Gavin made her feel: safe, cherished, redeemed as only love could do it—a heart at a time. She was glad she'd saved herself for a man like him. (Actually, she hadn't saved it. She wasn't a saint or made of particularly moral stuff. It just hadn't been asked for prior to this.)

Dorien's alter-ego (who liked to believe she was so tough) knelt in a corner of her subconscious, stuck not just two fingers or three fingers down her throat in the gag joke choke but the entire bulemic fist. Puked up roses and kittens and cooing doves. *Give me a break...*

(Fuck off, Id. This here's my moment.)

She stood in the tub as he toweled her off, then let him carry her to his bed. It was just a mattress with a bottom sheet on it and a single feather pillow. No top sheet, no blanket or quilt. He laid her down here and then began to kiss her. She let his fingers roam anywhere and everywhere they pleased as he whispered her name, "Dory, Dory..."

Almost sounded like 'I adore you.' Music. Fairy tale or wet dream, the heat inside her built until she thought her nipples and crotch would catch pink fire. Having sex for the first time didn't have to conjure up the images she'd seen on cable's soft porn. This was her own poignant torture and then frenetic release. It filled her with delicious grief, then emptied her out again. Made her buck with her sturdy pelvis until she lifted him right off the mattress. Slung herself upward and across the ceiling like some metaphor for orgasmic levitation, then made all her flesh turn into frosted peach jelly.

She'd bled some; virgins were supposed to do that, right? The hymen split by the man's erection and then a small amount of what felt like boiling scarlet spurted out with or without a startled feminine scream, juice of the proverbial cherry. Clinical, traditional, amazing. She rippled in all possible directions, out toward a contrapuntal combination of nervous laughter and freakish deaf-mute transcendence. She went blind for an instant, next saw the city's stygian shit straining at the window, matting itself in brown sworl against the panes, trying to desecrate this single pure moment of hers by passing through the glass by means of a feculent osmosis. It did enter the room, overtaking Dorien and Gavin, covering them in suffocating purgation until they froze in mid-thrust, fossilizing as ash-covered victims in Pompeii. It was evil coming in, determined not to let her escape through love, determined to drag them into the underworld which existed on a tide of worldly sewage.

Dorien bit her tongue, confused and angry. Where had that come from, so close on the heels of rapture? It was the baby submerged in monstrous scurf in the carriage, the old woman throttled with her own void. It was the damned brown night, arriving in buggery behind a bleeding asshole of a sunset. Because you couldn't help but be poisoned in a city like this, body and mind. Body, mind, and soul.

The hallucination, or whatever it was, fled. She lay nestled in Gavin's arms, inhaling the musk and spice notes of his cologne, his clean skin. Did she also detect something else? A foulness left behind from the lapse she'd suffered?

She let herself muse on sentimental schtick. They would never be apart. They would live together forever, never tiring of each other's bodies. Even if it wasn't true, she could imagine it for a while. And it might end up happening. Such things did occur.

She glanced toward the window again. For the first time, the night had changed. Not brown, not putrid with toxins and tricked out like a whore trying to hide her plague with cosmetics. It was black, velvet, clean. As if the apartment had been transported to somewhere far outside the city, far beyond the earth. She held her breath, it was so beautiful. How could it be that there was no light, no corrosion?

Gavin leaned close, nibbled her ear. He whispered sweetly, "Leave now."

She was distracted, confused. "What did you say?"

He gave her shoulder a little push.

"I'm finished with you. Get out."

She stared at him. He must be joking. But if he was, his face didn't betray the humor.

He shrugged. "Go away. Get out of the bed, get dressed, go home."

Outside, brown darkness against the window pane. Impure night. Inside, brief love affair with the "love" removed and "sordid" used to replace it. His game was not revealed to her but she crawled off the bed and, shaking, began to dress herself.

He also got off the bed, began stripping off the sheet and the pillow

21

case. Without looking at her—as if she'd already left the apartment, at least as far as he was concerned—he folded these neatly around the secretions their sex had left behind. He took a plastic bag from a drawer in his dresser and slipped the items inside.

She saw the bag bore a label with a name on it.

Dorien Warmer

So he didn't have trouble with her name.

And he had the bag prepared before bringing her there! He'd planned this humiliation?

He opened the closet door and laid it on top of a pile of similarly labeled bedsheets in plastic. His souvenirs.

He glanced back at her, arched one finely crafted eyebrow, and asked, "What? You still here? Would you get turned on by my foot up your ass? See these?" He indicated the bags of memorabilia. "This is all you are now. The sum total of your importance in this world. Get fucked, get sick with sores all over your body, get dead. I don't care. Just get out."

Dorien somehow made her legs work to carry her outside. She still dribbled virgin blood, warm in the crotch of her panties. The stinking night rushed to cling to her damp body. She understood she was just as defiled as the darkness.

++++++++++

Saint Francis of Assisi was reported to roll naked in filth. When he would do this he would cry out a welcome to Sister Death.

—Sacred Sepsis
Dr. Louis Godard and Dr. James Singer

CHAPTER
2

MT. KOSHTAN,
ZAGROS MOUNTAINS
1965

D r. Singer raised his chin, massaging the muscles in his neck, gazing up at the blue Persian sky where the sun had steadily been beating down on his head since dawn. He'd been too excited to put on a sensible hat, to even consider sunstroke as he carefully dusted earth from crackling bare bone. The air itself was icy cold as the expedition was thousands of feet above sea level. The Zagros range always had snow dusting its bleak tops. A man could freeze while still suffering a burn on his scalp.

The wind came up from a dead stillness. It seemed to suck all the air away toward some void he couldn't see. He briefly gasped for breath. It was easy to be short of breath up this high. One day, he scolded himself, he really ought to give up cigarettes. At least if he considered climbing cloud-covered peaks for the rest of his life. Eddies. Whirlwinds. Brown shapes dancing observed only from the corner of the eye, never straight on. If he let himself, he might hear gourd rattles, bells, flutes in such a teasing wind. The rustle of tassles on caparisoned animals gracefully crossing some ghostly meridian. The murmurs of captured women destined for a slave market. Oh, further back. Clash of metallic armor, the discordant cry of an ancient trumpet, not very different from the skraw of a buzzard overhead.

They had chosen this spot to begin digging for many reasons. Theories about decisive history, yes, there must be that. Some solid data to suggest *here* when so many others who were reinforced with myth and tradition insisted *there*. But Dr. Godard knew that Jim had sensations: of killing plains, death on a scale so monumental it left a psychic impression practically as concrete as a field of broken tombstones. Time skewed a bit, so that everytime he woke up there he felt dislocated, the way the body played tricks upon the mind just prior to passing out. The borders had a vigor to them, energy slightly electric, raising the hair on the head and along the arms. Even tugging at the hair between the legs, tickling his balls. When Dr. Singer felt that in a place, he knew there was something hidden he was intended to find. Waiting for him. Calling from the wind, flashing reviews of spirits passed nearby: sometimes dancing/sometimes bent and broken in dying mode/sometimes merely still and staring. He inhaled. Sandalwood. *Pimienta negra molida*. Rose. Lime. Mint. But that was faint. What else did he smell? It wrinkled his nose, rankled his midwestern sensibilities.

"Sir, sir!"

He looked up, the wind and its spectral natives and even the disturbing odor vanished. Moments of such locational phenomena were rare enough. He decided not to give in to being annoyed at the disturbance. After all, he knew he wasn't alone here. And the vision, moderate as it had been, might only have been announcing that the occult (read at its strictest definition: being "hidden") was about to be glimpsed. He grinned as Hassan came running to the edge of the dig. "Yes, here I am. What is it?"

"Dr. Godard say hurry," the youth declared, sputtering at the hole Jim Singer sat in. The boy's breath smelled of goat cheese and the bitter coffee the locals preferred. It took so long to make coffee at the dig, in the mornings. At this height among the skies, it took forever for water to get hot, even though it came to a boil fast. "He has found something he say is unusual."

Early yesterday Jim might have expected a chariot, or part of one anyway. Or possibly even a snarling bronze lion, like the ones used as standard weights at the royal treasury in Susa. Perhaps even a cache of gold darics, the coin from King Darius' realm of the fifth century B.C. If it hadn't been for what they dug up only ten or so hours before, that is.

The expedition hadn't made much headway at this location, in a scientifically unpopular attempt to forge a link with Mt. Koshtan and the ancient Royal Road which had run for 1,600 miles in the old Persian civilization. Everyone in the archeological community had laughed when Louis Godard and his young protégé proposed this mountain as a remote place where Darius had taken on the Scythians. The skeptics had pointed out that this was a long way from the Black Sea and Thrace, which had been the locational spearhead of Darius' offensive against the horse culture nomads. But the Frenchman and his American associate couldn't be dismissed, and indeed had been heartened by last night's unearthing of approximately one hundred skulls which had their tops removed and edges sanded. Something in the soil served to keep them from turning to dust. The Scythians were infamous for using the skulls of their battle-slain enemies as drinking vessels.

Jim sensed death here. Godard agreed, having seen the younger man's insight work on previous occasions, including when Jim had only been a student of his at the university. Much of reactionary theory must derive from inspiration. And the twenty-two-year-old (a rather tender age at which to have a doctorate degree) suffered a strong sense of *frisson* when near an authentic site of not only important history but bloody history. Death could have, and probably had happened, just about everywhere, but sometimes an event or events were so powerful that an imprint was left. Not really a haunting but a recording: the way that lightning sometimes etched glass, and atom bombs going off could leave a shadowy umbra upon a wall to mark where someone had been and then had been disintegrated. If this intuition sometimes made for rogue science, so be it.

The men had been ecstatic, had danced a jig together that left Hassan puzzled. Had the thin atmosphere driven them mad? But closer inspection had suggested that these bones were far too old. Possibly as many as twenty or thirty thousand years older than what they were looking for. Carbon dating would back this up. The expedition had found a verifiably ancient site all right, but it was a prehistoric one. Not Darius, not the Scythians. Not even young Persia in the time of Babylon or even the first of the bloody pyramids in Egypt. Back before silk, before linen. Before the wheel. Long before the Bronze Age and into the Stone.

This was not necessarily bad news. Millions of people had lived and died in the Paleolithic eras but only a few hundred of them had ever been dug up. Bones didn't always fossilize; sometimes they disintegrated and became part of the dust the singing wind cast into your eyes or lay far down as silt in the strata of the decomposed of ages. To find evidence of a community that old in this location was still a career-maker.

Many great discoveries had been made while the industrious were busy seeking something else. A lot of earth-shaking finds had been accidents.

Just look at the Dead Sea Scrolls.

Jim was so intent on what he was doing that it hadn't even occurred to him that Louis Godard had left to find a rock to piss behind several hours ago. Well, they'd both had a mite more than usual to drink last night. Each had brought spirits—not the wind-borne kind. Godard had carried brandy up the mountain and Jim Singer had packed Scotch. They'd been celebrating. Up this high, a man didn't ignore the pressure of his bladder. Like the water for coffee, it boiled long before it got hot.

Jim followed the boy up out of the dig, asking, "What is it, Hassan? More skulls? Or tools?"

"No, sir. Dr. Godard find a cave," the boy replied, quick bare feet beginning a steep climb into the tumble of jagged rocks.

"Really! Here?" Jim exclaimed, having visions of a Middle Eastern Lascaux. The colleges would do better than accept them now; they would make them gods. "Has he been inside enough to see if there are paintings?"

"No painting, just dead," the boy answered, hissing the words under his breath as if in awe. As if this sort of thing was not what he'd signed on for.

The opening was a crevice, barely perceivable behind a limestone outcropping shaped like a battlement of stone axes. The two wriggled into it, the boy snapping on a flashlight once within. But after getting through it, the cave quickly flared out, easily tall enough to stand up in, getting larger a hundred feet or so later. It was the kind of cave an entire community might have lived in. Or might have employed as a holy vault.

Louis was crouched with another flashlight over three figures, skeletons, laid out side by side next to a natural shaft into the bedrock. His eyes were bright blue, the color of lapis lazuli that the goddess Ishtar kept sacred. "Remember what Koshtan means in Persian?" he asked as Jim and the boy came up.

"Yes, it means *kill*," Jim replied, frowning as he looked down at the ritually arrayed remains.

"Curious," Louis stated, reaching down but not quite touching the first one. "What do you make of this?"

Jim knelt down, shorts crinkling stiffly, bare knees in the dirt. The well-preserved skeleton was female, belonging to a young woman in her late teens perhaps, on its back, the skull with jaws agape, remarkably whole for twenty to thirty millennia (providing these were to be included with the skulls they'd discovered outside)—as indeed every one of the three figures was in perfect condition. A clay phallus, shaped like a spherical sausage, was inserted into the mouth cavity, apparently applied with so much force that it had shattered most of the front teeth, and had been lodged into what would have been the woman's throat. In addition, there were smaller phallus statues in the eye sockets and a particularly large one—almost half a meter, a good foot and a half by standard American measurements—inserted into the pelvis. The leg bones indicated a splayed position of about three feet apart.

"And then this." Louis indicated the skeleton in the middle. Of another female, much younger than the first. A child of perhaps seven or eight. The jaws were also agape and the cavity filled with seeds that had fossilized in the arid environment. At least a hundred similarly dried primitive cherries lay scattered close to the bones, some fallen through the ribcage.

"And last but not least, this fellow," said Dr. Godard.

The third skeleton was male, at least twenty flint spear points among the bones. But the most curious—and ghastly—thing about it was the second skull imbedded in its abdomen.

"Ritual sacrifice," Jim muttered, scratching the dark whiskers on his chin. "Sex, harvest and war. I will guess that this man had an enemy's head stuck inside him before or, well that is to say, after he was speared. Interesting how the killers found so many spear points expendable, isn't it? A necessity for their hunting and self-defense, this must have been a very important ritual to give up something so precious."

Godard smiled even as the boy standing behind them shivered.

"And the seeds, I suppose she must have choked to death on them, poor child, even as the other one might have on the phallus. Although I suppose the older female might have bled to death internally from the larger, vaginally inserted one. Unless she was alive when they put the ones through her eyes and thus into her brain pan. Brutal way to go in any case, I must say."

Jim leaned very close to the child's skeleton, examining the minute fossils of the cherries. Why, he could almost smell them. Sweet. The wind shifted direction, howled through the cave's opening, ehoed along the bends and turns of the chamber in the rock, sounding not unlike the faint weeping of a child.

"Judging from the placement of these, I'd guess our little harvest girl had these fruits sewn into her flesh. I've never seen anything like any of this. It's quite exciting. To have evidence of this kind of ritual murder so long ago. It by far beats any of the nasty things we know of the Scythians doing."

(And it was hard to beat those Scythians. They had been masters of both dramaturgical and oblique violence. Ah, that was the way to secure one's reputation forever in history.)

"And the way they're lined up. Obviously a single offering, although multi-purpose in intent," Jim agreed.

Hassan was horrified, not only seeing the grisly scenario depicted there but also hearing how enthusiastic the professors were about finding it. Shouldn't someone say a prayer? Or do something to ward off whatever evil spirits might inhabit this place? (Is this what hissed in the wind? Angry at being disturbed without blood offered to placate?) Why would such things be done to someone if not to ward off demons?

The boy had sensed things ever since arriving at this spot on the mountain. Ever since the two men had pronounced, "This is definitely the place." He'd glimpsed movement to the side, djinn who disappeared when he'd turn his head to try to see them straight on. He'd heard the most primitive music. He'd smelled the bittersweetness of death and what died to decay even within death. Hassan couldn't believe the doctors didn't perceive what he did, or—if they did—they approached it with foolish curiosity instead of more appropriate, self-preservational terror. Now he inched away from the men, a bit at a time, thinking he might easily leave the cave altogether without them noticing, so focused on the skeletons were they. He could slip outside, get his horse, be halfway down the mountain before they realized he'd abandoned them. They didn't really need him anyway. What use did two crazy foreigners have for a sane guide?

Hassan wasn't watching where he backed up. Howling, he fell into the shaft in the rock.

"Hassan!" Jim cried out as both doctors jumped up. One tiny bone in the skeleton of the little girl moved a fraction of an inch, disturbed by dust moved from the toe of a boot. A single petrified cherry rolled like a marble.

They hurried over, Jim throwing the beam of his flashlight into the pit.

The boy had hit bottom at only about four feet down and didn't appear to be injured. But he was screaming at what he'd landed beside. There was the back of a skull visibly emerging from the rock. A partially submerged skeleton was on its stomach, arms and legs evidently once bound together behind with a single thong: ulnas, femurs, tibias and fibulas sticking up like a fistful of breadsticks. Except this rock was a very different color from the limestone.

Godard carefully dropped into the pit. Singer had always been overweight and he would likely have trouble getting out. But the Frenchman was athletic—even if he was quite a bit shorter (and older) than his colleague. He helped Hassan climb back out. But he stayed in, examining the remains.

"How do you suppose it became enmeshed in the bedrock?" asked Jim, running his hand through his longish hair to push it back from his eyes. He had the strangest—the strongest—sense of place and electricity he'd ever had before. And it actually frightened him, almost as much as it seemed to compel him.

"Oh, this isn't rock," the older doctor mumbled, feeling just a bit queasy, despite his usually detached perspective.

Jim Singer tilted his head, rubbed his hands briskly up and down his arms. He felt dizzy, getting the sense that the shaft for the pit really went down much farther, miles maybe. Into a vast underground network. *Well, it couldn't really be miles. It only felt that way, because that way came a sense of...not hell, no. Although hell was close by it, perhaps as close as a single layer of gauze or a waterfall. Yes, he thought he heard a waterfall...*

Jim thought perhaps he'd better step back from the edge before he fell into the pit himself. "What is it then?"

If the others had been sacrificed to primitive deities of sex, harvest and

28

war, then what possible personification of power would require a woman be trussed up and pressed down to suffocate in... For what even vaguely logical purpose?

Perhaps it was the beam of the flashlight but the Frenchman could have sworn he was seeing a womanly shadow flow across the stone. The corner of his eye, naturally. "It's fossilized shit, actually," Godard replied, suddenly wanting very much to get out of there.

+++++++++++

Buddhist doctrine esteems what is called "the foul sense". The student is enlightened while in the act of meditating upon decaying corpses. Through this act, the student will understand the process of birth and rebirth, realizing that what is pure and what is impure is interchanged.

—Sacred Sepsis
Dr. Louis Godard and Dr. James Singer

CHAPTER 3

SUBWAY TUNNELS,
1990

S he woke up, hearing the rumbling on the other side of a
wall. Parts of these tunnels had been begun and never finished; they started and then ended without tracks being
laid or stations being erected. Vagrants lived here. Sometimes
babies were born and grew up and died—without ever once
seeing sunlight.

She'd seen a sign back there. So she must have been at the
last platform. Perhaps she'd arrived at the platform on one of
the trains. The sign said Myrtle Ave. To her, it wasn't quite like
a map with an X on it, saying *you are here*. It was more like a
signpost in a dream, identifying the dreamer. *This is you*.

But she never dreamed. Did she?

"I am Myrtle Ave." She said it several times to fix it in her
head. "I am Myrtle Ave. I am Myrtle Ave."

It was as good a name as any.

She didn't know how long she'd been there. Well, she'd just left that platform and the sign which gave her what she'd call herself from now on. But before that platform? She wasn't blind or too pale so she knew she couldn't have been down there since birth. She could see in what illumination there was where she now stood, seeping around a corner from whence the rumbling came, that her skin was slightly dusky. It was soft and smooth. She must be young.

What was she doing there?

(No place to go.)

Where was her family?

(Didn't have any.)

There could be countless reasons why she had no memory. She understood this was a big city with hosts of evildoers, capable of crimes extreme enough to traumatize any young girl into the need to forget everything. No, not countless reasons. How did the beginning to the old TV series go? She murmured, "There are eight million stories in the Naked City..."

Not that she recalled how she happened to know that. Perhaps it didn't matter.

Out of the corner of her eye, Myrtle caught movement. A shabby creature shuffled into that circle of weak light. He called to her with greasy fingers tweaked and bidding, "Come here, girlie."

His voice was thick with cheap booze, breath rancid. His skin was a liver-damage grayish-yellow. "Come here, girlie."

"Hey! I seen her first!" A second guy jumped out of another ragged shadow pile.

"Ya did not!" the first protested, swinging away from her, directing that vile air in his mouth toward this other man. The second man launched into him, bending low, swooping in like a combination wrestler and cat. They began to fight. They bit and scratched and punched, rolling in the filth on the ground. They rolled toward a wall. One ended up on top with the other at an awkward position with back on the ground and neck bent to place the back of the head against that wall. The one on top commenced to repeatedly cracking the other's skull against this wall. The muscles in the neck twisted and she heard the vertebrae pop, even as the man on the bottom managed to pull a sharp object from his pocket and stab it into the top man's shoulder and side, once—twice—three times. The fourth time seemed to be on reflex only, but higher, into the top man's face, skewering an already bloodshot eye.

Myrtle hadn't backed off much, she was too mesmerized. She didn't move again until both men slumped, the top one tumbling sideways to the ground. She crept forward then, bending slowly in case one or both should show they'd only been playing possum and made a grab for her. She touched the neck of the top man. There was no pulse even though the body shuddered, causing her to jerk her fingers away. She noticed the object still embedded in the eye, not really deep but obviously far enough it had struck the brain. It was a fork.

She checked the bottom man. He still had a pulse but it was weakening. His mouth worked as if he was trying to say something, to cry for help perhaps. She wouldn't get close enough to listen. Whatever his last words were would never be recorded by anyone. They would enter the air as useless things, echoing down the tunnels forever in search of a confessor ear.

Myrtle went through their pockets. The top man had 27 cents and a piece of paper with a bright dot on it. The bottom man's wealth consisted of half a Payday candy bar and three quarters of a pint of rotgut gin. She ate the candy and the sugary dot, then drank down the gin.

Within an hour or so—time in the dark was hard to guess without a clock—she was hallucinating. She imagined herself with wings flying up and down the tunnels.

Myrtle found a pen somewhere and began to draw upon a concrete wall. Did she have any talent for it? No... But it was fun. It seemed to empty her mind out a little—even of things she didn't think she understood at all.

Brother
And She,
on the
Crapulent
Sea

CAN YOU COUNT HOW MANY
CROSSES? (†'s)

CHAPTER
4

SHEOL'S DITCH,
1972

M r. and Mrs. Cave were both so high neither parent even knew that three-year-old Jason was in the room, concealed in the closet, watching them get it on in their bed of tie-dyed sheets. They had illustrated each other in non-toxic, washable body paints, obscene with finger monkeys and knuckle sodomite clowns. Darker shades were changed to watercolor pastels as they smeared and diluted with saliva, sweat and semen. The room stank of whiskey sours, musk, Screaming Yellow Zonkers, and a stiffly unwashed pile of clothes in a corner reaching halfway to the cracking plaster ceiling. They grappled one another fiercely and languidly at turns, fingertips straying out to gesticulate dragons, to trace invisible gorgons into the air. They babbled sappy Aquarian Age endearments, Sumerian blasphemies, hippie homily idiocies as the L.S.D. rocked them through the night hours.

The stereo blared out Arthur Brown (from *The Crazy World of Author Brown*). The record was scratched and skipping, the worn diamond needle playing over and over like a growling mantra, "I am the god of hellfire…"

"I am the god of hellfire…"

From time to time Jason would giggle, suppressing it behind his hand. Lord, wouldn't want them to catch him in here, seeing all sorts of paisley scorpions and polka dotted humdinger cobras watusi-ing across the topsy turvy rumps of his humping progenitors. He'd snagged a precious square of their best acid test paper and was tripping the spider bite fandango. They'd actually given him the good stuff a few times, just to watch him go strange and try to eat the cat. But after he'd freaked out bad on the last jaunt, Mom and Dad had decreed no more lysergia for the tyke.

"Welfare will come haul your tiny pink ass away, Beast," Mom had explained solemnly, using her nickname for her son, her eyes crinkling up to mere slits with lashes drawn around them in dayglo lime.

"Too many nosy straights reported your screams to The Man," Dad had added vehemently, remembering the humiliation of not being able to shut his own kid up.

"They'll put you in a foster home full of butt fuckers with coke bottle dicks. As soon as you're eighteen, Beastie, they'll pack what's left of you off to Vietnam, to get your arms and legs blown off and your face turned to oatmeal," Mom had offered as a further incentive, knowing he'd seen on the six o'clock news the sludge that soldiers became.

They had found him in the bathroom, during that seizure, flushing the toilet endlessly and letting out a scrotum scrunching shriek each time. They'd tried to make him stop, short of actually physically pulling him out of the bathroom. Well, it was a weird kick, seeing him stand there like that, pushing down on the handle.

Whoosh! Scream. *Whooshsh!* Scream. Eyes huge and dark as the centers to shit tornados. They'd pinched him black and blue, slapped him, tweaked his little dinger, pulled out some of his babysoft hair, getting no reaction from him but *Whwhooooshsh!* Scream. Not even looking at them, just at the swirl of disappearing water.

Then it finally dawned on their own pharmaceutically enhanced mentalities that the child's fits were likely to rouse the neighbors into telephoning the fuzz. Because Jason was usually such a quiet kid.

Yeah, because they fed him downers so he'd sleep while they partied. Or stuffed him with speed so he'd play frantically in his own little dungeon, not wanting to eat and therefore not disturbing their own games.

"What did you see in there?" Mom and Dad eventually asked him after the cops let them go, the hospital released the child, and a social worker threatened to drop by unannounced whenever she fucking well felt like it.

Jason had just sucked his thumb. He hadn't exactly been an easy kid to toilet train anyway. And after this incident he resolutely refused to sit on the porcelain donut at all, relieving himself in the cat's litter box when he could hold it in no longer, which totally rankled the cat until it split.

But they'd been guarding him, watching vigilantly for two whole boring weeks of him, them, and a TV fixed on monotonous animated comics. The kid seemed fine now. They were in desperate need of some funky R. and R., so they locked Jason in his room with a peanut butter sandwich, down the hall, newspapers spread on the floor in lieu (loo?) of a litter box, then dropped some white lightning and got nekkid. Three-year-olds were such a bummer. Didn't know the little dufus had learned to pick locks with a paper clip. Had sneaked down the corridor lined with black light posters of cartoon characters improbably buggering each other, into their space, parental mutual distractions keeping their attentions elsewhere as Dad buried his yellow submarine in Mom's juicy-in-the-sky smile. Never noticed Jason licking an iridescent spot off the page and then slipping himself into the closet where their few clean clothes jangled on hangers. He didn't quite shut the door.

"I am the god of hellfire…"

"I am the god of hellfire…"

For hours of megacosmic thirty-one flavors screwing.

And then the front door burst open, kicked in by a troll in pendulum-swinging raven fringe, seeming to own three sets of silver fangs, clutching an automatic assault motor that spit rockets. The thunder knocked Jason to the closet floor, sound concussion temporarily reducing his hearing to a roar of congealing sibilance.

And it might have happened for any number of reasons.

It might have happened because his parents had an outstanding balance due on their party favors.

It might have happened because they'd sold some bad chems to somebody with no head for humor.

It might have happened because some conscientious psycho prick who believed himself to be the archangel of justice had heard they were child abusers.

It might have happened because the damned possessed stereo needle was stuck in the groove of "I am the god of hellfire…" and had repeated it so often in an arcane but powerfully numerological sequence that it had inadvertantly summoned a violent entity.

It might have happened because Jason's mother was once married to another guy. A dealer named Rosh who gave free acid to young girls just arriving in the Ditch. Several thousand mikes until they damned near went comatose. And he'd ball them while Mom took pictures. He'd take the girls out of the apartment, saying, "Gonna go dump 'em in an alley to freak it off." And she'd just assumed it was what he did. Until she found the shoe box Rosh stashed under a floorboard, with a favorite hash pipe in it and some Thai sticks and a necklace. It looked like a row of pink to brown nut meats dried and strung on a shoe string. She'd made an anonymous call to tip the cops when she figured out they were nipples, leaving the scene until he was packed off to prison. Rosh had been paroled, or had escaped, and now fired off a barrage of lead protests to loyalty's demise in the twentieth century.

Yes, she was missing a nipple. Jason could see that when he finally crawled from the closet for a tremulous look-see. But it might have just been blown off. There was no way to tell if it had been carried away. The room was too much of a mess. The blasts had caught the couple in full loin-fused coitus, ripping through both abdomens and turning sets of upper and lower intestines to gruel, virtually severing the two at the hips. The bed had been turned into a feculent cul-de-sac, the mosh of flesh and waste cooling into rippled curds of shadowy wax. A pair of legs dangled over the edge of the mattress. The still intact asshole (with nothing above it but a grimace of bony ham) squeezed out a final squirt, unfolding as loose brown parachutes.

The boy slowly crept forward, hearing *Whoosh! Whwhoooooshsh!* inside his buzzing head. The toilet on acid had truly terrified him, its mystic undertow seeming to pull him down with it, to some terrible subterranean place into which kids went when they turned up missing.

But this…fascinated him. As if they'd started mud wrestling and pulled each other apart. Their upper halves, arms outflung, twitched in the drugged corrugations of his swampy vision, oscillating, doing a jellied breast stroke in the blood and manure gumbo, waving him closer. The smell of burnt almond and pig-day-at-the-abattoir destruction lifted him off the floor by his nostrils, bearing him forward, trapped in some von Krafft-Ebing nightmare. *Psychopathia Sexualis* hallucinations in a language Jason's brain didn't comprehend but which his miniature penis apparently responded to, erecting as if to bury itself in a sodden Babylon earth, in a darkly swirling river of ruin.

He couldn't stop staring at it, somehow knowing beyond his years that this was the menudo of regeneration. The same atoms that in another arrangement had created him. He watched, expecting something to stir in it, to assume an alchemical shape. Surely it would tell him what to do. Or might it simply lure him nearer? And if he did get closer, then what would happen?

"I've lost them, lost it," he lisped.

But what did that mean? No one learned a damned thing from what they owned and kept. It was what they lost that educated them. Innocence equated with ignorance. Innocence gone meant knowledge, and by that the means to survival.

And they weren't really gone for there they were, spread out before him, radically transformed, but not bitching at him or pinching him livid or doping him up to keep him entertained by himself. And there was something so compelling in that transformation, as if pining for its original form gave passion back to what had become a numbing hell.

It was so bizarre that he'd felt empty before this and now could barely contain himself with the excitement inside him.

Lagoon. La Brea Tar Pit.

Space as the point of genesis.

Warm rain at midnight.

His first Halloween as ghouls bayed beyond the door.

Mystery Meat.

Abyss.

Jason put his hand into it, finding it wet. What was touching this substance if not touching the proxie of oblivion, coming back to life with its stench in your sinuses and its secret madness yours to flaunt?

He mashed it between his fingers, experiencing a roll of cold nausea in his stomach and a heated rhythm in his loins. He had witnessed sex in diverse positions but still didn't really know what it was, what mechanics made up the primordial rut, had no instinct for that spellbinding epiphany. He only felt inexorably drawn as if to an intuition of postdiluvian evolution. So he climbed onto the bed and into the swill. Not simply as a child enters his parents' room, asking for permission to sleep with them because he's had a nightmare.

He'd somehow expected it to be bottomless and that he would sink, sink into another existence far from Sheol's Ditch and the poverty and the infuriating helplessness. But the morass was only shallow.

++++++++++

Why did the cops come? The neighbors hadn't reported the shots—even though they were the same folks who had called when they heard Jason shrieking during the bathroom bummer. When did the cops come?

The killer had left the front door ajar. Perhaps the postman had alerted them, smelling the carnage—because that much feculent bloodshed stank, steamed out onto the porch in waves ridden by flies. A mailman might have been an army veteran, back from the jungles, recognizing in a shuddering flashback this stench. He might have staggered off the porch to sprawl on the unmowed lawn amid the dandelions which exploded like native huts, sending ghostly wisps to haunt the air. He might have begun screaming, an old—but not too old—wound seeming to bleed afresh, full of shrapnel and bone splinters doing a crimson-spattered ivory boogie through olive-drab uniform material. The neighbors may have noticed *him* and called the cops. Or maybe he'd stuck his head in the door and gotten a red/brown/black eye-full to match the snootfull of ruin.

The cops entered. One of them shook his head, clearly sick. "I know these two were lowlifes, but whoever this butcher was, did he have to do the kid, too?" Then Jason sat up, awakened by this comment. The policeman who'd spoken cried out, perceiving what he thought was a dead toddler covered in brains and guts doing a zombie jack-in-the-box. He was already retreating, halfway out the door before his partner shouted, "Get back in here, you piss-pants rookie!"

Then this one stepped toward the bed, a hand outstretched. "Son? Are you okay?"

"I had a dream I was there," the child told him.

"Where?" the officer asked, looking him over for signs of injury. It was difficult to tell without lifting him out of the swamp. There was so much gore on him but close inspection revealed it wasn't his. He didn't appear to be wounded but he had to be suffering from shock.

"The place where Mom and Dad are now."

The cop nodded. "In a better place, yeah. Whole again, not like this."

"Yeah, a better place. 'Cept they're just like this. Over and over," answered the little boy, smiling. He then curled up in the murder bed again, hoping sleep would return him there.

+++++++++++

Five years later. Jason dreamed he flew in a helicopter. He'd seen helicopters on TV and in the movies. It was the same blade-slashing drone except it surrounded him, threatening to buzz his brain into wrinkled, pink, tutti-frutti bubblegum-flavored ice cream. It moved through night, starless, linear. He managed to get to the doorway and look out, down.

Now there were some lights, far below. Or was he flying upside-down? The illuminated points might be overhead. There were cliffs and peaks and tortured rocky pinnacles. Everywhere bodies, parts of bodies. And creatures with silver jaws and flesh that hung in raven fringe who were free to rip anything at will.

"Take me there," he told the pilot who sat at the controls with his back to Jason. "I want to go there."

"Only **Superman** gets into that place," replied the pilot.

It was later that Jason realized the guy didn't mean the one from the comics.

+++++++++++

He lived now with an old couple, a great aunt and great uncle—although he was never quite sure whether they were related to his late mother or his late father. Merrice and Bowie Cursky didn't talk about the

Caves, ever. Jason called them Ice and Bowtie behind their backs. Boring folks, creakers, retired and living in a ratty old apartment building not four blocks from the house where his parents had been slaughtered. Yet he'd never met them before child services hunted them down to get them to take him in. Flesh and blood. Their flesh and blood. But he'd only ever seen their flesh. He wasn't convinced either of them had blood.

When not in school, he went to the library to read. No sense going home where Ice and Bowtie only had the television tuned to one channel. The city had designated some channels for public access for several years—since the late '60s—and this station always ran old '50s shows ad nauseum. Not just the usual suspects either, such as *I Love Lucy* or *Leave It To Beaver*. Obscure stuff: *Bachelor Father* and *The Life Of Riley*. Weird that the station never let the shows creep into the 1960s. For example, they showed only *Perry Mason* episodes that were originally run from the show's debut in 1957 to 1959, leaving out anything from 1960 onward—which was another six or seven years for the series! Talk about being lost in a time warp.

The two times he'd ever tried to change the channel—at ages five and six respectively, as for a brief second he'd been left alone in the living room—he'd had his hands slapped and then taped around the wrists behind him. After that, there was always at least one guardian there with him. He never heard anything about the space program or plane crashes or terrorists until he went to school. Of course, they usually only told you what they wanted you to hear.

So Jason learned about the world at the library. He could pick up the daily body counts by thumbing through the newspapers. He pored, fascinated, over photographs of fire and mayhem in the colorful news magazines, touching the slick pages like peels of enticing flesh. He found one older issue of *Time*, cover with children who had accidentally been napalmed in Vietnam running in agony up a road. It caused a peculiar tingle in him, so he stripped off the cover as quietly and unobtrusively as he could and ate it.

Eventually he began to prowl for books. It was cool in the library stacks, looking up anything he liked as long as he didn't ask a librarian for it. And they were too busy to keep an eye on a kid to make sure he wasn't reading material too adult for him. But he wouldn't be stuck with the crap they forced him to read in class. As if all he had were two brain cells and one was being roasted by the other with a flamethrower. How did they expect any kid to be interested in school with this garbage?

But the hour always arrived when he had to be home. Ice and Bowtie enforced a curfew. He didn't dare disobey them.

"You're dependent on us," Ice had drilled into him.

"You would end up in a foster home," Bowtie had instilled.

"Beast like you would eventually go to juvie hall," great auntie had furthered.

"And you know what's at those places?" great unc would ask. Ice had whispered, "Cornholers!"

Jason hadn't known what that was so Bowtie had defined it, "Screw you up the butt!"

Jason quivered at the idea of having to walk around with a corn cob wedged implacably up his tiny anus, twisted in savagely until he'd be quite bow-legged. So he always made sure he was home by seven for dinner. They locked him in his room by eight o'clock at night, and didn't unlock it again until it was time for him to go to school the next day. "It's time," his unc would tell him and then escort him down the hall—unless Jason was already in his room. In which case the door simply closed and he heard the key in the lock: *click-nick*. No "Goodnight, Johnboy" for him. No "Pleasant dreams." Not even "Sleep in fright, don't let the fanged baby-brain eaters bite!" that his mother would sometimes tell him. Just the phantom movement of the door out of the corner of his eye and the telltale, soft *click-nick*, a noise in two subtle parts. One evening he sleepwalked into his closet, woke up when he heard someone crying on the other side of the wall. That wasn't part of the Cursky apartment over there. He rapped his knuckles against the plaster and was surprised when a knock answered his.

"Hello?" he called out softly, not wanting to alert the aunt and unc to the fact he wasn't in bed and dutifully unconscious. Besides, he sometimes suspected they perched outside his door and listened, expecting what? That they'd hear leather wings rustling out from his shoulder blades and breathed-out flames flashing through the keyhole as nightly he turned into the devil they suspected he was? Or were they wanting to hear little shrieks as some behemoth dragged him by his eyes out the window, at last freeing them of this onerous responsibility which had been thrust upon them in their golden years? He whispered to the knock on the other side of the closet wall, "Are you there?"

He heard a muffled sob and a "Yeah."

The voice sounded young, another kid. But whether it was a boy or a girl, he couldn't say.

"Are you okay?" he wanted to know. Not that he had the faintest idea what he could do about it. He had no power; he was locked in his room.

"No," came the reply.

"Are you hurt?" was his third question.

It came through the material which separated the two rooms as a faint echo, tinny with distortion as a friend on the other end of a string linking two tin cans. "All the time."

"How come I never heard you before?" Jason asked.

A snuffle? Cough. "Gate's open right now."

"What gate?"

"The one the red-headed man here says there is."

44

This line wasn't getting anywhere. It didn't make any sense. These seedy apartments were in one of the worst areas of town. There were no yards and, thus, no fences and no gates.

"Is this some kind of joke or are you crazy?" Jason said with a sneer.

He listened but didn't hear anything else. He went back to bed. The next day, key in the lock. Better than an alarm to tell him it was time to get up and dress. Eat his bowl of cereal drowned in milk which always seemed lumpy. See Ice and Bowtie rigid before the TV, watching *Tic Tac Dough* or *Queen For A Day*. Before he hurried off to catch the school bus, he listened at the neighboring front door. Had he seen anybody coming and going from there? He didn't think he had. He paused at the row of mailboxes downstairs. There was no name listed for that apartment. Maybe they'd just moved in.

That night, led down the hall like he was walking the last mile to the electric chair. The closing of the door, the turning of the key. *Click-nick!* And not long after he heard the voice again, only it screamed instead of wept. It wasn't a loud, shrill scream but came through the wall as if from a great distance. *Poor kid's getting the tar whaled outta him*, Jason thought, sympathizing. It surprised him that he might feel any pity for another child. Usually his interactions with other kids were with him as aggressor. He could beat up any bully half again his size because he'd do absolutely anything to win, including trying to gouge out eyes or crush testicles into pudding—the last usually accomplished by grabbing hold with both hands and squeezing until he'd could hear 'em pop, audible even above the other boy's screams. Most bullies were generally cowards anyway. Jason didn't frighten easily. When you started off in life the way he had, it took a lot to push the panic button.

He knocked on the wall and called out, but there was no answer save for the buzzing he associated with the helicopter dream. It, too, sounded far away, sort of like the electric vibrator Bowtie used on Ice when they believed their charge was asleep. That sound always rumbled through another wall, less like a purr and more like a kitchen appliance—better living through technology. He knew what a vibrator was. There were books by Jacqueline Susann, Erica Jong, and Xaviera Hollander in the library. He'd even chewed a page from *Fear Of Flying*, simply to taste the word *zipfuck*. Jason continued to listen until he fell asleep, slumped in the closet. He dreamed about the kid, of breaking down the door and rescuing this boy. They would be best friends, especially since they'd both suffered. Jason would protect him and teach him how to be strong. He woke up in the morning with his back and neck very sore.

"Anything happen last night?" he asked his caretakers at breakfast.

"Like what?" Bowtie asked suspiciously. So maybe that drone had been the vibrator.

"I mean did you hear anything outside? I thought I heard a scream," the boy explained, trying not to cringe at the mere notion of these two old scabs fumbling with one another's secret places.

"This is Sheol's Ditch. There's always somebody screaming outside someplace," Ice commented as she set down a plate of burnt toast and scrambled eggs for him. Ice never cooked the eggs right and they were always runny as snot.

"No murders in the building last night?" he pressed on. "Next door?"

They stared at him, their expressions unreadable.

"You had a nightmare," Aunt Merrice said, her voice almost inaudible it was so low. And—was that a touch of disappointment? Because the night-mare hadn't claimed him forever?

That was it. They thought he was flashing back on what happened to his folks. They didn't want to have to speak of it. For that had been unspeak-able, hadn't it? Therefore impossible to utter aloud. Forbidden, taboo. The kind of phrases which might conjure up green, squiggly-faced gods with rotten oyster-breath who'd suck your brain right out through your asshole.

Downstairs he checked the mailboxes again. Now there was a name on the slot for next door. GARTH LISTO. The next night, he left the closet door open. When he heard the crying he threw off the covers.

"You again?" he asked, straining against the wall, chill plaster against his shoulder and cheek.

"Yeah."

"I'm Jason. You got a name?"

"I used to have one."

"That's stupid. What do you mean, used to have one? If you've been given a name, you always have it."

"I don't."

"Why not?"

"Names don't pass through the gate."

"Kid, what kind of gate is this?"

"There are lots of gates. This is the one names don't pass through."

"You know, if you don't quit jerking me around, I'll just go back to bed."

There were no more responses from the other side of the closet wall so Jason did just that, slipping back between the dry cold sheets that somehow seemed unnatural to him. He went to school the next day, skipped the library after, and came straight home. Ate supper with Ice and Bowtie, then said he had some extra studying to do and left them with their *My Son Jeep* and *I'm The Law* reruns. He stole a knife from the kitchen but waited until he heard the key twitch in the lock before he went into the closet. Slowly he began to put the tip into the plaster, chipping away tiny pieces and flakes. He turned it on its edge and scraped as if the wall were a fresh hide.

A few hours later he heard the crying.

"I read in Greek mythology about Odysseus and his men when they met the Cyclops. And the Cyclops kept asking Odysseus what his name was. But all the hero would answer was 'I am No Man'. I'm going to call you No Man, okay?" Jason told the weak little voice. "Sort of like No Man can pass through the gate."

He laughed, but then thought of the helicopter dream. Except that wasn't "Only No Man Gets Into That Place.'"

He continued to work with the knife, long since having destroyed the dry wall. He'd hit the edge of lumber between the two surfaces, that space rats and cockroaches ruled. "No Man," the voice repeated.

"Hey, are you a kid? 'Cause you sound like one. I'm eight years old myself," Jason persisted.

"I was."

Jason groaned. "You mean you got older? Sure. Isn't that the way it generally works?"

"Years don't pass through the gate."

"Not this again."

"Don't be mad. I can't help it."

Jason could hear more from the opposite side now. Voices he was certain must belong to other people in the next apartment. More weeping, and gutteral moans like he barely recalled his parents used to make when they got it on, the noise a wet sheet made when it flapped on a clothesline, and the buzz which reminded him of the helicopter in his dream.

"Listen, kid. I'm cutting a hole in the wall. We can talk easier then. Maybe I can see what's going down with you and I can get help if you want."

"Can't help."

"Let me guess. Help doesn't pass through the fuckin' gate."

Suddenly the knife slipped, slid as if going through hot butter. Jason's arm shot forward. He drew it back and stared at the knife. The blade dripped a mass both green and black and bloody.

"Oh, shit. Did I cut you, No Man?"

"No," the voice whimpered.

Jason shifted position in the closet, put his eye to the hole. Saw an eye looking back at him.

Something didn't seem right.

There was light all around the eye.

Jason put his hand into the plaster which crumbled more. He reached through the wall and touched the eyeball where it hovered in the air. "This is you?" Jason whispered, unbelieving. He had to have fallen asleep in the closet again. He must be dreaming this.

"Yes."

But where did the voice come from? It was just an eye. And how had the kid knocked on the wall the first night?

He pushed it slightly with a finger and it floated out of the way. Behind it he saw a broken landscape stretching back toward—what? There was no horizon. Just rocks, cliffs, slabs and steeples of stone.

How could there not be a point in perspective where land and sky crashed together?

A half a woman crawled past not ten feet from where he'd touched the eye-child. He could see the jerking end where her spine had been severed. She dragged entrails like an assortment of rusted chains. To the left a pair of mismatched legs curled around one another like mating worms. Someone in a black jacket—swinging fringe like a conga line of shadowy spider Rockettes—had his face buried between the cheeks of an ass without upper torso or legs. To the right, a naked, red-headed man with something like a bone saw for a penis rammed himself in and out of the rectum of another man, whose own dick was long and thin as a string and tied around the neck of a furious cat. The saw buzzed like a helicopter, lost without up or down in a negative space.

The red-headed man wasn't just a man with red hair. The entire head was crimson as a massive pimple. He saw Jason and, while continuing to thrust into this bloody chocolate buggershake of a victim, he grinned and beckoned with a free hand…someone else's, jaggedly removed just at the wrist.

"You come right along. Don't have to be like them. Be like me. But hurry. The gate's about to close."

Jason gasped, jumped up, left the closet, slamming its door behind him. He dove underneath his bed, screwing his eyes shut, bringing his hands over his ears. The mattress began to squeak above him, old springs full of rust. The blankets hanging nearly to the floor dripped red/black/brown. It trickled across the floor, sticky as treacle.

He heard very softly, "I am the god of hellfire…"

"I am the god of hellfire…"

He felt it, smelled it rotting back through his sinuses. He pulled one hand away from an ear and put it into the pool growing around him. Wet, the proxie of oblivion.

A secret madness. Would he let it take him or would he flaunt it?

He mashed it between his fingers.

Suddenly he was crawling out from under the bed, running back to the closet, picking up the knife, and stabbing at the wall trying to make the hole larger as fast as possible, to make it big enough he could fit himself through it. Harder and harder he plunged the tip of the blade into the plaster. He grunted, he screamed. He didn't care when the knife handle slipped and he sliced open his palm. He grasped the handle again and stabbed.

"What the hell are you doing?" Jason hadn't heard the door of his room being unlocked, nor Bowtie and Ice running in their slippers. His great unc grabbed him firmly by the shoulders and shook him until his teeth rattled.

The man—stronger than he looked after all—grabbed the wrist of the hand holding the knife, snapped it to make the boy let go of the weapon.

"Jeez-Louise, will you look at that? The landlord's going to have our heads," he exclaimed.

"What were you thinking? Are you nuts?" Jason's great aunt demanded. A curl of disgust on her thin lips suggested who she was comparing him with at that moment. "Bowie, I told you one day those drugs they gave the little beast would eat out his brain."

She didn't add *right through his asshole...* More of the unspeakable, the forbidden. People in '50s TV didn't say *asshole*.

Jason kicked the old man in the knee, hard as he could, hearing cartilage crackle as it ruptured. He jerked out of the guy's fists and rushed past the old lady. He fled into the living room and then swung open the door to run into the hallway outside the apartment. He began pounding on the unit next door.

"Let me in!" he bellowed. "I've had the intuition. I've seen the mechanics. I'm not afraid anymore! I'm not afraid..."

The front door there opened and a really big, yet young man with glasses poised on the bridge of a very narrow nose peered out at him. He wasn't really fat, just tall and fleshy. He wore a silky robe of oriental design.

"What do you want? Do you know what time it is?"

Jason pushed at the door until the guy stumbled back, silk material swishing around his legs. He ran inside the neighbor's place and stared at the dingy walls, the second-hand furniture. There was a table with very small trees in pots. They looked just like regular trees, gnarled branches and knotted, whorled trunks—except they were miniature. Like giant oaks and cypresses reduced in a magic machine. Next to these sat an assortment of scissors and pruning shears.

"Oh, no," Jason sobbed. He was too late. "The gate's closed."

"Huh?"

Jason shrugged his shoulders, mournfully shaking his head. "I didn't have a chance anyway. The pilot said only **Superman** gets inside."

The big man laughed. "Cool! Thus Spake Zarathustra!"

+++++++++++

There was a belief held by the Pythagoreans that animals living upon the moon neither ate nor shit. They existed solely upon diluted heat, air and vaporized moisture. They were considered the better for it, as opposed to animals on earth.

—Sacred Sepsis
Dr. Louis Godard and Dr. James Singer

CHAPTER 5

MOENJO-DARO,
2300 B.C.

Moonlight on the baked mud avenue lit up her footprints, making a pathway running between the brick-
lined gutters which ran on both sides. A cloud falling
across the moon like a lank of hair turned the boulevard and
her footprints dark, black as the shit that bobbed in the ditch
water. Only the lighter stuff floated on, the rest landing in catch
basins created underneath to capture detritus which might have
otherwise interrupted the proper flow.

This city was far ahead of its time. In most other places the
natives simply squatted by the side of the road. But Moenjo-
Daro already had an appreciation for the finer points of waste
management.

She heard the gutters gurgling in the shadows, the night air
redolent with the spice of human waste. Every now and then

clay pipes rattled between the buildings, sounding similar to peristalsis within a living being, the noise of consuming and digestion.

I used to be Eska, she thought. This emerged from nowhere she might discern. Was it a memory or a dream? That she had recently been a mortal woman named Eska? Her father had been a brick layer, and she recalled he was half blind from the gypsum used to mix the mortar. And he always smelled of the bitumen layered between skins of sawn brick used in much of the construction for the Great Bath. Where was he? Because he did not see well he'd stumbled against a kiln for firing clay pots and been burned. Of her mother she had no recollection at all. When she thought of the word *mother*, the only thing that came to mind was herself. Did this mean she had children? Oh, yes...thousands.

I used to be Eska. Soon I will have become somebody else.

She put a small, wing-shaped hand to her belly. Felt nothing save a yearning hollow. For she was empty. Looking up, she saw that Great Bath, one of the city's most imposing structures. It was the time of night when the moon was past its apogee. The time of night when the mating dance of the stars produced the strangest children. The time of night the celebrants emerged from the bathing pool in the bathhouse courtyard.

"Aralu!" they chanted, many of them still fondling themselves or one another. Some of them abused their genitals with the baked clay scrubbers, crosshatch inscribed for abrasiveness, or pushed them into anuses...their own, or others who bent forward to invite the intrusion—meant to plug up the orifices in the same way that a gold bit in the mouth kept the soul from escaping during sleep. "Aralu!"

They ascended the staircases on the northern and southern approaches to the pool, gripped by pain in their rectums and bladders as they struggled to withhold their receptive mass and water. They stretched lips into rictuses of self-containment, teeth clicking, hands clenching fists. Penises and labias were swollen with dew; buttocks trembled.

"Aralu!" they cried as she stood waiting for them, veil across her face, promising again to lead them to the land where they could pour out their joys and grief. They had gorged themselves on the blood and flesh of their loved ones: wives, husbands, parents, children. They had fornicated with every movable object they could find in the moments which thrived just after twilight fell. Calves and muzzled dogs littered the streets, some still faintly twitching. Others screamed with their insides hanging out through ruptured asses amid broken terra cotta statues. The celebrants smeared themselves with every grease known to inhabit biology's interior scapes. They had broken into the tombs of the kings and rutted with the corpses, singing as the cadavers split, burst, rubbed away into dust. Then they'd gone to the Great Bath to clean the outsides of their bodies for her.

She made the cloud release the moon, letting them see her. Her full-lipped mouth and vulva were the color of blue knots of intestine.

They immediately let loose all they'd been harboring of their feasting. Gourd castanets, drums, tambourines of excrement rumbled out. Flutes and whistles of waterfall urine sprayed. A few looked up in torment, having held it for so many hours, cramping double until bile—chunked with partially ingested anthropophagy—spewed, vomit cleary tracked with their sins.

It poured out, symbolic as many a rite was prescribed to be.

She inhaled the acidic nutmeg of it. She observed them laughing, rolling around in the stifling debris like swine in their own filth. The liquid music in moist lyre and rain harp, coming from the nearby sewers and from these befouled people, didn't cause her to tremble. The bronze drizzle of fervid marasmus, puckering to form a lewd ringworm kiss, didn't disturb her. For she was a humid queen.

"I am the gateway," she hissed and trilled.

"Aralu!" they shouted, not caring if their cries woke up the rest of the city who would be disgusted at this evil. They convulsed on the ground in the swill, wriggling up through it on their stomachs toward her.

She opened wide her arms. "Yes, to Aralu."

+++++++++++

Dorien's eyes opened. She was lying on her side in her bed, facing the window with the brown darkness beyond. Always that sewage air, prevalent and inescapable as a rotting rat tied about the neck.

"What the hell was that?" she asked herself, keeping her voice small just in case something awful might be eavesdropping.

Another bad dream. She'd been having them for several weeks now, ever since her encounter with Gavin. She was someone else in them, never Dorien Warmer. Always somebody else who used to be somebody else... There would be the omnipresent middens, the cesspools. Strange people vying for a curious gross-out one-upmanship. Committing abominable acts not even the most graphic porno movie could simulate. Some of those things didn't even seem possible once she had her real eyes open and could think about it. Except she didn't want to think about it. Dorien just wanted it to go away.

She supposed she oughtn't to be surprised she was suffering nightmares. After all, what Gavin had done to her had been akin to rape. Only this had been a consensual rape, manipulating her into a position where she couldn't have gone to the authorities that night to file a complaint. She was too embarrassed anyway. What would she have said? She couldn't have falsely accused him of forcing her: she had no bruises. No, only her pride had been bruised. He'd treated her like a whore. Worse, as if she'd been of no more substance or feeling than a tissue he'd jerked off into and then tossed into the toilet.

She might have sued him but then she'd have to admit to being such a pitiful thing. She'd have been the laughing stock of the college. And he'd still be big man on campus, with his closetful of seminally stained sheets. There was no law against being an asshole. He couldn't be labeled a sexual predator if she took off her own panties and begged for seconds.

The simple truth was that most people—at least according to television and the movies—were sexually active. If you hadn't had at least a single one-night stand then you probably looked like a gargoyle or were in the fifth grade...or both. Nobody would care except to tell her to stop whining and obsessing and get herself a makeover. It was better to have been shtupped, then spurned, than never to have been shtupped at all.

She'd drifted through the days, going to class in a fog, trying not to notice him whenever she attended the English Lit lectures. Not giving him the satisfaction of seeing how much he'd hurt her. She'd sit in the back with her head down, scribbling so studiously, pretending to be making copious notes. Not willing to risk looking up and possibly making accidental eye contact. For all she knew, he'd told everyone and they were staring at her, whispering, smirking. Or worse: pitying. Not especially pretty, no. Not especially appealing. Not like the bevy of lookers who she was sure had to be throwing up their lunches every day in order to keep so thin. Tits on sticks, she often thought of them. Several of them were in this class, popular girls. (Not women? Was Dorien guilty of making such a crass designation?)

A pair of these drop-dead-gorgeous types sat down across from her. She could smell hints of their big breakfasts and whiffs of bile, barely tangible under the layers of perfume. They wore hiphuggers and had their belly buttons pierced. There were shadows between their ribs that sighed when they sat down or got up. Gavin would always sing out, "Hi, Ladies!" as he went down the aisle toward his own seat near the front. And they would reply, "Hello, Gavin!" in sync, in harmony, like a pair of starved Barbies. Dorien would scribble and scribble. Nonsense. Squares and triangles she'd color in with black ink. Spirals leading from and going to nowhere. Meaningless symbols, names and places she heard in those dreams. Gateways.

Thresholds.

Underworlds.

She didn't hear a word the professor said. She didn't fare any better in her other classes. Dorien would surely flunk out that semester and have to start over. She might even have to spend the summer living at her folks' house again. The very idea gave her the shivers. Not that it was a hell on earth but Dad had always been creepy in the manner of very disappointed men, and Mom had forever been a babbling manic. Shudders, what if she had to get a menial job somewhere because she couldn't afford to start again? Someplace like food service where she'd work her ass off but get her meals for free and go home every night stinking of fried mystery meats.

Now she got out of bed, images from the latest nightmare barely faded. She stumbled into the bathroom to take a shower, feeling nasty from the dreams of filth and perversion. She glanced at herself in the mirror. Her skin had been just a little strange lately, as if it were wet all the time. Her hair, too. Maybe the pollution was starting to effect her, damp yet colorless Rorschachs of corruption, the mark of a modern Cain. She'd smell herself, expecting a sour perspiration. (She might be sick.)

But it wasn't sweat. It didn't pool in her pits or stain the V between her breasts. It was an even misting, as if she walked to and from the bus station and then to classes from the bus stop in heavy fog. But there was no fog.

The smell of it was sort of sweet. Flowery. A garden smell or a greenhouse smell.

This reminded her of orchids—a reek which had always permeated a recurring nightmare she'd suffered as a child. Suffered, as a matter of fact, until she moved away from home to attend college. A funny thing to dream badly of and to smell like now—orchids. There were hundreds—or was it thousands—of varieties of orchid. And they were parasites, weren't they?

When she woke up in the morning—having sweated this out all night—her sheets had turned dark with her silhouette. And when she came home at the end of the day, the inside of her clothes had turned dark. The way a shiny pot turned when eggs were boiled in it...or tea. "Maybe it's the dark night of my soul," she said aloud to the reflection and tried to grin. "Or the shadow of death."

Perhaps it was those dreams leaving a shit stain, mark of ancient Cain. Did orchids grow in shit? Her attempts at even gruesome levity failed. If it was a shadow, it came from insanity. She might be losing her mind. Weak and stupid—just because some boy broke her heart. Not even that! Dorien hadn't known Gavin long enough to become that attached. Okay—just because he'd shit on her then. Gross vernacular and not really true in the literal sense...not like the roving gang of killers who did employ this to every degree. But she'd let him get to her. He'd been between her legs and apparently had crawled under her skin as well. She knew she wasn't the most gifted of women but she'd never have taken herself for an abject loser. Yet there it was, toxic cloud looming over her, casting darker what lay in her wake. Casting her down. Underworlds.

Thoughts of death and corruption.

Was this the path to suicide?

Dorien started to cry. She wiped the tears from her cheek onto the back of her hand and stared. They were a yellowish brown. Like what washed off when she cleaned her windows. Definitely the pollution. It had infiltrated her body and now came out the pores.

If she could squeeze her flesh, how many bowls of poison would there be?

++++++++++

Going across the campus in slow motion, Dorien pressed her books tight against her chest. Talismans. Her breasts were swollen. Her period must be coming. They seemed bigger than usual. Did that come from losing her virginity? She didn't think so.

Actually her cycle was late. She really feared she might be pregnant. It might explain the mood swings. See, she wasn't really going crazy, just the hormonal variety of postal.

She imagined how that would go down. Walking up to Gavin. "I'm pregnant. What are you going to do about it?"

Because it took two, didn't it? The responsibility was shared by both partners in the act of conception. Not that she expected him to marry her. Gad, those days were gone and good riddance.

Then what?

She got a mental flash of a sheet with the shadow of a fetus on it, name scrawled beside: BABY WARMER. And of Gavin folding the sheet up and putting it in the closet.

She kept her head down, not meeting anyone's eyes. She only looked up when she passed a wall of the engineering building where workers were starting to clean off another remark left by The Shit Detail.

> "And thou shalt eat it as barley cakes and thou shalt bake
> it with dung that cometh out of man, in their sight."

Ezekiel, IV, 12

Dorien heard bits of conversations coming from kids and teachers who passed her.

"A priest who helped out at the student clinic..."

"Found him right there..."

"...his skull was cracked and the brain gone..."

"...excommunicant in its place."

"Don't you mean excrement?"

"Don't ask me, I'm not Catholic. Dominum, dominance. Whips, chains, and let my people out of bondage go! What's the difference?"

Dorien had stopped to read the biblical phrase before soap and a long-handled brush washed the wall as if cleaned of sin. Another campus worker began hosing down the nearby grass of blood and what might have been mud but probably wasn't. She spied a jet black rosary bead being pushed across the lawn by the force of the water. It might have actually been a pearl of impacted rodent shit but she knew it wasn't. A holy object—or intended as one to whoever believed in such things. For all she knew, The Shit Detail revered the dropping as holy but not the rosary. Some folks thought eating flesh and drinking blood was a sacrament; others viewed it as nothing short of cannibalism and completely disdained the act of communion at Mass.

She felt a tap on her shoulder. Turning, she found another young woman standing behind her, hair loose about the face and neck, hanging in the eyes. This woman tried covering up really bad skin with make-up but it only served to make her look worse. She looked as if she'd recently had a really bad sunburn, one that still left her blistered. It actually made Dorien wince as she considered she'd seen her before, in the cafeteria. Nobody ever sat with this person. Well, her skin wasn't very appetizing. And, while this close, Dorien also noticed an unpleasant odor rising from the young woman's body. Dorien congratulated herself upon managing not to flinch.

"Hi, I'm Neela Wilson. I saw you with Gavin Parrish at the movies a few weeks ago," the young woman opened with.

"Yeah? We did go out that one time," Dorien admitted cautiously. Two heartbeats, three. She awaited the purpose of this.

The young woman bit her lip. She blushed, which made the blisters seem even angrier, the edges hardening with a crackle, liquid centers pulsing red and white like the epicenters to tiny atomic explosions. She clearly wanted to talk about something that disturbed her. Dorien wished she'd just spit it out.

Then she did. "Did you sleep with him?"

Dorien snorted with aggravation, starting to turn away, blond hair swinging. "I don't see where that's any of your business."

She did toss an angry look back and saw as Neela shrugged self-consciously and then tilted her head. "I know. That's true from the usual perspective. And I'm sorry because I know you don't know me from Eve..."

Right, instead of *you don't know me from adam.*

Neela was so embarrassed she twitched around the rheumy eyes and the pimpled mouth. "Don't take this wrong. I'm not some religious freak or anything..."

An odd thing to say, given the murder of a priest that had gone down by the wall of the engineering building the night before. Dorien waited for her to ask something like, "Have you been saved, sister? God forgives everything. All you have to do is grovel a bit and you come clean."

Instead Neela said, "Gavin...he's a really bad guy."

I found that out all by myself, Dorien started to reply. She decided not to. This person might be an ex-girlfriend of his. She might be stalking him and on a mission to kill anybody he might have dallied with.

(Dallied? What happened to just plain old fucked over?)

When Dorien didn't say anything and even started to walk away again, Neela went on, keeping her voice down. If she was stalking him—or the hapless ladies he betrayed her with—she wasn't hysterically loud about it.

"He's hurt a lot of women. It's a thing he's into, charming them, setting them up. You'd think chivalry wasn't dead at all."

Dorien shook her head, not caring if this chick had a gun in her pocket, torn between committing suicide and going postal. She tried walking faster but the woman kept pace with her, almost putting out her hand, then not. Dorien thought if this creature touched her again, she'd knock the bitch in the head with her books and start running.

"He knows all the tender things to say, has all the right moves..." Would this creepette never get the message and go away?

"Jeez, I'm late for a class. Do you mind?" Dorien said irritably.

"You're late for more than that, believe me," Neela pressed, wheezing. Getting out of breath? Try shutting up! "You're so late, whatever your personal itinerary is, you'll never find the way back to it again."

The woman's body odor was making her sick. Definitely not flowers. She didn't want to resort to violence; she hated violence. But who the hell was this person? "Damn, girl! Don't threaten me. Okay, so I slept with him. Get over it. Not like it's going to happen again. We're through. Gavin and me—and you and me. Get lost!"

Neela stumbled, brushed against Dorien. Dorien gave her a disgusted shove. The young woman actually fell down into the soft new grass. Dorien gasped, appalled at herself, yet hurried on.

Neela called after her. "Are you one of the sheets in the closet?"

Dorien stopped for a moment, turning around to glare at the other woman who was awkwardly getting back on her feet. She spat out a hostile, "Screw you."

"Actually—if you are—then you're the one who's screwed. Gavin Parrish is HIV positive. He's giving it to every girl he can sweet talk onto that mattress. Get tested," Neela advised, rubbing a bruise which bloomed on her knee.

Dorien's jaw dropped. "I don't believe you," she said slowly.

"You'd better," Neela replied, not unkindly. "He gave it to me. He might not have it himself yet, but he can sure pass it on. I slept with him a year ago. Look at me now."

Dorien did believe her, realizing at last what the skin problem really was. And she felt terrible for having spoken to this unfortunate woman the way she had. For having pushed her down! See? Dorien was just as bad as everybody else in this stinking city.

"I'm sorry," she told Neela sincerely. "Don't take this the wrong way either. Are you sure it came from Gavin Parrish?"

Because naturally she didn't want it to be that way, turning a bad experience into attempted murder—what might someday actually be her murder for it. It was like being told the creep had jerked off in her mouth and she'd swallowed semen thick with cyanide.

Neela nodded her head. She folded her hands which Dorien noticed were in soft little cotton gloves, the sort a jeweler might wear. "I'm afraid so. He's the only man I've been with. Nobody before and no one since. I wish I hadn't had to be the one to tell you. But you had to know, right?"

Dorien reached out and took one of the gloved hands in her own. She very gently shook it, not wanting to hurt this girl—especially not anymore than she already had—just in case the gloves disguised bandaged lesions. Did the gloved hand feel slightly damp? She wanted to wipe her own on her jeans but didn't. Dorien had already been enough of an asshole.

Were her own hands wet right now? Yes… Would she soon be wearing gloves like these, her flesh gone from smelling of funereal orchids to smelling like the funeral itself? "Thanks," Dorien said, words choking in her throat. "How's your knee? I'm sorry. I do appreciate what it must have taken for you to approach a total stranger and reveal this. I suppose it sort of makes us sisters, doesn't it?"

Neela smiled. "Yeah. Unfortunately, it's getting to be a pretty big sisterhood."

+++++++++++

In the country of Ireland, farmers used to heap their manure just outside their door so they could keep an eye on it. It was considered to be so valuable (as both a fertilizer *and* a fertility symbol) that neighbors would steal it. On May Eve when it was believed the race of faeries was out to party and perhaps do mischief to the race of humans, farmers would stick a talisman twig from the holy rowan tree upright in the noxious pile to ward them off.

—Sacred Sepsis
Dr. Louis Godard and Dr. James Singer

CHAPTER
6

1975

Jim Singer indulged in self-pity. He'd fallen into a rut.
Once the wunderkind of archaeology, thought by many
academics to be destined for great things—for finding
great things, that is—he'd been relegated to the back burner as
a proponent of pop science. Make that poop science.

At the moment he sat correcting papers in his office, sipping bitter coffee, smoking a chain of cigarettes, disgusted
with his students. He'd tested them the afternoon before and
had asked in essay question #3 about the preparation of the
dead in Egypt. Far too many had answered that tanna leaves
were used as fundamental for eternity!

Their reference? Mummy movies.

Was it his fault because he'd rather be on a dig somewhere
than dying of chalk dust-in-the-crack-of-the-ass boredom,
trapped in a classroom in hell (in a podunk school in Iowa
where the sciences were extra credit courses only and most

kids were agriculture majors), full of fools who believed that the pyramids were signposts for an alien landing strip?

Their reference? Von Daniken books.

Ten years had passed since he and Dr. Godard had written of their discovery on Mt. Koshtan. Ten years gone since the part about the sacrifice in excrement had been deleted by the editorial staff of every prestigious archaeological journal. Ten years lost to him since so-called colleagues insisted the sacrifice was merely some clutz who'd suffered an accident in a prehistoric toilet, making sophomoric jokes about the elevation of latrine casualty to godlike pretension.

He recalled something he'd overheard at a conference in Boston that still left his ears burning.

"Two Egyptologists discovered an unopened tomb and once they got it open they found a pile of fresh shit inside. The first one said to the second, "Dr. Singer, do you think a cat crept into the crypt and crapped and crept out again?" To which the second one replied, "No, Dr. Godard, I do believe it was the pup popped into the pit and pooped and then popped out."

Never mind that twenty-one skeletons had been found in the manmade sanitation shaft which descended more than sixty feet into bedrock.

(Not a vast underground network as the one he'd been sure he sensed as he'd stood that day at the edge of the pit. But he'd never really expected to find such a thing, *not Hell but near...*)

The consensus was, "We don't really need archaeology to become publicly synonymous with scientific poop scooping."

Classrooms were full of girls in black silk and leather, dreamy eyed over the concept of dead men returning with undying love to rescue their equally-dead damsels.

Point of reference being Im-ho-tep and Dr. Phibes.

Hadn't yet to sit in the dirt under a hot sun and/or a bitingly freezing sideways wind until they lathered with sweat that rolled salt into their chapped flesh, wrinkling them prematurely so they resembled the preserved dead only a very small percentage of masters of this science would ever be lucky enough to unearth. The pit squatting alone caused lumbar spasms until they shuffled like old geezers by the time they were thirty. (A twinge caused Jim to shift uncomfortably in his chair. He put a hand to his lower back and groaned. One would think that working at digs would make a man fit, but he had never shed that baby fat. Now it was the bloom of a downright paunch and this aggravated his back even more.)

There were always one or two serious students in every semester or so. But they still came in with unrealistic expectations. Most archaeologists never found anything earth-shaking or career-making. (And if they did, the earth might make it known it didn't care to be shaken by *that*, thank you.)

When the docs were in Persia, it hadn't really been that many years since Jack Paar got into trouble for saying "water closet" on TV. Nobody wanted to know that the ancients on Mt. Koshtan had pushed their sacrifices face down to suffocate in feces. Yet Jim had been fascinated. What could be the religious significance? Or, if these were merely executions for a crime, then what transgression would mandate this sort of punishment?

The other remains discovered there—in astounding shape considering their age, as most bones decomposed after only a few centuries—had all been traceable to rituals based upon standard cyclic, Stone Age religious beliefs. Sex, harvest and war. It happened to be what motivated modern killings as well, the harvest equating nowadays with acquisitions of wealth, the war being the same old same old international pastime or based upon personal vendetta, and the sex…well, that was identical in any language/any era. The violence with which it was accomplished was so *de rigueur* and par for the course that it barely managed to be a footnote.

This was what Jim had always wanted to do, an adult's search for meaningful and symbolic treasures in the Cracker Jacks. But he wouldn't get that in the classroom. He was convinced there were no nuggets of wisdom—ancient or otherwise—to be found in the skulls of his students. And without being permitted to discuss his own experiences in the field, what he had to offer them was next to nothing…somebody else's artifacts. Old news. Blah blah. A kid playing in a sandbox stood a better chance of unearthing the past than he did now.

This idea brought on a memory, of Jim as a small boy, with his family on a trip to—where? Some Civil War site. Gettysburg? Shiloh? (Probably Gettysburg, since he'd grown up in Philadelphia. It would have been a state's history kind of vacation.) He'd been sitting on the bare ground as his parents spread a blanket for a picnic on a former battlefield, opening containers of biscuits and fried chicken where minie balls had flowered in organs and cannon shot had blown off arms and legs. He'd started to touch the earth, then to pick up dirt by the handfuls and sift it through his fingers. He'd sensed something in this substance. It ran pictures like a movie through his head. It frightened him as he imagined he saw that dirt he funneled through his palms turning from brown to dark red and from cold dry to a hot wet. He winced, almost hearing screams. Blue and gray shadows lay around him, many very still, others convulsing—gutshot, stench in the—*air?*—of black shit. And him standing somewhere, close, very close, seeing many of these guys were just kids, a few years older than he was. He wanted to be able to put his hands in their wounds and pluck out the lead, gently replacing the loops of viscera until they seemed mostly normal again.

Instead, as he reached out, he started to poke his fingers into the ground, digging. And found a greening brass button with an eagle emblazoned on it.

"Let's eat, boy!" his father had called out.

Jim had stood up and gone somberly to the feast set upon the blanket in the grass. His mother had already made up a plate for him and held it out, smiling.

"We can't," Jim had told them, backing away from the food, suddenly sick. "We can't eat on top of the dead."

But Jim had recovered from this notion. He'd come to see that everywhere a man might take a mouthful of bread was over a spot where the dead were. The entire earth was filled with death. The land was stratified with layer upon layer of decayed life. The grain which had been grown to make the bread had nurtured in a soil of dead things; it was blessed with them or tainted by them—depending on point of view and degree of suggestibility.

As he grumbled over marking an unsatisfactory grade on the fourteenth test paper in a row—wondering if he allowed his unhappiness to color how he measured the answers to essay questions and deciding that he was, but that power lay invested in every disappointed academician as a perk of being one of those who taught because they couldn't do—the phone rang. He stared at it balefully, sipping his coffee which tasted more like the ink in his pen, grinding his last cigarette out on the corner of the test paper, wondering if it might be Dean York calling to tell him the board had decided not to grant him tenure. After the seventh ring he answered.

"Jim?" came a familiar voice with a strong hint of accent. "Is this Dr. Singer?"

"Yes," Jim replied, surprised. "Louis?"

"The very same! I have received a communication about an unusual object which has been unearthed. Would you be up for an impromptu sabbatical to Mexico?"

Perhaps his thinking about his intuition at certain sites had been a psychic flash that his old colleague was about to contact him. (Uh oh, pseudoscience, pseudo-hoodoo?) Well, damn it, why not? Jim listened to the pitch and agreed to fly out at once to Texas to meet Dr. Godard. For the first time in a decade he felt excitement. What was more, he felt purpose. This might validate everything. The dean could screw his tenure. Singer would have his pick of colleges.

++++++++++

"A man came to see me," Louis told Jim when they met at Love Field Airport. In his fifties now, Dr. Godard had aged well despite the career disappointments. Jim positively envied the spring in the other man's step. "He works for a chemical company in the process of building a factory in a place called San Inmundo. It's about a hundred miles or so from Mexico City. While digging foundation they discovered an apparent Aztec shrine."

Jim's eyebrows went up seeing the mischievous gleam in Louis' faded blue pupils. "Apparent?"

"Well, the assumption had it that the shrine was comprised of hewn black basalt. But it turned out to be baked-to-brick hardness fecal material."

Jim bit his lip, then said, "I've never heard of that with the Aztecs."

"Nor have I," agreed Dr. Godard. "Nor has anyone else."

"Who else knows?" Dr. Singer asked.

Louis shrugged. "Frankly, I'm not sure. The man said that the company was trying to keep it quiet so the government of Mexico wouldn't confiscate the property for study. So much has been stolen from them, who can blame them? It's their heritage. It's a shameful thing when archaeologists act no better than the conquistadors."

"How are we going to get in?"

"Our man's a foreman at the site. He'll be expecting us." Godard already had tickets waiting for them for the flight to Mexico City. There would be no time to rest or see any of Dallas. They did want to jump on this before the chance evaporated.

"Is this all?" Jim wanted to know. "Have you seen anything to back up what he says?"

Louis chuckled. "He gave me…a relative term, *gave*. Rather he *sold* me a manuscript, written by a priest traveling with Cortés. I made a copy which we are taking along, translated into English by a friend of mine at the university. I'll show it to you on the flight down."

"And the original?"

"Is in my safe at home."

++++++++++

In 1519 I, Father Osvaldo Encarnacion Estrera, had seen the altars of Tenochtitlan, witnessed the harvesting of the red cactus fruit offered to strange gods to hold back even stranger beasts of the twilight. I had seen the bodies of victims thrown down the bloody steps of the temples, pulled away so that their flesh could be used to prepare dishes which the priests would eat. Sometimes the killing would go on all day and into the night, depending on which holy festival was being celebrated and which god was being honored.

I had gasped and genuflected at arms and legs sold as meat in the market place, swinging from tethers like the separate pieces of far-East wind chimes. Nearby would be baskets of tomatoes and peppers. Next to bundles of brightly colored feathers from green quetzal and blue cotinga, drums made from the shells of enormous Atlantean turtles, and ornate jewelry created out of silver set with brilliantly sky blue turquoise. I had observed people dancing half-naked in the street, bedecked as fiercely-plumaged birds or sinuous as serpents. I had tried not to judge for that is God's right alone. I only tried to understand their beliefs, savage and incomprehensible as they were. I learned quite a lot about their rituals of carnage and renewal, the meaning of life and destiny after death. I came to accept that there was more to this religion than the superficially macabre. It contained a thoughtful inner essence of sacred rebirth and the journey of the spirit, as well as a profound and ceaseless struggle to keep the demonic world from destroying the world of light, similar to my own Catholic tenets. Not that their methods of attempting to achieve this didn't completely horrify me, because they certainly did. I had trouble—as indeed any Christian would—reconciling such wholesale slaughter with a battle to defeat chaos. And surrounding tribes hated the Aztecs, since a major source of sacrificial victims were those captured by the Aztecs during war. These other Indians said the Aztecs were arrogant and vicious, and many joined Cortés to defeat them forever.

Tenochtitlan, a city more beautiful than all the best cities in Europe combined, was brought down in 1521—mostly with siege and starvation and smallpox. The Aztecs committed atrocities but what might I call what I saw Spaniards do? Plunder and rapine. Killing men, women and children together, sacrifices to greed and Jesus. And then they would come to me and confess—to much less than I had seen them do with my own eyes! I had to bless them for this was my function. And then I wept, burdened until some days I did not think I could stand up. The beautiful city was torn down.

All the gold within became the property of Spain.

But where had all that gold come from?

We Spanish heard rumors, of a mine in a valley amid the mountains to the west. Near a city called Temictlazolli, which was made up of those who had fled Tenochtitlan because their own theology was considered heretical. The Aztec refugees I talked to—through my interpreter, of course—shuddered when interviewed about this heresy. All they would say was that these followers of schism performed the vilest, most unspeakable of rites. No matter the coercion or persuasion, they would reveal no more.

I was troubled by this. What could be so awful that even the Aztecs would shun it? I could not imagine.

++++++++++

"I researched the name of this place. Temictlazolli is a combination of words, not unusual for the Nahuatl. Temictl is the word for dream and tlazolli means filth. It is 'the filthy city,'" Godard explained on board their flight.

"Who would name a city that?" asked Jim as he read from the translated copy of Estrera's manuscript, set open on a tray in Godard's lap.

"Well, actually 'San Inmundo' means approximately the same thing, which may or may not speak volumes of what the Spanish who named it were thinking. All I know is that I could not find Temictlazolli on any map of that period, nor any later. Nor is it mentioned in the Codex Mendoza nor upon any other manuscripts of Aztec writings."

The two men shared a look.

"Please don't let this be a hoax," Jim said, crossing his fingers.

++++++++++

In 1522, Cortés sent part of the army to investigate the possible gold mine. I accompanied them. We saw many terrible sights as we crossed the mountains. Near one snowy peak there was a village beside a narrow, deep lake so cold that on some nights when the moon was full it appeared to turn white. Birds the colors of rainbow frost drank there. The fish caught were like ice and if you dropped one against a rock, it would shatter. The people had a most unusual method of sacrifice. They placed the victims inside small handsewn nets and then squeezed until their intestines burst out. Another place employed an idea I had seen the Aztecs use. Victims were decapitated, rods inserted through the mouths to exit the back of the skulls. Then the heads were displayed upon a rack until they rotted and fell apart. It seemed an inappropriate place to see thousands of butterflies, gemstone wings like hands folded in prayer and riding upon the backs of jaguars.

A third appeared to be some sort of monastery erected in rock halfway up a sleeping volcano. Inside the stone abode were the mummified remains of some of the priests. The tops of their skulls had been sawn off and flowers grew out of the dusty gardens of their brains. Their chests were hollowed out where hearts had been removed and hummingbirds nested there.

At last the army neared Temictlazolli. We passed fields of corn twenty feet tall. It was black beneath the shadows of the mountains. The ears were each as long as a grown man's forearm. The smell was sweet, almost nauseatingly so.

I paused to pick an ear of the corn for examination. The kernels were black as beads of jet, of black jade, of midnight obsidian glass. I guessed it must be something from the nearby volcano that nurtured the corn into this color and caused it to grow so tall.

++++++++++

The pilot announced the descent into Mexico City.

"When does it get to the part we want?" asked Dr. Singer, seeing many pages left they hadn't yet reviewed. It wasn't that this didn't fascinate him but he hoped for a tie-in with what they had found on Mt. Koshtan.

"Yes, that is back here," replied Godard as he thumbed to a place toward the end of the manuscript, marked with a napkin. He forgave the younger man's impatience, understanding that what lay at stake was no less than their entire careers.

++++++++++

The interpreter said, "They think you look like well-fed maggots."

Referring to our white skins, no doubt. This was a far cry from having natives mistake us for gods.

I was familiar with Tlazolteotl-Ixcuiana, a goddess sometimes depicted wearing human skin flayed from a living victim. She was associated with the spring season and with fertility rites similar to those abominable rituals done in the name of renewal for Xipe Totec. The goddess I now saw before me was carved all from black stone and appeared to be garlanded in plump, sculpted loops of intestines.

It made sense with what I had witnessed the last several weeks. Outwardly this town was as the other Aztec cities we had seen, beautiful and sparkling. In Tenochtitlan we smelled blood, blood everywhere. Here there was a taint of something even more sinister—if it is possible to be darker and more evil than gore. We had arrived in time for the beginning of the harvest season. Victims were first encased in boxes with just their heads emerging, kept all in darkness, only pine torches at the entrance. They were stuffed with meat and sweetbreads for a fortnight to fatten, sitting in their own piling excreta which permeated their flesh with a septic odor. I could smell them even at the opposite end of the town.

Taking us as guests to the sacred place, we passed a shocking variation of the skull rack. There only the lower halves of torsos were displayed, legless, impaled through just above the pubes and out the rectum where the sphincters had prolapsed.

And then that lovely Indian girl I had been so taken with… She who I had nearly managed to baptise. She was their ritual "queen," brought out as the priests chanted, "Izca! Tla xihuallauh tezzohuaz tonatiuh tlazolli!"

"Behold! Come forth to be stained from filth!"

The Indians drank a mixture of pure cocoa, the preserved excrement of the first priest to eat from last year's corn harvest, and a snake herb called coaxiuth. They called this concoction *coatl chocolatl*: snake chocolate. They offered this to us and a very few of the men were curious enough or stupid enough to try it. The snake herb was a powerful hallucinogen.

I almost did not recognize the girl. She wore the fouled skins of the victims who had that morning been taken from their boxes and offered on that hideous dark altar. She bent to don the necklaces of their impacted bowels, feces smeared upon her lips and cheeks in the most obscene of rouges. She led a parade out to the fields where she was butchered, hacked into tiny pieces and strewn among the soil to fertilize the corn as the priests sang, "Tla xihuallauh, yayauhqui-Cihuatl. Otihuallauh nonan-Tlazolli!"

"Come now, Dark-Woman. Welcome Filthy Mother!"

68

We were sick at heart. The soldiers were ready to strike the entire population down. Not that this would be extreme for them, for they often massacred inhabitants. I had seen Spaniards with trophies of severed arms and legs from children in their hands, guts set as victors' laurel wreaths on their heads or around their throats. But how could I compare their hypocrisy with this new horror?

This was by far the most disgusting thing we had viewed since reaching the shores of this country. I began to understand why even the Aztecs abhorred the rituals of these people, these outcasts from their own group.

But then those who had drunk the snake chocolate began to shriek, plunging their bodies together in the vilest of orgies—what the Inquisitors of Holy Mother Church reported as done during witches' sabbats. Those soldiers who had drunk with them stripped off their armor and clothes to join the indecent mob. The others began to draw out their swords, faces grimacing, eyes blazing with indignation and bloodlust.

And then a shadow came out of the corn fields. It began to take the shape of a naked woman with flesh the color of smoke. She wore a veil across her face. The ground began to move beneath our feet—not as with the tremors of an earthquake but with a liquid sliding as if it were no longer solid earth but changing to another, horrible, element.

Mother of God, I turned away. I ran and did not look back.

++++++++++

Godard and Singer boarded a small plane in Mexico City which flew them to San Inmundo. There they hired a driver to take them to the site where the American chemical plant was building its new factory. The car bumped along bad roads, a plastic statue of the madonna swinging from the rearview mirror.

Dr. Godard said, "I discovered more than one reference to a goddess of filth in the Aztec religion. One is as Tlazolteotl. She is identified by a band of raw cotton on her headpiece and a dark spot around her nose and mouth. People who were guilty of having committed adultery, or who were what the Aztecs referred to as loose-haired prostitutes and who hadn't been caught in their sin, could escape punishment by making a public confession to this goddess. But there was a rule of only one confession to a customer. If they did it again they could be executed."

"I take it hookers who kept their hair up were okay," Jim joked.

"You never know." Louis smiled. "Another reference referred to four goddesses of love and filth. The singular for them is, incidentally, Tlazolteotl—same as the name given the goddess I just spoke of. Perhaps she was a later composite of the four deities."

Jim nodded. "Streamlined. Like some Christians lump all the variations of ancient demons into a single manifestation of the devil."

The driver kept looking at them in the rearview. Perhaps he understood sufficient English to be troubled by their conversation. It was a hot day yet the windows were rolled up, doubtless in deference to what might have been the finer sensibilities of these two tourists. With his weight problem, Jim tended to sweat buckets and he did now. But he still realized the windows being closed had to be a blessing, for through those windows both men could see squalor, garbage and waste everywhere. Pigs and dogs nosed into piles of every sort of steaming refuse, their own messes thick in the gutter. There was little proper sanitation here; the citizens were too poor and the government made no attempt to take care of them. It looked just like the worst areas of Mexico City where American factories built because they could get away with dumping their toxic by-products where they pleased, not to be concerned with being fined or with public outrage.

Louis could do nothing about this, so he simply continued with the conversation. "Precisely. The names of these four goddesses are Cuaton, Caxxoch, Tlahui and Xapel. I do find it interesting how love and filth are combined under one banner. It's unusual, isn't it?"

Jim laughed, a little nervously, while also trying not to stare out the windows. He'd seen miserable living conditions before, in other countries where his field of research had taken him. "Oh, I don't know. I've seen some men's magazines and stag films that did a fair job of putting the two concepts together."

The car drove through a dirty bazaar, vendors to either side of the street. There was one with bowls of a turgid, red chili sauce for sale, the vessels carved out of dark volcanic stone. It reminded Jim of the bowls the Aztecs had used to catch the blood of sacrificial victims. Here, too, brimming with bright red pulp. Another had a rack from which butchered chickens swung. He thought of the markets of Tenochtitlan selling human flesh, limbs jangling like far-East wind chimes. But the Spanish reports all agreed that the Aztecs had such clean cities, not like the filthy capitals of Europe at the time. Father Estrera even said that Temictlazolli appeared lovely and well-ordered...at least at first.

The car slowed to a stop as a group of nuns crossed the avenue from one corner to the next where there was a small, lopsided church. It looked as if it had been made of mud (or *coatl chocolatl*) and then melted. Seeing the nuns, then seeing the black-frocked priest in the doorway, caused Jim to shudder uncontrollably for a moment.

"Are you all right?" Louis asked him.

The shaking stopped and he nodded without speaking. Yet he mopped his face with his tie. Normally he never wore a tie to go to an excavation site, but he knew they were going to be dealing with officials and he didn't want to seem like a hippie.

Children chased one another around an Excusado, a public toilet, the only one they had seen since arriving in San Inmundo. It had overflowed and the kids ran through the raw sewage with their bare feet. A pitted stone fountain splashed an unappetizing yellow water. A man strolled by with a fistful of greasy balloons of grinning devils and tentacled octopi. Jim noticed a booth selling tiny silver replicas of body parts. He asked the driver about it.

"You choose one matching the area of your body which is diseased. You pin it to the skirt of The Virgin at the church and this—with prayers—will restore this member to good health," the man explained. Pretty good English at that.

"Yeah?" Jim wondered aloud. He said, half-joking, "Think they have one for fat?"

The car left the marketplace. After a few more blocks, the driver told them, "The plant site is just there."

They could see the chain link fence which had been built around it, ten feet tall. A few metal sheds were up and bulldozers sat silent. The work had been stopped because of the finding of the altar. Had anything else been unearthed?

Suddenly the driver yelled and braked to a sharp stop which threw both doctors forward.

"What is it?" Godard asked, rubbing his knees from where he'd collided with the back of the seat in front of him.

But the driver didn't reply. He opened his door and jumped out, his body shaking from head to foot, eyes popping. He genuflected.

"Look at that," Jim said as he pointed to the swinging statue above the dashboard.

It had begun to bleed a black liquid from its backside. Both docs wrinkled their noses.

The driver took off running back the other way. Leaving them and the car.

"It is odd," Godard commented, standing up as much as he could and leaning across the seat. He reached out his hand and touched the viscous fluid leaking from the plastic madonna. He sniffed it, rubbed it between his fingers. *"Merde!"*

He withdrew a handkerchief from a coat pocket and wiped his fingers clean.

"I'll refrain from asking," Jim said as the older man simply nodded with a wry face.

"Shall we see if our foreman is here as promised?" Louis suggested. "The odds should be in our favor for something going as planned. If the science concerning the ratio of probability and non-probability can have any meaning."

They got out of the car. Jim noticed as soon as his feet were on the ground that he felt strange. The old sensation coming back about something down in the earth. It vibrated into his leg bones. He reached down and picked up a handful of soil. For a split second he thought he saw the silhouettes of giant black corn on the other side of the fence.

It grew deep, deep into the earth, with roots in that proverbial underground network. Near hell? Or was this place actually hell?

Louis had stopped in his tracks, understanding that the younger doc was having one of his—what did Louis consider them to be?—*'Epiphanies'*.

"Feel something?" Godard asked him.

Jim nodded. "Yeah, a lot like on Koshtan."

Louis smiled. "Well then, this must be the place."

The two men walked up to a gate.

To their surprise, it was no foreman who met them but a pair of armed soldiers.

"*No entrada*," one of the soldiers told them, brandishing his rifle.

The other pointed to a sign on the gate.

"What does it say?" Jim wanted to know.

Louis sighed. "My guess would be from the few words I understand that it says the property has been confiscated by the Mexican government. *Merde! C'est la vie!*"

"Maybe the driver left the keys," Jim remarked hopefully as he turned around.

The two men peered into the front seat. The dark moisture now spewed from the statue, so much it could not possibly originate from such a small object. Yet there it was. It streamed down the dashboard and puddled on the floor and the front seat. It splashed the windshield. It stank even though the windows to the car were rolled up.

Dr. Godard stepped back. "I for one will walk, *mon ami*. Care to join me?"

++++++++++

The Zuni tribe had a brotherhood called the Ne'wekwe who performed a ritual dance during which they both drank urine and consumed excrement. These substances were believed to contain a healing magic. The men were also thought courageous for doing this and the tribe heaped praise on whichever man got the most down with the greatest show of enthusiasm.

—*Sacred Sepsis*
Dr. Louis Godard and Dr. James Singer

CHAPTER
7

SUBWAY TUNNELS,
1991

Myrtle thought she'd had it for a moment there. It was because it was Christmas and a bunch of drunks had been singing (if you could call that singing) carols as they passed around a couple bottles of Mad Dog 20/20 some generous yet misguided soul with a sudden urge to give a bit of charity had laid on them. She smelled the sour tang of putrified grape juice, like some potable from a church intended for mass that a mischievous choir boy has pissed into.

If this be their sacramental drink, what are they using for the communion wafer?

One of them made a joke. Apparently he was an old bugger who'd served in The War. (Vietnam? somebody asked.) (Naw, *the war*! Before long-haired hippie draft-dodgers and troops sent to save some businessman's portfolio, he grumbled. We knew what we were fightin' for!)

Number Two.

But back to the joke. They used to serve this chipped beef gravy on toast in the mess hall. Called it S.O.S. if they were being polite. Called it Shit On A Shingle when they were feeling bolder.

They passed around some cartons of take-out they'd found in a dumpster. Egg Foo Yung and spring rolls so frosty and old the stuff was as hard as the communal wafer and smelled of the dirty diaper which had lain next to the cartons in the trash.

They had rejoined in singing, and it had something to do with the religious sentiment and the way it floated unevenly down through the underground that made her strain to think what it reminded her of. It made her feel sort of sad and simultaneously comforted.

Fall on your knees! Oh hear the angels' voices!

This bunch didn't really sound much like angels or any kind of chorus other than that which might bay at the moon after a romp of mutual tail-chasing at the city dump. But it might have been that very gruff quality—unpolished and with dust inside the throat—that touched her.

She kept in the darkness, feeling her way along the wall, getting as close as she dared so she could see them.

Yeah, Myrtle knew these guys. They had attacked her only six weeks ago. They had raped her while the thunder of the trains drowned out her screams. They had taken turns with her on her back and on her stomach and forced into a position of prayer. (*Fall on your knees!*) She'd bled out her cunt so much they joked she'd started her period. And she'd got diarrhea so bad she'd had to stuff toilet paper in her rectum for a week. The old man hadn't even been able to get it up, no matter how much he made her suck. So he'd used a foreleg cut from a dead dog. He'd also commanded her, "Howl, little bitch! Howl like a mutt!"

Now they saw her standing there, watching them sing Christmas songs. Myrtle thought for sure she was in for it, never should have done anything but run the other way.

But nobody rose to go after her. They didn't even really turn their heads toward her. She just saw their faces as they stared down, eyes flickering a bit to the side. They'd stopped caroling and wiped their mouths, saying nothing, not even to one another.

One by one, they scrabbled to get onto their knees and began to crawl away, the opposite direction from her. Hands and knees down the tunnel, leaving the food and the wine. There was so much rubbish on the ground: rocks and broken glass and used needles. Were they performing some kind of penance?

"Atonement is where you choose to have it," she said to herself, softly, trying not to allow her words to echo. "But it's a performance art, impermanent and without any guarantee of salvation. No, redemption comes only after forgiveness. And who do I forgive? Not them, not anyone."

And she drew upon the wall, lines sometimes not sure because of the rumbling of the trains.

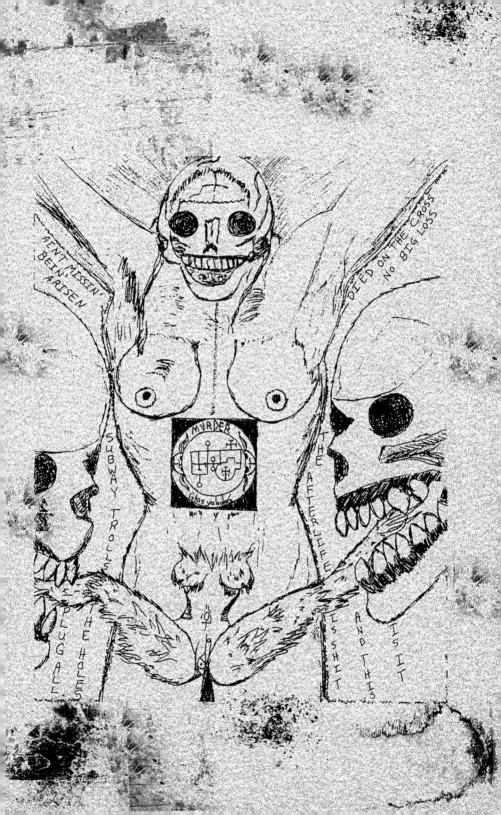

CHAPTER
8

SHEOL'S DITCH,
1977

The cheapskate landlord didn't actually repair the wall in Jason's closet where the boy had punched the hole with the knife. All the fellow did was cover the gape with a section of plywood. Big Garth and Jason worked together to make this removable without being obvious about it, enlargening the aperture so Jason could slip into Garth Listo's place while Ice and Bowtie believed he was yet locked in his room.

"You orient the plant in space," the young man explained to his neighbor, Garth's large frame in a silk robe of Japanese style.

Jason was so fascinated with those tiny trees! He moved all the way around a fully matured pine which was no more than three feet high. It even had fragrant, miniscule cones. He wanted to observe it from all angles, as if it were a trick of sleight of hand, performed by a magician with a talent for illusion.

"But why?" Jason asked. "Or is it just because they look cool this way?"

Big Garth laughed. "Beauty is always merely a secondary motive. It's really about power. I control the direction, shape, and size. I train it to do my bidding, contrary to its nature."

"So how long does it take to grow them like this?" the kid wanted to know.

"It takes several decades to really get them going. I acquired some of these about five years ago, already in progress. The others—the ones that aren't magnificent yet—I started about that same time," the man said with obvious pride, happy for the chance to show off his work.

Jason didn't have to feign interest. For weeks it was practically all they talked about. Trees so intricate, normally forty to fifty feet high maybe— why you'd have to be a giant to tower over them so. You'd have to be a god.

He showed the kid how to use the clippers. Where to put supports which aided in the bending of a plant. How it might be fastened to twist to his desires. "Bending it," Garth would say whimsically, "like a passive slave. Yet a cherished one, never to be abused."

Slipping nightly into Garth's apartment, Jason worked on the art of bonsai. He learned light utilization and the proper way to restrict nutrition, even as he pruned both roots and tops judiciously. Garth actually put him in sole charge of a tree. Nobody had ever trusted him with anything before.

B.G. peered through his glasses and pointed. "Train at the spot on the primary stem from which the branches grow. Look at the trunk as the tree's central axis, branches growing laterally up and down and around this stem. If you end the progress of the main stem, you force the growth through certain branches that originate near the upper end of the trunk. If we could film it for years and then speed it up, it would resemble a kind of tortuous ballet."

Jason learned delicacy this way—rather difficult for a child's immature, manic hands. He adopted patience he didn't think he had in him. And the result was so satisfying, even if many years had to pass before what essentially was a microcosmic sapling would become an artistic accomplishment, a personal definition of beauty laid upon a form usually only God had any say in. Yes, this felt like power. Not the brute force kind. Different, subtle, patient.

"Wow," Jason commented after about a year. "Imagine going further. Making them grow into anything you want. The shapes of demons maybe."

"Yeah, that's called topiary. The ancient Romans did that," Big Garth told him. "They had entire grotesque gardens, suitable for enjoyment by the most jaded patricians. Sometimes they had slaves that had also been twisted loping through these gardens like freakish fawns or crawling like mutated serpents."

Garth had only just moved into the place the night Jason cut through the closet wall. Since then, of course, the big man had finished unpacking. There were hundreds of books. He had samurai swords on display. And framed woodblock artwork from Japan he called *muzan-e*. These consisted of atrocity prints from the 1800s, of high-foreheaded Japanese men, usually in the process of torturing and cutting up Japanese women.

"This selection over here is rare. Yoshitoshi Tsukioka and Yoshiiku Ochiai," Garth explained. "See this one, with the woman trussed up in the air? He looks as if he's making a bonsai of her, doesn't he? He takes what might ordinarily be considered an outrage and deftly converts it into an art-form."

Big Garth made these comments so naturally, without pretention or maniacal eye-gleaming, that Jason couldn't fail to be impressed. It was most amazing, being exposed to this viewpoint from an obviously intelligent adult: could this be evil? Was there a third category outside of good and bad where you could be exempt from the usual moral dictates, based on education and a higher esthetic competence? Sure, that's why wealthy people and movie stars so often got away with things the law threw lesser mortals in jail for. How often had Jason heard it said that the rich were different?

"Have you ever done that?" Jason asked, ogling the atrocity print that Garth had compared with bonsai. He'd never thought of a woman and a plant as interchangeable before.

Garth slowly shook his head, rubbing his chin thoughtfully as he, too, stared at the piece.

He also had one of those newfangled video recorders. Invented in Japan! He seemed to have a thing for Japanese movies but not the Godzilla type Jason was familiar with. The boy saw titles on Sony Beta tapes. They were usually in Japanese first, then with the English version of the title. *Kyoso Joshiko (Death Of A Madman)*. *Niku No Hyotek Tobo (Screaming Flesh Target)*. *Gendai Sei Hanza: Zekkyohen: Ryu Naki Boko (Modern Sex Crimes: Fierce Screams, Wild Rape)*.

Sometimes when Jason slipped through the hole in the closet wall, he found Garth—in a kimono—watching these movies with intense fascination. Some contained violent sex acts but with a blurred grid so the viewer couldn't see any actual penetration. Yet Garth wore over his own glasses this funky looking pair that reminded Jason of the 3-D specs that movies handed out. With these he could see through the grid. (As if into another, forbidden, dimension.)

Seeing Garth do this was actually a relief. Jason knew what pedophiles were and had suspected this might be why the man had befriended him. Well, *really*, the big guy often wore those long silk robes that looked like dresses.

But Garth never laid a hand on him nor asked him to do anything threatening, not in the year since he and Jason had become friends. The man apparently preferred women—just not quite in the traditional sense. (Unless this was traditional for Japan. Jason didn't know. He'd seen enough brutality in his own neighborhood that this might just be normal everywhere.)

Often, outside Jason's door at night—on the occasions when he was there in bed—he'd hear that buzzing. Sometimes Ice would moan, a freaky sound like a fire engine's siren being strangled on qualudes. A morning after this, he saw a bright red circle all the way around her wrist as she set his cereal in front of him. She quickly pulled down her sweater sleeve to cover it up.

"I was a samurai, you know. In Nanking," Garth told him one night.

"You were?" The kid didn't know what he was talking about. How could he be that if he was an American?

"In my last life. It's why I'm so interested in Japan," he replied, serious as he could be. "I started to remember stuff when I was your age. I didn't even have to learn bonsai. I just knew how. Man, were my folks pissed. My dad served in the Philippines in WW2. He knew guys on the Bataan Death March."

That's how he said it: WW2.

He showed the boy tapes from 1938, taken by the Japanese after they invaded that Chinese city. A history lesson, yes. The Japanese soldiers grinned and held their cameras just like the tourists the boy saw around town.

There was film about these two sublieutenants who indulged in a beheading contest to see who could chop off a hundred heads first. Garth even had a copy of a newspaper, *The Japanese Advertiser*, which showed the photos of these guys on the front page.

He pointed to script and said, "This translates out to 'Contest To Kill First 100 Chinese With Sword Extended When Both Fighters Exceed Mark—Mukai Scores 106 And Noda 105.'"

Garth pointed to the guy on the left and said proudly, "That was me. I was him, right there. You can tell when you see a picture sometimes. Your eyes look into theirs and you feel a spark, like what it takes to continue a fire from Point A to Point B."

Jason had never heard of this. The Nazi concentration camps were covered in his school's history class. And Pearl Harbor when the Japanese sneak-attacked. But not one word about wholesale terrors done on the men, women, and children of Nanking where murder and rape were turned into a nonstop sport. Jason watched the atrocities as if it was just the movies. His memories of the murders of his parents were that way, like recalling a particularly grisly movie he'd seen. Like *The Last House on the Left* and *The Texas Chainsaw Massacre*. If it stirred anything in him, it wasn't fear or revulsion. A yearning maybe, one he couldn't quite place. Why would he want to crawl into the carnage piles and lie down? Why did he expect comfort there?

++++++++++

SHEOL'S DITCH, 1979

Jason just sat up one night, remembered what Garth had said when he first pounded on his door and demanded to be let in. Big Garth was seated on this very short wooden stool, paging through catalogs advertising women offering themselves as foreign brides. This was what passed for chairs in Garth's place. He'd explained they were traditional, classic Japanese. Jason found them uncomfortable and usually just sat on the floor when he visited.

Through the wall, Jason could hear that noise which he'd never heard before except for right outside his bedroom door. It was the buzzing sound which reminded him of the helicopter dream. And of the chainsaw penis of the red-headed man beyond the gate.

"Oh, no" Jason sobbed. "The gate's closed."

"Huh?"

Jason shrugged his shoulders, mournfully shaking his head. "I didn't have a chance anyway. The pilot said only **Superman** gets inside."

The big man laughed. "Cool! Thus Spake Zarathustra!"

"What's 'Must Shake Zza Zza Krishna?'"

Garth glanced up, hearing something, too. Except he looked back toward his own bedroom door first. But there was no sound coming from that direction. He frowned momentarily and ground his teeth. Did he even hear the buzzing coming from the Cursky place?

"Excuse me?" asked Garth, clearly perplexed and distracted. Yet he didn't act at all as if he minded Jason being there.

"You said that once," Jason told him, and then reiterated the event which had brought them together.

"Oh! Existentialism. It was Nietzsche and *Thus Spake Zarathustra.*" And then Big Garth quoted, "...my secret laughter: I suspect ye would call my **Superman**—a devil!"

Jason snickered. "Ye?"

"He often used archaic words." Garth shrugged as he marked his place in the catalog. Then he got up from the stool, padded barefoot over to a large bookcase, and pulled a volume. It was small, yet he hefted it in his hands as if it were an encyclopedia. "You get used to it. Just because it's stilted doesn't make it any less true."

He handed the book to the boy. "Verily, there is still a future even for evil!"

B.G. had believed him completely when the kid recounted what he'd seen through the hole in his closet: the eye that spoke, the landscape with no horizon, the brutality like a forbidden candy store.

"I felt sorry for No Man—that kid, I mean—and wanted to help him.

But then, when I saw this place, all I wanted was to be there. I wanted it more than I've ever wanted anything."

Garth nodded sagely. "Did you know that the Tibetans believe that when you dream you actually go to real places? Some shamanic religions see two forms of reality, the waking and the *other*. Each one is considered to be real only as long as you're there."

"But I was awake when I saw this," Jason argued politely.

"There are lots of accounts all through history of people who've glimpsed into other times and worlds. There was a teenaged girl who saw an ancient army on the coast of England. There are all those disappearances in the Bermuda Triangle that some say are due to a rift between the dimensions. Others conclude that sightings of spaceships and aliens are really seeing into the future, or maybe they're coming from the sea or from within the earth. There are the stories of Atlantis and Mu. And how about ghosts? Are we only glimpsing a part of the past, like a glitch in a record? You never know. You might have been seeing into the hollow earth, a popular theory for centuries. Might explain why there were no horizons. And just a few years ago, at the Great Serpent Mound in Ohio, *Ohio* for chrissakes!, some sociologist saw the leaves sneaking up on him, coming up and going down just like feet, then swirling around him like witches in a moon dance. Dude! This wasn't some ignorant trailer trash redneck with a chaw between the tooth and gum, and his finger at the crack of his ass. This was a guy with a college degree. Hell, shit falls from the sky: frogs, beans, fish... Where does it come from?"

How great was this guy? Jason wondered as he grinned, interested in everything that came out of Garth's mouth. In two years, this man had never bored him.

Garth took the Nietzsche volume away. "That's for a little later, I think. Tell you what, let's give you this one first." He bent to a lower shelf to retrieve a different volume. "This might be a good one to start with."

Jason read the title and knew Garth must be right. How could a boy such as he not be enraptured by something named, *The Book Of The Damned*?

He'd taken it home through the hole in the closet. Hadn't taken it to school with him for fear he'd lose it. He wasn't worried that his guardians would find it for he was sure they never went into his room at all. If they did, they would have questioned him about all the unusual things he kept in his dresser, under the bed, stuffed into the closet. Radios, cameras, wallets with cash, knives, a couple of guns (one broken, one not), expensive boots too big for him, silver/gold/maybe platinum jewelry and watches. Items he stole as he taught himself a valuable trade.

He salivated just thinking about that book as he sat in his classes, fidgeting, putting up with the mindless drivel his teachers thought it suitable for him to learn. Got into a fight right after the last bell—as he was trying to leave for home—with some hold-back from two grades who'd just moved into the neighborhood and wanted to establish dominance. Jason had felt the kid grab him from behind by the scruff of the neck and actually lift him an inch from the floor. Saying quite a lot since Jason was big for his age.

"You the necro feeler slept with his dead folks, right?" the Frankenstein-foreheaded boy demanded with a grin, showing a crooked line of lower teeth and practically no upper ones at all.

Jason hadn't answered but swung about, letting the collar of his shirt wring a raw-red corrugated crease in his neck as he punched his attacker right in the throat. *Pop! Crack!* He could actually feel the area fill with blood while his fist was still against the spot. An ambulance was called and, even though the attendants finally got the kid breathing again, he was still going to need emergency surgery for the tracheal injury. Jason spent two hours in the principal's office, wondering what might be in that book waiting for him under his pillow. The police went away after a school bus driver said he'd seen the other kid start it.

"Why do you suppose these guys jump you?" the principal asked him, weary circles under the man's eyes. "Been happening to you for years, hasn't it?"

"My parents were murdered. I was there. Everybody knows it. Children can be so cruel," Jason said, parodying some tragic little face he'd seen somewhere or other. Stuck out his lower lip and faked a sniffle. Come on, come on! He wanted to get home to that book. He wasn't some dumb-assed, oxygen-starved braindead punk who would never learn to tie his shoes much less read. This man was holding up the furtherance of his education.

"You don't exactly make yourself an unworthy target. You've got a hefty reputation for someone so young. Any kid out to make a name for himself finds out right away he's got to go through you first. Fastest gun in the west always had to prove it, usually died young." Was this old guy, like, trying to be paternal?

Jason chuckled. "You're right. Next one, I'll lick his asshole and let him be the alpha male. Okay? Can I go now? Because unless you're willing to actually start protecting me, then I have to protect myself. You said it yourself—they jump me."

The principal's shoulders sagged. He knew he couldn't protect anybody. Pelan Elementary in Sheol's Ditch was the most violent school for grades one through six in the city. There was no death row in the state anymore, but children graduating there would likely become the adults responsible for having the death penalty reinstated.

"Get out of here," he told Jason. "Thank God you haven't killed anyone yet."

Jason didn't contradict him. Only fools bragged.

He got home barely in time for supper. Meatloaf like a small red brick.

Covered in catsup too rusty-tasting to be trusted. The TV played on with its parade of squeaky-clean families and cities without trash.

He excused himself and rushed to his room, taking out the wondrous book.

Book of the Damned
By Charles Fort

Jason's hands were clammy. He opened it to the beginning of the first chapter.

'1

'A procession of the damned. By the damned, I mean the excluded.'

That was Jason, definitely. The excluded. He touched the yellowish-brown flesh of the pages.

'Some of them are corpses, skeletons, mummies, twitching, tot-tering, animated by companions that have been damned alive. There are giants that will walk by, though sound asleep. There are things that are theorems and things that are rags: they'll go by like Euclid arm in arm with the spirit of anarchy. Here and there will flit little harlots. Many are clowns. But many are of the highest respectability. Some are assassins. There are pale stenches and gaunt superstitions and mere shadows and lively malices…'

He read passionately, pausing only as the key was fitted into the lock of his bedroom door. Click-nick. And later he heard the buzzing drone. But all he did was go to his window for a few minutes, looking out and up, hoping for the sight of falling cold rocks. Or black rain. Or maybe showers of some-thing dead. But where his window looked out at the back of the apartment building, he could really only glimpse a small patch of sky. In a city rife with shadowy canyons, Sheol's Ditch was made up of bricked crevasses and gulches of crumbling brownstone/brimstone. The alley running between the buildings on this side of the block and the ones on the other side was what some might have called a "defile". A word which also meant to corrupt. That was a passageway between mountains. And here he was in his part of the mountain on the left, Jason *Cave*, a hollow little boy being filled lately with the most frightful of enlightening and defiling esoterica, looking up from a defile to try to find a patch of emetic night sky. Damn! He loved language!

And if he did manage to see…? Perhaps he'd see Melanicus, the Prince of Dark Bodies, navigating interplanetary space. Not really just a sun spot: nothing so simple and mundane, so utterly without drama. But what Charles Fort thought was Melanicus—a vast, black vampire that sometimes brooded over this earth and other bodies.

He wanted to eat just one page. Even just a single word—damned—off of one page. But there was no way he would damage this. It belonged to Garth; Garth had entrusted him with it. It was, in fact, a treasure!

He read the entire book that night, stretching out his right hand, biting the inside of his cheek with every stab of pain in the middle and forefinger. He hadn't told anyone but he'd broken those two fingers hitting that kid in the throat. He used the discomfort to keep him awake. He'd stretch them out, feeling: Pop! *Crack!*.......(blood filling the spot).......*Click! NICK!* It felt like a magical gesture of evocation. The agony made him dizzy, nauseous, ecstatic. He read, and what he read and how he stretched out that invoking hand made it seem as if magic were done with a few words and a spasm.

'27
'Vast and black. The thing that was poised, like a crow over the moon.
'Round and smooth. Cannon balls. Things that have fallen from the sky to this earth.
'Showers of blood.
'Showers of blood.
'Showers of blood.'

He half-expected to see that wondrous place again where hovering eyes spoke and there were no horizons to hold desire in check. If he saw it now... Hell, yes, he'd enter without hesitation.

'Rivers of blood that vein albuminous seas, or an egglike composition in the incubation of which this earth is a local center of development—that there are superarteries of blood in Genesistrine: that sunsets are conscious of them: that they flush the skies with northern lights sometimes: super-embryonic reservoirs from which life-forms emanate—
'Or that our whole solar system is a living thing: that showers of blood upon this earth are its internal hemorrhages—
'Or vast living things in the sky, as there are vast living things in the oceans—
'Or some one special thing: an especial time: an especial place. A thing the size of the Brooklyn Bridge. It's alive in outer space something the size of Central Park kills it—
'It drips.'

But no crossover presented itself. Still, Jason wasn't deterred. Even if these efforts didn't produce the place now—(and how he ached to!)—he knew he would see it again. Once it had summoned him. He would learn to summon it.

++++++++++

"What happened?" asked Garth the next evening, immediately seeing the broken fingers—which the principal had missed and the cops had missed. And the ambulance attendants and Ice and Bowtie had failed to notice.

"I received a slight injury whilst defending the honor of the damned," Jason replied, leaning heavily on the word *whilst*. He hoped he'd said it right.

Garth set the fingers for him, using chopsticks for splints.

Jason heard a slight noise from Garth's bedroom. Whimpering? He wouldn't be rude and inquire. It had always been an unspoken rule between them, that Jason visited as much as he liked but respected Garth's space and privacy.

"Have you started the book yet?" he asked the boy. If he'd heard the sound, he ignored it.

Jason grinned. "Started and finished. Cool! Got more?"

Garth laughed and happily provided. *The Lost Continent of Mu* by James Churchward, *A Journey to the Earth's Interior* by Marshall Gardner, *The Phantom of the Poles* by William Reed, and *The Bermuda Triangle* by Charles Berlitz. He had a whole library on strange phenomena and theory, from dusty old leatherbound tomes to cheesy paperbacks spotted with coffee stains and yellowed by cigarette smoke that he got cheap—about fifty cents apiece—at a used book store from a guy who smelled like a urine sandwich and had dead, stuffed animals hanging from the ceiling. He brought out the philosophy again, giving more reading assignments than even the teachers at school piled on—except this stuff was neat! Sartre, Camus, Kierkegaard, Kafka, and especially oh, yeah! Nietzsche. It made his head swim, got him downright giddy. Jason didn't even bother going to the library after school anymore. He just went straight to Garth's place. Adjourned home for dinner, let the unc lock him in at night, *CLICK NICK!*, and then it was back to next door through the hole in the closet. Months passed as he seemed to read every book Big Garth had. He never took a single mouthful save to read something softly outloud, rolling the word or words about on his tongue, and then swallowing.

"...why have all our fruits become rotten and brown? What was it fell last night from the evil moon?" Garth quoted from *Thus Spake Zarathustra*. Then he said, "God is dead and we are mandated to be strong, to be the new gods. You have to understand your own self in order to master anything. Nietzsche called himself 'a philosopher of the dangerous perhaps.' Kierkegaard held his 'Existenz at the critical zero...between something and nothing.' It's about death and power and being the guy with the keys to the other side. And you might go there as god or you might send others—lesser mortals—there as slaves."

Jason pursed his lips, scrunched up his forehead. Dare he contradict his teacher? He said carefully, "I'm not sure I read into it what you do. 'Course I'm just a kid..."

Big Garth was opening up a box of stolen merchandise. Jason had brought it to him, ripped off from a hospital. It could be useful to be a little boy. People often didn't bother to see him at all.

Glittery surfaces, keen edges that reflected in the lenses of Garth's glasses. Some items reminded Jason of roach clips for pot cigarettes burned down to the nubbies. There were plastic tubes, hypodermic syringes, sewing needles, and thread. He didn't really know what all was in there. He'd just snatched and run.

"Well, the writings are like the quatrains of Nostradamus. They're veiled as to content so that the slave masses won't suspect their real purpose. Consider them open to broad interpretation and not to be taken at absolute face value. You're meant to study and get out of them precisely what you need, no more and certainly no less. Then it's you who are transformed into the philosopher and the **Superman** you are meant to be."

Jason grinned, sure he understood now. He liked being classified as apart from other people. He was no loser—he had a destiny. He concluded aloud, "Do what you fuckin' well feel like is the only law there is."

Big Garth blinked at him, turning his attention from the medical equipment. "A paraphrase of Aleister Crowley. Do what thou wilt shall be the whole of the Law."

Jason crowed, "The craw, the whole craw, and nothing but the craw!"

(whimpering, softly, from the bedroom)

Garth nodded and went back to seeing what all had come in his medical grab bag. He loved to rummage through new toys but he was careful so he didn't get poked or sliced.

"He wrote a lot of books. One was *The Book Of The Law* where that statement comes from. Supposedly it was dictated by his Holy Guardian Angel, Aiwass."

Jason's eyebrows went up. "*I was?* Like God speaking to Moses from the burning bush? I Am That I Am?"

Big Garth took out a stainless steel bedpan, held it up to the light with a sly smile. "Ought to be a practical purpose for this other than the obvious."

"So who is this Crowley guy?" Jason asked.

"A magician. *The* magician. They called him The Beast."

"That's what my mother used to call me," Jason mused, remembering a snatch or two from babyhood. "And so does Aunt Ice sometimes, come to think of it."

Garth looked up again. "In his autobiography, Crowley says his mother used to call him that. And you paraphrased his *law*. I find that pretty interesting."

Jason picked up a scalpel from the things Garth set out from the box onto the table. He smiled at his reflection in the metal. "Think of the magic you could do with this..." And he turned and twisted it in the air, as if gutting a tall pig or carving runes into the wind. "I summon thee! Appear to do my bidding in all the other worlds! I am the master of the kingdom!"

Big Garth shivered, studying the boy with a newfound curiosity. "Little dude, I wonder if you might be Crowley's reincarnation."

"Did you say reincarnation?" Jason asked, then pulled a wad of cotton from the box and sniffed it. It had dark stains from betadyne or blood.

"Yeah, I did," Garth replied.

"I thoth tho," Jason lisped, then spit trying to dislodge cotton which had floated into his mouth.

Garth grabbed his chest dramatically. "Thoth? A slip right from the gods."

He put down the new toys and took yet another book from the shelves. He searched through it until he found a photograph of an intense young man in strange Egyptian-looking garb, including a leopard skin for a cloak.

Jason did indeed feel strange looking at the eyes.

++++++++++

"Nothing is unclean in itself."

—The Apostle Paul
quoted at beginning of *Sacred Sepsis*
Dr. Louis Godard and Dr. James Singer

CHAPTER 9

FRANCE,
14TH CENTURY

Face down in an open street sewer, a body lazily circled, a motion almost identical to the flies which roundly buzzed to light upon the decaying head. There were other dead in sight, sprawled in Parisian doorways and over the cobbles. Apparently the carter hadn't driven up this way yet on his daily collection route. Maybe he had perished, the seepings from other people's bubos drenching him to a stiffening plague bone. Someone would either take his place soon or else no one would. The dead would pile up more until the very buildings seemed to be erected from them. A true necropolis.

The body's swirling reminded her of a raven, sailing overhead, not flapping its wings but just letting the wind direct him. Ravens—descending to thrust their beaks into apple-rotten faces and pluck out the liquifying olives of eyes—had themselves died, feathered stones dropping from heaven with a good deal less fluid grace.

At the end of the block and across the park (also littered with decomposing French), she could see a sumptuous townhouse where the inhabitants had sealed themselves in, awaiting what would hopefully be the contagion's eventual surcease. Brocades hung in rose and gold thread barricades to the infectious outside world. Every now and then a tired-eyed face would appear there, slightly parting the heavy drapes, searching for a saint's sorrowful glimpse of hell, searching for a voyeur's peek of the miles-wide lazar house. Searching for *her*. She could also hear the dulcimer sounds of troubadour voices and mandolins as the wealthy in this mansion were entertained.

"Where does fire go when it goes out? Into the soul where warmth is drought, where love laments its icy doubt. Where does the soul go as black death creeps? Stealing kisses as milady sleeps, and claiming all the phantom keeps. Where does death go in dark water streams? In bloody essence and wet grave schemes, to Charon's river of cesspool dreams. Where does blood go when it has fled? Into the fire to make it red, into our tears when we are dead."

In the great house, she could see a hole in one stone wall of a bay which surely contained a privy. Refuse was falling from it into a stream which ran below, sluggishly carrying the muck to the heavily polluted river, itself clogged with corpses as if with logs.

A young woman rushed into the street from a bakery shop that had been out of bread for weeks.

"My child is gone!" she cried, wringing her chapped hands. "My little Guillaume!"

No one left their own homes to heed her. Their voices tricked through the wood chinks, clear as a chamberpot bell.

"Your boy died. Leave us alone. We've our own troubles."

"Dogs dragged him off, you silly madwoman. If he wasn't already dead then, he was soon enough."

"The dogs, too!"

A macabre chuckle followed this last. The woman went back inside. There was a damprot thunk as the door's bolt slid into place.

But she, in a nun's habit, scarf tied over her eyes as if the convent had been playing some forbidden court-of-love game, knew the child had been stolen. Had been carried up to that big house.

Emilie.

A name she thought she recognized. Perhaps she knew an Emilie. Another nun at her convent.

No, impossible. She wasn't a nun. She was nobody's sister. Her faith did not run to men nailed to planks taken from mangled trees. Nor did she think that those who did believe in this—with or without compromise—went to heaven after they died. Although some of them did end up going some-where...

Her own name was Emilie. No...*had* been Emilie but was no more.

And she only wore this garb because... She had been naked and needed it.

She'd walked a long way from her parents' farm, barefoot and wearing a dirty, torn dress. Her mother and father had died, starved to death. They had also bled, taking a knife to cut off their own flesh for her to eat. "You must live. You are young."

Bits from gnarled fingers, from shrunken breasts, from spare thighs. Thimbles full of warm blood, seasoned with tears.

They had made her eat and drink them, whispered to her to continue consuming even after she found them cold upon the floor. But she couldn't keep it up after they rotted, even as their staring eye sockets pleaded for her to eat, and the blowflies in their mouths echoed their last message to their daughter, "You must live. You are young."

She'd wanted to bury what was left but hadn't possessed the strength. She'd barely managed a prayer for each before leaving to go to the convent many miles away, severed green toes in patched pockets to give her some-thing for the journey. Her thin red hair had begun falling out, then had grown back red as ever but thick to boot.

Emilie had fallen asleep no more than a few feet from the front gate to the convent. Three soldiers found her, stripped her, took turns. They beat her, her formerly freckled flesh purpling into a single, all-over bruise.

They had treasures looted from the chapel. One of them had even borne away the stone statue of the baby Jesus from a nativity scene, and this he shoved up inside Emilie. They laughed and sang coarse renditions of hymns, making her give birth to it, straining to push it out, the tiny fingers and toes in rock scraping every inch on the way in and out again.

"Our little madonna!" they called her and laughed.

Emilie hadn't cried out to the saints to save her. Nor had she wept, for her eyes felt as hard as the statue. The light from the soldiers' fires hurt them; even the darkness hurt them.

"What's this in your pockets?" asked one as he probed her ruined clothes in the heap where they'd been cast off. He passed the toes around to the other men.

She didn't answer as these relics from her parents were defiled.

"Our madonna is a cannibal!" announced another soldier.

"You know how meat is marinated in wine so it will taste like wine?" asked a third with a chuckle. "This stinks sweet of death. Maybe she eats it to taste sweeter herself."

They took bites to test this theory, rubbing their faces in her grease, smacking their lips and sucking the shiny threads of her morsels from their teeth.

"Ugh! Same as every unwashed country madonna," the first one remarked. "Stringy and sour from slopping hogs."

"But I'll grant her this. Hasn't screamed once," the second pointed out with the barest hint of some twisted respect.

"Probably just a mute," the third suggested. He grabbed her, threw her on the ground on her back, knelt upon her chest, and forced her jaws apart. "Has a tongue."

He snatched it between his fingers — pinching it hard to keep it from wriggling away, slippery. Pulled it out as far as it would go, then cut it off. He let Emilie flop back, mouth filling with blood, choking on what gushed down her throat.

"Doesn't now," he said as he held up his trophy. "Perhaps she didn't need it anyway if she couldn't talk."

"And if she could, then she ought to have spoken up sooner," the first soldier chuckled.

They grew tired of her. She hadn't been their first diversion. So they departed, believing they'd left her for dead.

And maybe she had died, drowned in her own blood, and maybe she had not. She'd slept at least, and dreamed that the blood had dried into a hard, long, black clot. This was her new tongue.

When she awoke, she knew she was no longer Emilie. She went through the convent's gate. There were only two nuns to be found, both dead. (The others had fled or perished. Perhaps the plague had only spared these two.) They had been skinned and those skins spread upon the altar in the chapel, with two candles left burning on top. The bodies had been set together, with the fleshless face of each woman in the fleshless crotch of the other. And there was a priest in the corner, also naked. His throat had been cut. His penis was missing. In its place, solidly between the legs and pressed right up into the wound, the soldiers had put a large tallow candle. It still burned.

It was traditional to light a candle in church for the dead. The soldiers must have been at least a little superstitious to do this, even for victims they had outraged. Or they might have done this as a joke. After all, the candle for the priest had been left to resemble a pale erection, slowly melting.

It was there she'd found the habit she'd put on. She set a wimple on her head, blessed the three corpses with her new black tongue, then blew out their candles.

She'd walked on to Paris. She now stood before the expensive town-house in the ravaged park. Where the little boy, Guillaume, had been taken. Where many others had vanished behind the door.

The occupants there tried to shut themselves off from the sickness but they couldn't resist the youngest pretty faces, paled by hunger, mouths willing to do anything for a bite of clove-studded orange. Others had vanished in the city, too. But so many people had already died, most families didn't go hunting for them, didn't even weep anymore.

The house in the park, where the strolling ornamental peacocks and the turtledoves in the cherry trees had long since been taken for food, was a palace of venereal midden. Every excess which the Renaissance mind could devise was carnival there. The surviving townfolk put up horned fingers to ward off evil eye, seeing the grand mansion, believing that beyond the intricately carved obscenities on its silver filigree door was an entrance to another world. One where cruelty was as delicious as a truffle, and where the dwellers' hearts were so black that not even the plague could darken them further. A place where the dead rose up to mock God, with ulcerous lusting until their digits and limbs cascaded from them as the autumn leaves flesh of mating lepers.

But she knew that those in the house actually prayed for just such a door and world. They had gone so far from normal routine that they could never return to the manner in which they'd lived before the plague came. Could never rub their silks against the base lives of common men nor bow to the Church in either real or feigned reverence. They couldn't even bear the presence of other gentry without hitching their clothes up to hips or down to ankles at the first bloom of desire.

She saw that face at the window again. Vulpine, jaded. Searching for redemption or for degradation. Or searching for *her*.

"I am the gateway," she said, wimple framing her face like a glacier.

She picked her way down the carcass-heavy street, entering the park where the formerly carefully-tended gardens of fleur-de-lis, camellias and amaryllis had turned to weeds. She spied half a black rat beneath a wilted oleander, fleas and maggots swarming in competition through what remained of matted fur. A cat lay dead a short distance away, a single rodent foot sticking from the death grimace. Near that a litter of kittens were merely balls of dust, tiny as snippets of gray moss.

She went up to the silver door and wasn't surprised when it swung open.

Exotic beggars and once-beautiful children were draped, naked, in every possible pose across the gilded, cushioned furniture. There was a half-finished tapestry on a loom, upon it a scene depicting a broad-foreheaded woman squatting above an infant as a man in a knight's black-plumed helmet penetrated her from behind. It was unclear whether she'd just given birth to the baby in this position or was in the act of smothering it with her spread thighs or both. On the other side of the room were tables upon which a feast had been heaped. Golden dishes of smoked mackerel and eels, platters of bacon and stuffed grouse, bowls of ginger stew and peppered cheese, almond cakes and mutton pastries were overrun with rats.

She heard inhaling.

Sighing.

Inhaling.

Sighing.

Orgasmic gasping.

A door was open, leading down to a latrine reserved for the servants and household clergy. It was below the house where the refuse went through a stone ditch which eventually channeled it into an underground oubliette.

Here she found them, even with her blindfold up. The partiers were lined up along the open toilet, breathing deeply of the stench.

There was a belief prevalent that the odor of shit and piss acted as an innoculation against the black death.

But this didn't make her smile.

"Here is the gateway to Aralu," she told them in French, in Latin, in the ancient tongue of the Indian subcontinent, and in every other tongue.

A man wearing the currently popular pointed toe *poulaines*, the ends tied at his knees with precious metal chains (and wearing naught else), came up to her. With one hand he fervently worked the veined shaft of his carbuncled penis. With the other hand he boldly slipped down her blindfold.

++++++++++

Their mother called Dorien at the college and asked her to come home. Peter Warmer's cancer had returned. Well, her grades had been terrible lately. She'd already known she would flunk this semester out. It gave her a reason to say "the hell with it" and retreat for a while.

"You lose a little weight?" Mom asked first thing when Dorien came in. "You probably spend too much time studying. You don't want to get too skinny."

She'd held Dorien out at arm's length to appraise the changes. "I almost wouldn't have known you."

That was okay. These days Dorien almost didn't know herself.

"You're so thin and pale. That the new gothic thing I keep hearing about, girls as ghosts? You're supposed to be at college to learn a trade, not just lure boys," Mom added, trying to smile. "Don't want to starve. God didn't intend us to be skeletons until we die."

Mom realized what she'd just said and slapped a hand across her mouth. She'd meant it to be light-hearted, but the strain from finding out Dad was no longer in remission showed in every square inch of her face.

Dorien slipped an arm around her mother's shoulders and tried to give a heartfelt squeeze of support. Even if she very much didn't want to be there, with the old man a few feet away, his sleep noises like something which would roll out of the cave of a dangerous beast. (Besides…boys? If only her mother knew. Attracting men was about the last thing on Dorien's mind.)

Annet arrived only about an hour after Dorien. Five years older, Annet had always been a big girl. If Mom felt surprised by how different her youngest looked, she was downright shocked when the big-eyed, wispy stick walked through the door.

"Good grief," Mom managed to utter. "What have you done to yourself? You leave home a healthy girl and go out to California to turn into an alfalfa sprout?"

This from a woman who'd always displayed her love most through frequent home-baked goodies and second to third helpings you didn't dare refuse. A few extra pounds on her children told the world she could take care of them.

Dorien experienced a twinge of jealousy. She'd never envied Annet before, except as a child, and only then because her older sister got to do everything she couldn't do (but this had simply been typical pre-pubescent rivalry). But now Annet fit the popular anorexic icon from every magazine cover. Even though Dorien had also lost weight—but not this much!—she looked as if she hadn't slept in a month. She looked into the mirror and saw something ancient peering back. Annet lost pounds and looked younger than Dorien.

"It's my great new diet," Annet replied, posing, showing off in an outfit so snug its size had to be in the negative range. "I've finally purged the evil from my body."

The room smelled in a way not even the hospital's strong disinfectants could mask. Pete Warmer was hooked up to many machines, monitors, and respirators. And devices to bear his waste away. He looked very frail in the bed until he, too, resembled a child.

He moaned. His eyes flicked open, lids at half-mast.

"They have him on so much medicine for the pain, he's really far gone. Cancer's all through him," Mom explained quietly. Then she went over and bent down to give her husband a kiss on the cheek.

"Do I know you?" came a small, crackling voice.

"Yes, honey. I'm your wife," Mom told him. Then she gestured for the daughters to do as she had. Annet first, because she was the eldest. Mom murmured, "Don't let it bother you. He doesn't recognize anyone anymore. He just went downhill so fast this time."

"Hello, Daddy," Annet said, offering her obedient peck.

"Do I know you?" he asked again, staring at her, trying to place her features.

She moved back with a frozen smile as Dorien moved up to the side of the bed.

"Hi, Dad," she managed to whisper but couldn't quite fashion a smile. She gave the dutiful buss, ashamed because she was repulsed by the stench of ruin.

"Do I know you?" he asked a third time, not recalling he'd asked the same of the previous two.

Dorien didn't answer.

They sat there in the room much of the day. None would admit to suffocating. They didn't bother with the television as sound seemed to disturb him. Because of this—and the depression of their situation—they also didn't talk much. They read magazines or stared out the door into the hallway. There wasn't much to do during a death watch.

++++++++++

Dorien didn't return to her apartment at the end of the day even though it was just across the city. Instead she stayed in her old room at home. Well, she'd been living there until just two years ago when she graduated high school. She'd only been home once, during Christmas break of her freshman year, and that only because the doctors thought Dad was going to die and it would be his last Christmas. But then he went into remission. She'd felt just fine about being too busy with school and trying to be independent.

As much as she hated the polluted skies, she hated that house more. Both parents (and Annet) were heavy smokers. Annet began smoking in her mid-teens, having heard someplace that it was a great way to get thin. Now, combined with the pervasive smell of Dad's unavoidable incontinence before this last (and probably really *last*) hospitalization, the place reeked in a manner which made her think of primitives burning their own shit for fuel. Except Dorien had never personally encountered this so how did she know? Or had she seen this done by homeless people in the park during killer winters?

Everything in the house was yellow, seemed encased in amber. And she couldn't simply climb in the shower to wash it all away. The porcelain was just as permanently tainted with tar and nicotine. Once the tile, tub, toilet, and sink had been pink—way back. But now it was the color of a diseased salmon.

She resigned herself to having this miasma settle over her, covering and penetrating, as depressing as the malaise of smog outside.

She'd excused herself from supper—which had visibly upset her mother. Mom had prepared a lot of food, as she always did. And there were cakes, pies, cookies. Hoping to fatten her children up so that no one would mistakenly think she might be an unfit mother. Annet also begged off, apologizing profusely.

"I worked so hard to get thin, Mom," she protested sweetly. "Please don't take it personally."

And the night had fallen brown outside the yellow home. The house thickened into sepia, with the women in their separate rooms upstairs. Dorien lay stiffly in her bed, afraid to fall asleep because of the nightmares she'd been having lately. Afraid to fall asleep for fear she'd have the kind of nightmare she used to suffer when she lived in this place. Of being in the dark with only the sounds of screaming children all around. Nothing else, but it would go on and on until she began screaming, too. She never knew who the kids were supposed to be, only understanding they were in terrible pain and very much afraid. And there was a smell—always this same smell permeating the dream, drenching every unseen subcurrent.

As a little girl, she'd dream this. She'd start crying out in her sleep. Annet would be in the bedroom next door. "She's doing it again! Could somebody shut her up? I've got a big test tomorrow!"

And usually it was Mom who came in to hold Dorien and tell her everything was okay. Just a bad dream, sweetheart. How about a cookie and a glass of milk?

But there was this one time when Mom was sick, so Dad came down the hall. He opened the door and switched on the light. Of course, this woke Dorien up. She trembled a bit to see him there for he'd always scared her. He was a grim man, not mean but certainly hollow-eyed and unsmiling. The skin of his head and arms was spotted from having been injured when he was much younger, before either Annet or Dorien were even born. She didn't know how he came to be hurt because it simply wasn't spoken of, merely taken for granted and a certain measure of face value. Except the spots always made her think of him as some sort of leopard, creeping from a jungle. When she looked at him, it was a jungle she always sensed, full of dark leaves, eyes, hunger.

"Just a dream, Dory," he told her as he padded across the floor. In slippers, not on paws. He always rolled the r's, especially on Dorrrrry, until the name became an integral part of the growl. (It was the main thing about his speech which might make anyone believe that English wasn't his first language—yet she'd never heard him speak anything else.) "You keep doing this. What in the world have you got to have nightmares about?"

It came out as a challenge, as if she were too young to have suffered, to have developed tremors or any contraband grief.

She pulled the blanket up to her chin and shrugged. "I don't know. I just hear children screaming. I smell orchids."

His face darkened, the spots vanishing in a shadow. "Did you say orchids?"

Tonight, first time back home in over a year, yellow walls and stench of smoke and waste, she slept, dreamed of Paris, dreamed blindly of screaming kids and orchids. Woke up, unable to breathe in the nicotine fog.

I'm going outside. Bad as it is out there, maybe there will be a breeze. Just a few minutes of air that isn't a complete ashtray.

She left her bedroom and slipped quietly down the stairs. Noticed the light was on in the kitchen. Why was she so determined not to make any noise? It had to be her mother, probably already preparing for tomorrow's breakfast, even if it was only about 2 a.m. Mom often did this. Couldn't sleep so she dragged her insomnia to the stove to cook. Food to her was the definition of happiness. And right now she needed to celebrate, sorrow's composure arrested by the mandate to rejoice—death was only for the damned.

But it wasn't Mom. Dorien peeked in and found Annet standing at the counter, stuffing her face with all manner of chicken drumsticks and wedges of cheese, hunks of fruit pies and buttercream-frosted carrot cake she propelled into her mouth with her bare hands, licking each finger and sucking from under the nails.

Definitely don't want to walk in there. Looks to me like a private Hell in progress.

And why wouldn't Dorien try to talk to Annet about it? Because this looked just plain gross. Annet gobbled as if she were positively starved—which she actually seemed to be. Maybe it was due to being in the house again. Annet hadn't lived there in ten years. Maybe as Dorien suffered the nightmare she always had here, so did her sister in her own way.

And they had never been a family that talked about things, who interceded to help one another. Mom had always insisted there was nothing wrong, anywhere. To do so would be to admit to the possibility of danger, of imperfection. So they pretended everything was okay: Dad silent, Mom acting happy, daughters hiding whatever must be borne as if it were the challenge that proved their worth.

Dorien stood around the corner as Annet ate at a raptorial pace for a good thirty minutes, not always chewing, often washing food down with can after frosty can of soda pop. Dorien heard it effervescing in her sister's throat.

Then Annet opened a cabinet where vitamin bottles, cold remedies, and other sundry over-the-counter pharmaceuticals were stored beside drinking glasses. She just figured her sister had a belly ache after all that. (God Christ Almighty, who wouldn't?) But Annet didn't reach for the Pepto. She took out a clean glass, turned on the tap, filled it. Took a small bottle from her purse and poured in a few drops of some dark liquid. *then*…after eating all that junk…she mumbled a prayer, a blessing. After this she drank the water.

Dorien ducked backward into a closet as Annet turned off the kitchen light and went past her to the stairs. She followed after a minute or two, when sure Annet was no longer on the steps or in the upstairs hallway. Annet had gone into the bathroom and shut the door.

"I'm going back to bed," Dorien said to herself, disgusted. Her sister sure was a hypocrite.

Yet she knew better.

She stayed in the hallway and listened as Annet groaned, gagged and puked, farted, flushed, moaned etc. And did she hear chanting in the midst of dissonant wet rumbles and murky thunder? Dorien put her ear to the door, for what could she be saying in there? Could she actually be praying?

"I purge myself of evil thoughts and an evil world. I make myself an empty vessel. I make myself a pure child again."

Dorien shook her head. Went to bed. Dreamt about a hospital room with a patient hooked up to gurgling machines, reeking of waste and death.

But it wasn't her father in the bed. It was Gavin.

+++++++++++

The women returned to the hospital the next morning.

Mom bent to kiss Dad and he asked, "Do I know you?"

Annet leaned down and gave Dad a buss. He wanted to know from her, "Do I know you?"

Dorien thought that the reek of his waste and the bathroom that morning at home were a lot alike as he inquired of her, "Do I know you?"

He went back to sleep. At some point Annet excused herself and was gone for about a half hour. When she came back she brought take-out from some restaurant. The bag had a name on it: CANE. She sat down in the chair next to the bed and, when Dad woke up again, she began feeding stew to him. He readily slurped and chewed what she offered him.

"Lord, honey. He can't have that," Mom insisted.

Annet dipped the plastic spoon back into the large, styrofoam cup. "Why not? He seems to like it, doesn't he? If he's dying anyway, why shouldn't he have it? After all, food is comfort of the highest order. It's what you've always taught us."

Mom didn't even try to argue with this logic.

He opened his mouth for every spoonful, even as he still looked at his eldest daughter as if he had no idea who she might be.

+++++++++++

WALLACHIA, 15TH CENTURY

Dark forests, castle with towers fisting a glowering sky, skulkers in black abducting women and children and every kind of traveler on the road.

The local lord fancied himself a vampire of sorts. He visited his dungeon every night to torture victims and drink their living blood. He drank because he enjoyed the heat of it and its salty flavor of rust and copper. He never believed for a moment that consumption would grant him any spurious immortality. No, even though he was acquainted with fools who accepted as gospel old Romani gypsy fireside tales and other Transylvanian nonsense about a forever undead existence.

It was on the lightless pond in the level beneath the dungeon that he believed held the possibility for superhuman transformation. A natural water source over which the ancient castle had been built, encasing the dark icy water—so frostily turgid it seemed at first glance to be viscous, so black it might have been oil.

But it was only water.

Into this he had his servants throw the chopped apart remains of those who perished in the dungeon. Bones, flesh, organs from a couple hundred anonymous peasants, peddlers, soldiers, and religious pilgrims. The nearly freezing temperature of the water kept the human chum from decomposition, although the older pieces did develop a kind of ebon slime, which trailed in the liquid like threads of pitch albumen in a serpentine egg drop soup.

Once a fortnight he had the retainers set candles in a circle around the tiny pond and light them. He would then disrobe and plunge into the waters. He would swim downward, body caressed by masses of hair like jellyfish, tubes of undulating guts like the tentacles of an octopus, severed fingers and toes like schools of curious minnows. Severed breasts trailed tendrils of blood vessels—a strange anemone. There would be here and there enough of a female torso for him to fancy there were truncated mermaids spying on him. He'd go down, spiraling through the ever-chillier water, touching bottom, breath held in his lungs about to explode, brain a volatile cannon between his ears. But it was always only the muddy bottom of the pond. Never a threshold.

One night there would be enough souls present that the weight of their pain and terror would punch right through to the other world. Where someone with his power would be an emperor of demons, instead of just some local potentate over villages of rats.

She knew these were his thoughts as she watched the week's dead being brought down from the level above, carried in crates, dragged in sacks, even in the big soup kettles normally kept in the kitchen. She listened to each grisly splash as the henchmen tossed in that fortnight's total suffering with all the passion of those who held a reverence for travesties of flesh.

Her mother had been a Turkish captive, taken when the castle's lord had fought alongside Prince Dracul. One of these butchers was her father, although she didn't know which one. She sometimes wondered who he was, back when she'd been Olga and a member of the castle's contingent of sewing women. Not that it mattered. Every one of them might be him, just as all of them had bedded her. Half-Turkish girls had no status. If she hadn't been so clever with a needle and thread, she'd have been part of that watery abomination.

Recently she'd been more afraid than usual, shocked by dreams and changes in herself. She'd prayed to the Christian God with facsimiles of his bloodied corpse nailed to nearly every wall in the castle. She attempted to speak as she'd heard Turks do.

Salaam aleikum!

Now it didn't matter. Now she crouched where no one could see her. She had stripped her own clothes off and wore only the veil she'd made herself. She hadn't been required to wear one but she knew that proper Moslem women often did wear them. The lord and his men had thought it amusing, but she'd used it as a form of anonymity, keeping the thoughts in her head to herself, a way of cherishing her hidden soul.

That had been when she was still Olga. But she wasn't Olga anymore. She'd become an immortal creature, yet not a vampire of myth, not any undead shambling thing pitiful of desecrated churchyards and moonlight.

At the pond's edge, the master ordered the servants away so none would be there to witness his failure if—once again—the bottom of the pond didn't open up. He took off his clothes, his body filthy with blood from not having been washed since the last time he'd entered the water. He had an erection, so excited was he to be entering his liquid graveyard. He jerked his cock until a jet of semen went out across the surface, his signature of ownership over the spirits he'd trapped therein. Then he dove.

A moment later she emerged from where she'd been hiding. She jumped in after him. Somehow she reached the bottom first and waited for him, arms open wide. A severed hand drifted past, a single remaining digit (a thumb) snagging the edge of her veil to drag it away, as the flag of a submerged ship caught in a shark's fin.

She spoke to him in ripples, in bubbles.

"Welcome…"

++++++++++

Dorien shook herself to consciousness. Brushed her face as if trying to fold back some wet gauze clinging to it.

"Who's Aralu?" Annet asked. Then she winked knowingly. "That some foreign student you met at college?"

Mom had been gone for a while. When she returned, it was Annet who took a break.

"Has he been okay?" Mom wanted to know after the eldest daughter left.

Dorien tried to clear her head. She glanced at the flowers around the room. Roses in a green vase. Chrysanthemums in milk glass. Carnations and baby's breath in a jar painted in hypnotic swirls.

Nowhere did she see orchids. But she smelled them.

"Excuse me," Dorien said abruptly, getting up, also leaving the room.

She spotted her sister going down the hall, followed in a second elevator. Saw doctors and nurses smoking outside the building, looking like the tough kids at a high school with stressed-out eyes and yellowed fingers. Saw patients hooked up to IV's which they dragged around with them, some with faces that hung on them like wrinkled masks made from the foreskins of baboons, smoking there, too. Annet lit up.

She claimed she'd given it up. (Like she'd forsaken pigging out?)

Annet didn't linger. She got in her car and drove away. Dorien grabbed a taxi.

"See that Ford? Stay behind it," she instructed the driver, feeling foolish, as if acting in some television cop melodrama.

Annet went several miles away, to a short side street across from a local, unimportant park. She stopped in front of a restaurant that had a small, hand-painted sign which read CANE. She went inside this place. Dorien watched through the big front window as she ordered something at the counter.

Annet left with it, a styrofoam container in a paper sack. Same place she'd brought food to the hospital from before. Stuff she fed their father.

Dorien waited until her sister had gone before exiting the taxi. The driver had let her off near a place where the alley and the street came together. There was a dead dog in the road, one that evidentally had been hit by a car. Yellow grueled from its eyes, and the tongue was covered with ants. She sighed and entered the cafe, walking up to a woman at the cash register and saying, "Pardon me. See that very skinny woman who just left? Would you mind terribly telling me what she bought?"

The tiny woman smiled and shook her head. "Non capisco."

"Well, does anybody back there speak English?" Dorien asked.

The woman shook her head again. "Non parla inglese."

Dorien realized when she'd come in that the place was filled with people speaking other languages, what she guessed from tonal qualities to be French, German, Russian, Spanish. She also heard English. But when she turned around after getting nothing from the woman at the counter, the patrons had gone silent and were just staring at her.

"Anybody here able to talk to this lady for me?"

No response.

"How about anybody here speak English?"

Just blank looks. Silence.

She couldn't help but notice how thin they all were. Must be a new trendy place, popular with the chic sticks.

Dorien shrugged and left. She'd glanced about for another cab or maybe a bus stop. She saw a man in cook's whites scooping up the dead dog, then scurrying back with it down the alley, to disappear into the cafe's kitchen door.

There was a bus stop sign and a bench at the other end of the block, near the park. Dorien had to pass a flower shop to reach it. It was almost Mother's Day and the place was filled with orchids. The smell filled her nostrils as she passed the door just as someone came out, fragrance from many orchid varieties coming out with them.

All of a sudden she heard children screaming.

++++++++++

Nandi had been her name. But she had no recollection of family, of father or mother. She saw leopards moving gracefully through the jungle and thought that perhaps she'd been a child of theirs. Maybe she'd been orphaned by poachers. Or by the White Tomorrow.

Now she was not Nandi. She was a creature of tempest and still, of animals who killed on the veldt and mated by the river, of all the things which died and rotted and fertilized the trees in which orchids were parasites to.

She'd seen the men from the White Tomorrow moving through the undergrowth, creeping up like vines—like snakes on the unsuspecting families who had come out from the village to collect orchids for a wedding celebration. Neo-Nazi Afrikaners dressed in paramilitary camouflage, carrying automatic weapons, grenades clipped to their belts.

On an outing from Jo'burg. The slaughter of school children in Soweto hadn't been longer than a few months ago. Many in favor of apartheid had banded together to keep those "kaffirs" and their insidious "swart gevaar" from ruining South Africa.

Those gathering orchids never saw them coming. The "rooineks" opened fire. Children shrieked, everyone folded down like wheat, delicate flowers exploded. A white man threw a grenade, and a black kid picked it up and threw it back at him.

It landed, rolled to within a few feet of him, detonating, taking away most of his lower body into the long grass. A buddy behind him caught hell in the face and on his arms.

"Van Doorn is dead! Warmerdam is injured; he's bleeding!" another shouted to the other attackers, going forward to help his buddy. "You all right, Petr?"

"I think so. Hurts like a son of a bitch though. I can't see a fucking thing."

The man grinned and slapped him gently on the back. "Glad I won't have to tell your bride a sad story. But you'll have scars I think. Spots like a leopard!"

Blood ran in the man's eyes as this one dragged him back a short distance. Although there was no real need, for they had killed everyone. He reached into his pack, saying to the injured man, "I'll give you a pain pill," and produced a morphine tablet.

"Smells like shit around here," Warmlander complained good-naturedly as he dry-swallowed the pill.

When she came through the quiver trees, at first they brought their weapons up again, seeing her black skin. But they didn't open fire.

The injured man heard her murmur, "Aralu..." in a voice like a wind through sand. But he couldn't see her. Yet when he heard the other men scream he got up and ran, blindly. He tripped over the bodies of those they had murdered, slipping in gore, hands coming down into devastated orchids. He got up and fled again, running right smack-face into a tree. This knocked him out.

She who had been Nandi didn't care to pursue him. Those who came to her always did so in their own time.

++++++++++++

When Dorien returned to the hospital room, Annet was feeding their father whatever it was she'd bought at CANE. The old man took a bite, staring up at his eldest daughter, mumbling as he chewed, "Do I know you?"

The waste machinery chugged, working overtime the last couple of days.

"Where have you been, darling?" Mom asked the youngest. "You've been gone a long time. I was beginning to worry. Such a dangerous city we live in. People getting killed for no good reason."

"Lots of dangerous places in the world though, right?" Dorien countered as she set a small bag of her own in a chair. "And in most of those places, the reasons for killing are usually pretty lame."

Mom blinked, confused. But she still sparkled with a smile. "I—uhm—brought some cookies. There, over on the table."

Dad suddenly choked. Mom rose from her chair and hurried over to him. "Pete? Shall I call the doctor?"

She tenderly touched his bald, spotted head.

"Do I know you?" he asked her.

"Yes, I am your wife."

Then he spewed, half-liquid mass spraying chunks and puree across her. She jumped back with a screech. Some of it struck Annet as well. She ignored it, quietly staring at her father. He wretched but couldn't double up, too weak to spasm with the cramps. The tubes for the waste machine bobbed and twisted.

He did this for about a minute. It seemed longer than it really was. When he stopped, Dorien approached the bed and bent over him, leaning close.

His rheumy eyes tracked her, going wide as they could.

"I know *you!*" he exclaimed, voice louder than it had been at any time during her visits to see him. Pink and brown crud flecked his lips as he glared at her, terrified. "You were in the jungle!"

Their eyes locked as his spotted hands came up from the bed sheet, raking in claws at the air as if he was trying to push something horrible away from him. Then his eyes rolled up to the whites, filthy mouth hanging slack. The heart monitor shrieked a single high note to punctuate a flat line.

Mom cried out. Annet ran out into the hall, breaking her peculiar silence to shout for help. Mom punched the call button over and over again. Now it was Dorien who simply stood there, gazing at the man who had always frightened her.

"Help him! Do something..." her mother begged, tears springing into her eyes as she stared at her unmoved youngest child. "He's dying!"

"No, he's dead," Dorien corrected her, then retrieved the bag she'd brought in with her. She opened it and took out what she'd bought at the flower shop.

She set the orchid on her father's chest.

Her mother's jaw dropped and she trembled, looking at Dorien with guilty eyes. So, she'd known! She'd helped this monster heal, change the family name, move to America to hide.

Annet returned with aid but the old man was gone. She got her purse and took out a plastic cosmetic vial filled with gold glitter. She unscrewed the top and sprinkled some of this onto Petr Warmerdam's head and into the narrow fringe of his hair.

She said softly, "So the angels will know him as one of their own."

+++++++++++

The venerable Hindu spiritual leader, Mohandas Karamchand Ghandi, believed human waste to be as holy an object as that from any sacred cow. He used to take walks and he would pick clean the roadways. He would say, "Removing the excreta of others is a form of communion."

—Sacred Sepsis
Dr. Louis Godard and Dr. James Singer

CHAPTER
10

DECEMBER 21, 1989,
ROME

"Three days ago," the captain said to the his co-pilot, "we took her up and what the Italians call the *Tremontana* shook us until we were halfway to Albania."

The co-pilot was familiar with the northern stormy wind that blew over this country during winter. "Doesn't seem to have let up," he observed, the gusts striking the old DC-10 on the left side as it steadily increased its ascent, having just taken off from Aeroporto Ciampino, returning to Istanbul and flying into the sunrise.

People wanting to get to Turkey before the Christmas vacation rush started in a day or two (when seats would be scarce) had packed the plane to capacity. 346 passengers crammed into the McDonnell Douglas three engine super jet which was 181 feet long, seating eight people at every aisle.

The captain grit his teeth as the plane rocked, lifted,

dipped. They had only taken off five minutes ago. At this rate it was going to be an awfully long trip. He glanced at the altimeter. Right where it should be.

"Could be worse," the co-pilot remarked. "Could be snowing, as little of it as they get here."

"So, is this your first trip to Rome?"

The co-pilot nodded. "I met this woman at a club. An American, red-haired, big plastic breasts. She was drunk and walked up to me, saying, 'Hi! I'm from Ohio!' And I said, 'I am from Batman.' You know where that is?"

"Sure, not far from the borders with Syria and Iraq. Then what?" the captain asked.

The co-pilot shrugged. "Well, she misunderstood me. She shouted out, 'You're Batman? Hey, everybody, this here's Batman!' Laughed her apple ass off and then bought me champagne."

The captain chuckled. "She sleep with you?"

"Her and two other tipsy ladies. Same time. You know the new steward out there?" He thumbed back toward the cabin.

"Ali? Yes, I met him when we boarded."

"He joined us. I told them he was Robin."

The captain laughed and slapped his knee.

"It gets better."

"Better than that?"

"Yeah, they're all three on the plane, in first class."

"You're shitting me!"

"I saw them and said hello. Welcomed them to the batjet. They want to get together again in Istanbul."

"Maybe you should be the captain here," the pilot said as he noted they were now at 12,700 feet, ten minutes out of Rome.

Suddenly the plane lurched so hard the captain's hands were knocked off the controls.

No one knew the cargo door hadn't been properly locked. It looked secure when final checks had been made prior to take-off. The door to the lower hold blew open, luggage full of tourist trinkets and Christmas gifts were swiftly sucked out. Abrupt decompression forced a floor above the hold to heave, shoving upward through ranks of passengers. Four people, still buckled in, were pulled through this gaping breach, their shrieks siphoned off into the freezing *Tremontana*. At the same moment, every cable for the tail section, the engine, and the navigational controls snapped. Even as the captain tried to right the plane, it nosedived like a dove with a shattered spine. It cracked open in the air, dropping passengers like confetti into the wind.

A young couple—a Frenchman and his Italian fiancée—had driven out of the city just before dawn to go to Tivoli. They saw a fireball and thought the sun had risen twice. An enormous black plume of smoke came next, accompanied by a noise like an approaching thunderstorm dogging the steps of an earthquake.

"Gerard! Oh my god," the woman began, then crossed herself with a soft prayer.

"It's only a couple of miles away, Linda. Hang on," he told her as he floored the accelerator and began racing to the disaster.

They arrived at a field, wreckage everywhere, gruesome chunks of meat unrecognizable as having been people fused with burned metal. Some trees were on fire, many had become just broken matchsticks. Others were full of body parts and blood fell to the ground like rain. Clothing flapped in forked branches like panicked bats. Linda screamed, seeing two halves of a woman hanging in two different cypress trees. She choked on a ghastly stench of incinerating resins and jet fuel. She was reminded of something she'd read in school, that the cypress was a graveyard tree, considered a symbol of death. The cross upon which Jesus had been crucified was said to have been cypress.

An object plopped from one of these and rolled lopsidedly to her feet. It was so mangled she couldn't tell what it was until part of it sprung and she saw teeth. Somebody's crushed head.

The DC-10's severed nose had plowed through the grass and evergreens for almost 200 feet, carving a deep furrow about twenty feet down into the ground. Almost as if there really had been an earthquake and this was where the land had opened up along a faultline. The grass at the edges of this trench smouldered, just beginning to burn. Gerard jogged over and looked down. Earth and rock had been scraped and shattered, an evisceration. But not far from where the nose had come to a halt, he spied a tunnel. The tendrils of roots and grasses hung down across the entrance, creating almost a bead curtain of natural threads of varying thickness and clumps of earth. Squinting, focusing until his vision virtually telescoped (giving him one hell of a headache) he caught sight of a bit of smooth stone. A step, and then another.

It was a tunnel graveyard. He was positive! It was an old catacomb.

He heard a cry for help down there. Was this even possible? Could anybody have lived through such a crash? No, he knew they must have all died—if not as the plane broke apart in the air then surely due to the fall. The cockpit had virtually disintegrated. No one had survived that.

Yet he was certain he heard someone calling. Linda came alongside him, trembling, tears on her face.

"Do you hear something?" he asked her.

"Yes, a voice—female. Calling for us to help her," she replied. "We should go get someone…"

"No time," he explained, glancing about for a way to climb down.

Linda shouted, *"Súbito, signora! Présto, fra póco!"*

Gerard swung back to his fiancée and said gently, "I'm not sure she'll understand you, *Chéri*. She's French."

"No, her cries are in Italian," Linda politely insisted.

Both of them were college students majoring in business. Gerard spoke no Italian and Linda no French, but both were fluent in English. This was how they always communicated with one another.

He cocked an ear and listened intently, then shook his head. "That's definitely French..."

Linda put a hand on his arm. "Wait. Tell me exactly what you hear."

He obliged. "She repeats, '*Aidez-moi. Je me suis perdue. Depéchêz-vous. S'il vous plait...en bas.*'"

He started to turn away again to climb down. She tightened her grip, saying, "I clearly hear her calling '*Aiuto! Mi sono smarrita. Fácia présto. Per pavore...a in giú.*'"

Gerard blinked, then gazed back down into the pit where he could see the damage and then the entrance to the catacomb. "It is odd that I hear her saying she's lost. Not that she's hurt—but lost."

Linda agreed. "That's what I hear, too."

The hackles rose on both of them. The fine soft hairs on Linda's arm stood up and traveled in rippling, tingling static to raise the hair on Gerard's arm where she held him fast.

"There is no way I'm letting you go down there," she said, voice shaking but adamant.

They both realized at the same moment that, despite the burning debris in the trench and fire spreading in the grass to either side, what air rose from it was cold. Colder than the *Tremontana*.

"We'd better get out of here," Gerard told her. "We don't want to get trapped by the fire, and it will soon be out of control in this wind. Let's find a telephone and get real help."

Knowing as he spoke the words that all of these wretched souls were beyond rescue.

They sped back up the road toward Rome, stopping at the first petrol station they saw. Linda rang the authorities. Then Gerard Godard called all the way to the United States to talk to his cousin, Louis Godard.

Humanity and six degrees of separation.

+++++++++

Jim Singer slept on the plane. Nightmares. Stained glass windows which, to him as a boy, had seemed as unnatural jewels while he tried to pretend he was anywhere but with the man in black, behind him but with big hands coming around to the front of him—and down. Never able to talk about it for fear it would turn out he was ratting on God. The term "Father" was a double-edged sword, Father to whom you confessed your most wretched crimes and Father On High who could throw a lever and drop you into Hell. Make you drink His holy water, a special communion of blood and flesh no one else must ever know about, pain/fear/shame.

Raised a Catholic in Philadelphia, he had no faith now and no religion. He thought he'd outgrown this, it had happened so long ago, in the '50s when such things were never even breathed. When a kid didn't dare tell his parents for being such a dirty little butterball sinner. Because he wouldn't be believed and he'd end up excommunicated and the devil would possess his defiled ass without the sanctuary of the blessed Jesus. Jim had thought the terror was over, yet perhaps no damaged child ever really let it go. Some betrayals went too deep.

He moaned in his sleep, in his dream having run down the aisle past gleaming mahogany pews, racing for the altar where he expected to be safe but with the stained glass windows of tormented saints casting blood shadows on him. In his dream there were more pews than the church really had, and the aisle was long, going on for miles perhaps. As dark as it was and with a regular ceiling instead of a vaulted one, it seemed like a tunnel. And all down the aisle, on both sides in the pews were children, endless numbers of them, their faces a blur of tears and pain. He ran and glanced left and right. Man, where did they all come from? They were different races and wore clothes from a lot of time periods.

"Don't leave us!" they cried out to little Jim.

"Fix us!" they begged him.

But eventually he made it to the altar. The stained glass shadows cast on him had changed from blood red. Now they were simply dark and disgusting. The man in black who pursued him smelled of roses and Ivory soap, hands cold as the bells over the roof.

Hands on his shoulder…

"Wake up, Jim," Louis said gently.

And he opened his eyes, found he was sweating even more than he usually did. Jim forced a chuckle.

"I hate these long trans-Atlantic flights," he said, yawning with exaggeration.

"Bad dream?" the other doc asked him.

Jim chewed his lip. "Why? Did I say anything…"

"No, nothing," Godard replied with a smile. "Simply whined like a puppy. And the flight is almost over. Rome is below."

Louis rolled up the map of known catacombs he'd been pouring over. The disaster site wasn't on it. The catacombs the plane crash had revealed had been undiscovered for over a millennium.

"This is my chance to do something important," Louis said.

"You've done lots of important things," Jim countered. "The powers that be simply chose to ignore them."

The older man sighed. "This time it will be different, yes?"

Jim grinned. "I feel it's going to be very different."

But he was uncomfortable from the moment he got off the plane. It was Christmas Eve. This might have accounted for why he saw so many priests at the airport. The black suits made him twitch.

++++++++++

"Hello. I am Dr. Godard and this is Dr. Singer. We are here to help you if we may."

Their passports were examined. Yes, papers identified them as doctors—but didn't say of archaeology. They were added to the large team sent to the crash site. Volunteers had come from all over Italy and other countries to assist with the tremendous job of cleaning up this tragedy. There were guards to keep spectators and scavengers beyond the perimeter. The catacombs were not even a consideration at this point.

"I know it is terrible to misrepresent ourselves," Godard admitted in a hushed voice. "But they aren't letting anybody in who isn't with the crash team. I am afraid if we don't get in now, we never will. The more time goes by, the more chance grave robbers will destroy whatever real history there may be."

Singer didn't argue, just as excited about the prospect. But neither of them had truly been prepared for what they saw once they reached the field where the DC-10 had gone down. Only a few days had passed. There had been time for emergency personnel to verify there were no survivors but not for the bodies—and the many pieces of the bodies—to be picked up.

The stench was horrible. Jet fuel. Blood. Carnage. Even though both wore masks, Godard felt so dizzy he stumbled and Singer caught him.

"I just became a vegetarian," the old man said, trying to breathe through his mouth.

"Will you be all right?" He was worried about Godard, who at age seventy was no longer a man in his prime.

"Just you keep a hold of that bag," Louis rasped.

They'd had to show the contents of it, of course. But they weren't the only men there with both regular and video cameras. Used to record items for identification by the families, whether it be a half a finger with a signet ring or a glass eye the color of a sapphire or a jawbone with a tooth imprinted with a gold crescent moon and silver star. And others had flashlights, too, for looking inside wreckage and down in the holes in the ground the wreckage had created. It was going to take a long time, for the area had to be gridded and then every single piece—whether McDonnel Douglas or human—had to be recorded as to exactly where it was discovered within the grid.

It seemed like a dreadful lie, employing a ruse after such a tragedy to be the first into this catacomb. Dishonorable. But they had both suffered so many career disappointments. Hell, Jim knew this would likely be Louis' last hurrah.

Going into the trench which the plane's nose had carved didn't elicit any unwanted attention. They slipped away, descended carefully into the crevice, away from the severed nose of the plane. A miracle it hadn't caused a cave-in. They set their feet into the ancient tunnel, and didn't even consider turning back.

++++++++++

First thing as they stepped into the darkness, the two docs stepped on bones. Turning on their flashlights and aiming *away* from the entrance, so that hopefully they wouldn't draw attention to themselves, they saw narrow, steep steps going further down toward a bottom they couldn't see.

"Should there be remains at this point?" Jim wondered outloud.

"Hmm. Not human. They look canine," Louis said.

Jim chuckled.

"What is funny?" his friend and mentor wanted to know.

"You ever see *The Omen?*"

"Pardon?"

"Never mind."

They went down the steps, slowly, creeping toward a pitch blackness that virtually swallowed their lights after only ten to twenty feet. It was much colder once they reached the stairway's end and crossed a threshold. It was a good thirty to forty degrees below what it was just outside in the trench. They were glad it was December and they'd both worn coats. Grappling with the flashlights, they began to walk down the silent passageway, stopping now and then to snap a picture of some simple carving in the tufa, the softly porous stone which had commonly been used in catacombs, it being easy to work with.

"The niches are closed. The tiles limed over their entrances are intact," Louis commented. "This columbarium has never been disturbed."

"It's very plain," Jim noted. "I've seen photos of others with colorful tesserae and stucco artwork."

"Those are tombs for patricians." Louis turned his light, revealing a crude yet lovely painting. "Still, look here. A fresco of The Good Shepherd and his flock. This marks it as definitely Christian."

"And this etching here, of a wheel and a fish," Jim indicated.

"That is not a wheel..."

"Just kidding. I know it's round bread. Loaves and fishes."

They stood inside a large quadrangular chamber. It was centrally supported by a large pier. There was row after row, nine in all, of arched "loculi" rising up to the ceiling, plaques carved with the names of those interred. There was a bench that went around the base of the chamber wall. Into it were two rows of jars set into the stones.

Every ten feet or so, Godard used a piece of chalk to draw a small arrow, pointing back the way they had come. It was just too easy to get lost down there. Catacombs were often miles long, with various levels and turning with separate chambers like a minor maze. They came to another set of steps and went down, teeth chattering with the cold, breaths hazy.

The passageways were so cramped, often no more than a meter wide, and Jim felt claustrophobic. (Was this that vast underground network he'd dreamed about so often? Not hell, near hell?) He told himself to calm down. After all, it wasn't as if he hadn't been in snug regions before, inside tombs or in ancient caverns too small to turn around in, much less do the hokey pokey. But this place felt so oppressive!

Naturally, it had been closed with thousands of dead for anywhere from fifteen to maybe twenty centuries. Archaeological sites—especially subterranean ones—were usually stuffy at first. Many a student—and professor—had suffered a cavernous unease. It wasn't unusual for a place to be sticky and damp and possessed of the sense of "crawl."

And if this place held the remains of martyrs who had suffered the most heinous torments, then it might be no less psychically disturbing than touring through Auschwitz.

Jim had boned up on the subject after Louis received the tip from his young cousin, Gerard. There were dozens of catacombs known throughout Rome, although many more were thought to lie hidden from the modern world. At least sixty miles of them had been excavated, the earliest dating back to the Emperor Augustus.

There were the catacombs of St. Agnes. The story had it that Agnes had been a great beauty. At about age 13 she refused all offers of marriage, claiming she'd have no husband save Christ. Spurned suitors publicly denounced her as criminally Christian and she was dragged off to a brothel. Many young Roman men showed up to take advantage of this but were so awed by her spiritual presence that they couldn't bring themselves to abuse her. Only one rotten kid attempted to rape her and he was immediately struck blind. She was eventually put to death in Domitian's Stadium.

There was the St. Celilia. She was another who had vowed her virginity to God. She was ordered to be burned but the flames didn't touch her. So they settled for beheading her.

St. Sebastion had catacombs named after him as well. Supposedly he was showered with arrows that failed to kill. His persecutors did succeed in beating him to death.

They turned a sharp corner, ninety degrees, and both stopped, catching their breaths. What an awful feeling! Both of them experienced it.

114

"Whoa!" Jim exclaimed in something akin to a startled blues shout. He grabbed at his gut which rumbled and sloshed. He almost bent double with a seismic cramp. He was genuinely afraid he'd have to excuse himself to find a dark corner to squat down in. Then it passed as quickly as it had come.

"*...le ciel m'en preserve!*" Louis said, his old body farting loudly. "Oh, *excusez-moi.* I don't know where that came from."

Jim chuckled nervously. "I think I do. Getting ready to change, isn't it? And you feel it, too..."

"Indeed. And that is unusual for me. Ah well, I am an old man. Perhaps the closer one gets to one's own end, the easier it is to feel the mortality of others."

Around that corner was another square room. But here the jars in the bench had all been broken into, whatever had been inside dumped onto the floor. They were now filled with dust. And everywhere were large bowls and buckets. There were also entire skeletons, some in fetal positions. Others were stretched out and twisted as if in positions of writhing when the people had died.

"Look at this," Jim pointed out in more than one of the bowls. "The same kind of bones we saw at the entrance. Dog, you said."

"This is not right," Godard replied, scratching his head. "These are serving dishes. Were they eating dogs, down here?"

Another doorway and flight of steps. How far below the surface were they now? An uneven corridor was adorned with a complicated fresco. Repeated appearances were made by a radiant skeleton of a girl (named as St. Aureola in a history which had been inscribed beneath the artwork). She had long yellow hair and an exquisite/prerequisite halo. A little dog yapped at her feet. She was shown in positions of prayer, of eating flowers, of crouching to shit light into a bucket.

Aureola, from *aureum*...the Latin word for "golden."

The docs stared open-mouthed at this and then turned to one another. They hadn't been expecting anything of this nature. But what were the odds that, of all those in the world who might have made this discovery, it fell to these two?

"This is our kismet," Godard told Singer. "Our eureka that will astonish the world."

++++++++++

According to the Renaissance Italian traveler, Marco Polo, there was a pious order on the Indian Malabar Coast whose solemn members never ate a living thing. Their dietary restriction wasn't limited merely to animals but also included living plants, since they believed that fresh vegetation contained souls. They did, however, eat dried plants. They eliminated their waste on the beach, then mixed it with sand, breaking it down as much as they could. Their goal was to destroy the waste so that no worms could be generated in it, only to perish for having been born from the order's sins.

—Sacred Sepsis
Dr. Louis Godard and Dr. James Singer

CHAPTER
11

SUBWAY TUNNELS,
1992

In two years Myrtle Ave had filled the whole wall with her
drawings. Vagrants from all over the city came to see them,
pressing into the tunnel, filing by as if at any uptown gallery.
They whispered reverently or laughed out loud. Kids on dates
braved the dangers to go see the sewer art. That's what folks
were calling what she did: sewer art — despite the fact the location was the subway and not the city sewer.

Maybe they called it that because there was this one big
piece she'd done in which she used the phrase sewer-sybil.

Like this:

s
e
w
e
razorekshun
y
b
i
l

And Myrtle knew she wasn't any kind of real artist. Not a da Vinci or a Picasso. She just did images from her head, cathartic doodling. Little frenetic poems without style or grace. A kind of dirty, underground manifesto or—dare she contemplate it?—a bible of darkness. Cheesy cartoons, when you got right down to it.

Last week there had been a minor gang war in the tunnel. Members from two rival factions had decided to come down for a viewing at the same time, somebody carrying a big radio which hammered out a Blam blammmm ta-ta-ta-tingting ughgh hughgh! Somebody chanting behind this rhythm as if knowing the daily grind reflected in your nightmares and setting them to rhyme. Guns were drawn, heads blown halfway to pink cotton candy and cherry slush, bullets ricocheting to kill a few hapless strays and digging a canyon across part of her work like a finishing touch from the visiting specter of Jackson Pollock. The flashing of the muzzles like cameras going off, like the lights from a train suddenly *POW! POW! POW!* down a formerly pitch-black tunnel. *POW! POW!* Are you blind yet?

(How's about deaf?)

When it ended there was blood everywhere. The vagrants quickly descended to rob the dead and dying.

As for Myrtle, she stayed with her face pressed to the cold ground for more than an hour after the killing had stopped. She shivered, eyes squeezed shut, not shamed at all that she'd shit and pissed herself. That was just the body's way of saying, *Okay, I'm cleaned out. I'm ready to leave the world as the empty vessel I came into it as.*

How much later than the gangbanger thing was she practically kidnapped?

A month?

Two guys grabbed her, stuffed a foul rag into her mouth, and started lugging her down the tunnel.

"Listo'll like this one, I'll bet. Once he scrubs her down," one of them said.

She jerked every which way trying to get loose.

"Should we check to see if she's a virgin? He pays more for those..."

118

"Who'd fuck anything this filthy?"

"Still…"

They set her down. One of them stuck his fingers down her crusty panties and probed her hole.

"What d'ya suppose he'll cut offa her? Both arms? Both legs? Maybe make her a new cunt in her left butt cheek?"

Myrtle freaked. Who wouldn't? She vomitted so hard the rag was forced out of her mouth. She also lost complete control of her sphincter.

Noxious, toxic tides from each end forced the men back from her.

"Jeez!"

"Gross!"

"Let's get out of here. A few things done died inside her!"

"Yeah! Big Garth'll cut our nads off, we bring him somethin' doin' that *before* he fixes her."

Myrtle lay there quivering, helpless in her own waste. But she was thinking, "Hey, I didn't know you could use this stuff as a weapon. Cool…"

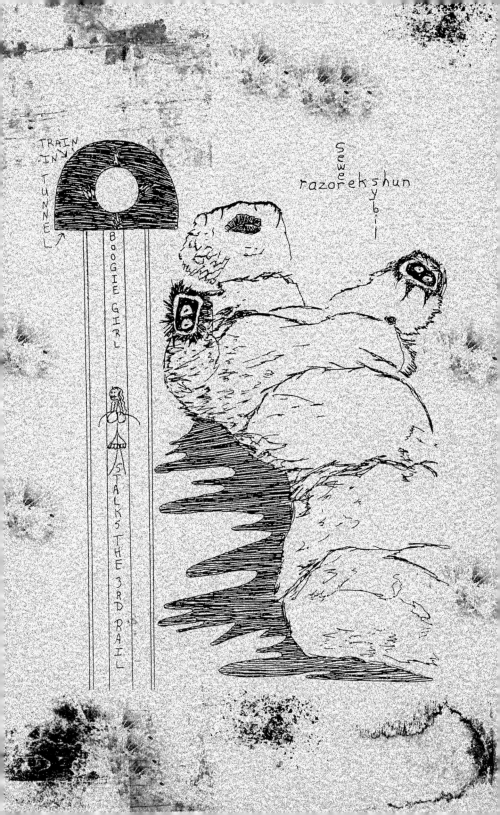

TRAIN
IN
TUNNEL

Sewer
razorekshun
ybil

BOOGIE GIRL
STALKS THE 3RD RAIL

CHAPTER

12

SHEOL'S DITCH,
1981

he Millionaire. The 77th Bengal Lancers. The Buccaneers. Crunch And Des. Oh! Susanna. Doc Corkle.
Shows from the '50s. Jason started to notice that whatever funky cable channel his aunt and unc were watching, it didn't seem to be part of anything anybody'd ever heard of. He checked Big Garth's cable and this channel wasn't there. Even the ads were '50s. No modern station identification.

Even the news was from the '50s. Sputnik. Russians putting down a revolution against Communism in Hungary. Pres Eisenhower this and Vippy Nixon that. Edsels for sale. Korean War. Elvis…a sleek, gyrating sex machine—not the sweating self-caricature who'd died a few years ago.

"You ever hear of a TV channel that's all '50s all the time?" he asked Garth one evening.

He'd come in through the closet hole. There was a new pot in amongst the bonsai trees. The only thing that emerged from the dark soil was a woman's elegantly manicured hand.

"No," B.G. admitted, not seeming to notice the bright red blossom on the sash of his kimono, the only one amidst the predominating pattern of blue chrysanthemums. "Call the cable company. Number's in the guide over there on that table."

There was a book over on that table, too. *Microsurgery.* Jason only glanced at it before picking up the cable guide. He dialed the number and asked the operator the same thing.

"We don't have anything like that," he was told.

Jason then asked Garth, "Do you ever hear a buzz coming from our apartment?"

His older friend shook his head. Interesting. Garth had formerly sported a full head of hair. Tonight Jason noticed the man had shaved the top off, balding himself front to back. He was starting to resemble more and more the Japanese men from the atrocity prints. "Afraid not. You ever hear screaming or gasping coming from this one?"

Jason smiled. "If I'm not over here, I'm at school or asleep."

Garth smiled back and shrugged.

But Jason was hearing that buzzing outside his bedroom door every night now. It aroused both contempt and curiosity. Had he been wrong to assume that this was a vibrator Bowtie used on Ice because he was impotent? In his bedroom, he perched at the keyhole, trying to see out into the hall. Mostly darkness. He'd think he saw a red light, too, but he could never get a fix on it. His eyes would water and then he wouldn't be able to see anything.

He listened. Were there whispers? Aunt and unc seemed past the prime for sweet nothings. He strained his ear against the keyhole and thought this sounded more like dirty talk, erotic and violent. Shot through with a low-key giggling and a voice hitching, sobbing. Not enough so that he could really make out any of the words, which he found truly frustrating.

Next morning at breakfast, Aunt Merrice gave him his cereal as the television showed the McCarthy hearings. He tried to study her for signs of injury. He didn't want to be obvious about it. (After all, the crying could have come from Garth's apartment, couldn't it? He was making use of that surgical stuff the kid had given him. Maybe the buzzing Jason heard these days—or at least part of it—was a bone saw.)

Nothing wrong with Ice. Jason stuck his spoon into the cereal, noticed something weird floating in the milk. Had she changed from flakes to granola?

Still flakes. The extra bit was a nipple.

Jason stared at it, floating pinkly among the golden flakes and black raisins.

Might be an albino raisin.

Then he noticed Bowtie rubbing his chest, a spot of blood visible through his pajama top and robe. Better red than dead, Jason thought with a wry face.

Jason cocked his head, then dug out the nipple and put it in his mouth. He bit down. It would just taste like meat, right?

It was harder than he expected. And it tasted completely spoiled, as if it ought to be green instead of pink. And it…stung. As if he'd put a scorpion in his mouth. He spat it out into his napkin.

"I-I don't feel good," he said. "I'll pass on breakfast."

"What about school? You don't go to school, you go to prison. Know what's in prison, don't you, beast?" asked Ice.

"Yeah, cornholers. Cornholers and holy rollers. I'm going to school," Jason replied, getting up from the table.

"Don't sass your aunt," Bowtie snapped.

That night when Jason sat at the dinner table, he carefully forked through his food, not really managing to put anything in his mouth. He'd been ignoring the television as much as he could, just wanting to get the meal over with so he could sneak next door. But he happened to look up. He didn't know if this was an episode from the first season of *One Step Beyond* or if it came from *Inner Sanctum*. It couldn't be an early *Twilight Zone* he'd never seen, could it? (He thought he'd seen them all over at Garth's.) He'd missed the beginning.

There was this strange landscape, loopy and melted as if Salvador Dali had designed the set—an artist's rendering of surreality almost too good for low budget fifty's fantasy. There was an eye floating around. An overvoice (narrator? or was it supposed to be coming from the eye?) said, "Hurt all the time. Gate's open. Names don't pass through the gate. Years don't pass through the gate."

And there was the kid, '50s traditional towhead with freckles and a striped T-shirt. He was on his knees, reaching forward to touch the eye as if it were some freakin' butterfly.

Jason blinked, feeling his flesh freeze. But after the blink all he saw was a game show. Several people on a panel, and four teasers each saying in turn, "I am Charles Fort."

The first was a guy who looked an awful lot like Friedrich Nietzsche, in a frock coat, mustache bristly as an exploding catepillar, one eye too wide and the other crackled like a fried marble—evidentally after his breakdown. The second looked somewhat like him but fairer and maybe a trifle heavier, glasses with lenses like thick dull toenails across his eyes. The third was General Hideki Tojo, in uniform replete with shiny medals as when he was Hirohito's minister of war. The fourth was an enormous cockroach in a snap brim hat, sitting upright in the chair and twiddling its feelers.

Jason knew Nietzsche and Tojo were dead, the former at the turn of the twentieth century and the latter hanged for war crimes after WW2. Was the giant cockroach supposed to be Kafka? He wasn't sure who the second man was (but given the nature of the program, he guessed by process of elimination).

The panel asked questions which he couldn't hear for some reason. It came out garbled, as if there was something wrong with the sound. It came out in whimpers and groans and giggly half suppressed gusts of naughty talk. The panelists marked their cards. When they held them up, every one of them had written the word DAMNED. Eventually the command was given by the host: "Will the real Charles Fort please stand up!"

It turned out to be as he'd suspected—the second man. The fellow rose and opened his mouth. Out came shrieking wind, the noises of pounding artillery and hissing firestorm, the sounds of millions screaming. Out of it blasted deformed frogs, locusts, chocolate kisses, luminous splinters of metal, and black slime.

Jason dropped his fork.

Sudden switch to commercial. Two people in a sedan sped down the highway. There were Burma Shave ads around the bends.

The first read: Do What

The second read: Thou Wilt

The third read: Shall Be

The fourth read: The Whole

The fifth read: Of The Damned

Passing this fifth sign, the car spun out of control to plunge over a cliff. As it burst into flame and the people trapped inside died a horrible death, the freckled towhead in his striped shirt and the hovering eyeball crept close enough to get (what? an eyeful?).

Jason jumped up from his place at the table. Jesus, had Ice drugged his food or was he only flashing back on the stuff his parents used to hop him up on so they could party?

He staggered to the television, his hand shaking so hard that, even though his two broken fingers had healed by now, they sounded like they were full of chinkly broken glass.

"Boy, what the hell are you doing?" Bowtie cried out as Jason touched the channel dial.

"Leave that alone, you little beast!" Ice spat out, chunks of meatloaf brick spewing from her yellow teeth.

Yet he did turn it, again, again. Nothing else. Just darkness and a buzzing static all around the dial. Was there only this one channel?

"No, don't do that..." Bowtie shouted.

"Stop the little beast, cumcakes!" Ice urged. "We'll send him to the cornholers!"

The knob felt full of blood, as had that spot on the kid's larynx when Jason punched him in the throat. It thrummed beneath his hand. It discharged a jagged static that he could see twisting around his fingers and wrist, a chaotic interlocked knotwork raising the hair up his arm. Stunned, he turned it off. The square screen went black, like the patch of sky above the defile between the mountains at night. Where a hollow boy searched for Melanicus to be gliding from one world to another, carried by a dark wind that roared between stars.

Bowtie had left the table, too, and now grabbed the boy by the ear.

"Need to learn some respect," Unc said as he began to drag him down the hallway to the kid's bedroom. With his free hand, he pulled his keyring from his pants pocket.

Jason jerked in the man's grasp, kicking him like he had when they'd found him cutting the hole in the closet four years ago. He'd just turned thirteen and was as big as a high school linebacker. Bowtie was just a frail old man. How had he ever allowed this old coot to lock him up? Not anymore.

Bowtie's leg bent entirely wrong in the middle of the calf. Jason simply pushed him into the couple's bedroom, then stalked back to the kitchen table for his aunt. She put up more of a struggle, hissing and spitting like a cat, her gray hair standing on end, thin lips shriveled back to bare her corn-like teeth. He reached down and scooped her up, throwing her across his shoulder, wrinkling his nose at her flaky old lady stink, shuddering at the way her backbone coiled like a slinky toy hidden within a ham. He carried her to that bedroom and set her down, not all that roughly—considering. Unc was turning around and around on that knobble of a leg where it lay with the inner part of the calf horizontal and pressed to the floor, spinning on it as if trying to invent some weird new dance craze.

"You fucked up good, boy!" Bowie Cursky told his grandnephew, squinting so hard it seemed there was nothing in his eye sockets but egg shells.

"You better start learning to bend over and spread 'em, because that's how they pray in prison church!" Merrice Cursky added vehemently. "You're going to find you ain't seen nothin' yet. No matter how bad what you already seen was, it won't compare..."

"Yeah yeah," Jason muttered as he wrenched the keys out of his uncle's hand, walked into the hall, and closed their door. Then *Click NICK!* What a satisfying sound. For once not hearing it as he was locked into his room but only as he locked them into theirs.

Jason went to his own room and entered the place next door via the hole in the closet.

"Garth?" he whispered.

There was no reply.

"Are you home, Garth?" he called louder.

Now he heard a frantic yet muffled whimpering coming from Big Garth's bedroom where the door—as usual—was closed.

His friend wasn't there. He crawled back through the closet aperture. He wanted to stay close, just in case his guardians started to scream for help and the neighbors called the cops. Because if the cops showed up, they might find that cache of stolen goods in his room.

"Shit," he said to himself, biting his lip. "Am I going to have to kill them?"

Well, they had never liked him. Was it possible they could refuse to take care of him anymore? Was it true what they had always threatened him with, that he could end up in the juvie? Not that he didn't believe for a second that he couldn't hold his own against the teenaged rapists and the callow cripplers and the adolescent zombie flesh-eaters. But he'd be separated from B.G., just when he was learning so much.

He read in his room but couldn't really concentrate. He tried to lie down but couldn't sleep. He paced the floor, going to the window from time to time, looking out, hearing noises in the alley down below: cats fighting, rats fighting, some hooker being whaled on by either a john or her pimp, drug deals in raspy whispers, a drunk or addict seeing shoggoths as he threw up on some homeless guy's cardboard hut and the homeless guy pretending to be Cthulhu—scaring the literal crap out of the fool in a thunderous fart which echoed off the apartment walls like a gunshot.

Hours had passed. Jason hadn't heard a peep. Not cursing aimed at him nor the usual buzzing. Maybe he'd handled them too roughly and they'd developed blood clots and died. Maybe they'd tied the sheets with blankets together, escaping through their window—or tried to escape and were now lying in a broken heap of scabby limbs in the alley.

He unlocked their door and looked in.

The room was empty.

But the window was still fastened shut. As a matter of fact it was stuck so hard he couldn't open it to look outside and down. It smelled in their room. Of rotten eggs and bread thick with black mold. Of mildew and summer roadkill.

Jason checked the rest of the apartment but didn't find them.

On a whim, he turned on the TV. Before he even saw a picture, he heard the low thrumbling blues-shout of "...I am the god of hellfire!"

" ...I am the god of hellfire!"

Then with brilliant clarity there was the place he'd seen through the hole in the closet wall, four years ago. He sat down and watched, all the rest of that night, shivering, making fists, sweating ice water, his mouth taking turns giggling and chattering the teeth. He listened to the buzz, weep, and vile murmur, watching the terror which had no horizons.

Aunt Ice had been right. He hadn't seen nothin' yet.

At dawn, the television set caught fire. He put it out with a cushion from the sofa but it never worked after that. Might as well have been just any old piece of shit from a second-hand store.

He never saw Ice and Bowtie again. He didn't tell anyone this but Garth. He sold his stolen goods and paid the rent himself. Nobody ever found out. Hell, lots of kids fell through the cracks. Some of them crawled through and nobody was ever the wiser.

++++++++++

Egypt's scarab beetle, revered as sacred, was a dung beetle. Dung beetles breed in manure.

—Sacred Sepsis
Dr. Louis Godard and Dr. James Singer

CHAPTER
13

Ring!
She didn't bother to pick up. She let the answering machine take it.

"Dorien? It's Annet. Mom's really depressed. Why haven't you been back?"

Ring!

"Hi, it's me again. The funeral is tomorrow at noon. I assume you'll be there. Right?"

Ring!

"Dorien, how can you do this? Especially to Mom? Do you know how she freaked out when you didn't show at the church? Or even to the graveside? Has something happened to you?"

Ring!

"Ms. Warmer? This is the clinic. Your test results show negative. No signs of abnormality. Probably just stress. Give us a call though if anything changes you want us to take a look at."

She didn't even glance in the direction of the phone. Or at the many blinking lights indicating messages she'd never played. She'd been sitting right there when they came in, so she knew what they were. That is, when she was awake.

She'd been sleeping a lot. Having those dreams where she was somebody else, a series of others who deep down were really just one mysterious, incomprehensible woman.

(Not a woman.)

Yeah? What then? A goddess?

Ring!

"Ms. Warmer? The clinic. Test was negative. Congratulations. Dr. Ramil says you'll outlive us all."

Two tests. One for pregnancy and another for AIDS. Of course she'd outlive them all. Goddesses didn't die, did they? Well, this one apparently flitted from incarnation to incarnation like a girl skipping stones in a river.

Last night (it had been last night, hadn't it?) Dorien took a bath, frothy with gardenia-and-rose-scented bubbles. She had a few candles burning, not merely for asthetic effect but because the electric lights burned her eyes. Mostly she wore sunglasses even when inside. But she felt stupid having them on in the tub.

Dorien had just sat back with her head resting on a vinyl bath pillow, letting the perfume and hot water soak the sin out of her. Gardenia, a white flower, and that had to be (symbolically) as clean as you could get. Rose, a saintly scent if ever there was one, unsullied and pure.

But was she sinful? In those dreams seeking out—no, summoned to and called by—the most atrocious people. All the shit humanity was capable of. Yet she wasn't evil herself.

Outrage was simply the bell that called her forth, walking along the curbs beside sewers, stepping lightly through scenes of carnage where entrails had spilled. Looking for those who were both wasters and waste. The attraction was perhaps symbiotic but not sympathetic.

Dorien had watched the water change, darkening, gurgling around her, semi-solid. Gardenia-rose tilted into a darker substance which might have been used to fertilize them. Grossed out, she couldn't move, couldn't stand up to shower the filth off. It caressed her breasts, nipples hardening against her will. It tickled her between the thighs, infiltrating by millimeters the entrances to both vagina and rectum.

There might have been a logical explanation. Sewer backing up through the drains. The old building had lousy plumbing. And an even lousier landlord.

But the plug was in the drain; she felt it with her foot. So how was this coming up to taint her bath? (And her?)

It wasn't an infusion of crud into the fresh water she'd drawn and had dropped the bath oil beads into. This was the water itself altering: perfume becoming rank, milky going brown, liquid slowly assuming mass.

She caught the chain between her big and second toes and pulled. Then she sat there, fixated as blackening bubbles screamed down the drain, exploding like defiled little heads.

Her own skull throbbed. It felt like an overworked anvil in a blacksmith shop. She knew better than to try taking anything for it. Nothing would help. Not aspirin, acetaminophen, ibuprofen, or Jack Daniels. She glanced at herself in the mirror as she finally got to her feet. She couldn't look at her eyes.

Turning back, prepared to scrub the porcelain even though that would surely be a disgusting job, she spied no sign of the muck. There wasn't even a ring around the tub. It sparkled, whiter than the gardenia flower she'd imagined and as without sin as the rose.

She stayed awake as long as she could. This might merely be a psychic contagion brought on by the shock with Gavin. She didn't care to have to think of herself as being so sensitive (i.e. weak-brained) that she could be hurt this deeply by one cruel boy, enough to send her into a neurotic tailspin.

"I'm having a breakdown."

She'd been lucky to miss the other disease he was carrying. She'd heard of psychic vampires who drained the emotional stability out of people. Why couldn't there be psychic werewolves, seemingly decent at first, then whirling into hideous manipulators, able to wreak havoc in the spirits they touched, mangling the minds until…your own mother wouldn't know you—you didn't know yourself.

She drank pots of coffee and attempted to read the nights away, pages rustling in her caffeine-jittered fingers. She bit her tongue whenever she started dozing off, tasting something mineral-based that definitely wasn't salt or iron. She stuck a pin into the palms of her hands to startle herself away from sleep, but then she stared in wonder (and not too small an amount of fear) when blood didn't show at this pricking. What oozed wasn't red; it was like the brown rain that ran down her windows during city storms. (Now why couldn't this have shown up while she was at the clinic?)

Not that she saw the rain anymore since she'd used duct tape over every square inch of her windows, blocking out the insolent and unwanted outside. So she didn't know if it was day or night when a knock came gently at the door.

A familiar voice called, "Dory? Little sister? Are you in there? Please let me in. I brought you some food just in case you're hungry. I'll bet you've been holed up in there because you're down about Dad and all, huh? Bet you haven't had a decent meal in a week."

Dorien put her hands over her ears.

"I've decided not to go back to California. I'm staying with Mom because she, like, needs someone, you know? I've met some nice people and have a new job. I'd sure like for you to meet them. Dorien?"

She groaned very softly, had a pain in her jaw. But managed to keep very quiet.

"Hey? Mom's worried; I'm worried. What do we have to do, call the cavalry?"

Dorien frowned, put a finger inside her mouth, poking at a soft spot. She then spat a tooth into her hand. Then she spat another. The AIDS test must have been wrong. How soon before she had lesions like Neela's? It must be the reason her blood looked and smelled different. Why her subconscious was obsessed with images of plagues and pollutions.

The doorknob rattled. "Hello?"

"Go away," she whispered almost silently. She tried to will the woman in the hall to leave. If Dorien wasn't really Dorien anymore, then Annet couldn't really be called her sister. And she needn't feel guilt at how she'd abandoned her mother. Especially considering what Mom had done, protecting that monster, that child-killer.

"I'm going to guess maybe you really aren't there," the voice beyond the door said. "Which means I must sound silly still talking, right? I'm going to leave this bag of food here. It should heat up fine in the microwave. Call us or come by. Just get in touch. We love you."

There was a pause as if Annet hesitated.

"I don't love you," Dorien murmured. The word itself, "love," stuck like peanut butter to her gums and the roof of her mouth.

Footsteps grew distant. Dorien felt herself tilt sideways. Didn't even realize it was sleep sneaking up.

++++++++++

"And while Satan and the prince of hell were discoursing thus to each other, on a sudden there was a voice as of thunder and the rushing of winds, saying, 'Lift up your gates, O ye princes; and be ye lift up, O everlasting gates, and the King of Glory shall come in.'"

—Nicodemus, Chapter XVI, 1
The Lost Books Of The Bible

ROME, 399
THIS WAS HOW THE STORY WENT:

Aureola was a beautiful, golden-haired waif who was evicted with her group from their communal chapel. The councils in North Africa at Hippo in 393 and in Carthage in 397 had established canons of both the Old and New Testaments and the Apocrypha, deciding on the tenets which would be acceptable to Rome's new church. Of the New Testament, only the gospels from four apostles were to be included: Matthew, Mark, Luke, and John. All else—the gospels of other apostles—was to be discarded from the Christian side of the Bible.

Factions had their favorites and had been warring with one another, even willing to do violence to have their theology win out. Aureola's group had become unpopular for believing that animals had souls and for preaching from the book of Nicodemus about Christ in Hell. The patriarchs apparently felt it was counterproductive to admit that the Lord had set foot in the underworld after his crucifixion and before his ascension. Besides, there was already a story in which Jesus succeeded in winning the battle of wits between Satan and he, taking place during the forty days in the desert, told by Matthew, Mark and Luke.

Driven into the night, separated from her brethren in faith, Aureola found refuge with a pack of wild dogs. They kept her warm. One in particular, that she named Frater, always brought her back the best garbage from his foragings. Some of the other Christians chastised her for living with unclean beasts, but she argued eloquently that they were God's creatures—as the ravens who'd fed Job. The dogs had proven their brotherhood by giving her charity.

There were many orphans in Rome then, as incursions by barbarians and disease (and squabbles over doctrine) frequently killed parents. Some of these children had begun tailing after her and the pack. It was feared her following might grow into a problem. So she was arrested on charges of vagrancy and bestiality and thrown into prison.

She starved until a guard pretended to take pity on her, for she'd grown thin as a skeleton. He brought her some meat which, being in a state so weakened, she ate gratefully. Then he admitted she'd just eaten Frater, her dog. Horrified, she reached out of the small window of her cell to grab handfuls of blossoms from an Egyptian cassia plant. Eating these caused her to undergo a forceful catharsis.

She prayed for many days and nights, tearfully pious and pure, until Frater arose from the matter she'd expelled.

Hallelujah.

The next morning all the dogs of Rome—thousands of them—had gathered outside her prison. They howled. They had brought scavenged garbage in their jaws. Drawn by the noise of the dogs, people came together. Wasted, the cachetically thin girl could be seen at the window. She held her hands up to show open sores on the palms. "I bleed for the souls of the animals!" she explained.

And she held up Frater so he could bark.

When the guard who had killed and fed Frater to Aureola came to the end of his shift and was replaced by another, he began to walk home. The dogs chased him down and tore him to pieces.

All were impressed by her beauty. Many arrived every day to pray outside her cell, others camped out to be witnesses at all times. They watched as her fasting caused her to grow smaller. The more she starved, the more ethereal she seemed in martyrdom. Even though she was a grown woman, she appeared childlike, returning to innocence without the curves which belonged to the mature lady.

"That Aureola," they would say reverently, "she grows lovelier each extra day she suffers."

The church fathers were petitioned to let her go. It had become too dangerous: to release her might have given the appearance of sanctioning her beliefs. They gave orders she be forced to eat so she wouldn't die. But she would pluck cassia blossoms from her window every time. The authorities had the plant stripped away again and again, but by dawn it had always grown back. Another guard responsible for carrying out her waste bucket was bribed to show it to the crowd. Her excrement was always pale, never dark. It had a golden color, the hue for the holy.

Soldiers were dispatched every day to chase away the dogs. Sometimes they resorted to killing them. But more returned at daybreak, howling, all the best garbage in their jaws as offerings.

One morning the nearby entrance to the sewer began to bubble and then flood up from Rome's Cloacus Maximus, bringing out a tide of crapulent bilge.

A sign!

"Free Aureola!" some folk began shouting, cries blending with the baying of what were now thousands of dogs. In the stink from the miasms of sewage, dizzy people spied shapes in the steam and gases, glimpsed images of martyrs and apostles. "Free Aureola!" they demanded.

The guard, fearful for his life, quickly unlocked the cell, then fled as the sewage rose across the yard.

Aureola appeared at the doorway, little Frater in the scoop of one reed-thin arm and a bunch of cassia flowers in the other. Her skin was stretched tight across the bones. Sores ringed her skull like a crown of thorns. She smiled wide and floated out, walking upon the feculent waters.

Someone hissed, then said, "Filthy! Corrupt the body, pollute the soul!"

Aureola's head turned. She stared unblinking at this person. "All that is of the body is made by God, and all that has been created by God is sacred."

Then she tilted back her head, lifting her eyes to heaven, jaw creaking in her beatific smile, and burst apart into a flurry of cassia blossoms. Frater did this, too.

The dogs stopped howling. Everyone gasped, then sighed. Even the dogs sighed.

Then someone near the jail's doorway shouted, "Aureola's body is still in the cell!"

They looked, having to wade through the slop which had just ceased to churn up from the sewer but which still oozed across the ground. There she was, lying on her back in her own excreta, quite still. Dead and cold for hours with the corpse's grin. Flies squatted in the portholes of her nose and skated across the frozen ponds of her eyes. Her golden hair was matted with yellowish waste.

A great cry went up. "God has even turned her shit to gold!"

When they went to lift her up, she weighed so little she might have been measured with a few feathers plucked from an angel's wing.

"She's become as a child again," a woman commented softly.

"I don't understand," wondered another. "We all saw her outside."

"It's a miracle, that's what it is," yet another told them, as if it ought to be plainly obvious.

"She's a saint!" the shout went up.

They tried to take her to the cemetery but were refused entrance by another faction disgusted by her stench. The rivals claimed she was a suicide who had starved herself to death.

They tried many places but no one would take her body, especially seeing the dogs following in a number not unlike a horde of invading barbarians.

In one place, two soldiers came out.

"We will make sure she's dead," they declared and one drew his sword.

Another test for the martyr! Proof of her holiness!

Her followers cried, "Yea, verily! Plunge it into her side, like they did with the body of Jesus!"

The soldier with the sword scoffed, turned her body so it lay face down in the dirt, then slashed her back open with the blade, down and across in the manner of a reaper with a scythe. Then the faithful were permitted to bear her further-insulted corpse away.

Eventually they carried her to a graveyard tunnel outside the city.

A sect began, the members emulating her spare beauty, starving themselves, always taking cassia leaves if they chanced to gorge in weakness (as both a penance and a sacrament). The Church began to persecute them, so they held themselves secret.

Men and women both began to turn their bodies back into the pure child. They even began kidnapping fat Christians and dragging them down into the area which came to be known as the Catacombs of St. Aureola. They forced these prisoners to eat dog meat and then made them consume large amounts of cassia and other herbs, praying deliriously as their victims suffered terrible bouts of vomiting and diarrhea. These were the new sacraments, dog flesh and cassia-infused wine. "We are made in God's image and it means our bodies are temples like unto the Lord. And what comes out of those temples is holy, for nothing profane can exist within the sacred."

137

DREAD IN THE BEAST

The waste was never discarded but kept as relics, yea every bucketful until the reek in Aureola's catacombs could be detected above ground. Many of the dead (except for Aureola), some who had been there since the time when pagan Rome had persecuted Christians, were taken elsewhere and dumped, in order that their niches could be used as latrine troughs.

And who was she? Taking the steps down into the cold earth, following the noises of people in deadly cramps as they strangled on the upward tide of their own stomachs and squatted over buckets, following the soft simper of prayers ringing around the unfortunate prisoners snared with fecumenical bullshit. The remains of dogs decayed at the entrance, down the narrow corridors in black rot rainbows.

Who was she this time? Not the golden one. An Egyptian woman whose father was a wealthy trader in precious substances for temples and medicines. Oil of cinnamon in her hair, frankincense and myrrh ground into powder across her breasts, and the gold material of her dress imbued with kuphi (an incense for the dead). She had no memory of what she'd been called, only that it might have been similar to one of the ten thousand names for Isis.

She saw no prisoners here. No, they were in another vault, toward the opposite end of the catacombs. And those that tended them lay with them on the ground, dead, visited by others only a few hours ago while these here had hidden and listened to the echoes of their slaughter.

She knew there were two halves to this unholy group. Soldiers had come for the first, the mad children. And now she had come for the second, the beasts.

The worshippers in their throes saw her and thought she was an angelic messenger.

"I am the gateway," she said. "The threshold to Aralu..."

They believed she said, "the threshold to Aureola..."

But she hadn't.

And they followed her to their sacred, thunder mug heaven.

Amen.

++++++++++

Dorien woke up, so startled she fell off the sofa. Whose trashy dogma was that? She'd been raised a good Christian and this profane schism shook her down to the atoms.

Right, raised a good Christian by a racist child-murderer and his loving, complicit wife.

Lies were everywhere you cared to look. And where you didn't want to see them. Besides, she had no real reason to accept anything she'd dreamed as having a basis in reality. They were the midnight ramblings of a tor-

138

mented mind. The human brain stored all sorts of things and then spewed them orgiastically into dreams, the bowel movements of the subconscious.

"I have to get out of here," she told herself. "At least for a while."

She glanced at the clock and it said it was 11:00. a.m. or p.m.? Didn't matter. She peeled off her tacky robe, also the man's sleeveless undershirt and sweatpants she used for pajamas. She pulled on jeans, a black cotton turtleneck, and slid her feet into tennis shoes—no socks. She grabbed her handbag.

Dorien opened the front door and found what Annet had said she was leaving. Brown paper sack. CANE printed on it. She picked it up, set it inside the apartment on the nearest table, then locked up.

Turned out it was p.m. A tad dangerous to be walking about, alone, so late. She reckoned to remain on the street, not straying off toward the park where there were too many lonely darknesses to get waylaid in. Not that true evil laid in wait only in such areas. She could be run down on the sidewalk with others about only a few feet away. She could be raped and murdered where dozens stared out their windows into courtyards.

Dorien walked, not thinking about how far she was going, not moving toward any special location. The nights weren't as cool as they had been a few weeks ago. Had it really been almost two months since she slept with Gavin?

She wished she had a car, then she might have been driving aimlessly. Which was wandering for lazy folks. Except it had to be safer, at least more private. She recalled the most recent trips she'd taken on the bus or in the subway. In mass transit you were at the mercy of people's smells. Those with their heads in the lap of death, somebody with colon cancer who didn't know it yet, someone else with a deceased rodent up their asses, yet another with human flesh digesting in them…several even digesting dog.

(Wondering, "how do I know this?")

Tomorrow she would get a paper for the classifieds and try to find herself a cheap car.

She neared a closed liquor store, sign off but bright enough under the streetlights—even through her sunglasses. There was a girl in the loosely-darkened doorway. She huddled under a blanket which she held just down to her neck, as if she were inhaling strange medicinal vapors. It completely concealed her face except for hints of what might exist below from the seeping of pink mucous and smears of gray cottage cheese in dozens of places. Even as far away as Dorien stood, she could tell the girl stank of the lich house.

A teenaged boy in an I Read *The Bighead* And Can Still Eat Solid Food T-shirt was stumbling away, eyes large and round from sickening revelation, ecstatically frightened. His fingers jerked as if he'd stuck them into an electric socket.

There'd been a few of these recently, strewn about the neighborhood.

Selling glimpses of deformities for loose change. Freakpeep. She always passed by, even if she heard a soft, "Wanna see? Wanna see me?" Knowing it wasn't a sexual come-on. (Not exactly…) She'd seen those who took the bait, those curious, those jaded, and those just downright mean.

Yet for reasons she didn't dare pry into, Dorien suddenly decided she wanted to know what lay beneath that blanket. So, even though she'd strolled past, she turned on her heel and walked back.

"How much for a look?" she asked in as steady a voice as she could manage.

"Two bucks," answered a phlegm-heavy voice, the diction of someone wearing a full metal jacket-dental brace, until the regalia they sported resembled the rigging for a circus trapeze act.

Dorien snapped open her purse and dug for the money, all the while glancing about to verify she wasn't going to be knocked on the head for it— or seen by anybody she knew. She produced a pair of wilted dollars she'd accidentally washed with her best black jeans about a week ago. Gray money. (Just as well…money was filthy!) She tried to control her hand so it wouldn't tremble as she held them out.

Very slim fingers emerged to clutch the bills, drawing them away where Dorien couldn't see. Then she heard a most unsettling snuffle and sigh, which perhaps meant there was now no turning back (for either of them). The blanket was raised up, slowly revealing the head of the wretch beneath.

Dorien might have fainted as she did on those two occasions with Gavin, the mind so avid to escape that it briefly and abruptly turned off the five senses and temporarily cut the strings to the legs as well. She might have screamed and run off down the street, lips stretched in almost comical rictal shock-schlock. She could have laughed nervously, totally inappropriate to both human decency and charity. (Yet, seeing this, Dorien knew there was no such thing as either human decency or charity.) She could have vomited when presented with such a savage tableau. But she didn't do any of these things; she simply tried to make sense out of the mixture of wound and tattoo.

Slick new orifices to either side of the scalloped splinter of the nose leaked twin rivers of snot over the rattlesnake pattern needled into the bottom lip (there being no upper lip). Eyelids were trimmed back until they didn't close anymore, tear sacs flooding through conduits carved down to both jaws and inked a jaundice yellow. Tiny yet intricate fanged serpent heads had been drawn open to encompass each eye. Were the unrestrained tears intended to represent venom? The hair, including eyebrows, had been plucked, ears pruned like the eyelids, the area adorned with miniature panoramas of a variety of snakes in the act of swallowing rabbits, cats, cherubic children. Or in the reverse of disgorging useless bones.

All Dorien did was stare in silence, strangely detached, as if she'd seen it all before: the degradation, the unfathomable heart of cruelty, how revulsion companioned with the arousal of sick fascination produced the queasy/rapturous emotion treasured by the most hardcore voyeur.

—Yet, did she feel any of this? Did she feel anything?—

She and the poor human wreckage gazed back at one another without comment. Eventually the freakpeep rearranged the blanket to cover herself and then shuffled away.

++++++++++

From LEVITICUS, XV: 2-9:

"When any man hath a running issue out of his flesh, because of his issue he is unclean.

"And this shall be his uncleanness in his issue: whether his flesh run with his issue, or his flesh be stopped from his issue, it is his uncleanness.

"Every bed, whereupon he lieth, who hath the issue, is unclean, and everything, whereon he sitteth, shall be unclean.

"And whosoever toucheth his bed shall wash his clothes and bathe himself in water, and be unclean until the evening.

"And he who sitteth on anything whereupon he sat who hath the issue, shall wash his clothes and bathe himself in water, and be unclean until the evening.

"And he who toucheth the flesh of him who hath the issue shall wash his clothes and bathe himself in water, and be unclean until the evening.

"And if he who hath the issue spit upon him that is clean, then he shall wash his clothes and bathe himself in water, and be unclean until the evening.

"And whatsoever saddle he rideth upon who hath the issue shall be unclean."

And the horse upon which he rideth on…

—Sacred Sepsis
Dr. Louis Godard and Dr. James Singer
(italicized text not in Bible, provided by Dr. Singer)

CHAPTER
14

ROME,
1990, JUST INSIDE THE NEW YEAR

"I'm sure this isn't right," Godard said, holding his flash-light to examine the chalk arrow.

"You don't think someone came down here behind us and changed them, do you?"

Jim found it hard to believe that they wouldn't have heard another person crawling about the catacombs. They would have—must have—seen anybody else's light. And anyone down here would have to use a light, wouldn't they? Not just prowl about in the pitch blackness...not unless they were either blind or a demonic mole.

Yet the chalk marks did seem different. And Jim Singer was sure they'd walked a lot farther going out than they had coming in.

But what they had discovered! They had a video tape and many photos of the mural and text in front of the chamber which purportedly held the remains of St. Aureola. They had entered that tomb and found—as elsewhere—very old bones. Also, an epistle on paper...flaking, very fragile parchment. It wasn't contained in a proper box but in a piss pot. Similar as the text for the mural, it told in greater detail of her imprisonment, the howling dogs, and the miracle walk upon the sewage. A most bizarre find. Gawd-uh-mighty, a most bizarre *story*.

"You know, it is remarkable when you consider how long it must have taken the artists to paint that mural," Louis said. "It was difficult for any of the artisans who came down into catacombs. Very poor light...and the stench of thousands of corrupting bodies with no ventilation to disperse the poisonous vapors which must occur. Such miasms were known to kill people. And in these catacombs, with its doing double duty, so to speak, as a privy?"

Jim made a gagging noise in his throat. "I'm glad we have masks."

"The tunnel has been opened for several days since the crash. Hopefully it has had sufficient time to vent any deadliness."

But it was taking so long to get back to where they'd entered. They were positive they'd walked for several miles in the wrong direction. The air was very bad down there, even with the special masks they wore, the feeling so oppressive. Godard coughed and Jim scratched, feeling invisibles crawl across him with itchy little legs. He tried not to think about those legs as being covered in the dust of those who'd perished from cholera, smallpox, plague. Not that remnants of this could sicken him; it was just gross.

The very worst sensation for both men had been as they reached a certain chamber, just prior to finding the final corridor which led out. There was a wave of static electricity, snapping and stinging at the tip of each hair. They thought they heard shouts, screams, the noises of ripe fruit being split and wet sheets being torn.

The room was heaped with human bones, similar to the one before, only this time their deaths were marked as having been other than excruciating dysentery. Skulls were cleaved as if with swords or axes and had been pierced as if with spears. They hadn't already been through here, yet the arrows had led them this way.

About a quarter of a mile then, straight and marked with yet another arrow (which Louis couldn't have drawn as they simply hadn't been down this way before). The passage turned out to be the narrowest they'd seen down there. It reminded Jim of a shotgun hall in an early twentieth century house he'd once seen while visiting Memphis, Tennessee. The corridor was lined with shelves for the dead which held nothing but strange curliques of dust, spirals of fossilized clay. What they knew must have been the matter expelled at both ends by Romans. Had they actually crawled into these spaces, intended for corpses, to do their nasty ritual?

"It's almost Zen," Singer pointed out.

"Oh, I do not think so," Godard politely argued.

Jim wiped tendrils of muck from his chin and forehead, knowing that a millennium and a half ago, this stuff might have been somebody's semi-processed meal. Some household dust was made up of things like human skin.

"I don't mean literally. I do mean, you know, how the Buddhists will contemplate rotting corpses in order to grasp concepts of rebirth. Can't you just picture them, squeezing into these niches, going through this awful business of contortions and self-abasement in order to be—according to what we've read—innocent as children again? How grueling, how humiliating, and how fanatically faithful they must have been to put themselves through it."

"Yes, now I see what you mean," Louis replied. "And yet there are no bones in these. So perhaps if anyone died while undergoing the septic-sanctum mini-martyrdom, their remains were taken to another part of the catacombs."

It was how they found the other entrance, following that last chalk arrow, climbing up the long flight of black steps, struggled over debris of what must have once—an age ago—been a stone wall constructed to seal the entrance. They pushed through a thicket of vines heavy with rotten grapes. And then discovered they were no longer at the crash site. It was a different field, and beyond it—if the rumble was any indication—there was a highway.

++++++++++

The docs had rented a car, not bothering to return to the place where the DC-10 had come down. That ruse was at an end. They doubted the crew would contact them, wondering why they hadn't shown up the next day. Assuming they had seen more than they'd bargained for in the grisly field. Doubtless, using that excuse, they weren't the only ones.

They returned several times to the catacombs, recording what they saw on film, taking hundreds of photographs. They had the epistle and several sealed ceramic vases. Other than this activity, they disturbed as little as possible. They wouldn't do much else until they could arrange for a proper archaeologic investigation.

But they would have to get permission. They had already gone outside proper channels. It was time to do the expected thing and inform the authorities, requesting the necessary permits to start an excavation. They realized they would probably have to share this opportunity with Italian archaeologists.

In their hotel room, the docs had ordered up room service. When a knock came at the door, they assumed it was their food. Godard was taking a nap on his bed, but opened his eyes at the sound.

He said as he sat up, "Good. I am so hungry. I could eat a..."

"Dog?" Singer finished for him, grinning. He'd gone to let the waiter in.

"I have eaten many dogs," Louis admitted.

Singer chuckled as he made a face. "Yeah? Hot dogs, right? With mustard, chili, onions…maybe some saurkraut. Or—ooh lala—snails perhaps?"

The old man shook his head. "No, I mean ones that go bow-bow. During the war, the Nazi occupation of my country, I was a partisan. I told you…"

Jim nodded.

"Well, sometimes meals weren't so easy to come by. And right after the war, I worked on my doctorate in Indochine Francaise…now Vietnam, Laos, and Kampuchea. Also, we have been many places together where we were served dog and you didn't know it. But that flavor, I recognize it."

Jim's jaw dropped. "And you didn't tell me?"

"Sometimes I knew we were not supposed to know. Places where we weren't always welcomed with open arms, they fed us dog because they thought that's what we were. They fed us dog because they could. Other places…would you rather have starved or been reduced to—not only insulting our hosts but having to eat river reeds and bugs?"

There was a second knock at the door, a little louder than the first.

Godard's eyes sparkled so that his colleague wondered if he was even telling the truth about Jim having been fed dog. "Hurry, Rover is best served hot, yes?"

Upon opening the door, he found three priests standing there. He managed not to glare at them. (Can't blame them all for the actions of one scumbag.)

"Doctors Louis Godard and James Singer?" one of them asked, smiling mildly.

This one was the eldest of the trio, with very white hair and very black eyebrows. The other two were both young men, what Jim thought of as young—which generally meant just younger than he was. He was in his mid-forties and not a good judge of age for anybody visibly less than mid-thirties.

Somehow, in Rome, he'd thought they would all be in the classic long black cassocks. Of course, he'd seen clergy at the airport when they came in, as well as a few who had accompanied the clean-up crews to the crash site. So he knew better. Still, the black suits made him think of undertakers. Or underworld assassins.

No, they didn't. He knew perfectly well what they made him think of. Stained glass and blood shadows, tormented saints and altar boys, being pursued down the aisle so long, endless, connected to…yes! The underworld. Underworld assassins not so far off, after all.

"That's us. What can we do for you guys," Jim asked, stopping himself from calling them, *what*, Fathers? That double-edged sword.

Godard trotted up in his stocking feet and peered into the hallway, his eyes round as those of a marmoset.

"May we come in?" requested this older priest. "We promise not to take up too much of your time."

146

"Can't you just leave a pamphlet for us to throw away like the Jehovah's Witnesses do?" Jim asked sarcastically but stepped back.

He almost added, *We'll either read it or use it to wipe our asses with. Either way it'll serve its purpose.*

Jim turned around and noticed that Louis had thrown a blanket over the video camera and the piles of film cassettes and photographs. The epistle had been carefully boxed earlier and was in the bathroom. He wanted to leave the door open, not that he could have told why he felt this way—and strongly, too. The mere notion of being in a closed room with men wearing Catholic collars made him want to hide under his bed.

But one of the Fathers closed the door, after they were all inside. It shut like the entrance to a vault. Apparently they were concerned about privacy.

"I am Father Malvezzi," the senior priest said with a bigger smile now. Then he indicated his companions. "This is Father Cubberly and that is Father Paolo."

"To what do we owe this honor?" asked Godard, smiling back, matching the man tooth for tooth.

Malvezzi sucked his smile back in but still gave the outward appearance of cordiality. "It has come to our attention that you had been trespassing on Vatican property. By which we mean the catacombs where the unfortunate Turkish flight crashed on December 21st."

Jim grunted, noticing the younger two never smiled at all. They were rather big for priests, he thought. But why couldn't clergy work out? Maybe the Vatican had a state-of-the-art gym, to make the priesthood stronger for grappling with Satan...and little boys. "You mean the Catacombs of St. Aureola."

He didn't say it as a question. He meant it as a correction.

Malvezzi frowned now. "There is no saint by that name."

True, only the Church could decree someone a saint. Probably only Aureola's followers had believed her to be that.

Louis shrugged. "We found these catacombs to be—-to all appearances—abandoned, apparently forgotten. I researched and found nothing to indicate the Vatican had any claim here or even any knowledge of it. We do, naturally, apologize, if this is in error."

Jim interjected, "We were going out tomorrow morning to see about proper permits to do our scientific thing."

Malvezzi blinked. "There will be no scientific...'thing'. Aureola and her followers were outlaws of the cruelest order, dangerous blasphemers. They committed heinous acts and even killed people..."

"And then were killed themselves, right?" Jim concluded out loud, thinking of the chamber strewn with bones, skulls with obvious breaches by sharp weapons. This wasn't simply where niches had been opened and the contents dragged out.

Godard cleared his throat, making Jim wonder if perhaps he shouldn't have said this. Considering the mural, text and epistle, it was easy to leap to the notion that these Christians (however wayward and, oh what the hell, *freaky*) had been murdered by other Christians, a deed perhaps sanctioned by Mother Church itself, such as it was in those early years.

"Anything that you have seen...we would consider it a great favor if you would not report it," Malvezzi told them.

"We're scientists. We don't sit on history to please anybody," Jim retorted, feeling more uncomfortable the longer these priests remained in the room. The closed room, he reminded himself. He was beginning to feel as claustrophobic as he had in the catacombs. "Come on, guys, it isn't like it's the first time in history the Catholic Church has shed blood for dubious interests."

They gave him such a look, one that silently called him a dirty little butterball sinner. One meant to show their power here. God's team. Malvezzi probably figured him for a lapsed Catholic the moment Jim opened the door and reacted.

"The interests in this case are not dubious," Malvezzi replied.

Godard sighed. "Dr. Singer is right. We publish our findings, whatever they are. You shouldn't take it so personally, Father. It happened a long time ago but it is still history. The world has a right to know the past, it being the only way to enter the future with any hope. Wisdom can be a warning to the wise, and vice versa."

Jim had to admit to himself that Louis put it better than he did, not getting defensive and not snapping. And not acting as if he suspected they had the tools of the Inquisition under their somber coats. (Are those thumbscrews in your pocket, Father, or are you just glad to see me?) In the over twenty-five years he'd been working on projects with Dr. Godard, he'd never had occasion not to admire the Frenchman. He even understood that he would never measure up to this man.

Malvezzi argued blandly, "The world is full of children, young and old. Not equipped to deal with some topics. We must protect them as we always have. We *will* protect them."

Jim laughed now, mostly to cover the incidence of his profuse sweating. Was the room too hot or what? "Is that a threat?"

And he was perspiring—sluicing saltwater might be a more appropriate term—because he kept seeing this priest in front of him but feeling him behind him, smelling of roses and Ivory soap, hands cold as bells...

Malvezzi shrugged. "It is not your fault that the entrance was opened after so many years under sacred seal. The tragedy of the Turkish plane crashing was the cause. The catacombs will be sealed again tomorrow morning. The plane's foremost section..."

He glanced at the other two priests.

One said, "The nose."

The other said, "The cockpit."

Malvezzi nodded. "Yes, this has been removed by crane today and so the canyon it cut in the ground can be filled back in. After we seal and bless the entrance. But there is more than one way for evil to escape and that is through the dissemination of information. This is why we are here. To request your silence."

There was another knock at the door. Malvezzi opened it this time. There stood the waiter with the docs' tray.

"Good evening, gentlemen. I hope you enjoy the rest of your stay in Rome. As archaeologists, you might want to consider visiting the Vatican. We have some of the finest museum facilities and collections in the world. Of course, I'm afraid many things are kept separate. Not for public or profane view."

The Fathers left.

Jim signed the waiter's slip and tipped him. Then closed the door.

Louis had started changing clothes.

"Hurry," he told Jim.

"Why? Where are we going?"

The older doctor pulled a long, comically incredulous face. "To the catacombs. He said they would close them tomorrow."

Jim grinned. "And we have tonight."

+++++++++++

Malvezzi had said the entrance would be sealed. And then he'd mentioned the crash site. Obviously the Church didn't know about the other entrance. The docs boxed up everything they had so far. Louis called his cousin Gerard to come pick it up, leaving a key for him at the hotel desk.

They drove out to the second field, a good four miles from the crash site. They descended the steps with flashlights, looking carefully about, seeing no one and no sign that this entrance had been disturbed since when they'd left it, earlier that day. The fact that there was no guard here helped to assure them this doorway was unknown to the Vatican.

Their plan was to take one or two things more, choosing carefully. Items which might bolster the findings they would later publish. So what if the Church was embarrassed? They already had some pretty convincing evidence. Perhaps the Italian government would overrule the Vatican once they saw the video tapes on PBS. (Jim didn't know if Rome got PBS. Yet he was sure they'd hear about it, after the Americans ran the piece. He wouldn't even permit himself to consider that PBS would turn it down.) Yes, Italian archaeologists would champ at the bit, he was sure. That is, he couldn't picture scientists without the same drives he and Louis possessed.

(Even if there had been plenty of scientists who'd looked at their past finds and merely thought the docs *possessed*. But times had changed a lot, hadn't they? Well, there had always been a few treatises by anthropologists writing about so-called primitives and their personal and peculiar views on substances the so-called civilized world considered unclean…as long as their premises weren't too prurient. It was in the same manner in which nudity on the cover of *The National Geographic* was acceptable. As long as the subjects could be viewed as uncivilized. Then they could be put on par with animals. And animals ran around with their naughty parts showing, right?)

"I feel like a thief," Godard confessed. "No better than a tomb robber."

"Yeah, so do I. But we haven't been given much of a choice," Singer admitted. "Once they seal this up again, they'll make sure it's for good. At least for another sixteen hundred years."

"But perhaps they'll only seal that other entrance…"

"I think if they're that worried, they're going to go through with a fine tooth comb. They'll find this soon enough. As well as whatever other entrances there might be that we haven't seen."

Louis stopped briefly to touch one of the chalk arrows. It wasn't any of those he'd drawn on that first day they'd investigated.

"Are we so certain *they* didn't put these here?" he wondered out loud as he rubbed chalk dust between his fingers.

Jim sighed heavily. "No, we're not."

Louis patted his friend on the back. "Three's the charm, *mon ami*. Now people won't turn away. We shall have the recognition we deserve."

Through that horribly cramped passage, tall enough Godard could stand up but Singer had to bend forward a little. It was probably the reason he saw the coin, because he was hunched over and looking at the light to see where to put his feet down.

"Hey!" he said as he picked it up, not quite in a shout but with enthusiasm. "By God, it's a gold solidus!"

He passed it to Louis who paused to hold it under his flashlight for examination. "That is the portrait of Emperor Honorius on it. It means late fourth or early fifth century. That, then, for certain. It's what we suspected but without yet carbon dating the epistle or the ceramics…"

Jim nodded. "Might have been dropped by one of the cult members. Or maybe by a soldier who was part of the kill-squad."

Of course, ancient coins were not particularly rare. One could buy them from mail order businesses that supplied various minor antiquities.

Jim slipped it into a sandwich bag, along with some of the dust for comparison with the few other items they'd already retrieved. This went into his coat pocket.

Louis started to walk again but then stopped, gasping, cocking his head. "Did you hear that?"

"What?"

"A voice. A woman's, I'm sure of it."

Jim did hear something. Someone. Decidedly feminine.

Godard made two fists and set his mouth in a thin line as he listened intently. *"Aidez-moi. Je me suis perdue. Dépechêz-vous. S'il vous plaît…"*

"I'm lost. I'm hurt. Please…"

The two men glanced at one another.

"This is what my cousin Gerard told me he heard. He and Linda. I take it you hear this in English as I hear it in French," said Louis.

"Yep," Jim affirmed, nodding his head and then thwacking it on the tunnel's low ceiling. If they went only another 100 feet or so, the roof would go up as the corner turned in to the chamber where the slaughter had been carried out.

Then Jim saw a glimmer out of the corner of his eye. He swung his light. It came from one of the chalk arrows. They had passed it a moment ago and it was as before. But now it glowed. It had changed color to a neon yet dirty yellow. It flashed, on and off, slowly, then faster, strobing.

Suddenly it winked out.

Aidez-moi…

Help me…

They turned the other way, toward the sound. Before it had not seemed to have a proper direction. But down where they were, so far under the surface, in the chill air, a voice could easily seem disembodied. Why, even when they spoke to one another…

They swung their flashlights that way and the beams jointly illuminated a bare stripe of mist, silvery with frost. It looked like a naked girl—no, a woman so thin she resembled a starving child. Her eyes were large and icily luminous, face and frail body framed by yellow hair. She looked right at the docs and each heard, "Help me," in their own language. She curled the other direction as if crying to somebody behind her, "I'm lost." Her back showed a savage gash from her left shoulder down to her right hip, a bloody arc through which ribs and spine showed with splinters and spleen. Anyone might have thought at first she had a dark red ribbon tied about her waist with the bow behind her, but it was only her kidneys falling out through the wound.

I'm hurt…

Then she faced the archaeologists again and repeated the entire thing.

It tore at their hearts. She seemed so helpless, such a waif. They knew she was only a ghost, a spiritual repetition, a fragment of a song replayed over and over in a record with a scratch in it. (Might she even be Aureola herself? Wouldn't that be something! Well, no matter who it was, it was amazing.)

It was interesting that Gerard and Linda heard her right away but that it was the docs' fifth—and final—visit for them before this little revenant addressed them.

Jim thought about a popular sci-fi movie he'd seen in the '70s. *Star Wars*?

A hologram or some such thing coming out of a robot, in which a space princess repeated over and over again her recorded plea for help. The other day, entering the catacombs and finding a dog's skeleton had made him think of the jackal bones in *The Omen*. Actually he didn't see that many films.

Suddenly she blurred, moving in and out of focus in their flashlight beams. Then her smoke turned all of a hard blue as she growled at them, her face becoming lupine, eyes shining a dirty yellow like her hair.

Her growl turned into a hackle-raising howl, magnified until a crack appeared at the roof of the tunnel. It startled both men, being such an animal thing, beyond language.

The sound of the first explosion immediately followed. (Could a mindless glitch in time's dimensions do that?)

"Jesus!" Jim yelled, clutching Louis' shoulder. "Back! Back to the entrance!"

The explosions might have originated from the crater-site doorway but shook the ground the entire four mile length, harder with every one which thundered after the first. From the sound, the first might have detonated in the initial chamber where they'd found the intact niches, then another where the dog bones in bowls had been discovered, then in Aureola's chamber. Of course, it might have begun in the saint's vault. The clouds of black dust rolled toward them like a mob of black ghosts, replete with shadowy faces, the thunder in such voices actually a howling for blood.

They fled, dust everywhere, not able to properly see as Louis' flashlight went out and Jim's barely showed them where to put their feet. They could have sworn they heard the whole place shake like a giant box full of bones.

Then the explosions stopped as abruptly as they had begun. The men probably hadn't run for more than a couple of minutes yet it had seemed much longer. Godard was shaking, out of breath, the mask across his nose and mouth flattening against his face as he gasped for air. Jim put his arm around the old man, the ground still trembling below, around, and above them.

"Damn those sons of bitches!" Jim cursed. "They said they were sealing the entrance, not blowing it to Kingdom Come."

The steps going up were not far away. But they were dark, descending too deep from the surface for even a full moon to help brighten them. And was there a full moon tonight? Jim didn't know.

"It's okay. I've got you. I'll get you out," Jim promised, afraid for his elderly colleague. Godard was now showing every one of his seventy years (and then some.)

"I just can't believe they would blow it all up," Louis said. "Such a find. What a waste."

When the ground and walls began to shake again, it wasn't from another round of explosions. What remained of the ancient tunnel started to collapse. It came down in a wave, as if the cave-in were deliberately chasing them.

Jim hoisted the old man over his shoulder and began to sprint. In doing this he dropped the flashlight but never heard it if it broke. Racing through pitch blackness and blinded by dust, he went on instinct. The roar of the disintegrating catacombs deafened him. Disoriented him, too. He'd seen the steps—that way? Stumbled, felt crumbling stucco and tufa knocking against his head and arms, feared what it might be doing to Louis. Felt the first step under his right foot and fought to go up. Jesus Hoppalong Christ hurry up...

Then he heard a cavernous, groaning *HHHHHAAAAA-AAA!* A few million tons of earth, dissolving stonework, and whatever force had gathered enough momentum, caught him and blasted him up the rest of the steps as if he and Louis were flies caught in a great exhale.

He lost consciousness. When he opened his eyes again, he told himself, *yes, there is a full moon tonight.*

The force of the cave-in had thrown both men all the way up the steps and into the field. It had also blown out a great deal of stonework. Jim was pinned under something; he couldn't move his legs. He saw Louis next to him.

The old man had received a barrage of sharp pieces of masonry in his lower back. These had been propelled like shrapnel through his intestines until they were hanging out of him. Louis' shoes and protective mask had been blown right off him and now his eyes and mouth were open, all full of blood and dust. Jim tried to cry out but had swallowed too much dust (he'd lost his mask, too, and he guessed that his feet buried under rubble were probably bare). He flashed back on that vision he'd had as a youngster visiting Gettysburg, of gutshot soldiers and the smell of black shit. He wept, tears running very black on his face. He slipped his hands to the mess to try to put it back inside his friend.

This is the landscape of the underworld, not hell, near hell...

Somewhere. very distant, he thought he heard a waterfall. But it was just the roar in his ears from the collapsing catacombs.

++++++++++

The ancient faithful of the pagan god, Baal-Phegor, were trained to consume excrement. The Church (once upon a primitive time) mandated that ascetics be required to prove symbolic self-mortification by the act of pious coprophagy.

—Sacred Sepsis
Dr. Louis Godard and Dr. James Singer

CHAPTER
15

SUBWAY TUNNELS, 1993

The fat man blinked.

She figured her language had caught him off-guard. Because she'd asked him, "You come down here to fuck me? See my drawings and think I'm some sort of freak whore using a subway wall as her calling card?"

She repeated it.

"No," he said slowly, swallowing hard. "I am so sorry if I offended you. Actually one of my students told me about your art. So I came down to have a look. I'm a college professor."

Myrtle tilted her head, sizing up the older man. She could tell he didn't have a hard-on. Most of the men who came down there looking for sick thrills had erections that told on them no matter what they said. And women who did the same stank of estrus, like animals in heat.

"I'm the one who ought to be sorry," she told him, biting her lip. "But try to understand, my life down here..."

His forehead wrinkled and he sighed. "How long have you lived in this place?"

She shrugged. "I don't really know. Three years or forever."

He looked away, seeming to be listening to something.

"That's the rumble of the subways," she explained.

"Actually, I think I'm hearing a waterfall somewhere," he said, his attention far away. Then he smiled. "Come out with me."

She shook her head, frowning, snorting. "Ah, that's what I thought."

"No, I mean, let me give you a job. I could use a secretary. No strings. No touchy-feely crap. I'm always telling myself how much I want to help someone. Maybe this is my chance to put my money where my mouth is. I can't just walk away and leave you. It isn't..."

She finished it for him. "Christian?"

"No, it isn't Christian."

Myrtle thought about it for a moment. "No strings?"

She saw nothing of the hungry vagrants or the caroling rapists in his eyes. He wasn't a horny tourist or a would-be sugar daddy.

"No strings," he told her.

Somehow she believed him.

And she did want to get out of there. Destiny in the underground could only go so far.

CHAPTER
16

EGYPT,
AT THE END OF DESERT STORM

Corporal Jason Cave was in Cairo, ready to be entertained after the let-down of so-called battle, high on amphetamines he'd scored from a couple Navy pilots, his live wire grin burning in electrode dimples. He walked around at dusk, amazed that anyplace could smell so good and so bad at the same time. Cumin and unwashed sweat glands, ginger and heat-percolated toilets, sex acts live on stage with semen and piss stains everywhere, bellydancing boys in crotchless silk baggy trousers whose assholes were shiny with rose attar. At sunset the rounded tops of mosques gleamed golden breasts in the sky, turrets of scalloped erections bringing the rest into balanced perspective, singers crooning devotion to Allah as Jason went about his recreation.

What a groaner this war had turned out to be! Nothing on

the scale of the World Wars and Korea or even Vietnam. And over way too soon. He'd expected stimulation, kickass games. The practice of humanicide and all for a good cause. But mostly he'd just sat around on his butt, behind a computer in a tank. Only twice got to shoot at something and one of those had been a mistake, turning out to be another tank full of more Americans. (The term ruefully applied was *Friendly Fire*, but Jason hadn't considered any of them to be his pals.)

He saw many dead Iraqis, in twisted sprawls or burned in or around their gutted vehicles. He was ordered to help bury some of them in the sand—a duty many of the G.I.s hated, although Jason didn't mind it. It gave him a chance to examine them closer. But, really, it wasn't as if he'd never seen or smelled corpses. In the last few years he'd been exposed to quite a few. It's just that those who'd perished in battle were different from the victims he'd known. The definition of active rather than passive being tacked onto demise...he'd been curious as he approached the battle dead: would there be a marked and proud alteration in expression (when there was a face left to hold an expression), an aroma of power in the blood (even if it had turned to blackened brittle), a certain *je ne sais quoi* of aura extant in the remains (even if scattered) which might point to one who'd been a **Superman**.

Jason thought he'd found one, torso splattered to the four winds from having caught a minor rocket in his midsection. But the shoulders and head were there and that head smiled, more than the expected rictus. The eyes were starting to glaze but still blazed with a manic fury, that even at the moment of mostly physical incineration had told the world *FUCK YOU!* No birds had yet touched this one, to pick at flesh and pluck out orbs. No birds had dared.

Jason had touched the third eye center of this forehead. He felt a rush of aggression and contempt. Someone who had been blown apart yet wasn't vanquished, his head unbowed (even if almost all that remained). Jason received an image of him inside his mind, of the man whole again in an infernal paradise, working an assembly line of houri virgins, first deflowering them. Then proceeding to perform full infibulated pharaonics on each, excising the clitoris, labia minora, and most of the labia majora. He then handed them off to a female djinn to sew up the mutilated vaginas, leaving a tiny opening preserved with splinters of fragrant cedar. She took the scraps of sundered flesh and scooped them into a basket.

This female djinn seemed to sense Jason watching. She glanced up at him, out toward the red clouds where he spied. Her face was very pale for someone from this part of the world but she had dark freckles as if she'd been splashed with an anisette. She was so beautiful he gasped and this was what brought him back to the desert and reality.

He bent and kissed this third eye on the dead Iraqi, and whispered a quote from Aleister Crowley, "I yield him place: his ravening teeth Cling hard to her—he buries him Insane and furious in the sheath She opens for him—wide and dim My mouth is amorous beneath..."

Another American soldier saw him and shook his head. Practically no one of Jason's unit cared for him. He'd expected camaraderie, to find men of like spirits. But they were mostly mama's boys, thinking their most exciting night was a case of beer in a sports bar and a blow job from a willing cheerleader.

The single exception was a grunt named Michael Roheim, as big a man as Jason. Constantly in trouble, he was a violent man who believed himself to be on a mission from the angels. He might have been a **Superman** if he'd had more self-control. Jason alternately was amused by and disgusted with the guy.

Someone once said that war was hell. Actually, it was a bore. He'd gotten a lot more action back home.

He'd joined up looking for an hourly opportunity to blast somebody into the fourth dimenson. Races to see who could slaughter a hundred meaningless enemy in a given time frame.

Big Garth Listo had thrown him a party before Jason left for overseas. Vietnam had been Garth's war.

"I was younger than you," he'd told Jason. "This will be a furthering of your education. I went to Tokyo before I was shipped home. You have stops to make, too. I know when you come back, that light will blaze from your open mouth. You have nothing to fear. You are The Beast."

Jason had nodded, but the Aleister Crowley step on his part of the incarnation wheel was over as far as he was concerned. It was nice to know. He'd needed it when he was growing up. But now it was time for Mach 2.

"You're not too old to come along, you know," he said to his mentor.

"I've become too Japanese," Garth replied, gesturing down himself with a tinge of self-deprecation. "They'd never let me bring my swords."

"I have a gift for you," Jason told him, bringing out a small box. "In case I don't return, you know? Because I'm having too much fun to come home? Something to remember me by."

Garth was touched, smiling as he unwrapped the package and opened the box. Inside was a beautiful *netsuke*, a Japanese ornament—usually used as a button or other fastener—carved intricately from bone or ivory. This one was bone and Jason had strung it on a fine red silk cord. The figure was of a naked man sodomizing a naked woman whose head was a chrysanthemum blossom.

"I saw that and she reminded me of sort of the ultimate bonsai project," Jason admitted.

"It's gorgeous," B.G. declared genuinely and put the cord around his neck. "I'll always treasure this."

161

Big Garth had spoiled him on tales from Nanking and Saigon. Now Jason had gone through the Gulf War without a scratch, very disappointed in the hype of age-old traditions of butchery. He promised himself he'd have some fun. This trip just couldn't be a total waste.

He'd visited the usual sights: the Citadel, the Egyptian Museum, the 14th-Century madrasah of Sultan Hassan, a Coptic church in Misr al-Qadimah. He'd even gone to see the Pyramids—which, upon the magician's first visit, Aleister Crowley hadn't bothered to do, saying, "I wasn't going to have forty centuries look down on me. Confound their impudence!"

Jason even bought a copy of the Koran, a paperback of it anyway. He vowed to eat a page of it every day that he was there, to give him dreams of seventh heavens and battling infidels and demons. It made him a bit consti-pated—scriptures of any sort had that capacity, eh? But the local cuisine more than solved the problem.

He'd even gone to Sahara City, south of the Gizah Pyramids, an open complex of nightclubs complete with Las Vegas style neon lights. Mostly watched bellydancers in spangles and tassles, drank a lot, tried unsuccess-fully to score some hashish, and only barely avoided being arrested. Didn't land even a single punch and saw no blood. Yawn!

So that afternoon, he'd descended into the slum of Bulaq where he'd heard that there were as many as 300,000 people per square mile. He slipped a few bills to a man to tell him where the real shows were. Took the man's cab in which a radio blared the voice of a muqri', a Koranic reciter. It reminded him of the nasal evangelists belting out Bible lessons in America, gimme that ol' time religion. (You hear that, Roheim?) Urchins climbed aboard the running boards and back bumper for a free ride, staring at him through the cab's windows. Normally they flocked to the soldiers, chat-tering, offering matches or flowers or plastic combs for sale. But these kids wouldn't speak to Jason, just ogled him as if not sure exactly what he might be.

Cairo, from al-Qahirah. The oldest term for it was offered by the fel-lahin, the native stock, They called it Misr, Umm al-Dunyah: Mother of the World. Misr was an ancient Semitic word, meaning "big city."

The Mother of the World sprawled in mud brick and concrete, so hot it wisped the breath away, reached down to inscribe the lungs with its massive pollution, snaked in-between the legs to incite like a feather fan.

The cab passed canals along the railroad tracks. Children were playing, splashing in the fetid muck only a few feet from water buffalo. There were goats, donkeys, sheep in the streets. A cart rolled by, laden with vegetables, its wheels six feet in diameter. A blind man tripped over an array of sugar cane cages in which chickens squawked. Reeking pools of water overflowed from sewers.

At dusk Jason arrived at the bar. The driver spoke a few words to a guard at the door and Jason was admitted. He watched a woman, down on all fours but with her abdomen up, arching her slinky spine. The long rope of her coffee-colored hair, braided with silk cord, lay on the floor like a fakir's cobra about to rear up for the fatal strike. A fat eunuch inserted a slender wire into his flaccid, nutless member and then wiggled this pop-up joke into her vagina. He shook up a bottle of fermented camel's milk and let this spew into her to simulate his seed.

Then she was fucked by a donkey, by an Ethiopian dwarf with a dick longer than he was tall, by the head of an asp, by a customer wielding a fish caught in the sea which she afterward fellated before he filleted it. Throughout all of this, her face betrayed no sense of presence.

Jason was impressed by the mastering of her emotions. Not that he believed that all emotion could or should be reined in, or that everyone should have to control their passions. Fear and pain ought to be regulated by those who felt that such forebearance might please their masters. And, of course, **Supermen** like Jason were those masters, and the only discipline **Supermen** needed to know was what they themselves meted out.

(What a shame the army didn't see it that way. Hardly existentially-enlightened, the military. Made no sense to him, considering the lessons death could teach you. They offered you a chance to be all that you could be, but in the end all they did was teach you how to march in the procession of the damned.)

He waited until the club shut for the night, wee hours of the morning. He hid across the street until the woman left. Then he followed her down past the closed booths of falafel vendors and aphrodisiac peddlers, narrow and mean like the edifices of outhouses, temples to nether gods, sepulchral with slime. They walked a long time, hours, eventually leaving the slum and entering an area of the city where modern construction gleamed lurid and monolithic in streetlights.

He'd already visited innumerable places where raw sewage was everywhere. With the building of the Aswan High Dam, Cairo's water table had risen a great deal, causing the city's ancient drainage system to almost break under the stress. But this area of the city was more modern, designed for universities and museums and a higher class of tourists.

The woman slowly marched past a new treatment plant. Water shimmered there in the dark as silent fountains before some medieval caliph's palace. Moon and lamp lights floated in zigzag squiggles like some kind of sentient, luminous bacteria. The pumps hummed, grinding out the swill-mashers song as the modern part of the city's offal was micronized and sanitized. The reflection from the pools played those miniature germinal thunderbolts across her voluptuous silhouette, as if these microbes were jumping out of the fetid impetigo to caress her.

Could there be a goddess of toilets?

More precisely, of waste?

Of defecation and micturation?

Feces and pee?

It amused Jason to think so.

But that was not this creature, who was paid nightly to be humiliated. Who was nowhere near anyone's definition of a superwoman.

Therefore, Jason—as a **Superman**—could take her.

Could take her apart.

(Upon that stage, looking into her face, he'd seen how dead her eyes were. He simply brought the rest of her up to speed.)

And when he was finished doing that, the pieces of her floated in those pools, the mosque of her face up, eyes staring in much the same manner (no manic fury, no *FUCK YOU!*) as they had on that stage, being as Jason saw them last. The way she'd looked at him as he grabbed her. Turning toward him, so tired, almost stony as a pillar carved with cartouche out of the frozen past. Turning like a prayer wheel for someone caught between worship and penance. Perhaps relieved it was over, she did not try to scream. Her undergarments were already full of blood and other secretions from the bar's several unnatural acts.

Jason quoted Kafka to her, although she spoke no English. (Which was all right, since Kafka hadn't written it in English.)

"A first sign of nascent knowledge is the desire for death."

The next night he followed another woman beside the Nile. Black smoke had started drifting that far, from the distant Kuwaiti oil fires which the Iraqis had set as a final, violent gesture before their ignominious retreat. The moon and stars were obscured. It made the sky smudged thicker even than was usual for Cairo's smog of car exhaust, constantly blowing sand, and greasy vapors from the omnipresent food stalls. It turned it into an enormous cesspool, like the colostomy bag to a sphincter-cancer world. Definitely not the symbol of lovely Nut, Egyptian goddess of the sky, her body forming the vault of heaven as she bent to incestuously embrace the earth, her brother Geb. According to ancient belief, they were only separated by Shu—the air's embodiment, providing the universe its shape.

(There was another story that told how Shu—and Tefnut, Shu's sibling—were born. They were produced when the great god, Atum, masturbated. Cream of the crop.)

The Nile churned, a black hole taffy-stretched into a light gobbling ribbon. The woman, dark matter. In the gloom, her bare feet left the tracks of a cat.

And cats were animals who ate their own dung as they groomed themselves. Sacred, according to the old ways.

Jason had seen this woman in the market, helping her family sell carpets to tourists—or in this case to the U.N.'s soldiers. The central mandalas were confounded with vortices, or were labyrinthine with adorned pathways concealing some *Cloaca Maxima*, the stench of which rose up as an elixer of peccant incenses. And always within sight of this squalor were the most fragile minarets, obelisks, steeples and turrets. People lived in cement boxes but within sight were carved domes, starting with simple ribbed patterns, going to fluent chevrons and then into flowered arabesques, intricate lace in limestone with interlocking stars.

A magic maze of fairyland beauty complicated by gray misery. There, late at night, beside the Nile, one or two fishing boats still out on the water. Men cast nets in the moonlight. What did such midnight fishermen seek? That which came up from the black mud. Somewhere amid the many suqs— or specialized markets—probably in the Old City, was a bazaar open only long after sunset, specializing in the dark catch.

Jason smiled to himself, thinking *here is my dark catch*.

She fought, trying to cry out. He struck her in the mouth with his fist, breaking many of her teeth, cutting his knuckles. He would have hieroglyphs of scars across them as a memento. He leaned in after subduing her and murmured, "Shall I tell you a story of an Arabian Night? Sometimes there are no sugar-coated build-ups, no idyllic preludes. Sometimes the darkness begins immediately."

He kissed the tip of her nose and added, "It begins now."

This time Jason was more inventive, leaving a pyramid of her on the sandy bank, torso as the base, legs then arms, head at the top. A tomb fit for a slum Cleopatra.

The third night he caught sight of a woman in the severe traditional Moslem garb. The yashmak veil with the vent for her eyes fluttered next to him. She coyly allowed her gaze to meet his, unheard of for an orthodox Mohammedan. At least he thought she was staring at him. He couldn't see her eyes. The vent for them was a grid of gauze.

The more modern Egyptians (including the many Christians) adopted western dress. He caught a whiff of patchouli and heard the soft rain-like tinkle of cheap jewelry beneath the chador.

He saw only a glimpse of beauty and was reminded of that female djinn sewing up the defiled women of hell. This might have been why he chose her. Because she might be that djinn, come to lead him to the other world without horizons.

She moved off into the crowd which buzzed in several dialects about the murders of the previous two evenings. The authorities were sure the killer wasn't from Cairo. They believed it was a soldier, and they were anxious to apprehend him before the various countries sent their military contingents home.

People brought up in the States had no idea what foreign cities with their poorer quarters smelled like. Not even those U.S. citizens from the worst ghettoes could readily identify with the reek of rampant bilge. In a country of scarcely two centuries, it was hard to perceive the choking gag of places where the millennia of outside latrines had drenched the environment with pungent human slop. Even in the arid desert, relics of mummified turds from the time of the pharaohs, of Moses, mingled with the newer resins of ejecta. Or maybe it was just him, able to detect such things, sensitive nose eager to find it out. The true **Superman** must investigate every nuance before he could understand—and then control—damnation. There was another place of suffering and joy. Where dominion existed for the truly despotic at the end of the puzzle of arterial miles and unraveled bundles of nerves.

Victims always called to their beasts, by gesture or simple expression. By pheromone or faint echo. Usually without their conscious realization of this on their part—but it must be subconscious. Death wish or the craving for a nihilistic sex which would rescue them from the gray, useless/sense-less/hopeless lives most lived.

Jason followed the woman through the old city, many stretches still surrounded by ancient battlements. They passed the crenelated walls and militant towers of the enormous mosque erected by al-Hakim, ruler from 996 to 1021 A.D. This caliph had been a member of the famed Fatimid Dynasty, claiming descendence directly from the prophet Mohammed through his daughter, Fatimah. It was said that al-Hakim was insane, with staring blue eyes that terrified all who saw him. He would buy slave children, play games with them for a short time, and then disembowel them with his own hands. Not far from there, they went through the Khan al-Khalili, the high-priced bazaar for the idiot tourists with more money than brains. Last they passed the al-Azhar Mosque, where the world's oldest functioning university lay.

Jason watched the rolling muscles in her gazelle ass, the ample melons of her breasts beneath the black linen of her garments. She would occasionally...furtively...glance back at him.

As if to see if Jason still followed.

And was she frightened or reassured to find him there?

Perhaps she was going to lead him out of the city completely. Out onto the moon desert. What the ancients used to call the Land of the Dead. And maybe under all those swishing, rustling robes was the body of an unearthly, gorgeous Isis.

Or perhaps under the yashmak was the head of Hathor—a cow.

Jason tried to get close enough to catch the patchouli perfume again. Like a mysterious tease of paradise in a concentration camp of fecal horrors.

He recalled that the desert was to the west of Cairo. They were walking east where the city was hemmed in by the somber cliffs of the Muqattam Hills.

But they were indeed entering the Land of the Dead. Or rather, one of the Cities of the Dead—the medieval, Eastern cemetery. Here were straight, intersecting streets and lifelike houses built for bones. Some of it was neat, clean. But many families were squatters living in these tombs. Some had been there for generations. Grandfathers, fathers and sons living their entire lives in this graveyard. Ragged kids ran between the mausoleums. Garbage was piled high outside many. Jason peeked into one place and saw an old lady in wrinkled black gauze chopping melon upon a marble cenotaph.

His quarry glided through mobs of black-eyed, swarthy men in white cotton galabiyahs (which just looked like women's nightgowns to him). They turned slightly to observe her, as if her beauty had briefly stuck to them. She disentangled herself from obstacle courses of cripples crying for alms. She floated between streaks which seemed to reach out from the sunset, flapping scarlet bandages of cloud like a bloody dysentery.

Suddenly she darted into a tall crypt. This wasn't one of the well-kept ones. Anti-American, anti-European, and anti-Israeli slogans had been written in a mortar of fingerpainted crap. The door's hinges sounded like a Saracen's curse.

Jason followed her inside.

She just stood there, as if she'd known all along he would come in. As if that had always been the plan.

He had no problem with letting her see the bayonet right away.

"You are an evil man," she said in perfect English. There wasn't even a trace of that clipped, singsong accent he liked.

"You ever hear of existentialism, baby?" Jason asked, leering. "One of the great existential minds was a guy called Berdyaev. And he said, 'Without the freedom of evil, good would not be free; it would be determined and imposed by force.' Can't have one without the other, see?"

She dropped something on the floor. Jason took a split second to perceive what it was. A badge. She was a policewoman. She'd lured him there to arrest him. Was that it?

Jason laughed, it rattling from his chest like a long range missile along its track, anticipating firing.

He brought the bayonet across his own arm, splitting a nest of needle marks, spraying blood.

He said, "Ooh, I like it rough. Let me get started for you. There! Maybe you'll be more fun than those other two. I respect sincere conflict."

He saw the object on the floor. It had only seemed like a badge. It was gold, imprinted with hieroglyphs and a queen's profile. Not a cop. A smuggler maybe. Yeah, she ought to know some moves all right.

But she made no attempt to draw a concealed weapon, to position herself for a fight, or even to call out for whatever partners in crime might be waiting in this stinking outhouse of a hovel. She lifted the hem of the chador from the ground, bringing it high to her waist. Not grabbing for a gun in garter or boot top. Nor did she give him any sign that she was supernatural. She opened no gateways to exalted horrors. She slowly revealed herself, the eyes behind the gauze in the yashmak's vent were just a blur in the dark room.

Jason's jaw dropped. All he could think of was one of those giant chocolate Easter bunnies that were hollow inside. The heavy dark brown body hung together for a moment, as if carved from cocoa candy, as if sculpted from a heap of Arabica coffee grounds. Then it began to slide floorward, the form of pure shit losing volition.

++++++++++

The Code of Jewish Law said not to enter any house of prayer with even as much as a speck of waste inside the anus. It also said you mustn't pray anywhere near a soiled baby. And you mustn't even THINK of holy things while you were in a toilet.

—Sacred Sepsis
Dr. Louis Godard and Dr. James Singer

CHAPTER
17

The clock went off, playing music, something of relentless percussion and a baritone chanting the most violent obscenities about bitches in general and some whores in particular.

Dorien fought her way out of the darkness, sat up in bed, trembled hard.

What was that?

Just another perplexing dream. Being someone else. Being someone else who became the now-familiar goddess.

But in the other nightmare excursions, she was always in a past era, a clearly separate incarnation. (That is, assuming that these things were actually connected to her, part of her.) This one was during the Gulf War and she'd been alive, as Dorien Warmer, even if just a little girl. She'd had no such dreams as these then. She'd have remembered anything so unsettling. After all, she'd never forgotten the nightmare of the screaming children and the smell of orchids.

(And that had been connected to her—even if only in the case of an after-the-fact.)

The recent dreams had made up a sort of crazy logic. Now that was gone. For the time reference here was all wrong.

This one began as she'd passed through a tomb in ancient Egypt. Or maybe it was an ancient tomb in modern Egypt. At any rate, a tribute to an unknown queen. Sealed in, it was so dark there her eyes didn't hurt anymore. She found some ornament on the floor, picked it up, felt its pure metal vibrate through her skin, slipped it into some clumsy robe she wore.

And then suddenly she'd passed through the walls and was in a marketplace, leading some strange man toward a reckoning.

Well, she had lately been aware of a male presence in part of her dreams. But she never really saw him. So she couldn't say for sure if this GI was him or not. She only knew that the male presence was important to her somehow, at least peripherally.

Peripherally in-a-reckoning-kind-of-way? Not that she knew what that would have been. The alarm had sounded, waking her to get ready for court.

Dorien had received the summons to appear as a witness. What would happen? What would she have to admit to? How would she be forced to demean herself, taking down even further what little dignity she had left?

But she got up and dressed. Pulled on pantyhose. Odd material. Something she'd never thought about before. That stockings were from some petroleum-based synthetic. Oil black and viscous, from dead things which had piled up and then decomposed over millions of years to ride so close to her flesh. Pressed against her steamy crotch, some saber-tooth cat...or a slope-headed man barely away from walking on his knuckles to seek his food by bashing its brains out with a club. The polymer in her inexpensive dress was the same, a winding sheet from a primeval graveyard. She stuck her feet into shoes of man-made fake leather, feeling the insides as humid tongues of prehistoric ant-eaters and hummingbirds.

By the time she was finished and glanced in the mirror, she had an idea of herself as an insect encased in amber, nothing more than another dead prisoner.

Dorien sniffed. Why did the place smell worse than usual? On top of the brownness which had crept past the duct tape on her windows and the reek of those who lived in the apartments around her?

That stew Annet had brought and left outside the door, she'd tossed in the trash.

"Guess I haven't taken the garbage out in a while," Dorien said aloud to herself. She made a mental note: garbage should be taken to the chute more often than once a month, especially if there was food in it.

She hadn't eaten any, of course. (Didn't seem to have many teeth to eat with lately, had she been so inclined.) She'd seen that restaurant her sister frequented. But how had she known the aroma was dog? Some time between her father's death and Annet's delivering the bag from CANE, Dorien's senses had sharpened until she recognized the species of meats both simmering in the early summer heat or putrifying in someone's bowels.

Dog.

CANE.

Not as in Kane with a long 'a' and silent 'e'. But as in Cah-nay. A Romance Italian word out of the Latin root: canis.

(Dorien knew how long she'd known. Ever since she had the Roman dream.)

Her sister had been there last right before she'd had that dream. If Annet had come afterward, would Dorien have smelled dog inside her sister?

Going out of the building, she had to walk down to the car park. This was where she kept her cheap, creaking old but cute little Volkswagen. Only had to pay about four hundred bucks for it since it was forty years old and three different colors. Still had the tacky shapes from where some love child back in the late sixties (during an uncontrollable seizure of Herbie The Lovebug-itis) had stuck dayglow rubber flowers to it, probably the kind folks used to put on the floors of their bathtubs to keep from slipping when they showered. Never could be completely removed.

She turned the key in the ignition and heard it grind before it finally started. She had to let it warm up for about five minutes. The car emitted a tiny fart from its exhaust that sounded like a piglet full of beans.

She drove down to the courthouse. There were cops all over the place by the entrance to the main parking lot across the street. Media, too. And the usual crowd of voyeurs. She saw the body just before the wagon crew shoveled it onto a stretcher (couldn't blame 'em for not wanting to touch it) and covered it up with black plastic (more petroleum from the tar pit).

She smelled it a block and a half before she got there. Even with the car's windows rolled up and the exhaust's farts smelling of sausages ground with coal, she caught the strong stench of human excrement.

"Another victim of The Shit Detail," someone said. Maybe a cop or a reporter.

The victim (or VIC as the current chop-em slang went with word abbreviations, nominally etymonistic decaps) had been found spreadeagled beneath a populist mural of Blind Justice (commissioned by the city from some civic-friendly artist who didn't do the hoity-toity, cocaine-up-the-snobbish-leftist nostril, anti-religious smut that an earlier mayor had so campaigned against). No one ever mentioned how big Blind Justice's cha-cha's were, painted on the side of the building where one had to take a number and pay ten bucks for a parking spot.

The VIC had down her throat one very long, hard turd which had been excreted and then sprayed with a quick-drying polymer...(which might have passed for a dildo in any number of underground porn films to be found on the *web*). There was evidence of lientery all over the body. And there was the ubiquitous saying left smeared upon the mural about two or three feet above where the strangled face stared up at the sky with its peculiar eyes.

"Art happens—no hovel is safe from it..." Whistler

Even the dot-dot-dots were there, sordid and brown in their biffy punctuation.

Dorien blinked, read the saying. Thought to herself, *actually I would have said, "Art should never outlast its usefulness."*

She recognized those peculiar eyes. For the trimmed eyelids that couldn't have closed no matter how much this unfortunate girl might have wanted to close them and wish the attack away. The same one Dorien had paid two bucks to for a glimpse of her personal tragedy.

"Who do you suppose she was? There's no ID," Dorien overheard one officer tell another.

"Just another vagrant. One of the lost," another said tiredly, speaking through a handkerchief pressed across his nose and mouth. Ah, sensibilities.

Should Dorien come forward and say she knew this young woman? But she didn't, really. What would she tell them? That she'd purchased entrance to a freakpeep a few weeks ago, in a moment of moral weakness?

She shivered, the smell of that shit...well, there was a facet to it that disturbed her. She refused to think about it. Hell, she didn't know what it could mean and didn't have the time to mull it over.

Instead she drove down to the next lot and paid, put her card on the dashboard as she parked, locked up, walked toward the courthouse. Smelling shit in the brown wind.

Neela Wilson was in the waiting room. In a wheelchair, thin as a skeleton and twice as weak. Yet she managed to smile when she saw Dorien. Dorien went to sit next to her.

There were women everywhere, some visibly ill, others not as much. There were sniffles, coughs, dry husky murmurs. Heads under scarves, heads under wigs to hide patchy scalps. Lots of sunglasses—the only thing Dorien had in common with them other than some missing teeth. She felt guilty because she wasn't sick.

(Not sick? *Not sick?!* What would you call somebody who didn't eat anymore, didn't shit anymore, turned her bathwater into sewage just by sitting down in it, and who could smell what kind of meat rotted up your ass?)

"Hi..." Neela managed softly.

Dorien touched her hand and smiled. "Good to see you."

"You still look terrific. Radiant actually," Neela said. "Did you get tested?"

"Yes, I did. I'm negative." Well, so far the teeth she'd lost had come from the back, so it didn't show when she talked. Probably gave her great cheekbones.

Neela's eyes shone. "Thank God."

"Are all of them...?" Dorien jerked her head at the other young ladies. Was the one who'd filed the charges there or was she in the courtroom? Perhaps she'd already testified and now watched from a seat in the back, near where the jury could see every lesion and hear every cough.

Neela nodded, painfully. "Yes, we're the Parrish sisterhood."

Dorien was glad she had the sunglasses on. She couldn't bear that Neela be able to see in her expression that Dorien knew Neela would soon die.

Hell, every woman there was going to die long before what should have been her time.

Everyone but Dorien.

Dorien ended up the last to be called but she sensed the scene as it proceeded without her. Through the doors swinging open onto the large yet somehow claustrophobic chamber, like a vault, like a crypt. There was Gavin himself, in the defendant's seat, arrogant (or did it still pass for a kind of charm?), good-looking like a biohazard Ted Bundy. He turned around and flashed a forty carat grin at the women. (Should that have been measured in roentgens?)

"Hey, face this way," a guard told him sternly.

"All rise!" announced some officious uniform.

The judge entered, black robes rustling like a raven's wings.

Naturally, some of the women couldn't rise, those who'd already testified yet who remained to increase the daily number of his accusers. Neela surely couldn't after she had her turn and was wheeled to the back, near the jury, her skin like a dark lace, every cough a poetic line in a ghastly eulogy.

Dorien saw them through the walls, producing the sheets encased in plastic, with the names of women (VICS) scrawled in magic marker. She heard in sough and static as every lady was brought to the stand to testify about how Gavin Parrish had given them a deadly disease. When the prosecutor finished with each, they were turned over to the defense. They had to repeat what they'd just said: how they met Gavin, when they went out with him, not if but when they went to bed with him. But this time they had to go into the details of sex (embarrassing, shaming because every one of them had never had another man before Gavin Parrish).

They were made to look nerdy and needy by the defending lawyer. Possibly spurned and vengeful women trying to maintain a false propriety when they might have simply said 'No.'

He never asked whether or not Gavin Parrish had told them he was H.I.V. positive. No, that had been the D.A.'s question.

Piece-of-shit lawyer: "Did Gavin Parrish rape you?"

And they had to admit he had not.

Piece-of-shit lawyer: "Did he put any pressure on you to have sex with him?"

Well, no.

Piece-of-shit-lawyer: "Did he slip you a drug?"

He had not.

Piece-of-shit lawyer: "Did he get you drunk?"

Nope.

Piece-of-shit lawyer (with shit-eating leer): "How many men have you been with?"

Red faces. Not because the ladies had slept with dozens but because they hadn't been with anyone else. And that simply wasn't the standard these days. Sluts were normal, virgins were weird.

Piece-of-shit lawyer, drawling, tongue in cheek like a turd clinging to the side of a toilet bowl: "Did Gavin Parrish treat you like you were just another pretty face?"

D.A.: "Objection!"

Judge: "Sustained."

Dorien was finally called in, that door swinging open, sounding as if it were cast from a single block of steel. She went to the stand and was asked to swear to tell the truth. Gazing over at Gavin she wondered if she knew what that was. (Let's see. What is truth? Well, it's what rumbles out of us without force, a physiological/spiritual/irrepressible dynamic. It is the by-product of precise sciences and of correctly interpreted dreams. But not of religion. Religion might spawn dreams but never produces accurate formulas. No, what religion makes is purely masturbatory.)

But Dorien assured them she would tell the truth. Solemnly.

How bright it was in the court. She felt it even through her dark glasses. So she closed her eyes. What did it matter? They couldn't see her eyes anyway.

D.A. (after establishing Dorien Warmer had shared the same brief, unpleasant relationship with the defendent the other witnesses had.): "Are you now H.I.V. positive?"

D. Warmer: "No."

The turn of the defense (like the turn of the truculent worm in succulent ordure...).

The lawyer asked her the same things he'd asked the others. Some of them had broken down on the stand, weeping, humiliated. But not Dorien. She sat in the witness box like frost chipped from some half-recalled ice age, opening her eyes into slits behind her sunglasses, fixing her covered gaze upon Gavin until he fidgetted. She showed little emotion when the same questions were put to her.

It was because she felt so detached from that event now. As if it were no more real than the dreams she'd had lately. Wait! As if they were less real than the dreams...

Piece-of-shit-lawyer: "If you're not H.I.V. positive, why are you present in this courtroom? This case is to determine the guilt or innocence of a man accused of willfully and with malice infecting a woman, one Jesmiah Monroe, with the AIDS virus."

D.A. "I object. Ms. Warmer's name was on one of the sheets found in the defendant's possession. All of the women whose names appear on those pieces of evidence were called to testify to the defendant's character and mode of manipulation."

Judge: "Sustained."

Piece-of-shit lawyer: "Did Gavin Parrish rape you?"

D. Warmer: "He seemed to want me. I offered him my body. Then he fucked over my spirit like a crocodile with a dick."

Piece-of-shit lawyer, feigning exasperation: "Your Honor..."

Judge: "Ms. Warmer, please refrain from obscenities."

Piece-of-shit lawyer: "Did he put any pressure on you to have sex with him?"

D. Warmer: "We'd just witnessed a murder, of a homeless woman in the park by The Shit Detail. I'd freaked out and fainted. He took me to his place, gave me sherry and a hot bath, then carried me to his bed. I was vulnerable as hell and he damned well knew it. We're taught in this society to..."

Piece-of-shit lawyer: "Just answer the question, yes or no."

D. Warmer: "...respond to sensitivity, to this romantic bullshit ideal..."

Piece-of-shit lawyer: "This isn't part of my question... She's hostile, Your Honor."

Judge: "Ms. Warmer... I don't want to have to cite you..."

D. Warmer: "...and then some Typhoid Marty with a psycho agenda comes along like Lochinvar, like those nonexistent Harlequin cover sugar-pricks, and..."

Judge: "Young woman, I'm giving you fair warning." *Gavel slam!*

D.A.: "Wait. Your Honor, I think the witness is simply overwrought. All of them are. I can't blame them."

Judge: "Well, that may be, but a certain amount of decorum is expected even from the overwrought."

D. Warmer: "...it most surely is a kind of rape because everything in this society programs us to respond to it, to accept it with our legs spread and our asses raised. And if you dare to ask how many men I've been with instead of punishing him for how many innocent women he's been with, then I'll tell you *just one*."

Judge: ".....cite you for contempt!" *Gavel slam, slam!*

D. Warmer: "I wish I hadn't, wish that I were still a virgin, not some misguided child who thinks the pretty girls on TV who fuck everything in pants are *cool*, that it's expected of them and that if they haven't spread their cheeks for every sweet-talking, prancy, boy's band, soul-patched cock, it's because nobody in their fucking mind could possibly want *them*, even if there are some men out there that'll nail down anyone who isn't steel, and they have to accept it because everybody else appears to accept that the only thing worth being in this world is desirable..."

Gavel slam! Gavel slam! Gavel slam slam slam! Oh, that hammer of justice.

Judge: "Officer, remove the witness!"

D. Warmer: "...And if you can't be that, you might as well get cut and twisted and sell peeps under a blanket for two bucks a look."

A strong hand landed on her shoulder. She was pulled up and led out of the courtroom. Gavin smirked, his lawyer standing there with arms folded akimbo, trying to suck a stray pussy hair out from between his teeth. The women watched her leave, awed, wondering if they could have said what she did.

Neela applauded, cheering softly, the lesions on her hands bursting with each clap. She then held them up to show her stigmata.

+++++++++

The character of the Trickster from the Winnebago tribe in North America had the ability to use a magic trick to make the planet out of shit, mud and clay.

There was one particular story: the Trickster had been warned not to eat a root which would fill his gut with gas. He did it anyway, and with every fart he was taken higher into the air where he helplessly flailed his limbs and grew very dizzy. He summoned people to come hold him to the ground. They hurried to help and all the thanks they got was to have his last broken wind scatter them across the earth.

—Sacred Sepsis
Dr. Louis Godard and Dr. James Singer

CHAPTER
18

ROME,
1990

Jim woke up in the hospital. The first thing he did was look
down.

Have I lost my legs?

If he had he would try to kill himself. Take a good hand
and yank out the IV in his arm. Wriggle to the edge of the bed
and unplug machines that kept him breathing.

Where were they? At first he'd been on breathing
machines. Too much dust. Somehow he recalled this and the
smell of pure oxygen.

Not anymore. But the IV was there, all right.

He looked down. There were two extensions past his hips.

Wait. Had he looked up to see them last time?

Yes, both legs had been in traction for a while, suspended
from the ceiling by pulleys and ropes.

Well, just how long had he been out?

Jim knew he'd been conscious for a short time. First, after having been blown out of the collapsing catacombs, ghost hissing in his ear. He'd seen Louis Godard's body and tried in a not-thoroughly lucid state of mind to put the old man right again.

He'd not been alert when found, when loaded onto a stretcher and brought to the hospital in Rome. But he had been awake for a short time, after his legs had been operated on, as they swung like cement monkeys from the ceiling.

But he would have been in traction for weeks, wouldn't he? So, why had he been out long enough to not be in traction anymore?

He didn't pull out the IV. Well, why should he? His legs were there. All of him seemed to be present and accounted for. Thank God, because he had trouble figuring out how he could be an on-site archaeologist without legs.

Jim did find and press a call button.

What a flutter! Nurses and doctors came running.

He tried to ask them but found his tongue uncooperative, dry as dust. Just a relic of an organ of speech. A nurse began to give him cool water through a straw. They seemed to understand what he wanted to know.

"You have been in a coma for two months," a Dr. Cabrera informed him a little sheepishly, an expression tempered with obvious relief. "We knew nothing of your medical history and you had a reaction to a medication."

A call was placed for him. Jim had no family of his own but Gerard Godard came to visit.

"We have everything," the young man told him with a smile. "Quite safe."

"Not here I hope. After what they did at the catacombs, I'm afraid the Church would go to any length… You could be killed," Jim replied, not believing for even a second that he was overreacting.

Gerard shook his head. "No, in Paris. When you are well, Linda and I will take you there. You will have everything you need."

Jim choked up, put both hands to his face. "I can't believe what they did to Louis…"

He wasn't ashamed of the tears. He'd known Dr. Godard for thirty years, since he was eighteen and first pursuing an archaeology degree in college. What he did feel now was shamed by his inability to save Louis. He'd been going up those steps leading out, they were almost safe…a half a minute away from it at the least.

The explosions and the cave-in had carried stone and other debris far into the field. They wouldn't have made it without a good ten minutes lead.

Yet, Jim also blamed himself for being so rude to the priests who'd visited the docs at the hotel, to warn them off. He'd been combative, determined not to be brow-beaten no matter how nervous they made him feel.

Gerard touched his shoulder. "I have brought something for you," he said. "Perhaps you will get some use out of it before they release you. You know, working on notes for whatever you will do with the information you and Cousin Louis found here."

It was a small video camera.

Jim would put it across the room and tape himself as he told the story of the two docs and the Catacombs of Saint Aureola. He felt a little uncomfortable at first, talking to the thing, but he soon got over this. He found he had quite a lot to say in the way of tribute to his late colleague. This was what he was doing, in fact, when the door opened and Father Malvezzi entered the room.

Jim glared at him, unhappy with the interruption but moreso at who his visitor was.

"What the hell do you want?"

"To see how you are doing," the priest replied, mild as ever.

"Getting ready to write a book," Jim told him. "Are you going to kill me like you did Louis?"

Malvezzi sighed. "What happened to Dr. Godard was a terrible thing. You have my deepest sympathies. But I must still caution you against making public your findings."

Jim was incensed. "Oh? What'll you do? Blow up the college I teach at? Or the offices of whatever publishing company buys the rights?"

Malvezzi folded his hands across his stomach and tried to say quietly, "You do not understand who you are dealing with..."

"I think I do," Jim argued. "My career specialty seems to have been shit all along. And, brother, do I know it when I see it."

The priest seemed about to say something more but then simply left the room.

Jim stared into the camera which he'd noticed with glee hadn't been spotted by Father Malvezzi.

"Didn't exactly deny it, did he, sports fans?"

Eventually out of the hospital, on a trip to Paris with Louis' cousin and charming fiancée. Then back to the States. He sent a copy of that video tape to Father Malvezzi, C/O The Vatican. Jim included a note which informed the priest that copies of this tape were in several secured locations and would be released should anything of a sudden nature happen to Dr. James Singer.

Then he wrote the book, *Sacred Sepsis*. He shared the authorship with Louis, putting the other doctor's name first. He also gave half of all royalties to Godard's family.

Times had changed. He had success professionally with it. He also found a curious popular notoriety out of it. Sort of von Danniken-ish. A few years before this might have rankled Jim, but now he didn't seem to mind. At least he was being respected for his shit.

DREAD IN THE BEAST

William James wrote, "God is not necessarily responsible for the existence of evil. The gospel of healthy-mindedness casts its vote distinctly for its pluralistic view. Whereas the monistic philosopher finds himself more or less bound to say, as Hegel said, that everything actual is rational, and that evil, as an element dialectically required must be pinned in, and kept and consecrated and have a function awarded to it in the final system of truth, healthy-mindedness refuses to say anything of the sort. Evil, it says, is emphatically irrational, and *not* to be pinned in, or preserved, or consecrated in any final system of truth. It is a pure abomination to the Lord, an alien unreality, a waste element, to be sloughed off and negated...the ideal, so far from being coexstensive with the actual, is a mere extract from the actual, marked by its deliverance from all contact with this diseased, inferior, excrementitious stuff."

Yet Paul the Apostle said, "Nothing is unclean in itself."

And then James Frazier wrote, "Taboos of holiness agree with taboos of pollution because the savage does not distinguish between holiness and pollution."

Therefore, what is holy and what is evil? What is sacred and what is sepsis? The distinctions blur: black versus white = gray; right versus wrong might be as simple as intention or as complicated as a nation's declared manifest destiny.

—Sacred Sepsis
Dr. Louis Godard and Dr. James Singer

CHAPTER
19

CAIRO,
2001

Jason hadn't returned to the United States with the rest of the army. He'd spent the ten years after Desert Storm going around the world, supporting himself selling drugs or slaves or performing assassinations (some being paid hits and others being the act of rolling rich drunks). Apparently Big Garth Listo had connections which introduced Jason into certain circles he would otherwise have been viewed with suspicion from.

He'd enjoyed India, Southeast Asia, and South America, delighting with the things buyable and stealable in Calcutta, Bangkok, Buenos Aires. He'd visited every place in Europe that Crowley had been, including staying at the Villa Cefalu in Sicily, where Father Perdurabo set up his infamous abbey. He even disguised himself and visited Mecca, which Crowley didn't do. He stood on spots where magick had been done and tried to summon up the old power. Attempted to use it to open the gateway to that place without horizons. But he didn't see so much as a twinkle of darklight peeping from there, although—depending on what narcotics he might have recently ingested—he did sometimes feel tingling in his scrotum and across his scalp and smelled the odor of his own burning blood. He did find a piece of paper written in Crowley's own hand, buried under floorboards, lost for decades.

He believed he'd left it there for himself, as the Beast knowing that one day the **Superman** would come along and discover it.

Jason did not even read it. He commenced immediately to eating it. He collapsed to that floor and had a seizure which must have lasted days. He woke up with beard stubble and soiled clothes, finding he'd scratched into his left arm the numbers 666 and into his right arm the numbers 777. He'd flown! He'd fucked gods! He'd laid waste to worlds cloaked as Melanicus!

Interesting that when he shit the paper out, it wasn't chewed anymore but whole again. It no longer was a brownish page from Crowley's writings but a white page from *The Book of the Damned* by Charles Fort.

Crowley is no more. I'm Jason Cave and my magic (sans 'K') is of an earthier nature.

Each incarnation was intended to teach the wanderer something specific. Having learned it, you died, were reborn, and went onto the next item on your spiritual agenda. That didn't mean he wasn't still The Beast. He was every bit of that.

Like Crowley, he found he couldn't stay away long from Egypt. It had nothing to do with Osiris or Horus or even Thoth. (He was more of a Nietzschein anyway. Crowley had once said, "Nietzsche was to me almost an avatar of Thoth, the god of wisdom..." Jason simply turned it around, with Thoth almost being an avatar of Nietzsche.)

It was the draw of the delta, extravagant with the **Superman**'s passions, and it was the desert, severe as the **Superman**'s justice. He loved the wonderful and horrible smells, the press of so many sweating—mortal—bodies, the availability of ancient pleasures.

Jason kept returning, hoping to catch a glimpse of *her* again: the djinn or the disintegrater, marzipan demon or shit goddess. There were moments when he thought *there she is*... In a swirl of long black skirts, the flutter of a veil, a pair of surely magnificent eyes—or of eyes that seemed hidden behind mist.

But it was never the one. It was always just some ordinary, mortal cunt destined to live a brief time and perish even quicker between visible horizons.

It was while on his last journey to Cairo, walking about another of the Cities of the Dead after dark, whispering from Crowley again, "As I came through the desert, thus it was. As I came through the desert..."

He saw his old army buddy, Michael Roheim. The man seethed, stalking swirls of dust, one eye cocked to the vision of his leviathan shadow cast against walls lining the cemetery street. He bore a weapon in his hands ready to purr, to speak to him, caressing its steel teeth and the mesh of its oracle in circuit.

Jason heard him growl, "Catch me now, you burning chlorpromazine fuckers, needle dicks in the hands of starched harlot deities disguised as staff doctors…can't fool me…no, I can see the dusty scorpions of desert goddesses behind your faces."

Jason smiled. He wasn't afraid of Mike. But perhaps it was just as well the numbers 666 on his left arm were hidden under his sleeve.

"Hey there, grunt," he said just loud enough to be heard.

The man turned, chainsaw at the ready. His eyes glittered in the moonlight like new pennies put upon the eyes of the drowned dead.

"Cave?" Roheim muttered. "That you?"

"Yeah. Where you been, you in such a state, boy?"

Jason walked slowly toward him, no sudden moves. He was armed a damned sight better than a chainsaw. The lack of finesse wasn't even the consideration. It was speed that mattered.

Roheim chuckled, the sound deep, gutteral, scary. "You ever heard tales about Americans ending up in madhouses in this part of the world? Not the most up-to-date methods of treatment for prophets and archangels. I flipped out in a cabaret and cut a dancing girl into so much falafel. Fuck it, man, I knew she was Babylon, Ashtoreth, Lilith coming in moons from the white sands to seduce me. Michael, wielding a modern sword that sings on a string. They dragged me by my ankles through the filthy streets to the hospital. My barred window overlooked this boneburg."

Cool. Jason nodded, never losing his smile. "So how'd you get out?"

"You recall all those candies we did in the service?"

"Shit sure. You have an immunity to most of it now, right?"

"Dude, I pretended to be out, then first chance I got I broke the back of some greasy orderly across my thigh, stabbed another through the eye with the needle intended for the archangel. Mmmmmm, the long white squirt arced through the air like a seminal sigh. I took back my chainsaw, slipped outside."

So he'd gone from believing he had angels protecting him to thinking he was one. Well, why the hell not, if Jason could be The Beast?

"So what are you going to do here?" Jason asked, nice as you please. Voice even and soothing because Michael's face kept twitching, contorting. And if it wasn't the drugs the doctors had given him, then it must be stark raving madness.

"I'm on the next Crusade against the heathen, brother Cave. The last Crusade." And he stumbled off into the maze of ancient tombs.

Jason shrugged and followed.

They both eventually saw the woman in the—for want of a better word—alley between two rows of crypt buildings. She wore no headdress. Her hair and face were bare. Even at twenty feet away Jason could tell she had dark freckles that turned orange in the wisp of some squatter's coal oil lamp. Her dress was of some translucent stuff, similar to strips of silken bandages, similar to veils worn by Salome seeking Baptist heads. These floated even though there was no breeze tonight.

Roheim touched the string, making the saw speak to him again, Michael's shining sword reeking of bar and chain oil.

buzzzzzzzzz

Jason gasped, recognizing his djinn. Should he rush forward to protect her? He could simply draw the gun from his pocket and shoot Roheim.

But then he thought, *I've been fooled so often. If she's really my djinn then she will be able to take care of herself. If she's not, then why can't he just have her? And with that chainsaw just half her?*

So Jason stayed where he was, even slipping back a little into the shadows. He could watch from there.

"Jezebel, Rahab, Sheba!" Michael cried as he repeated the names he heard his weapon speak to him. He leapt into the narrow alley with the chainsaw howling gutteral threats, links in jackal ratchet, the modern holy hatchet man.

The freckled woman turned slowly, one slender arm up and out as if offering a handful of precious earth to him.

Michael sliced down with the chainsaw, taking off hunks before she could even react. They came off in a cloud of misty skin, bone, and sanguine rain.

Michael laughed with an insane chortle, waiting for her to fall. He stepped back and waved the chainsaw in the air in grisly triumph, licking the salt spray of her from his lips, savoring the moisture of it in the arid atmosphere.

Yet her flavor was dry. It smacked his mouth in dessicated slivers. Before he could slash again, she spun on the ball of a dark-spotted foot, grabbing the weapon from his careless hands with the one arm left her. She plucked it from him easily as if he were but a naughty child with a dangerous toy. It still chugged along in its sacred voice that only Michael heard, gurgling its lean celestial hunger in an echo that filled the alley, sending rats and cats scurrying to seek Saracen holes to hide in. She took it and swung it toward his hips. But she was weakened as blood flew out of her wounds, and so the chainsaw only hacked about three quarters of the way through his right leg.

She was injured (yet fighting grandly!). The spray of blood meant she must be human. Jason was tempted to help Roheim now, because the fellow had nearly been a **Superman**. But maybe almost really only counted with horseshoes and hand grenades (and chainsaws). He decided to stay still and continue watching.

Both woman and archangel fell to the ground in an identical instant, in a hellish slow motion as if this were a race between single-celled creatures. If the earth shook when they struck, neither of them heard it: Michael because he was overcome by his own shakes and hearing a memory of tanks, jets, and missiles—the woman because she knew the earth as a serene and gentle vessel. She landed with her one arm reaching toward the street and the crumbling facades of tombs, and...yes, outstretched with soil falling from her fingers.

She staggered to her feet. Michael was still pumped from his religious zeal, his eyes wide, unable to believe she could stand at all after what he'd done to her...the roar still grinding pounds through the night...yes, the kind of flesh lightning it was...voices in thunder telling him to smite this one as he had the dancer with her stomach undulating in the bar...but her getting up getting up getting up...

Jason held his breath. Because he couldn't believe it either. She was getting up!

Michael couldn't rise but the alley woman did, wobbling, clutching the rag of her shoulder, gouting scarlet slipping in an oddly muddy pulp through her slender fingers. She poked at the white hasp of cut bone and grimaced. She blinked at the flattened place where the left breast had been, a hollow next to the swell of the right. She put her palm out as if to cup the missing curve, hefting an astral weight. It had left lines in varying shades of henna and tan, like the strata in some canyons.

The woman faced the archangel, her legs widely spaced in a sailor's gait to keep her steady, despite the massive trauma of the severed arm and tit. Her eyes were a wide sienna in which no debilitating shock was revealed. Her mouth was set in a small pout: no more, no less.

"Why have you done this to me?" she asked Michael. "My people are no threat to the living, and the dead need no protection."

Jason heard her voice with its peculiar accent, sounding nothing like the way modern Egyptians pronounced English. It was similar to the way the oldest fellahin pronounced it, the ones who still relied upon the ancient tongue. He reckoned that Napoleon on his campaign through Egypt probably heard this accent when the ancient spirits of the old gods howled around his tent. And Richard the Lionhearted probably shivered as it sang through grains of sand as he tried to sleep before battle. Devils employed by Saladin might have spoken this way, chanting spells against the invaders.

She stuck a finger down her throat and gagged. She doubled over and choked, the flat belly undulating beneath her gauzy dress, single breast fluttering like a fish's gill. Something large began filling the slim tube of the neck.

185

She stared at the archangel all the while, finger on the sickening trigger. She stared at him when he wouldn't answer. She saw she was reflected in his vein-serrated pupils. He was in a state of marvel as well as sublime agony, the partially amputated leg jittering a dance as a nicked artery beat time with spurts.

Finger down her throat and the abdomen jerking in the twist. Esophagus rolling, convulsing, the taste of a chalky unnatural bile. She pulled the finger out as the product came up. A clotty paste of gruel slithered across her tongue first and she spat it out—or tried to. The blockage in her throat made it hard to expectorate, especially since it held no true moisture. Spitting was an action which required some control and now she had none. She couldn't breathe...felt her face turning blue with effort. Reflex and a fist, parched with strangulation. She punched herself in the stomach, grabbed her neck, gaseously belched trying to get it out of her. Withered threads of acid goop hung from her lips as her jaws popped as wide as they could go.

Michael trembled and Jason damn near hyperventilated with ecstasy. Both men watched as the blob slowly squeezed out from between her lips. Hitting the air, it blossomed, fingers uncurling like the petals of a cactus rose. The wrist attached to it gesticulated sinuously as this slid out behind, trailing with a forearm. Dehydrated gobbets of slime the color of green shadows on blue bottle flies clung to the skin in a wicked cross between dusty spew and placenta. It caught between her front teeth in taffy strings stiff as blown glass. Nothing flowed cleanly like a river, red and watery and drenching. It flopped, loosely as empty locust husks.

She made a horrible noise as the crook of the elbow jammed, like one wrong log in a floe. She hacked and sputtered, her eyes bulging. She grasped the vomited wrist and pulled, turning it, trying to work the obstruction free. While on the ground Michael shrank away as much as he could, trying to slither off on his backside—only his one good leg refused to help him and the other was worse than useless. If he could only reach the weapon, perhaps he could finish her. Perhaps he could do *something*.

But the woman was between Michael and the voice of thunder. Even now the chainsaw sputtered in the wind-down, catching on itself the way a child's breath hitches when it's crying. It whimpered and stopped.

Sulphuric sputum flew as she pulled the elbow out with a corky plop. The rest of the arm came smoothly free. Snot spattered the ground like balls of juiceless mercury. She slipped in the dust of her own blood and saliva while affixing the end of the upper arm with the wound into her shoulder.

The pieces of flesh squirmed in a maggot waltz, merged the knitting atoms, crackled with electron firefly spin. There was a noise of meshing no louder than a buried murmur. She winked out a few burnt almond-colored tears which struck her cheeks with the noise of cymbals, her face screwed up in pain and concentration.

And then she stuck the finger down her throat again, the delicately freckled hand clawing as the lump of unleveled flesh came up. She put this to the place where the breast had been, patting it, plumping it, fashioning a new one, twirling the thumb and index finger to form a hazelnut of a nipple. She stroked it and quivered as the new bud erected beneath her touch, massaging the unwounded one as if to compare them. The new hand strayed down the flat belly to the umbra triangle between her thighs.

Jason marveled at how strangely beautiful she was…yes, weird with the freaky terra cotta hair in a mummified plait down her back…brown eyes the color of Jericho ruins…the gauze of that thin little dress that had so captured his attention earlier crisp as the caul seers are born with…the prenatal sac which wrapped a baby's head…yes, what it surely was and not a real garment at all…extensions of patches of her skin transparently suspended from her shoulders and down her spine. It rustled like taffeta, like the wizened skin of a dappled fawn. If she danced in it, bells on her feet, surely all the cannibal demons summoned by perfumes and tambourines would bay.

Jason thought of a fragment of a poem written by the Islamic poet Ma'arri in medieval times. "This world resembles a cadaver, and we around it dogs that bark; And he who eats from it is the loser; he who abstains takes the better part. And certain is a dawn disaster to him unwaylaid in the dark."

She stroked her new breast, thumbing the darkness between her legs. She gasped and a flood of shadowy matter streamed to the ground. Jason frowned, certain it was shit. Then she couldn't be his djinn but the other one.

The substance hit the ground in an arabesque pattern, titian with drought. Dirt, not shit. She had shed a motif of clay beneath herself.

She examined the new arm. She said (whether to Michael Roheim or to herself, did it matter?), "It isn't the same color as the other. It is a pallid pink and quite hairless. That will change with exposure to the carrion blanket. It will brown some when I lay back in the dirt."

She tilted her head with a birdlike satisfaction and patted the crackling seams around the replacements. She brushed off flecks of loose flesh that hadn't quite melded. The gaping wounds were no more; not even the cracks bled. She flexed the fingers as she stepped closer to the injured man on the ground.

He tried to twist away. "Cave? Man, help me here. Don't let her get me… Cave? Are you still there?"

Roheim tried to scream…not a brutish protest or an animal shriek of terror…his sour gasp was nearly silent…seeing now the soil between her toes, up the softly marble pillars of her legs, wedged in the womb as a nurturing moss but dry as an old brocade pillow in a tomb…even up both her nostrils like topaz plugs.

It clung to her scalp in clods. Sprinkled her eye lashes. Stained the lacy patches in the skin that hung from her shoulders and spine.

Jason made not a move to help him. He felt Michael's eyes briefly on him, making his silhouette in a shadow. He felt the accusation of a man betrayed by another man in the face of the inhuman.

"God?" Roheim then switched tactics. "Jesus, help me!"

Jason would surely have expected the madman to cry to heaven first, since he was supposed to be an archangel.

The freckled woman knelt beside Romheim and stuck a finger into the geysering wound in his right leg...the same finger she'd put down her throat. He tried to reach up to shove her away, to keep her from touching him. His arms were heavy as millstones. She slipped the entirety of the new pale hand into the bloody crevice and smeared it with red juices.

She shuddered and slung the gore away from her in surprise.

"Wet!" she muttered in dismay.

Michael screamed now, bellowing in fury and torment, seeing stars winking hotly all through the alley, even though few shone overhead in the slitted spot of sky visible between the tops of the vaults. His cry dwindled down to a grunt, weaker by the moment...powerless as his cold chainsaw, not speaking to him anymore, helpless as any tool of God among the unbelievers.

"Don't touch me! Unclean! *Ghul!*" Michael shouted, using the Arabic term for what he knew she must be.

Jason's jaw dropped. He shook his head, grinning. *Why didn't I think of that? Not a djinn but a ghoul!*

She shook her head and clods of earth came down from her hair, so much more dirt than it seemed it should hold. She'd come by it by burrowing into graves for her food. Romheim looked like he expected to be buried under an avalanche. He choked as soil slipped into his mouth and nostrils, gritting like a sandy glass into his eyes.

"You have heard tales but they are not true," she told him patiently as she sat next to him. "We do not attack the living. We only eat the dead."

She drew her knees up, grave-soiled toes carefully beyond reach of the enormous pool of his blood the nicked artery in his leg created. A sea...yes, a dead sea soon. Michael wept, waiting to hear her creep toward him. But, of course, he would never hear it.

Jason waited. Once Michael was dead, she didn't wait long. She ate so delicately! He thought of the way movies depicted zombies, as slobs in a buffet of guts. But, well, a ghoul wasn't really a zombie. A zombie was the raised-up dead and she wasn't dead, just from another species.

He let her finish and then calmly stepped from the shadows.

She had already started to stand up and now turned to face him. From the look on her face, it was obvious she'd known he was there all along. She didn't act as if she would run. Why should she? Clearly she had no reason to be afraid.

"Good evening," Jason said. "Have you ever considered going to America?"

++++++++++

The fascination with bodily waste may be purely puerile. It goes back to our roots, when we are infants, before we've been toilet trained and are given our parents' stern commandment *don't play with that!* This is also when we are at our most innocent and—according to some religions—at our closest link with the spirit and/or God. Therefore, purity becomes equated less with cleanliness and more with sinlessness. Yet beyond the infantile state, the only persons so pure must be saints. Those of us who are adult and, to at least some degree, discerning, must eventually realize our failings. We can hardly be said to be without fault, so we adopt a scapegoat for our impurity. Our waste becomes a symbol of that, one which we daily—sometimes almost ritually—shed in an act that is a combination of physical contrition and purifying penance.

—*Sacred Sepsis*
Dr. Louis Godard and Dr. James Singer

CHAPTER 20

Dorien hadn't been allowed back in the courtroom. So she wasn't there when the judge dismissed the case. Some fucking technicality. A mistake made when the authorities took the evidence from Gavin Parrish's room. And now he just walked scot-free after deliberately passing on his plague to all those hapless women.

Neela cried when she called Dorien to tell her. (Dorien had Caller ID so she knew it was safe to answer. It wasn't her sister again.) Dorien stood there with the phone in her hand, feeling dark, seeing darkness plume around her in shades of jaundice yellow, sooty browns and grays, and moonless/sunless black. She knew she murmured something, words meant to be a comfort. But how did you comfort somebody who'd been poisoned unto death and lingered long enough to understand she'd never get justice?

The only remark she actually recalled making was, "The world is shit." Spoken flatly, dull of sheen and emotion.

"Don't I know it," Neela said softly on the other end of the line. "But I have to believe that somehow this will catch up with him. There must be forces that right wrongs, if not here on earth then after it."

She paused, suffering a bad coughing fit. She sounded as if she might be strangling. Dorien closed her eyes and wished it would stop. When it did, quite abruptly, Neela gasped.

"I'm so sorry. I hope that didn't hurt your ears!"

"I'm fine. And, yes, I also believe in reckonings."

"Sarah Stanner practically had a seizure in front of the judge, she was so mad," Neela told her, laughing hoarsely. "Later she told me she was taking up a collection to go after him again. I gave her a few dollars. I don't imagine she'll go through with it."

Neela tired so easily these days that she didn't stay on the phone very long. After she hung up and the dial tone buzzed like a swarm of summer locusts, Dorien just held the receiver for a while, feeling the plastic in her hand, thinking *deadthingdeadthingdeadthingdead thingdeadthingdeadthing.*

Then she stumbled to the bathroom, startled by a lurch in her belly. She hadn't eaten in weeks so what could be down there that wanted up?

Leaning over the toilet, Dorien heaved painfully. There was no scorch of bile. Perhaps her body no longer manufactured any since it seemed to have no need of food or digestion for food. A black tide rushed up and out, spilling into the porcelain bowl. Once down there it squirmed, turning out to be comprised of hundreds of insects.

Beetles to be precise.

They had a unique shape to their backs.

They were scarab beetles.

Where had she read that scarab beetles mated in shit?

She started to flush them but her finger paused on the toilet lever. It wasn't as if they would do any harm. They weren't a bit like Hollywood portrayed them, as horrendously voracious as a school of piranha. They began crawling up out of the bowl.

"Go where you may," she said quietly. Wondering if what she was becoming could somehow be mother to such creatures.

They overran to the toilet tank and went up the wall or spilled onto the floor and scurried every direction.

The phone rang and she cringed, hoping it wasn't Annet again. It rang four times and then her answering machine picked up.

"I can't come to the phone right now. If you're a telemarketer, I hope you rot in the worst hell available on this earth. If you're a creditor, you might just as well be trying to sell something as get any money out of me. I'm broke. Anybody else, leave a name and number and if I'm still alive later to hear this, well...we'll see..."

There was the ubiquitous beep and a female voice said, "Hi, this is Vashti from Grom's Market..."

Dorien remembered she'd had a call from Vashti yesterday. And had there been another the day before? The week before? Who was Vashti?

Ah, the one before (not sure whether the last one or the one before that) had asked, "When are you coming in?"

Why would she come into Grom's Market when she didn't eat now?

But this time Vashti said, "Sorry, we had to replace you. Hope you just blew us off and didn't fall prey to The Shit Detail."

Replace her?

Dorien slapped a palm to her forehead. That's right. She'd gotten a job! She'd had to, after quitting school for the summer. How could she forget a thing like that?

How long had she been going to work anyway? It scared her, doing things she couldn't remember afterward.

Dorien knew she suffered blank spaces. She'd find herself coming home at night, stumbling through the door with a splitting headache. Behind the eyes, always in the eyes. She'd go to the bathroom to splash cold water in her face and sometimes find a little blood on her cheek, or maybe trailing in a teardrop from one of those eyes. How'd that get there?

(Hey, maybe she was the butcher's assistant at Grom's Market. She held the baby goats down when somebody ordered cabrito. She arranged the piglet heads all in a neat row. She swung dead chickens over her head. Gross!)

She'd have amnesia...

Aw, come on, working at a market couldn't be that bad, even if apparently she'd been scheduled for the night shift.

(Everybody knew this was when the strangest customers hung out.)

So, why'd she quit?

"Guess I didn't," Dorien told herself. "I just stopped coming. Or forgot to go."

So, how badly did she need money now?

(Didn't matter. Or rather, *soon* it wouldn't matter.)

She heard a knock on her front door.

"Dory?"

Annet again. Damn, wouldn't she ever give up?

"I know you're there. I checked the college and they said you haven't been to classes in a long time. And your name is still on the mailboxes downstairs. Landlord says you live here, even if you are behind on the rent."

Dorien was glad she hadn't flushed the beetles, else Annet might have heard the sound in the hallway.

"Why won't you talk to me?" Annet's voice whined, wheedled. "I can help. I've met the nicest people and I think you'd fit right in. We'll even help with the rent and whatever bills you're having trouble with. I read about that Gavin Parrish guy and what he did to you and the other girls. Why didn't you tell us? No wonder you acted so strangely while Daddy was dying!"

Dorien crept into the living room and very slowly sat down on the sofa. She sniffed the air. The sunglasses didn't betray the expression in her eyes to any possible ghost in the room. She didn't hold her breath. Did she even have to breathe anymore? She did breathe but it might have only been out of habit.

She could hear Annet putting both palms flat against the door as if trying to will Dorien to answer, as if trying to pass through in an osmosis of both physical body and psychic determination. Those palms were hot and damp. The pulses in the fingers were fast, throbbing like a hummingbird playing drums. How weird that she could hear Annet's pulse that way. It filled Dorien's head, going round and round, rhythmic thunder captured and descending down long copper pipes, clatter clank rumble. It got so loud she feared she might actually cry out. (Mustn't do that! Annet will know I'm here.)

She already knows.

Dorien grasped the sofa cushions under her, squeezed polyester stuffing, stifling her scream.

Suddenly it was simply gone. As if she'd made it stop, as she might have Neela's choking.

"I'm leaving something for you. Right outside the door. Promise you'll get it and take a look?" Annet chuckled. "It's…well, you'll see. Maybe you really aren't in there, hiding from me. It'll help you just like it's helped me."

Dorien sat there, waiting. Knowing that Annet had walked a little ways down the hall and stopped, to see if she would open the door. She shut her eyes, let time flow away from her and here. Imagined underground rivers and conduits, thresholds and tunnels. If she started counting backward— beginning with a number in the trillions perhaps—would she go back so far she could never return once she hit zero?

Eventually she opened her eyes again. They were so sore behind the glasses. Annet had come during the day. Not that it was all that visible with the duct tape Dorien had sealed the windows with and the black electrician's tape she'd recently layered over that. But she felt the darkness, because it was as sentient as any god. And with all the poisons the city poured into it, it might even now be a devil.

Dorien knew Annet had left hours ago. She got up and walked across the room, opened the door.

She'd expected another paper bag with stew. She wouldn't just throw it into the trash this time. She'd sneak downstairs and put it in the alley for the strays. Dogs eating dog. At least it wouldn't be wasted. Everything that lived had a right to see its death be for a decent purpose—such as part of the food chain, nature's recycling.

But it wasn't more take-out from CANE. It was a book, much-read and (dog-eared?).

Sacred Sepsis.

"It isn't a comfortable subject. But it comprises who we are as well as who we were and will be. Every by-product is a metaphor for the end and a place for a genesis. The goddess of shit is not evil but possesses the duality that many mother deities from world religions have been said to personify: light and darkness, life and death, the sacred and profane."

Goddess of shit?

Dorien's heart stopped beating. (That is, provided it still did at all.) She realized she'd opened the book in the hallway and read a tiny passage in the introduction. What if Annet came back?

She heard a television (or maybe it was a radio) blaring from a neighbor's place. A news report of another recent grave found desecrated. Then a report of a series of crimes like those committed by The Shit Detail, only some of these were on the opposite side of the country and some were in Europe.

When had Dorien last seen or listened to news? For all she knew, another war might be going on (and on...) Wasn't there usually one somewhere? She might go outside to find the sun had shriveled and dissolved into the moon. (No, she felt it when it pressed against the covered windows, sweating like a dirty lover on top of the building.)

Dorien quickly ducked back into the apartment and closed the door, locked it, deadbolted it, put on the chain.

Goddess of shit?

It was the book's subject. First she paced the floor. What? For hours? Then she sat down, legs folded beneath her like a cat. Going through the pages, dry as a dead fly's wings against her thumb. Reading in the dark.

"Our history is the nightmare, full frontal and posterior exposed, outrage by outrage. Decency doesn't enter into it. Decency only mandates shame, smothered with guilt, the pain festering until it has turned to cancer. Our trial by fire and obscenity, except that humans don't want rational decay; they prefer a flushable riddle. We are oppressed by our toilet habits, by the mere notion that there is no choice but to submit to this undignified action, nature's ultimate intimidation. I do not mean to suggest that the goddess of shit intimidates us. Rather, I propose that 'nature,' as it or she or he is perceived, is solely a construction of mankind's, created with scatalogical and improbable nomenclature by rough beasts slouching toward nirvana.

"There were more religions in the past that had underworlds but didn't have heavens. Hells which were a sense of place more dismal than the earthly plain, where suffering surpassed nonexistence.

"In Ezekial it says, 'And thou shalt eat it as barley cakes and thou shalt bake it with dung that cometh out of man, in their sight.' Sublime or relentlessly scriptural? Whatever, it is yet undeniably intended as sacred.

"And then this, purely septic, possibly classic bit from Arthur Rimbaud (before he authored *A Season In Hell*):

'A small black angel getting sick
From eating too much licorice stick.
He takes a shit, then disappears;
But as the empty darkness clears,
Beneath the moon his shit remains
Like dirty blood in dirty drains.'"

Dorien tried to lick her lips. Surely they had cracked and bled. But her tongue wouldn't come out.

"This book is intended to encompass a full range of archaeological and socialogical information and commentary on our obsession with waste. It will include findings by Dr. Godard and myself at the sites, as well as mythology, art and literature. It may appear to be sensational but it was never my intention to simply shock. Those who find they are too easily offended by the information imparted in this treatise may wish to examine their own motives for unreasonable stricture and anal retention.

"When we accept that there is nothing which is part of us too small or too mean to have been created by God, we set ourselves free."

"Who are these guys?" Dorien said out loud.

According to the book's jacket there were two authors: Dr. Louis Godard and Dr. James Singer. But the introduction admitted the book was written after Godard's death. (In the Catacombs of St. Aureola! And she'd dreamt of this place. She'd been in it with the cassia flowers and the stink of dog inside bowels. There were photographs of the murals inside the tomb, and it chilled her to the bone to see the resemblance with how Annet appeared now.)

The text showed a copyright date of 1993 and numerous reprint years following. She had to talk to this Singer. He must have answers for what she was going through. Well, actually he'd probably think she was a nutcase but Dorien knew she had to try.

The biographical information didn't say where this archaeologist could be found. But she bet anyone with a book this popular might be listed on the Internet. She actually did own a computer, a creeker of an old redo she'd bought cheap to use for her school work. Right now it was covered with dust. But she wiped off the screen, blew at the keyboard, and got it up and running. Connected to the Web, went to GOOGLE, typed in Dr. James Singer, and hit *SEARCH*.

A long list came up. Apparently there were quite a few doctors in the world with this name. She tried *Sacred Sepsis*. Bingo.

Goddamn, the man taught at a college across town. Not her own but close enough to drive. What were the fucking odds?

Maybe there were no coincidences. Everything that really mattered to you might just be lined up and waiting. They called that fate, didn't they?

Dorien finger-combed her hair, grabbed her purse and car keys, and headed out the door.

+++++++++++

She'd stopped at a red light across the street from the park where she and Gavin—and others—had been walking after the movie. Where they'd witnessed The Shit Detail's murder of the old homeless woman. The lights along the road glowed like dirty yellow rainbows in the dark smog. The Volkswagen coughed as it idled, purring cat-on-its-deathbed coronary occlusion-rhythms to make up for her not having the radio on. Piece of shit, but it was all hers.

Another car rolled up next to hers, the bass in their music so loud she actually felt it dissolving marrow in her bones. Its windows were down—as were hers since the funky air conditioning had expired. It was August and steamy hot. So hot the pollution at night seemed to mate with itself to spawn shadowy dinosaurs of poison, which stalked the roadways and climbed the skyscrapers and fought in the widest alleys.

There were four young men in this car. They ogled her and one smiled with a whole mouthful of moonstone teeth. He said, "Baby, you lookin' like some mighty tasty shit."

Another told her, "Built like a brick shit house..."

"Why you wear those sunglasses at night?" asked a third.

"So everything I see will be dark," she replied. Not the truth but what the hell. What was the line from the famous film? It amounted to the fact they couldn't handle the truth.

"No shit?" countered the fourth young man, grinning.

"Oh yes, definitely shit," she answered with a curt nod.

The light changed to green and they took off, squealing tires, leaving streaks of black rubber like rankled skidmarks in equally dark underwear. She started to take her foot off the brake, to step on the gas, but something at the edge of the park made her pause.

What was going on there? A mugging. Not rare for this city.

Happened all the time.

One man had another on the ground. The one on the bottom tried to scream but only managed to whuff-whuff. Gag in his mouth or maybe he'd been chopped hard in the throat, collapsing his windpipe. Yes, there was a bit of the bubbly whistle in the whuff-whuff. (Amazing she could hear this but her senses had sharpened lately. Goddess senses.) She considered helping until she understood the man on the bottom was dying and would indeed be dead very shortly.

The man on top was much bigger than his victim. He'd jerked down the smaller man's jeans. Dorien stiffened, not really wanting to witness a rape, homosexual or otherwise. But then the one on the bottom turned his head just enough that some of the illumination from a reasonably near street light cast its yellow glow on his face.

It was Gavin Parrish. Not sneering now, not arrogant. Just whuff-whuff-whistling. Violet foam at the mouth and nose.

So, maybe that woman had collected enough money to put a hit on him. Didn't necessarily take a lot of dough. There were guys who'd kill for the price of a cheeseburger. Or maybe the attacker was a brother to one of Gavin's names-on-a-sheet.

A blade flashed in the same light, crisp and keen. The whuff-whuff whistle went up briefly so high in pitch it could have shattered glass. Then all Dorien heard was a gurgle.

The assailant looked out. Did he make her, there in her car, sitting through the green until it was first yellow, then red again?

Yes, he did. Dorien knew she ought to go then, fast as she could. So he didn't get her license number or maybe just come over to slit her throat. But when she tried to change gears and stomp on the gas, all she heard was that piglet fart and then the car choked. You get what you pay for.

He was coming, yes. Strolling across the black sea of mostly invisible grass like he had all the time in the world. Time was his friend, his co-conspirator.

Dorien just watched him, wondering how Neela would feel about it when she read about Gavin's murder.

(Are you kidding? She was going to laugh and pop wheelies in that wheelchair.)

(Yeah, and how would she feel when she read about Dorien's?)

Killer coming… A big, big guy. Shoulders so wide he probably had to turn sideways to go through some doorways. A smug expression harder than Gavin's own, more self-possessed.

"I've seen you before," she started to whisper. "You followed me down dirty streets in a dream."

Into a City of the Dead. No, she couldn't do this now. Whatever it was she was meant to do…or have done to her. It wasn't the right moment.

She might have jumped out of the car to run. (Was it possible she could have willed herself to vanish?) Instead Dorien slipped down a little in her seat until all he could really see of her were the dark glasses. It was in the hands of fate.

He was saying something as he neared the Volkswagen. He had something in his fist and he murmured, "Nietzsche said, 'Out of your wild cats must tigers have evolved, and out of your poison-toads, crocodiles…'"

Huh?

"Present for you, honey," he then told her and tossed what he held through the car's rolled down window. Then he chuckled and swaggered away, not giving a damn what she thought or if she planned to run shrieking to the cops. If she'd have been going to scream, she probably already would have. So many people cowered, mute witnesses, terrified to become involved or just so jaded that nothing phased them anymore. Dorien realized this beast of a man probably just assumed she'd pissed her undies in fear of him and would be virtually comatose long enough for him to get away.

She looked down at what had splatted on the passenger side seat.

It was Gavin's cock and balls.

Dorien picked them up and hung them from the rearview mirror, then drove on. Looking back at the place in the park, she saw a woman in a long robe emerge from the bushes and walk over to Gavin's body. She crouched down and bent toward it.

Dorien frowned, not knowing what this woman was going to do. But she was sure the female wasn't going to give the dead man a kiss.

+++++++++++

"If without knowing it one eats what is polluted by blood or any unclean thing, it is nothing; but if he knows, he shall do penance according to the degree of pollution." Penitential of Archbishop Theodore of Canterbury A.D. 668-690. This was the same learned man (only three centuries past Saint Aureola) who demanded that women who had given birth spend forty days in purgation—as if admitting new life into the world was a sin. He further insisted that any woman who had entered a church while she was menstruating do a fast for three weeks as a penalty. Not that he mentioned how anyone was to know she was menstruating. Perhaps the powers that be struck the offending female with a pink thunderbolt.

—*Sacred Sepsis*
Dr. Louis Godard and Dr. James Singer

CHAPTER
21

SHEOL'S DITCH,
ONE YEAR AGO

Big Garth Listo glimpsed his old friend through the security peep hole in his front door and opened it immediately.

"Jason! It's been fifteen years since I last saw you," the big man effused.

First thing Jason noticed was the *netsuke* around B.G.'s neck. He couldn't help but smile. Garth hadn't known he was coming, so he couldn't have put it on simply to please him. Garth really did treasure it.

In his fifties now, Garth's large frame had fleshed out so much that he almost resembled a sumo wrestler. (He really was BIG Garth now.) He wore the classic kami-shimo, a samurai costume consisting of full trousers and a jacket with wide wings across the shoulders. He had the traditional two swords in his belt: the katana (or fighting sword) and the shorter wakizashi. It didn't look as if he actually shaved the top of his head anymore for there was no stubble. He'd grown genuinely bald and what hair remained he'd drawn back into a tight queue.

Jason looked his old friend and mentor over, then nodded with approval. Yes, Garth had gained weight but he still looked fit enough to single-handedly take on any average gun-toting-because-they-didn't-have-class-or-style-enough-for-a-*real*-weapon street gang.

It didn't matter that Garth was still into his Japanese warrior mode, caught on the wheel of incarnation. Maybe it simply wasn't time for him to progress to the next level. For the most part (save for minor excursions more out of curiosity than being-in-a-spiritual-rut) Jason had put Crowley behind him. In this life he was Jason Cave; he had new lessons to learn and anti-laws to will into being.

"You got my letters though, right?" he wanted to know.

Garth nodded once. "Practically from every port in the world. How long you been back in the States?"

"About..." Jason glanced at the Rolex on his wrist, taken after a poker game with some French champagne salesman who'd considered himself a high roller, "...sixty-six hours."

"Two thirds the number of the beast," Garth commented. "Didn't have any trouble finding my house, I trust?"

"No. This place must have set you back some."

"Always have to pay more when you want a lot of privacy."

Garth had stepped back so his guests could enter. At first he'd thought Jason was alone. Jason also happened to be a big man, though none of it was fat. He looked like he ought to belong body and soul to the Worldwide Wrestling Federation, muscles hard as concrete blocks. Then Garth saw the freckled little woman behind him and his eyes widened some.

Jason smiled. "I'd like you to meet Rose," he said. "My bride."

Garth looked doubtful. "You got hitched?"

"Met her in Cairo. She's from a very old native family. No Alexandrian Greek and no Euro-trash."

They had all gone inside and Big Garth closed the door. Jason beamed as he glanced around the living room. One entire wall was filled with an impressive array of Japanese cutlery: Aikuchi and Tanto, Daito, Tachi and Shira Tach. Tassled, finely engraved steel, scabbards of ivory/cinnabar/gold. There were three gaudy suits of lamellar armor on mannikins, comprised of many strips of iron scales arrayed horizontally and then lamenated and laced together to form plate. Not exactly cheap trinkets bought for a song at some local flea market. Garth was obviously doing well at whatever was his current underground occupation.

"And you say her name is Rose?" Garth's eyebrows went up and waggled.

Jason knew what he was getting at. "Actually I have no idea what her real name is. I call her Rose after Crowley's first wife. But you'd already guessed that."

Rose's nose was in the air, sniffing, having detected an aroma she wanted to find the source of.

"So, this seems to be quite a large house," Jason stated, clasping his hands behind his back and rocking on his heels. "Taxes killing you yet?"

"I got it for very little. It was right on the verge of being condemned. The previous owner was going to turn it into apartments, a lot like our old building. Most of these places in this part of the Ditch end up as cubicles for the slum rats."

"So what happened to him?" Jason wanted to know.

Big Garth shrugged. "Oh, he had an accident. On the stairs over there. Fell down four flights of 'em. Over and over. Bet you could've heard them bones breaking like a marathon pig's knuckle stew."

"Have much of a back yard to it?"

"Yes, I have a lovely little Japanese garden there behind the high walls. Rocks and waterfalls, chrysanthemums and roses. Naturally, my greatest garden is 'inside' the house though."

The two men exchanged looks.

"Care for a tour?" Garth offered.

Jason grinned. "I thought you'd never ask."

Up the staircase. On the walls of the hallways were atrocity paintings, mostly prints but a few rare and very collectible originals. There were also stills from such modern Japanese ultraviolent pink movies such as *Entrails Of A Virgin* and *Guinea Pig 2: Flower Of Bloody Flesh*. More recent Japanese underground punk films like *Rubber's Lover* and *Tetsuo*.

Peering into a bathroom, Jason saw a film running, perhaps on closed loop so that it endlessly repeated its 45 minutes of gruesome mortality. Jason recognized it as being the documentary *Death Women*, Japan's answer to the monumental success of the American real-gore fest , *Faces Of Death*. He'd seen the film in Taiwan. The scene up was the one where a woman had been crushed by a bus, her corpse virtually disintegrating when taken from the wreckage.

Jason had taken Rose to see it, wondering how she would react to the sight of all those savaged bodies. He'd escorted her to films as they traveled around the world, including movies which incorporated some genuine act of homicide. So far she'd only sat, gazing stoically at the screen, images playing across her delicate features, cinematic blood seeming to caress her red hair like a ghastly starlight.

He'd wondered, then, if *Death Women* might arouse her? Would she be filled with an abrupt all-consuming passion for a snack? Might she run amuck in the audience, ripping off heads and sucking out all the organs through the straws of necks?

She'd done nothing. Perhaps she was like a cat with a mirror, not responding to the visual stimulis because it lacked the scent of reality.

He'd been disappointed. But at least she didn't try to keep him from following her when she went out to feed. He always kept a discreet distance to allow her the illusion of privacy as she trolled to cemeteries and funeral homes. He'd even accompanied her to a city morgue and assisted by knocking over the head an attendent who arrived at an inconvenient moment.

He'd grown accustomed to watching her dine, to observing as she used a long nail to slice open a cadaver's abdomen, reaching into the trunk's cavity to pull out intestines which she then squeezed to push out whatever shit they'd died with. In some guts—fresher ones—this ran out like pudding. But in those dead and maybe even buried awhile, the matter might have fossilized, turning into stones of topaz, amber and jet. (Never sapphires. No, there were never any stars here.)

Jason was a little disappointed, knowing from his vision with the Iraqi's head during Desert Storm that she was a creature from the other side—or who at least had access to the other side. He'd seen her sewing up the vaginas of ravaged virgins in that (seventh?) hell. He'd even performed rituals Crowley had written of, placing Rose in the ornate circle's center as a focus, as the offering's reverse, as the demon seeking home. But nothing ever came of it.

"You get contacts?" Jason asked, remembering Garth had always had glasses perched on the end of his nose.

"I had laser surgery. Lasers are just amazing," Big Garth enthused. "Wish I could afford to use 'em in my own work."

"Well, maybe someday, right?"

It appeared to have left Garth with a slight squint which made his gaze seem all the more intense.

Jason glimpsed a couple other people gliding noiselessly about from one room to another. He couldn't tell if they were male or female or one of each.

"My assistants," Garth explained. "Medical students, both of them. Getting experience here they could never have anywhere else. One plans to go into ER trauma and the other into graphic reconstruction."

He opened doors for his guests. On hand were delicate oriental antiques of subtle pattern or grimacing demon—then indelicate manmade prodigies: grimacing, no subtlety.

Jason's eyes lit up. Here were a human's darkest will imprinted upon reality. Regardless of what path destiny might have intended for these people, the true **Superman** had diverted and recreated their fates to serve his own vision. Where, then, did the line between god and man break? Ordinary man made history yet god planned out the future. Only a deity-in-the-flesh could generate their own personal procession of the damned.

Rose looked into each room but he read no expression on her face. Visions of visceral shock and suffering apparently didn't phase her. Jason already knew this, having her present during quite a few of his sojourns into wisdom-seeking depravity.

Yet B.G. expected a reaction: a female's natural empathy for other women, or maybe arousal if she weren't the sympathetic type. She might at least perspire a little, flick her eyes, bite her lip, make a secret fist, press her legs together...something to show emotional response. Yet she didn't sweat or flinch or blink. As if she saw through the freak show into another realm, a place better equipped to hold her rapt (raptor) attention.

Jason, however, was impressed. This was surely near to the mastery and beauty available in that horizonless place. It was almost as close as anyone on earth could reach.

God created a violent planet of disease and murder and atrocities-beyond-murder. Humanity invented the pretense of peace—the Pax-not-bloody-likely. Sweetness and light was not and had never been intended as man's natural condition. The **Superman** understood the universe's mandate and even improved upon it, not thoughtless cruelty as any predator animal employed on innocent instinct but a masterful merging of ego and evil, furthering the soul's ambition to triumph over the commonality alotted to most spirits.

It seemed as if the great philosophers preached a non-violent course. Jason knew better. He knew to *read between the lines!*

They had to cloak their messages in order to get them published at all. One had to FEEL for what they were really saying, spotting and interpreting the symbols in their language that announced *You are one of us, of the few. Do what thou wilt shall be the whole of the law.*

You are the law.

Read between the lines!

(The old God is dead; You are God now. Read between the lines! You have always been chosen.)

Professors and fools claimed it meant something else which they, in their terror and jealousy, called lofty. But they either didn't know or were too whipped to recognize it aloud.

This poetry of blood in the free form, night's blank verse/blank stare/onward into a place without horizons, without rules. Where scorpions and maggots and beating hearts fell from the sky in constant deluge. Where the grins of **Supermen** were turned up to the darkness, watching for Melanicus, the Prince of Dark Bodies, and where the possession of the damned was served up eternally for the tiger's palate.

Read Between The Lines!

"Jason?" Big Garth spoke softly, knowing his former pupil had been pushed into deep revelation. This flattered Garth, understanding it was due to the room after room of gorgeous bonsai. But now he'd taken them to the top floor which consisted of a single, large room. "This is my greenhouse."

Jason saw long silvery tables, needles and suture threads, Fogarty catheters, bipolar cauteries, vascular clips of varying sizes, jewelers forceps, microscissors, microtipped vessel dilators, microirrigators, fiberoptic lights, bone saws and bone screws, introosseous and intramedullary wires. It was awesome, not in the trite way that kids used the word, but in the way it was truly meant: overwhelming one with wonder and respect that made the head dizzy and the heart pound and the bladder leak a spontaneous sixteenth of a teaspoonful of urine.

He heard Garth gasp. Rose had wandered over to a bin marked BIO-HAZARD in a corner. (Actually at first Jason misread it as reading ALHAZRED.) She'd opened it to find all the 'scraps' of Garth's medical trash. And she'd begun nibbling.

Jason's old friend was taken a bit aback. He turned to Jason for an explanation.

"She's a ghoul," he said quite plainly, without inflection. One did not overstate truths or people might suspect the truth was being invented. Leave the drama out.

"Cairo, you said?" Big Garth asked.

Jason nodded.

"A genuine ghoul! So, is she from some bygone era? Does she harken back to the time of the pharaohs or does she personally remember Napoleon? Anything like that?"

"I have no idea," Jason admitted with a crooked smile. "Apparently it isn't cool to ask a female of any species what her true age is."

Garth chuckled. He next got a hopeful gleam in his eyes "I don't suppose she's shown you the doorway?"

But then, had she done this, Jason wouldn't be standing there to answer, would he? For who would return—if they could return—after managing the crossover?

Jason shook his head sadly. "No. Not yet."

++++++++++

"The religious enthusiast Antoinette Bouvignon de la Porte used to mix with her food excreta in order to mortify herself. The beautiful Marie Alacoque licked up with her tongue the excrement of sick people to 'mortify' herself, and sucked their festering toes. The analogy with sadism is also of interest with this connection because here also manifestations in the sense of vampirism and anthropophagy arising from disgusting appetites of the organs of taste and olfaction produce lustful feelings. This impulse to disgusting acts might well be named *koprolangnia*."

—*Psychopathia Sexualis*
Richard von Krafft-Ebing
quoted in *Sacred Sepsis*
Dr. Louis Godard and Dr. James Singer

CHAPTER
22

Jim Singer left off ever fooling around with any of his female students. They always expected him to be so far out, perverted, exotic: an American Marquis de Sade. The result of his lectures which were the most exciting on campus, packing the lecture hall with scores of kids (many not even enrolled in his class) who flocked to listen to what they perceived as a counsel of a counter-morality.

In the past, when the book first came out and the notoriety was new to him, (finally escaping the previous ostracization which had equated with social and professional euthanasia) he'd actually given in and allowed himself to be lured off by some pretty freshman. Then he'd turn out to be into the missionary position and she'd be so, like, disappointed. Dude, didn't all that bizarreness teach you anything special?

And the male students who rubbed up against him—how to let them down easily. Getting the point across that he wasn't into the whole up-the-butt thing. He fumed at rumors that

Louis and he had been lovers, seeking some archaeological validity for mutual attraction to the Hershey highway.

When Jim thought about how often, early on, their controversial work had inflamed parents or faculties into trying to get the docs' positions (no pun intended) revoked, it made him want to chuck it all in the can and retire to some dig in the most primitive and remote site available. Among the dust, relics, and quiet shadows where he could study without grievance.

Yet now he was a minor celebrity. He'd appeared on PBS, the History Channel, The Learning Channel, The Discovery Channel. His photograph had graced the covers of *Archaeology, Discover Magazine, National Geographic*. He'd even been interviewed about the recent Shit Detail murders. He had tenure (finally!) and a measure of respect from colleagues, even if it was tinged by jealousy. He never tried to tell himself that *Sacred Sepsis* didn't lean into the venue of pop science. He'd given up those feelings long ago. He knew it was popular now but his legacy for posterity might end up shelved at Half Price Books between *100 Jokes for the John* and *The History of Farts*.

(But the relics Louis and he had delivered from the catacombs would forever be in a museum with their names upon the finds. The epistle of St. Aureola, a few old trinkets, the jars, two of which had held dregs of cassia-infused vinegar and, curiously, stained yet preserved crosses carved from wood—with a figure of a dog crucified on them in place of the Christ, and the third filled with dried human offal (an examination of which had showed the person who had excreted these had, just prior to dying, eaten a meal of underripe melon, onions, and dog meat.) These things, as well as the manuscript of the priest who'd served with Cortés—telling of Temictlazolli's sickening ritual—and the skeletons, spearpoints and clay phalluses found on Mount Koshtan.)

Apparently he'd also given up that baby fat. About time, since he'd reached sixty. Since the book had come out, he'd lost fifty pounds. Not through any attempt at dieting or exercise. Maybe it was moving up the scale of self-worth that did it. He'd even chucked the smoking habit and it hadn't cost him an ounce.

The photo on the first edition of *Sacred Sepsis* showed a pudgy, boyishly awkward dweeb. The picture on the back of the most recent (last year) reprint was of a slim, almost rugged (if not good-looking at least not homely) outdoorsman. He did go to excavations at least three months out of twelve. He'd been hoping to garner enough material for a second book but lately he'd started thinking about investigating The Shit Detail and writing about the psychotic copromaniacs.

Sometimes he wondered why he'd gone for so much irreverent humor in a book which was supposed to be a scientific treatise. He used to be such a serious fellow. He used to be straight as an arrow. But Jim had changed a lot. He viewed much of his work now as a dark comedy. Not much was darker than shit, right? He got hurt too easily when he was as he once had been. This way, it told the world he didn't give a damn anymore. And if it offended some of the old guard in his field as he made money hand over fist, well he'd cry all the way to the bank.

Bathroom humor. It was universal.

Then the package arrived. He couldn't help but be very suspicious about who had sent it to him...and why.

"Have we heard back on the mystery document?" he asked Myrtle Ave, his secretary.

A few weeks ago, Jim had received an odd parcel. In it was what appeared to be a very old manuscript. Containing additional information about the 'criminal' Aureola.

It started off with a historical retelling of Emperor Theodosius The First's crisis with the city of Thessalonica. In 390, Theodosius was informed that one of his generals (some accounts said it was the governor) had been murdered during riots in Thessalonica, which was the capital of the Roman province of Macedonia in northern Greece. Furious, he gave orders that everyone within that city be massacred. The army was sent. They entered the city and shut the gates. According to most accounts, the slaughter was not complete but the soldiers did kill for three full hours. They hacked 7,000 people to death before they stopped.

The emperor had been away for a while. He returned home to Milan and left to attend services in the cathedral. But Bishop Ambrose halted him at the door, saying, "Go away. Go away, until you are ready to confess your sin and do penance for it!"

Theodosius was irked at being told he was responsible for any wrong-doing and refused for nine months to do as the Bishop commanded. He stayed away from the church, complaining about how he'd been mistreated.

"The Church of God is open to slaves and beggars," he whined. "To me it is closed, and with it the gates of heaven."

State officials pleaded with the bishop to withdraw his demands. But eventually the emperor came to the church's door. He prostrated himself on the ground, confessed with heartfelt *mea culpas*. Ambrose received him back with an equally ardent *te absolvo* and permitted the prodigal caesar to take communion.

Theodosius went to the front of the cathedral during the service, mounted the steps, preparing to present an offering at the altar. Ambrose stood in the way. He told the Roman leader, "The purple makes emperors, not priests."

Theodosius The First tucked tail to slouch back to his seat among the other worshippers.

According to this mystery document, Aureola was from Thessalonica. A little girl in 390, she barely survived the slaughter. She watched as her family was killed, living herself as a scavenger for weeks among the dead. Ambrose had sent a commission to inspect what had happened. She was taken by them to Rome. Later, those who'd taken her in died and she was homeless again. During this shattering period Aureola—now just into her teens—was abducted from the streets and put into a brothel where she was badly used. Already petite she was starved to look even younger to appeal to pederast clients. She was forced to perform in a staged sex act with a giant dog from Germany the brothelkeepers called Frater. Later she and the dog escaped. Living on the streets again, she attracted other young disaffected people who had no love for the empire. Aureola built a gang of thieves and murderers, all of whom claimed she was their patron saint, taking care of them when both Rome and new Church failed.

By now Honorius was emperor. Aureola had spies tracking down soldiers who had taken part in the Thessalonica massacre, those who had retired back to Rome. Or, in the case of those still in active duty away to some distant part of the empire—their families. She sent in these feral kids to kill in a grisly fashion, leaving messages in scripture behind to confuse the authorities into thinking the motive was Christian in-fighting.

Eventually someone talked under torture. Aureola was arrested and thrown into prison.

The document claimed that the dogs which had chased down and killed the guard responsible for feeding Frater to the girl hadn't been dogs at all, but a mob of her inner-core followers.

It was during her incarceration that she preached to those gathered outside her prison about purging to achieve purity. She struggled to make herself appear the martyr as opposed to the hardened criminal, hoping to incite a riot to free herself.

It also said that after her death an extremist group of her faithful went about at night acting as a pack of dogs, like the mob that had murdered the guard. They would select a single victim which they would then pursue, degrade, and kill in an act so bestial that eventually all of Rome was terrorized.

The group had taken refuge in the catacombs, shielded by other cult members who were only guilty of abducting people to starve and emeticize into thin salvation. Not really able to distinguish one from another, the soldiers sent by the Church had slaughtered them all. (They assumed all were destroyed, since the murders and abductions ceased immediately after.)

"Have we heard back yet on the mystery document?"

"Not yet, Jim," Myrtle replied. "The lab promised to e-mail us as soon as the carbon dating results are clear."

Jim had never regretted taking Myrtle under his wing. His colleagues had thought he was nuts (well, they'd thought this before, hadn't they?) when he showed up with this dirty adolescent girl in tow, saying she would be his secretary. She turned out to be bright and a quick-learner. And, eventually, indispensable.

210

Myrtle had never lost her thinness from her time living in the subway tunnels. She always seemed like she was about to snap in two when she stood up from her desk. She rose now and grabbed his briefcase.

"Don't forget this," she said.

He'd been about to do just that. He had to hurry off to his lecture and if he'd forgotten the briefcase, he'd have had to return for it. Jim remembered how much he used to hate teaching. But now it was fun.

"Don't know what I'd do without you," he said.

She smiled. "Thanks. It's good to be appreciated."

She did everything for him, from his correspondence with publishers and other universities, to arranging all the particulars (including student crew) for the next dig, to getting his dry cleaning out. If he'd just been attracted to her he supposed he would have asked Myrtle to marry him, despite the sizable difference in their ages. But he knew he could never do that, even if he did eventually decide he'd fallen in love with her. He'd saved her from that terrible place by promising "no strings."

"Oh! Your pager..."

He took it. "Anything else I'm forgetting?"

"Let's see..." She pretended to appraise him, looking him up and down critically. "No, you appear to be the total professor."

"Page me if the lab notifies us..."

"Will do."

"Or if the post office comes through with that trace on who might have sent it..."

"Yup. Better get going, Professor. Bet the hall's already full to bursting. They'll start howling if you don't show up soon."

++++++++++

THE SEPTIC HONEYCOMB,
TIME UNCERTAIN

Lights flashed on, motion-detector triggered, like tall-contact seeking lightning. Then they winked out, idyllic with relief, because no one wanted to see what lay on the walkways of these fungal tunnels. Not even she, perhaps. But to her more than to anyone were they dedicated. The billions of humans who'd lived since the beginning had spawned this place of concrete culverts she now walked. The dimensional result of homo sapiens' psychic fatigue. Similar to metal fatigue that used to cause planes to fall from the sky, back in the days before they realized that steel grew tired. What happened to a race when that happened? How did it crash from exhaustion?

She was underground in an endless maze of sewers, containing the accumulations of every moment when people were at their most studied unsophisticated. Where every ounce and inch of the redundant by-products of civilization ended up, unwanted by the rest of space and time. The lowest common denominator counterpart to higher spiritual realms of rosewater and star-bright auras. Underground, yet there was wind, roaring—or breaking—as it rushed over the swampy contents in the canals, rippling them slightly.

The ley lines were really nothing more than all the conduits and sewers of nature and history, connected to form a considerable network of power.

Everywhere she looked were bodies, cluttering the walkways, or slowly turning in the churning water of turbid channels which ran unchecked to infinite lengths, forward and backward, left and right. For some reason they all looked like children to her, perhaps because the vastness of the place made everything seem small. Or maybe everyone just reduced in size with death.

These people were dead, weren't they?

No, she saw many moving. They didn't move much.

Was it possible to be both dead and moving?

(I am goddess here. Does this mean I perceive them as children because they are *my* children, being those under my care or power?)

These were not the dead who had been mourned, buried, forgotten. These were not the dead who had received proper attention—depending on the rituals of their family and location.

These were those who'd been lost, unaccounted for, missing in history's action either from major catastrophe or trolling tragedy. And no matter who they had been when they'd been eliminated from the world, they became as children again (to her). The lost always returned to the most helpless state.

Old bodies, in wrinkled nakedness from having been folded into graves of burned leaves. In patches of redundantly fine silk that mocked their dry flesh. In reaper black and crone white, skulls and hip bones so frail these had gone from opaque to translucent, many hieroglyphed with fractures from both disease and cruelty.

Prime of life bodies: mothers and streetwalkers, teachers and thieves, farmers and shepherds, prophets and moneychangers and construction workers. Soldiers in every tattered uniform.

Then actual children's bodies. So many faces from milk cartons, shopping bags, fliers tacked to telephone poles and taped to the windows of convenience stores. Hundreds, thousands, no trace. Had to go somewhere: must go someplace. Nothing organic vanished.

And she knew, seeing them in the maze, in animal skins and togas, Oshkosh ByGosh overalls, play suits, patched jeans. Clothes too adult for them, in halter tops, see-through lace, tight leather. Clothes too young for them, growing limbs bursting through frayed seams. In school uniforms and Sunday best and hand-me-down worst. Naked. She knew they'd been squeezed through the gutteral conduit, becoming trapped in the temporal pathology of a species' waste. For what reason, she couldn't answer.

She walked on, lights coming on before she reached the section ahead, going out as her bare feet graced that slippery patch of path.

The bodies were damaged, visibly ruptured through the orifices. Blood and pus and silverfish. Rubbery nodules of extruded internal organs and cockroaches. Legs splayed and arms outflung as if in Raggedy Ann lotus, making even the very old seem very young. Mouths open, lips hitched sideways, ears punctured, nostrils flared as if Egyptian embalmers had been removing corpse brains with a hook, holes in the tops of heads like pop tops in cans of childhood.

She'd found herself here a lot lately, walking down the conduit, returning from somewhere else. It was the place she had to pass through to reach the world again after she'd been to...

Aralu?

She heard the plumber making his rounds, swaddled in stench-mask and rain poncho until he resembled some modern sewer rat-Phantom beneath Paris. His drain auger rumbled, its ratchety echo bouncing off the shit graffiti in void syntax on the nitered walls.

It was a machine called 'the snake' in vernacular. It ground out a long, thin, spiraling metal member to clean out obstructions. Except this one went through the plumber's fly and was attached to his groin. And as it vibrated, he grinned like there was no tomorrow.

(She thought, there isn't a tomorrow, not down here. Not for them.)

It caused her to sob, thinking *my children*. But goddess or no, there was nothing she could do. She wondered why she couldn't do anything.

She saw him, but he was so covered in unspeakable slime that she couldn't see his face. Did he have a face?

The plumber muttered, spotting clogged points everywhere, like bloodclots threatening to stick in the brain or in the heart. Except they were made of shit and grease, hair and toilet paper. He paused at this and that "child's" recumbent form, jabbing at them with the auger's tip and smiling fiercely, then making the iron cable end burrow and climb. Trying to free something up: a passage into a brilliance he thought might be eluding him, a passage out of his psychosis. He worked like a maniac, his whole body shaking with orgasm as they wept and tried feebly to squirm away.

"See? Wasn't I right? Wasn't I right about this place?" he asked them as he drilled long and deeply.

Moaning, lost little fish trying to wriggle away toward the sea. There had to be a sea. He heard it, roaring and wet in the distance. In waves. Or perhaps those were waterfalls where the sewage gathered like a sea and plunged down steep steps and breaks on the other side of one of these curved walls.

"The truth is crap," he whispered to them, almost gently, almost paternally. "Didn't I tell you?"

Groaning, shock.

213

"Stop fidgeting! I'm only trying to bore some enlightenment into you!" he commanded as his hips jerked and the auger ripped.

Every now and then he would stop, turn off the snake, rush over to a ladder suddenly revealed on one of the walls. He'd grope his way up, then cry out when he found it simply ended without meeting a manhole cover to the outside. He'd climb back down, pick up the auger, begin drilling for the source of another blockage, a hemorrhage being preferable to an embollism.

She walked on, never really passing him by for long before he showed up again. She didn't wear a veil down here, nor a blindfold, nor sunglasses. In this one place she didn't have to. She felt tears on her cheeks. Such a waste, so much void. Were they tears or did the wind just whip stray droplets from her eyes? What were tears if not empathy's moisture?

She thought of the elitist dumpers who philosophized on killing God but who swore their shit didn't stink. She watched the crazed plumber trying to translate his rage on the bodies of the lost. He assassinated not God but only the notion of a being of Light who could let Darkness happen. It was a foolish conceit, the idea that makers of shit could question the motives of deities.

He opened a teenaged kid up and pulled out the intestines, lifting them to festoon a jackal-shaped sconce with. He sang morbidly, moronically, "29 feet of guts on the wall, 29 feet of guts. You pinch a bit and down it with spit. 28 feet of guts on the wall…"

He did pop a piece into his mouth, like an afterthought, and swallowed. Then he shrieked as a cramp doubled him over. He hurriedly unfastened his trousers and squatted, auger dangling like a heavy dick, banging awkwardly against one thigh. Sweat ran down his face in grimy rivulets as he strained to force out a hard lump.

It fell behind him, rolling off the walkway's ledge to splash in the sewage trench. He made a grab for it, missed, and jumped in after it. She watched as he went down, then bobbed back up shaking strings of mucous from his head, blowing grumy bubbles out of his nostrils. He sank back down.

Chilling voices came from every body, dead but not quite motionless, drilled but dreaming. They called after him plaintively, "Don't leave us!"

They were calling for him, weren't they? For they didn't seem to actually see her, even if she was their goddess, their mother.

Was it possible they cried for somebody else?

She watched him surface and submerge again, the nihilism inherent in the shit act, the wish to restore what was lost. It was, after all, the body which gave it up. Thus these diamond-hard bricks and pools unbearably golden must be the keys to immortality.

She knew he'd never find that piece. In so much—oceans' worth, galaxies' worth—how could he? He'd climb back out as he always did. Resume his grisly work. But he'd forever be aware that he was boring what had already been squandered and jettisoned, conscious in what floated past.

++++++++++

Dorien woke up in the Volkswagen. She threw her hands up as the sun struck her in the eyes, even through the dark glasses.

She'd managed to get the car started again after it stalled at the light—as the killer approached. He'd left and she'd started it easy as pig fart pie. She drove for a while, then parked at some point and fell asleep. The night had ended. Damn! Her shoes were muddy. So she must have been out of the car at some point. She glanced in the rearview mirror and saw a splotch of blood on the side of her nose.

Where was she?

There were any one of a number of slums in this city. Which one was this?

She peered through the windshield at the nearest street sign. Corner of Rilke and Buber. Where did she know that from?

Only about a month ago some cop had been killed here. It had been all over the news until a Shit Detail crime took its place in twelve hours. This was Sheol's Ditch.

She giggled. "You mean I've been asleep and alone in an old sardine car, parked at a curb in The Ditch, and I'm still alive?"

But—mud on her shoes (she hoped that was mud) and blood on her face. What happened last night?

She noticed the grisly appendage hanging from the mirror. Gavin Parrish's perishable jewels. In the August heat they were already starting to steam and smell.

"What the hell do I want this for?"

Well, she might give them to Neela as a trophy.

"Why? The guy was diseased. And now he's dead. Dead things should return to the earth."

She took the meat down and tossed it out the window, just as cavalierly as the severed cock and balls had been thrown in by the assassin the night before. It caused her to think of Lorraine Bobbitt who'd mutilated her husband, then driven down the road a bit to throw his severed penis into a field. But that was recovered, and John Bobbitt had it successfully re-attached—enough so that he could become a minor porn star.

Gavin wouldn't be so lucky; he was dead. Maybe even eaten up by the woman Dorien had seen approaching the body after the killer had walked away. Dorien had sensed the strangeness about this female—as alien as she herself had become? Perhaps those without humanity knew one another.

She thought back to the night before. Had this woman looked up at her while bending toward Gavin's still-warm corpse? Had their eyes met briefly, sharing an understanding about the necessity of the scavenger in a world which would perish under its own waste if not for pigs and jackals and ghouls?

(oh my!)

No Bobbittisms here. Gavin's penis and balls lay in the dirt and gravel, already attracting the ants and flies of full-blown summer. Maybe a couple of crows circled overhead, round and round, like the proverbial and ad nauseum circle of life.

Dorien thought about her dream. The underground tunnels where the lost ended up. Was Gavin there now, lying in sludge alongside missing children far more innocent than himself, awaiting a visit by the plumber?

Maybe not. She didn't get the feeling this was a place for the evil to be punished. It was more of a...what? A purgatory, a dimensional sewer trap for those time accidentally lost its grip on.

On the other hand, she was sure (without understanding how she knew) that Gavin hadn't ended up in Aralu. That required a special pass from the goddess of shit. She wished she'd given him that, but she hadn't. She'd witnessed his murder and knew she'd had nothing to do with it.

There might be many hells. What had that book said in the introduction?

There were more religions in the past that had underworlds but didn't have heavens.

+++++++++++

"We repaired the hole, having been informed that in the adjoining room, the one selected for his activities, there was a pierced chair and beneath it a chamber pot we had been busy filling for four days and in which there must have been at least a dozen large turds. Our man arrives. He was an elderly tax farmer of about seventy years. He shuts the door, goes straight to the pot he knows to be brimming with the goodies he has ordered for his sport. He takes up the vessel and, seating himself in an armchair, passes a full hour gazing lovingly at all the treasure whereof he has been made the proprietor; he sniffs, inhales, he touches, he handles, seems to lift one turd out after another in order to contemplate them the better. Finally become ecstatic, from his fly he pulls a nasty old black rag which he shakes and beats with all his might; one hand frigs, the other burrows into the pot and scoops out handfuls of divine unction. He anoints his tool, but it remains as limp as before. There are moments, after all, when Nature is so stubborn that even the excesses we most delight in fail to awake a response."

—*The 120 Days of Sodom*
The Marquis de Sade
quoted in *Sacred Sepsis*
Dr. Louis Godard and Dr. James Singer

CHAPTER
23

SHEOL'S DITCH,
SIX MONTHS AGO

The party showed no signs of winding down.

That wasn't to say that some of its members didn't become too spent to leap to the next game. For them it was possible to rest, recupe, and indulge in voyeurism while others labored.

In a corner of the room was the tattoo genius, Boreolo, who paid all sexes to let him fuck and intaglio them, both activities applied strictly to the face. (He examined them thoroughly beforehand, to assure himself that they were clean and smoothly unmarked below the jawline first. What they did afterward to the rest of their bodies was their own business.) Most of them were homeless, unemployed, starving. When he was through, all of them could make a tidy living charging gawkers two-to-five bucks a glimpse. You'd see them in the park, on the piers, with lint-frazzled sheets draped over their heads, but pulled forward a bit because breathing was hard for some of them once Boreolo had his way. The folks in line would tiptoe up with their proffered sweaty sawbucks, getting a nauseating peak, lurching away with wild eyes, clutching their guts and groins.

Tonight, of course, Boreolo hadn't been required to pay for his canvas. It had been supplied him by the same benefactors who brought all the treats to the party they sponsored. His scrawny backside jiggled and became taut, jiggled and became taut. The runaway lay beneath him, face obscured and revealed in momentary increments as the man rhythmically thrust himself into the quivering mouth. The rest, visible from the neck down, was thin and slack. The anesthetic and whatever pain managed to leech through the soporific fog ensured the boy wouldn't get an erection of his own. There was the smell of burning flesh from the hot needles, the tiny buzzsaw skree of whirring blades, the scrape of very slender scalpel against bone. Boreolo's hands worked faster than his cock. Every now and then a muffled groan escaped the boy's plungered lips.

Jason marveled at how Boreolo could do this without excitedly slipping with the instruments. But he never missed a beat, made no mistakes in his vision for the boy's mask. A tray sat nearby with antiseptics and antibiotics, so the final product would heal properly. Boreolo wanted walking, talking galleries—not fatalities.

In a cubicle behind a translucent gauze curtain of shocking pink, Big Garth's girls were available to the party. Recently he'd patented a white noise machine. Those suffering from chronic insomnia sometimes used such machines to help filter the outside world and create a drone to even their stress with. Traditional ones employed tapes of surf, waterfalls, rain. But Garth Listo had just begun to market one for the underground, with tapes of whimpering dogs, crying babies, screaming women.

But he'd been known for years as another master of the makeover, some of his tools larger by necessity, others with points or wires so fine they almost escaped the naked eye. Even though the man who feigned the samurai persona was never called a pimp to his face, he made more money peddling crunched-up ass than most of the state's crack dealers raked in. Some of his subjects he acquired from an abduction ring that traveled through Canada, the U.S., and Mexico. But he also met whole runaways at bus stops and on street corners, bringing them home to his do-it-yourself grind-em-up and turn-em-out business. He did such a booming trade, he'd had to hire assistants!

But he was capable of producing stumps with ends in the shapes of roses, an origami of bone splinter and folded flaps of abbreviated skin. No mere purveyor of random scars was he. The appeal of his stable was to connoisseurs of more than simple trainwreck erotica. His customers—many of them influential people everywhere in the world—paid amply for the gen-teel human bonsai, manicured of the extraneous limb, artificially turned to a concept of microcosm sexuality. Not mere lovers of the quirky blunt, they appreciated the beauty of the ends of the stumps themselves, turned as if on a potter's wheel, sculpted, *blossomed*.

The political of the world (when in private), knowing of his penchant for the samurai pose, often referred to Garth Listo not as a chainsaw procuror but a Japanese gardener. And his blank-eyed females were amputee geisha.

Jason had brought Rose to the party and was now among the throng who'd been watching Boreolo work. He saw her across the room, sitting by herself, aloof, ignoring the creatures who crept up to her to flirt. She usually dressed in such a way as to hide the long veils of flesh that hung from her torso. It had been completely necessary to do so as the Caves traveled the world and then as she came through immigration as the bride of an American former GI. It had taken every connection Jason knew to keep her from having to undergo an inspection. And, once back in the city, he'd had a pri-vate doctor falsify documents, claiming she'd passed all the physical tests that immigrants had to have. Grade A human. She could never be seen on the street unless she wore a long-sleeved, loose robe that hung to her ankles. Fortunately, being from Cairo, it could be claimed she was a proper Moslem and preferred to cover herself fully for this reason.

But tonight, Rose had worn only a long coat which she removed after coming into the house. Jason wanted to show her off. He knew the word had gotten around about her true background. People were curious. And as far as people in their criminally-based circle went, it didn't hurt his reputation a bit to have a trophy wife like this one on his arm. Who else could boast a ghoul?

They had all heard about the desecration of recent graves in the news. Of cadavers disappearing from morgues, hospitals, and funeral homes. And she came in handy for disposing of anyone Jason had been hired to kill.

He wondered if a ghoul had been the reason nobody'd ever found Jimmy Hoffa's body.

Convinced she could take care of herself if anybody got closer than she liked, Jason swung away from Boreolo's spectacle. He remained suitably impressed as always but he'd seen it before. He passed the curtain where the girls flapped short meat flippers and undulated lumps of squat marigolds.

"You resting, Mr. Cave?" a tall, shaven-headed woman asked him. Red fetal tissue boots went all the way up to her wide hips, clinging to the hard muscles of her legs like wet Play Dough.

"I never need to rest, Simone," he replied. "I just find observation of another's invention to be stimulating."

He studied her, nude save for the boots and a matching strip of leather about her chunky waist. He was more casually attired himself: jeans, muscle shirt, Doc Martens, brass knucks elegantly revealed above the breast pocket like a monogrammed handkerchief. He glanced about for a mirror to see himself in but the one across the room had several people primping in front of it.

"You seem to have acquired something new in your repertoire." He pointed at the black penis skin-grafted to her white pubes.

"A doctor on Jaspers Street who sidelines in pirated organs did it for me. Hasn't been any tissue rejection so far," she explained, holding it in her hand to examine it. "It's so big and thick that, even if I can't crank it up, it's a formidable truncheon and stocking stuffer. It's never exactly soft. Sort of completes the wardrobe, don't you think?"

Jason's head bobbed up and down sagely. They looked up as two men with heavy gloves began laying down a wide coil of razor wire. At the opposite end a couple, the woman's hands tied to the man's feet, were about to be forced to crawl a gauntlet through it. Ah, it must be one of Everson's little diversions. Known as the Vigilante of Love, Everson created amazingly entertaining labyrinths of torture, designed especially for couples and out of which few ever emerged alive…and none unscathed. Jason recalled the cage of bones the man had erected not long ago, every bone end sharpened. A couple crawling through had first been separated from each other by a bone partition, and then—as the additional bone walls began to come down in sequence, making their individual spaces narrower and narrower—were soon separated even from themselves.

"Reminds me of something Camus wrote in a little item called *The Plague*," Jason said and then quoted, "'…Rieux believed himself to be on the right road—in fighting creation as he found it…'"

"Man, Cave, you should have been a professor," Simone said. Without looking, she raised a stiletto heel and brought it down on a finger of the slave on the floor, hooded and suitably leashed. She ground the heel against it until she heard an audible crackle and pop.

The slave didn't scream, not even a meager whimper infiltrated the rubber appliance over the mouth.

Jason noticed the dyke's slave wasn't really on the floor but on a low, wheeled cart. As Simone tugged slightly on the leash, the little wagon rolled an inch or two, the wheels also making no noise at all. She kept her accouterments well-oiled, so it would seem. He wondered if the woman in restraints was dead. In another room was a guy dragging around a dead dog on a chain. It had obviously been deceased for several days and left shreds of its greening self as he yanked it from place to place.

"I *am* a professor," Jason replied. "My students complain I never grade on a curve."

"Hopefully you enforce their claims into silent ones," said the dominatrix as she nudged the tits of the supine slave with the pointed toe of her boot. The nipple on the right breast wore a ring with a penny nail dangling from it. The nipple on the left one was missing, replaced with a single teardrop ruby.

"I like noise," Jason replied, spreading his large, scarred hands. "Every shriek is a metaphysical revolution."

Big Garth emerged from behind the vulva-colored curtain. He slapped both Jason and Simone on their sturdy shoulders, the tattoo on the back of his hand (not Boreolo's artwork) was of a Willendorf Venus—one of the very few exceptions to an otherwise all-Japanese motif. It was one of those fertility symbols with the tits, big belly and hips. Only the necessities. Not much of a head and certainly no face, no arms and legs to get in the way. He nodded, wriggled fingers, the nails of which were so eternally blood-stained it resembled polish.

"Speaking of Camus," Garth added, "he also said, 'Metaphysical rebellion is a claim...against the suffering of life and death and a protest against the human condition both for its completeness, thanks to death, and its wastefulness, thanks to evil...'"

Simone absent-mindedly scratched beneath the black dick, as if it had balls. "Sounds like psychosexual hyperchondria to me. Kind of *my dick hurts, therefore I am.*"

"More of an extrospective satyriasis," Jason argued, "humping anything that farts or bleats."

"Everything's a sheep to you," Big Garth joked.

Jason grinned. "We're all seeking an animal to merge with, and a refuge for that hybrid."

"If such a refuge were to exist, I'd be the first to hand over to the devil at the door every man, woman and child on this stinking world so's I could get in," Simone affirmed. Her eyes flicked from wall to wall as if half-expecting this offer to cause just such a passage to open, pluming flesh-colored fog and reeking of plenty of free, passive pussy.

"And every time I get an invitation to a party like this, I can't help but hope that when I get to the door, it'll open on the bloody Kyoto of my dreams," Garth agreed.

"But seriously, Cave," Simone said. "I would think you'd found your animal to merge with. Not meaning to insult your lovely bride. And does she have nothing to say of this fabled place we all crave?"

Jason looked away, toward Rose sitting across the room, surrounded by admirers. Someone had gingerly plucked flecks off the razor wire for her and she nibbled it like popcorn drenched with too much butter.

How could he admit that he'd never had sex with Rose? They wouldn't understand. He'd wed her hoping to be shown the threshold. But, as yet, the only glimpses he'd had of that extreme paradise had been when he was a little boy. He'd come to believe, despite her resemblance to the supernatural female in the hellish vision from the dead Iraqi's head, that Rose was (ghoul or not) a creature from this plane only. Just a rare specimen from a predator species, whose major claim to interest was the ability to vomit up new parts for herself: a bile starfish.

But, well, she'd turned out to be good for business. This was why he put up with her disdain. She'd only married him to leave Egypt, wanting to go to America and fresher haunting grounds. He hadn't pressed the issue of a husband's rights. He'd seen how she could take care of herself.

So he didn't comment, not because he didn't also pine for such a butcher's cloister—which at least he'd seen when none of them had. He just felt it was pointless. As reachable as it was (not), it might as well be a figment of the libertine's mind, the chimera groin at the end of a decomposing rainbow.

"How's that greenhouse gift I brought you?" he asked Garth, deciding to change the subject.

"Got to admit she's got verve," replied Garth. He turned to Simone. "Can you believe it? He leaves a quad on my doorstep, veins and arteries tied off with nary a drip, like he'd done this all his life. My assistants are med students and were they jealous! And that thing with the eyes, stroke of pure genius. Your bitch on the cart there with the jewel nip? You should see how my patrons go for black sapphire pupils. Stars in them. Those stones must have cost a fortune. And forking the tongue? Inspirational without being the least over the top. You ought to check her out, Simone. She's in the last crib on the left. Free tonight. Best advertising is word of mouth, I always say."

Simone wrapped the leash of her carted slave to a coffee table leg, like tying a horse at a hitching post, and parted the curtain.

"Generous of you," B.G. told Jason.

"Waste not, want not," he replied.

Jason recalled the night he'd found the woman, not long after he'd moved back with Rose to Sheol's Ditch. She'd been injured in her car, wrapped around a telephone pole, legs crushed in the little Italian tin can convertible. No internals though. She'd thought he was a brave fireman, pulling her out just as the flames erupted. Hearing the gas tank go up as it covered the sound of his hearty laughter. She'd thought he was a paramedic, winding careful tourniquets to keep her from bleeding to death. She'd sobbed in his arms, in agony and shame, knowing she'd lost everything in her bowels and bladder when the car skidded out of control and then slammed into the pole. Worse than helpless. She'd thought he was an angel, interceding where only heaven could, gently cutting off her ruined clothes, bathing her with cooling water he carried cupped in his own two hands.

Her rude awakening had been scrumptious. He hadn't used pain killers as both Boreolo and Simone did, depending instead upon the state of shock she was in to provide a haze across her mind. As a matter of fact, it was miraculous she hadn't *died* of shock, especially after he fucked her, then sawed off the damaged legs followed by the merely bruised arms, fucking her again.

He'd given the throwaway parts to Rose who'd not come into the room once. His wife had stared at him, unblinking, probably unimpressed with him as she ever was. But what the hell, she'd only married him for the green card, right? Some guys complained their foreign brides weren't the slaves they'd expected. Boy, was that right.

The woman decided he really was a demon, and that she must have perished in the accident. She screamed for forgiveness for whatever sins had landed her in hell. Jason only dumped her on Big Garth Listo's stoop after he'd finished with her, the Hieronymous Bosch novelty wearing off like the shine on the kind of jewelry you could buy from guys on the corner. He'd done it to tickle his mentor as Garth saw how Jason left a bone showing through flesh on each stump, dressing its end with a fancy scalloped paper crown like Thanksgiving turkeys bore.

"Did you wish to meet the ladies?" Garth offered, gesturing to the bonsai garden beyond the pink gauze. "It's an all new seraglio since the last time you saw. Save for the one little gardenia bush you gave me."

Jason shook his head, seeing Simone in a primrose crinoline diaphane, dicking some girl who was no more than a turtle on its back, black apparatus longer and thicker than any appendage the vessel had. He began to walk away, hearing Big Garth quote again from Camus to perhaps no one in particular, "'Convinced of their condemnation and without hope of immortality, they decide to murder God.'"

Jason pondered that. And what of genius in the beast? Surely Garth knew that it wasn't that God was dead but that He practiced copraphiliac cunning, making Him to shine with rhoid stigmata, and then inventing the world for Him to hunt in?

This was the true **Superman**, divorced from society's mouth-zippered mask and manacles, humiliated no more by original sin, not circumcized for the desecrations of his fathers. He was the one who truly remade himself, fashioned after not some cartoon of crucifixion but an icon of prehistoric purgation. Out with everything not of pleasure, not of immediate gratification. Godzilla gangbang, T. Rex huge, flattening by radioactive fuck the jungles and the diorama Tokyos (or, better still, the crotch-cosmic Bangkoks). Frankenstein's monster shaking the planet by its short pubic hairs, not afraid of the world because he won't be around for doomsday, since his bags are packed and a special doorway awaits.

He didn't obsess, didn't hermit himself away in a rathole apartment surrounded by newspaper clippings and a dozen stolen TV sets all tuned to the news. The millennium's arrival hadn't meant diddly to him. He Juggernauted through apocalypse every day, blood-bathed through *Revelations* nights, understood implicitely how holocaust was an hourly venture, requiring a profundity of animal animosity.

Some synapses never rested and did not burn out. They insisted upon attention to their constant firing, like a rapist who repeatedly nicks with a knife the already purpled surface, so his victim won't fall asleep between outrages.

Some nightmares didn't fade with dawn but ingratiated themselves, as an abusive yet charming lover one cannot bring themselves to shut out.

Jason thought of the Camus line he'd quoted Simone. "Rieux believed himself to be on the right road—in fighting creation where he found it..."

If Jason couldn't fuck and kill it, sodomize and eat it, puke and shit it out to make the earth and mortar of his own planet, he didn't want it around.

He spotted a woman being auctioned off in the library where every tome was a holy book or collection of nursery rhymes that someone had masturbated in, spit in, or defecated in. The woman was a little older than the wide-eyed innocents usually swept here. She was an Asian if the almond-shaped eyes were to be believed. But she was a total albino: snow skin, platinum hair, pale cherry touchstone eyes. Her limbs were like white jade, her small breasts moonstones surmounted by pearl papillae. The curls at the juncture of her thighs resembled the froth on new milk. There wasn't a single freckle, not a solitary soiling blemish.

She was too clean, too perfect. Jason found himself tasting thick salt, and tasting copper as he chewed the inside of his cheek. Salivating like Pavlov's dogs, trained in a sadist's cellar, drooling every time they heard a bone dislocate or a ligament snap apart.

He pulled a thick wad of bills from his wallet from having done a clean-up on some gangster's cheating wife. Added the heavy gold belt buckle he'd taken from the wife's paramour who he'd also diced. Threw in the ten carat emerald ring he'd been keeping in his asshole to warm him and keep him sharp.

He led the woman upstairs and force-fed her a massive dose of laxative. There in a bed swampy with senna and ipecacuanha, himself feeling frisky on Ecstasy, he wasn't interested in passing her some date rape ether. He preferred nails and teeth to the passive blow-up doll. He invented some new position invasively tracheal, doing a convulsive set of purgative sexual manuevers like an epileptic kama sutra. He studiously focused on censoring the cathexis, a desire concentration as he practically swam in her supreme despoilment, no speck of the lily left about her, flux even washing across those pink diamond eyes to smudge them out.

And he thought about what it would take that he'd not already tried (both in this incarnation and as Crowley and as the line of sorcerers Crowley had claimed spiritual descent from) to conjure up the key to that smoky

Eden, where every barbaric offense to a jealous god could be offered up, the risen Atlantis of debauchery where the wanton crapulence was so outrageous that if God wasn't already dead, this would finish Him off. Extreme magic was always reputed to take sacrifices and acts of soul-saturnalia.

How many beating hearts had Simone, Everson, Big Garth, and Boreolo (and all the other serious sociopathic misanthropes at this ruthless get-together) yanked from living chests, offering them for the meagerest hope of opening a portal into that infernal utopia? How many throats had they slit or fistfuls of duodenum necklaces pulled from steaming bellies, calling upon the Beasts of the Twilight or priapic incubuses or ancient tentacled mentors to lead the way to an idealized death-lewd wonderland?

Jason didn't know, had lost count of even his own attempts at conjuring up the celestial-cidal window which had been open to him so long ago—and so briefly. But he knew as he rutted in the albino's indecent sea, lathered in her catharsis as she died from cramps, dehydration and drowning, that somehow in this act he'd come as close as he ever had to an actual sum-moning. He'd almost had a soiled epiphany, of a woman lifting her skirts to reveal what composed the lower half of her, dissolving beyond his reach. Before, what was left of the woman in Cairo had swirled around his feet like an omen, an invitation, a warning. And, unlike any other specimen of man save the **Superman**, Jason hadn't recoiled in disgust and fear. He'd fallen to his knees and embraced it by the handfuls. As he did now with the albino, even though she was flesh, not shit. Even though she was just a dead woman, unable to offer passage.

++++++++++

"punkslapping
mobsucking
gravypissing poppa..."

—from 'F is for foetus(a'
e.e. cummings
quoted in *Sacred Sepsis*
Dr. Louis Godard and Dr. James Singer

CHAPTER
24

Dorien heard laughter as she walked down the hallway of the Science Building.

"Sounds like somebody's doing stand-up," she said to herself. "How come my professors aren't funny?"

This college was more expensive than the one she'd attended last year. They could afford to pay a tenured comedian.

"Is that where I'm going? Does Dr. Singer thrill his students with scat?"

Pauses. Then eruptions of giggles and guffaws. More pauses. She could hear a lone voice during these, muffled through the walls. A rising, falling cadence of somebody accustomed to frequent public speaking. Someone with confidence.

She found the room the author of *Sacred Sepsis* was scheduled to be lecturing in, discovered by peering through the door that it was he, and slipped inside to take a position at the back of the room. The place was packed, other people standing at the back or sitting in the aisles, some taking notes, many too engrossed to do anything but listen.

Damn, were all these his students? Or had a few sneaked in—as she had?

"Now let's progress to another myth," said the older but rather handsome man at the front of the room. His hair was gray and he wore it long, even though this shaggy affectation was out-of-style. He was thin except for a slight paunch at the midsection, and it made her frown, smelling something signature inside him. Yes, he was a sick man. Did he know it yet?

He didn't sit behind the available desk but kept on his feet, bouncing lightly and then taking off to pace with more energy than she was sure he ought to be capable of. But this was what some people did: kept going until the last second possible.

"There is an old Jicarilla Apache story," he told the class, smiling with just one side of his mouth. "Once upon a time there was a wicked creature named Kicking Monster. Kicking Monster had four daughters who were the only women in that early era of the world to have vaginas. That's to say they looked like women but really were only vaginas. There were vaginas fastened to the walls of their house, with square nails and the primitive equivalent of staples and an ancient super glue made from spider webs and coyote snot. But these particular four vaginas had all the other female things and limbs, having faces besides."

Male students snickered and a few of the young women raised their eyebrows, perhaps as a precursor to moral outrage.

"I'm not making this up," Dr. Singer explained, seeing a mind or two starting to shut down. "This is legend. You may consider it shit if you want to, much of what passes for truth is. Take it with a grain of salt as you should everything any institution of higher learning attempts to teach you. But remember: if you use too much salt, you'll end up constipated."

He stroked his chin with his fingers. "Where was I? Ah! Just hearing about these vagina darlings brought men from everywhere, out of the woodwork, up from canyons, down from mountain tops, away from the flocks of sheep by the lakeside—but we won't go there. The men would arrive at the house, tongues hanging out and throbbing, only to find Kicking Monster who would boot them inside. They were never seen again.

"Along came a handsome young hero, so virile he had more hanging out than his tongue. His name was Killer-of-Enemies. No, kid. I see you wrote that down wrong," Singer said, squinting and turning his head to peek—or pretend to peek—at the notes of a boy in the front row. "Not Killer-of-Enemas...*enemies*! Good. Yes, I read upside down. That's what taking your Metamucil every day will do for you.

"Now our hero had declared he'd fix that rascally Kicking Monster. And Killer-of-Enemies fools Kicking Monster (the myth doesn't say how, maybe next term I'll make something suitably cinematic up), and gets into the house without the customary monster-foot-in-the-ass. The vagina girls hurry up to him, fluttering and fawning over his biceps, hoping for some hero action."

Dorien scanned the audience, froze when she saw a familiar face down front. Annet, sitting with a girlfriend as emaciated as she was, hunching and shivering shoulders in apparent delight to be so close to the author of the book she'd left for Dorien. You'd have thought the old guy was a rock star or a guru. Or just a man who really knew his shit.

Dorien moved behind some other people standing at the back, just in case her sister turned around.

"But hero that he was, he only asked them, 'What happened to the other guys? The ones who got kicked in here? There've been thousands, so it's not like they're all in the bathroom. And don't try telling me they left because I have my sources. Everyone agrees the men were booted in here by Kicking Bitch outside.'

"'Oh, we ate them,' the daughters admitted. 'That's our favorite thing to do. We're very oral.'

"They started to kiss Killer-of-Enemies, rubbing themselves up against him, the temperature in the house rising. But then he shouted, 'Get back! That's not how you use a vagina!'

"The girls sulked prettily. 'Well, what is the right way?' they all wanted to know.

"'First you have to eat this medicine made from sour berries,' he said. How lucky he just happened to have some of these very same berries in his pockets. Four different kinds—one for each daughter, I guess. 'The vagina's sweet this way.'

"Well, the girls ate the berries which puckered up their lips. But they kept eating because he told them to and he was handsome and this was long before women knew better than to listen to any damned man preach about what constituted femaleness, as if he couldn't possibly have an ulterior motive. They popped more and more into their mouths, lips parting wide and then constricting with each tartly succulent, full-to-bursting fruit. Eventually they couldn't chew anymore—even if they could swallow." And here Dr. Singer waggled his eyebrows suggestively. "The acid berries dissolved their strong teeth, leaving their mouths undefended and no threat. They couldn't possibly eat up a man this way.

"And Killer-of-Enemies said to them, 'Now you're ready.'"

After the laughter died down, Singer nodded. "Okay, those of you who really do happen to belong to this class need to read Chapters 9 and 10 in your texts. Those of you who aren't students but sneaked in here for a cheap thrill, goeth out into the world and buyeth my book."

Dorien realized people were starting to leave. And since Annet didn't happen to belong here, she and her friend were already halfway to the door. Dorien might be seen.

She hunched down behind a tall teenager and slipped out into the hall. Annet was probably only ten feet behind her. Dorien ducked her head and turned through the door of the ladies room.

But they followed, still talking excitedly about Dr. Singer's lecture.

Dorien hustled into a stall and closed the door. Should she put her feet up so they couldn't tell she was in there? She tried to do this but it wasn't as easy as it looked in the movies.

Why do that, though? It wasn't as if they were making sure there was no elsc in the bathroom. They weren't talking about state secrets. And Dorien doubted her sister could recognize her by her shoes and ankles alone. She'd just stand there and wait for them leave.

But, damn it, she wanted to catch the professor and talk to him before he left the building. Not that she was certain he was going to go somewhere else. Maybe he had another class coming in. It had been luck on her part that she'd made it to this one. The man's secretary had been about to step out of the office herself when Dorien arrived. She'd stayed long enough to tell her where Dr. Singer could be found—until 11:00.

Dorien had thanked her. But she'd done it while keeping a good distance, wrinkling her nose.

"Isn't he amazing?" Annet was saying to her companion.

The two women had gone into the toilets on either side of Dorien's.

"I could listen to him forever," the other agreed. "But I wish he'd talk more about Aureola. So much of his lectures is made up of unsuitable, unrelated details."

"That's just to appeal to outsiders. It throws the uninitiated off," Annet explained. "Same's true of any genuine apocryphal text. The infidels take it at face value. Isn't meant for them so what the hell, right?"

Dorien heard them as Annet pulled up a short skirt and pulled down death panties of petroleum-based fabric, and the other girl slid denim jeans. Further down, at the end of the stalls, somebody else moaned as inaudibly as possible with cramps, tights like a black snake coiled around her ankles.

Apparently they didn't care if anybody overheard them. The sign of the true believer.

The groaner pulled her tights back up, flushed, and left. Two more girls came into the room, one taking a stall, the other fussing with her hair and lipstick in the mirror.

Dorien huffed. How long was this going to take? She knew both were bulemic. Such acts normally took place at home, at a secure location. It wasn't as if they had that much business to do in here. *Leave, already!*

She heard Annet and her friend mumbling the same litany Dorien had heard Annet say in the bathroom at their parents' house. "I purge myself of evil thoughts and the evil world. I make myself an empty vessel for you. I make myself a pure child again." Said in babydoll voices, no less. Dorien thought she'd puke. She couldn't, of course. Not only did she not have the interior stuff to do the deed but she didn't dare—or they would hear her.

Not that Annet would be likely to recognize her sister by the sound of her vomiting.

The last two to enter the bathroom left. Shift change, three more came in. Then *they* left. Still Annet and her friend stayed. Obviously this was like Mass for them. A social and religious event not to be rushed.

Well, Dorien was tired of it. She needed to hurry or she might miss her chance to talk to Dr. Singer. And *that* was important.

Dorien twitched a smile, fanned the fingers of both hands into something like a sunburst. And then jumped up to stand on the toilet seat, hunkering down just enough that her head and shoulders didn't show above the top ledge of the stall.

The toilets began to overflow.

She heard Annet and the friend and whoever else was in there cry out in disgusted dismay. They were hurrying now, damn it.

Dorien waited until they were gone, water gushing over her shoes, then she opened the stall door and left. People had gathered at the far end of the hall, watching the water pour out of the ladies bathroom. She spotted the professor with them so she made her way toward him.

++++++++++

Jim had just put all his papers and books together and was about to head out. He saw several young women come screaming out the the ladies room and observed the water chasing them.

"Professor!" Myrtle came down the hall, waving, smiling her quirky little smile when she saw the flood. "I'm glad I caught you! A man called, says he just arrived from Europe? I gave him an appointment to talk to you. It's in an hour..."

He'd turned away from the flood and toward his secretary. But then something made him look back. At another young woman who was wading out. She wore dark sunglasses. She seemed to flutter at the edges, like very old film some cinematic preservation society was trying desperately to reclaim.

And all of a sudden he was feeling the oppression of that dreamed-of underground network. Tunnels so far below, not hell/ near hell/smell of black shit. And a roaring as of thunder trapped somewhere...or of waterfalls.

He thought he'd been turned upside down. His stomach lurched and he experienced a spasm inside his gut which curled and then contracted, curled and then contracted.

Myrtle followed his gaze. She shuddered involuntarily although she couldn't have said why. She'd met the woman at the office earlier and had no such reaction.

"Dr. Singer?" this young woman with her eyes hidden said, walking up with her hand out. "I am Dorien Warmer…"

Jim's own hand stretched out on extinct. Their fingers met. And now Dorien suffered her own epiphany. For a moment she was back within that underground maze. She saw her lost people and the faceless, evil plumber. Pipes rattled and there was a rumble deep and below.

She realized it was actually coming from underneath the floor.

"Run!" somebody shouted, and then someone else picked it up. "Run! Get out of the building fast as you can!"

Myrtle grabbed Jim's arm and began pulling him toward the front door of the Science Building. He reached back for Dorien but almost couldn't see anything for his terror. He flashed back on the catacombs exploding, caving in. He didn't even realize it was Myrtle he picked up as he ran toward the door. In his mind it was Louis again.

But afterward he came back to himself. He'd hurried with everyone else into the next building over and climbed stairs to be on higher ground. They pressed against the windows on all the upper floors to look out. It seemed as if all the sewage in the city was being forced up through a rent in the floor of the Science Building. Kids laughed nervously and covered their mouths against the stench which permeated even the walls and glass of—where were they?—oh, the Engineering Building.

Myrtle smiled as he glanced down at her.

"Man, I thought I was saving you," she said, eyes bigger even that they usually were, shining with downright girlish awe. "Pretty good sprinting and lugging for an old prof."

He and Myrtle stood with about ten others, up on the fourth floor. God, he hadn't actually carried her up several flights of stairs, had he? Surely he'd gotten them into an elevator and then set her down.

Most of the kids standing with them were female. They all grinned at him like he was some sort of Hollywood action-film god. He figured they were wondering, gee did he take vitamins or Viagra or what? How embarrassing. And he had to just hold his breath, waiting for the heart attack which must inevitably follow.

They heard sirens and knew help would be there any minute. How could such a thing have happened?

"Did you see if the woman with the sunglasses got out?" Jim asked his secretary.

Myrtle shrugged. "No, I didn't. I'm sorry."

"Look!" one of the young women at the window cried. She pointed outside to the appalling tide of foulness which still spewed from the doors and windows of the Science Building. "I can't believe it!"

Jim stared. The one with the sunglasses was floating out upon the mass of sludge, borne aloft like a very steady surfer, upright upon the rippling current. Rats swam around her, washed up from the sewers. She didn't seem to even be touched by it, her shoes and the hem of her dress only being wet from the water which had overflowed first. She was like a goddess, that's what she was. Botticelli's Venus coming up to the beach standing in her shellboat.

Jim heard several of them sing out at once.

"Oh, my God…that's my sister!"

"She's Aureola! She must be!"

"It's a miracle, that's what it is!"

"It's a sign!"

Quivering, these people dropped to their knees.

Jim's jaw dropped open. He gaped at them. Was this a joke? Could it be possible that Aureola had a modern cult following?

He looked back outside. The woman riding the crest of sewage was there one moment. Then the next she disappeared, as if she'd dissolved into it.

++++++++++

The tribe of Nyakyusa have a death ritual in which they liken dirt with insanity: being that those who are out of their wits consume filth. Apparently there are—in their estimation—two forms of insanity. The first is given by God; the second happens to you if you don't perform your required rituals—a terrible thing, since any sense you have of what is good and what is bad is a knowledge arising out of those very same rituals.

The Nyakyusa define filth as anything to do with shit, mud, frogs, froggy shit. They equate the insane person eating their detritus as consuming death itself, the waste being the dead body.

Ritual keeps you sane and alive but insanity (from not performing the sanctified duties) brings shit, mud, frogs, etc., and a form of death. And if that's what you want, then you must be crazy.

This tribe has strong rules which must be followed to keep from touching bodily waste which they consider to be hazardous and toxic material. They call it *ubanyali* and it is basically derived from anything to do with sex, also the female particulars of menstruation and child-birth. It comes from dead bodies, including the blood of enemies.

Yet the people of the Nyakyusa welcome filth during the ritual for mourning those very same dead. They broom it onto the grieving. They symbolically eat the waste to sort of immunize themselves against later going insane. All the rest of the time they avoid it and think anyone who doesn't is mad. Yet when faced with the death of a relative or friend, they will say they have consumed this same anathema, just as the insane do, so that they will be able to safeguard their sanity.

So, to recap, madness is a penalty for those who do not perform their rituals. Yet the tribal members will go insane if they fail to do this ritual of consuming filth but, paradoxically, they will remain sane if they do the ritual.

Odd as it may seem, the Nyakyusa are not a partically stressed-out people.

—Sacred Sepsis
Dr. Louis Godard and Dr. James Singer

CHAPTER 25

He'd heard them whispering when they believed he was in another part of the house.

"Between the two of us, baby, we can do this ourselves."

"Yeah, what does he know you don't? You've seen everything on the table. You know every procedure."

"And you can keep the girls in line."

"Shock does most of that. But, well, it does help that they see me as one of their own."

"Yeah, but you never had that brain-scrambling problem."

"I'm from good, strong stock. Nothing phased me much before—and nothing after either."

"I love you, baby."

"I love you, too, sugar."

Big Garth fumed. So his top assistant had been going behind his back, wooing one of the geishas, getting it on with her and plotting to start a competing business.

He thought about bursting into the room and throttling that med school punk with his bare hands while she watched, helpless to do a damned thing about it until it came her turn. He wanted to carry her up to the operating room and show her how much she had yet to lose—and just how long it could take to die with a little bit removed at a time.

But he managed to stay restrained, creeping downstairs to avail himself of one of the fine blades on the walls. He'd just showered and only wore a simple robe. No armor, no uniform pieces, no weaponry.

Big Garth clenched his fists as he made it to the first floor. He'd been just about to call Jason with a curious proposition. Jason had told him about the frost between himself and his Cairo-born wife. So, what if they put Rose in underground theater, pruned yet self-renewing? She'd be a hit, a smash, a legend inside of a month. And Jason could garner some husbandly revenge for having been frozen out.

Shame, that. Had to be some interesting meat, with those flesh veils trailing off her. What would it be like to screw her? Bizarre. One or two steps above an animal and only one or two steps—maybe—below demigod.

But now this. Hell, Garth was master here. He couldn't let this measely stump-grinder undermine his authority.

Garth had only started to look around to choose a blade when his cell phone rang. He pulled it from a silken pocket, glad it hadn't done that as he stood outside the geisha's door upstairs. The conspirators would've heard it and known he'd just learned their plans.

"*Moshi-Moshi*," he said curtly.

"Garth…"

It was Jason. Speak of the devil.

"B.G., listen. I got a tip two seconds ago. You know your assistant, the one you said yesterday had gone missing?"

This wasn't the traitorous retainer upstairs but the second one. He'd left three days ago to attend classes and hadn't been back.

"Yes?"

"He's been arrested. And word has it he spilled his guts and I don't mean *seppuku*. Cops are coming. Get out…now! I'm already on my way there. I'll get you to my place. Meet me out front or in the alley behind the deli if the cops arrive before I do."

"Will do. *Arigato*!"

Garth hung up. He knew better than to waste precious minutes sulking over this calamity in his fortunes. He grabbed the nearest weapons, a katana (or the standard fighting sword) and a wakizashi (a shorter sword usually used for committing hari-kiri). He didn't intend to use either of them on himself.

He also had no intention of leaving anybody behind to talk about him—or to betray him further. Garth grimaced like a character in Kabuki, rushed up the stairs to the floor where the geishas were housed, and burst open the door where his first assistant had been plotting with one of the 'girls.' The kid jumped to his feet, trying to get his pants up. Garth slashed down with the katana, cutting through the right shoulder, splitting him all the way to the hip. Then he beheaded him. The geisha shrieked, cursing Garth as he then turned on her with the shorter sword. She cussed him all the way to hell as he disemboweled her, leaving entrails across the ornate couch, as if a whole crate full of joke cans containing festive paper snakes had exploded.

He stalked down the hallway, kicking open each door and dispatching each of his pretty little bonsai babes within. Ordinary decapitations here were in order, being the quickest method. Most didn't even scream, being unable to as they were drugged to the gills or simply too catatonic from shock and abuse to respond.

He felt pumped, knew he had to resemble one of the mad samurai from his atrocity prints. He was covered in blood and stank of death. *Oh, Nanking, I have come home!*

But who was that bitch standing at the end of the hall?

Not a part of his inventory. No, she was whole, voluptuous even, with two arms and two legs and blond hair down to her ass crack. Man, if he wasn't on the run, he'd be considering adding her to his repertoire. Yet who was she and what was she doing there in his house?

A cop. Sure. He hadn't heard any sirens but they must have zoomed onto the street without them. Maybe they were all through the house now.

He raised the long sword and pulled back the short one, prepared to let her have both, a chop and a gouging thrust.

But she said, "Here. This is the gateway. Enter…"

And she took off those sunglasses.

++++++++++

"…he bid his wife eat sparingly, because she was near her time, and that these tripes were no very commendable meat. They would fain, said he, be as the chewing of ordure, that would eat the case wherein it was. Notwithstanding these admonitions, she did eat sixteen quarters, two bushels, three pecks, and a pipkin full. O the fair fecality, wherewith she swelled, by the ingrediency of such shitten stuff!"

— *'Gargantua'*
(From Chapter 4, 'How Gargamelle, being great with Gargantua, did eat a huge deal of tripes')

Francois Rabelais, former Franciscan priest, former Franciscan transferred to Benedictine Order, former Benedictine adjourned to secular priest wandering about the world, former medical student, medical lecturer, master of anatomical dissection, actor and creator of a fish sauce, playwright, novelist, and eventual returnee to the Benedictines

quoted in *Sacred Sepsis*
Dr. Louis Godard and Dr. James Singer

CHAPTER
26

Jim wasn't feeling well. The cramps he'd experienced earlier were worse. And then to find out who the appointment
was with—could this be the visitor from Europe Myrtle
had told him about?

Jim walked into his office to find Father Malvezzi waiting
for him. The man still appeared much the same, except that in
1990 his hair had been white and his eyebrows black. Now the
eyebrows were white as well. He was without his two Blues
Brothers bodyguards.

"What the hell do you want?" he asked the priest less than
cordially.

The man from the Vatican lifted those heavy eyebrows.
"Well, I did not exactly expect to be welcomed with open
arms. I trust, however, that the document I sent you arrived in
good condition?"

Jim ground his teeth. "YOU sent that? Then it must be a
load of muck and a pack of lies. It looked real enough. I've
sent it to a lab to be authenticated."

"It will be found quite genuine, I assure you," said Malvezzi.

Singer had entered his office with his secretary.

Myrtle had opened with, "Oh, you must be the noon appointment."

"Yes," Malvezzi said mildly. He'd always been mild, hadn't he? Understated and cool.

"Well, can I make some coffee?" she asked, looking from her employer to his "guest," obviously sensing tension.

"No," Jim replied. "That won't be necessary. He'd require snake venom and we haven't any. Why don't you call the lab? It's been weeks. See what the hold up is."

"Will do, boss," Myrtle answered and made herself look busy to the point of being fussy with the telephone.

He went to the entrance of the inner office and gestured for the priest to join him there. He closed the door slowly, resisting an impulse to slam it.

"Why did you send me that?" Jim demanded. "To get me to pull a retraction out of my butt?"

Malvezzi managed a small smile behind one hand. "I do not believe you would do that. Your book has already been, shall we say, far too influential for a retraction to make any difference?"

"What is that supposed to mean?"

"Dr. Singer," the priest began, "I sent you this ancient document because I believe the cult of Aureola is active again, having become so in the years since *Sacred Sepsis* was first published. Do you mind if I sit?"

Singer huffed and gestured to a chair. He didn't sit himself down. He wanted to be ready to launch across the desk at the man's throat. (What? You carry a small, skinny woman out of a flooding building and suddenly you're a comic book hero? Leaping tall pieces of furniture in a single bound?)

Besides, from what he'd seen that morning, he already knew Aureola had new followers. But could that be attributed solely to his book?

What else could it be?

"You do not look surprised," Malvezzi pointed out.

"So there are anorexic girls calling her their patron saint...?"

"Oh, no, son," the priest argued, cutting him off, wagging a finger. Jim really cringed when the man called him "son." Hey, this creep wasn't his dad. "I do not mean simply followers. I refer to the dog cult. Surely you read that document I sent you before you passed it on for verification of antiquity?"

Malvezzi had been toting a large manilla envelope. He opened it and pulled out several news clippings. He wet a finger on his tongue and then began to flip through them.

"Let's see. Oh, yes. These vile people leave behind text at each scene. Let's list a few... 'Why have all our fruits become rotten and brown? What was it fell last night from the evil moon?' That is by Nietzsche. Quoted in your book on page 12. 'Nothing is unclean in itself', Paul the Apostle, quoted at the beginning of your book and also in the introduction. Then there is da da da, here it is…'I will even appoint over your terror, consumption and the burning ague, that shall consume the eyes and cause sorrow of the heart: and ye shall sow your seed in vain, for your enemies shall eat it.' From Leviticus, quoted on page 46. Here's another. 'During the Thirty Years War marauding bands of soldiers would attack villages. Trying to get the peasantry to tell where they had hidden their food, they would torture them by forcing them to swallow human and animal waste.' Page 173 of your book. And this from the introduction again, 'When we accept that there is nothing which is too small or too mean to have been created by God, we set ourselves free.' And another gem. 'A small black angel getting sick from eating too much licorice stick…'"

Jim felt all the color and warmth drain from his face as he listened. Every item which had been written at a Shit Detail murder had also been in *Sacred Sepsis*. It must be a coincidence, he told himself. It had to be.

What? Even material Jim had written? That was a stretch, boy.

He glared at the priest. Guy was sure enjoying this, wasn't he? "All right, all right! You made you point. I guess you're saying those murders are my fault?"

Malvezzi stopped, shaking his head. "No, I'm not saying that at all. But I did want you to see the connection. The cult is spreading abroad. I happen to believe you can help. Obviously you are a man of great influence with these people, because you are the one who discovered Aureola's catacombs…"

"Which you blew up," Jim accused, "killing Dr. Godard. Guilty of a little murder yourself. Did you quote something appropriately scriptural as you set the fuse?"

He was sweating, the pain in his gut moving low, twisting his insides. If he could, he'd attack Malvezzi. He'd do it for Louis. He glared hard at the man, expecting him to glance away, damned by the accusation in Singer's eyes. The priest ought to at least look down at the floor with shame. But Malvezzi did not do this. He maintained a steady gaze, eye to eye with Jim.

Feeling perfectly awful and determined not to show weakness to the priest, Jim sat down. He could actually double over a little and make it seem as if he were merely leaning forward at his desk. Must have been the pizza rolls he'd had at that faculty function yesterday. These or the deviled eggs. If he could get rid of this asshole, he'd see about swinging by the student clinic. If it was food poisoning, he might need antibiotics, not to mention an industrial strength Pepto.

The priest sighed. "No, we never did that. We were going to seal the entrance, that was all. Aureola built her strength for more than a millennium and a half. If humans may become saints of light, why not saints of darkness? Demons, even? She found her way out."

"I don't fuckin' believe you!" Jim shouted. But he thought back to that scene in his hospital room, weeks after the explosion and cave-in. Malvezzi had visited him then, too. And had been confronted with the truth.

But was it the truth? The man hadn't denied it. Nor had he confessed. He may have simply given up trying to talk sense to Singer who he could tell was in no mood to listen.

(He'd sent the Vatican the video tape of that visit. As insurance. As blackmail. They'd done nothing about his writing and releasing the archaeological evidence from the catacombs and elsewhere.)

Maybe there'd been nothing to do.

Maybe they'd never actually dreamed the cult would begin anew.

Did most of the modern Church believe in devils? Or did they merely view them as symbolic, not to be taken in any literal sense?

(And all those times Jim had been on television, grinning into the camera and talking about the finds, about science. Hoping like hell that this guy in black and his cronies were watching and frustrated because they couldn't stop him. Jim had been smug, sure this was just the sort of avenging of which Louis would have approved. Non-violent, but getting those self-righteous bastards right where they lived. Had he suffered the sin of pride?)

The priest spread his hands before him. "I know you've never believed me. I am sorry for that. The Church has been responsible for some terrible things in history: The Inquisition, the persecution of those of differing faiths, the suppression of accusations of child abuse among certain members of the clergy..."

Jim squinted at mention of this last. Yes, butterball sinner. Running down the long aisles of gleaming pews. Tormented saints in stained glass, blind-folded and gagged. The smell of Ivory Soap and roses and fear. Did Malvezzi know about how Jim had suffered as a little boy? Was that item mentioned to gig him or simply to guarantee that the priest held his attention?

Malvezzi continued, "But in the case of Aureola, we only ever acted to protect the innocent. And she with her dog cult were anything but innocent. We did not explode those catacombs. We had nothing to do with the unfortunate death of Dr. Godard."

Jim laughed, harshly. "I don't know. It sounds too convenient, too much like a bad movie. Crazed cult goes bozanga on say-so of demon."

He touched the bridge of his nose. His sinuses hurt. From the odor of that overflowing sewer. It might be that the gases he'd inhaled were why he was being so combative. That, and whatever was trying to backstroke into his colon.

Malvezzi shrugged. "Look at Manson and his 'Family' for a modern counterpart. They were supposedly Christians, even believing that Charles Manson was Christ. Those who killed Sharon Tate and her friends and who

242

killed the LaBiancas claimed they were ordered to do so with love. The inhabitants of Beverly Hills were terrified they would be next, just as the citizens of Rome were."

Jim wondered, *Could the woman with the sunglasses, floating out on all that sewage, then vanishing…might she actually have been Aureola?*

(He'd considered briefly that she might be someone else, far more ancient/primitive. The archetypal dark figure he'd pursued—at first by accident and later absolutely on purpose, with a purpose—for most of his life.)

Then he experienced a cramp so severe he actually screamed and slid to the floor. The priest bent down over him.

"Oh! You poor man… Help! Miss Ave? The professor is ill…call an ambulance!" Malvezzi cried out.

++++++++++

"O fairies, O buggers,
O eunuchs exotic!
Come running, come running,
ye anal-erotic!
With soft little hands,
with flexible bums,
Come, O castrati,
unnatural ones!"

—From '*Satyricon*' *Petronius*
quoted in *Sacred Sepsis*
Dr. Louis Godard and Dr. James Singer

243

CHAPTER
27

Jason had watched for the police but seen none. Was it possible they were waiting for a judge to issue a warrant? It was two in the morning. Maybe they couldn't find a night-owl judge this time. Or they could be on their way...

Tacked onto telephone poles and taped on the windows of the closed deli were more posters for missing dogs than he'd ever seen at one place and one time.

Jason got out of his car and stalked across the street. Big Garth had given him a key. Garth had always trusted him and this made him feel very honored. Normally those with brains knew never to trust *anybody*. But Listo and he went way back. Surely they had known one another before in a previous incarnation. They must have been brothers—or lovers—or both.

He'd been thinking of proposing a business connection. Jason was mighty tired of Rose and her monster-disdain of him. (Hell, Crowley had driven *his* Rose insane.) He thought that Garth and he might exhibit her. The voyeurs of the world would pay damn near anything to see a real *ghul* eat the dead.

Or—if that failed—what would the U.S. government—or any interested, rich government for that matter—pay for a near-human specimen with such an ability to create new body parts for itself? Wouldn't she be furious?

Although actually he'd never seen her when she wasn't granite-eyed and marble-slab cold. It was why he'd never tried to force her. There was no pleasure to be had from such an icy fish-fuck. But her people never killed—she'd said this and for the years he'd known her, it had proved to be true. Even Michael with his prophet's chainsaw had only been injured just enough to stop his attack on her. And he'd quite died on his own of those injuries.

Jason entered Garth's house, smelled anger in the air. Rage had pheromones every bit as potent and distinctive as those of fear and sex. A whirlwind had flown upstairs and he decided to follow it.

"Garth?" he called out as he raced up the steps. They might not have much time. "You ready? We'd better split."

No sound. It was a big house; how could there be no sound at all? At any moment at least one geisha ought to be twitching or moaning.

He checked each room, every floor. Found the one with the assistant's head on a different side of the room from the assistant's body. And the woman he'd thought of as gutsy-because-she-ain't-got-much-left…those guts were still hot, still steaming on the couch and floor. A lengthy section squirmed with peristalsis until it might have been an eel. Garth wasn't in the room but clearly he had been.

Every place else, if there had been a living (even if severely truncated) person there, now there was a dead one. Cleanly but swiftly decapped. No time to spare on formalities or last minute cruelties. Heads sat wherever they had fallen: on couches, on beds, on floor pillows, in chairs, on carpets. Origamies of skull and death mask.

Jason felt extremely peculiar on the top floor, looking down the hall. Blood had trailed to the end of that corridor and then stopped. A man who had just slaughtered more than a dozen might have this much blood fall off his hands and clothes and weapons as he walked.

But where was that man?

Gone to the end of the hall and then just disappeared?

There had been many disappearances lately. Acquaintances and colleagues of Jason's. Too many.

He spied something else at the end of the hall. Jason walked over and picked it up. It was the *netsuke* he'd given B.G. before he was sent to fight in the Gulf War. The bone figurine of the naked man back-dooring the naked woman whose head was a chrysanthemum flower. It was bloody and it vibrated; a subtle electric charge thrummed through Jason's fingers. Not really as from a live wire. More like a low level snake bite.

Jason put it into his pocket. It buzzed slightly, as if it were a pager and had just gone off silently. It moved, as if the man really were thrusting into the woman.

"Garth?" he shouted again. The sound of his voice and that one syllable echoed back at him.

Fancy frames hung upon the walls of that hallway. Some were stills from Japanese films. He spotted one of the atrocity pieces Garth had been so proud of. Looked like a first made from the woodblock. Probably worth a small fortune.

Yoshitoshi Tsukioka.

What fine sleek paper like a maiden's skin, ink sublime as blood squeezed out of weeping midnight.

He hung his head a moment, permitting a moment of silence out of respect for his mentor. He knew Garth was gone. The samurai had made it to the end of the hall and then left, somehow, some way.

"I hope you are given your own palace and procession of damned."

Then Jason took the frame from the wall and busted it, smashing the glass, lifting out the *muzan-e*. He crumpled it in his fist and then stuffed it entire into his mouth. An electric current stronger than the one in the *netsuke* burned across his tongue but he wouldn't spit it out. He chewed, swallowing. Not so difficult. He'd bitten off and swallowed larger pieces of quivering flesh. It danced through his veins and his penis erected, then ejaculated: surely a stream of ink and *akurei*—demon—moonlight. A beautiful figure waited for him in this pale glow, seen behind his eyes within a field of jasmine. Perfect, too perfect, unsullied, a bride for him to debauch.

The sound of the front door downstairs being broken open brought him to his senses. He heard boots stomping on the stairs and voices yelling.

Jason knew a nearby door and the staircase behind it that led to the roof. Quickly he headed there, climbing up fast and as quietly as he could, not quite sure what he'd do when he got up there. He tried to recall if there was a fire escape to take him down again. This was an old brownstone. Surely there was a fire escape.

No, no...Garth told him it had been removed by the previous owner due to disrepair. It had been more than fifty years old. Garth planned to replace it but it wasn't as if they were available for pickup at Home Depot.

There was no other roof close enough to jump to. What would he do? Leap to the ground, several stories below? **Superman** from the old TV series? And like the '50s hero, not ever entering the '60s? That pretender had killed himself. Jason wasn't that **Superman**. He was also no ghoul. He couldn't simply cough up new legs and a new spine. (Probably a new neck would be needed, too.)

Jason pulled both guns he'd tucked into his coat as he was leaving to go pick up Garth. Okay, he'd shoot it out if he had to. They could only come up the same stairs and through the door one at a time. He'd go for head shots, figuring they were wearing Kevlar vests. He'd shoot out eyes and blow off jaws, teeth scattering like bits of pearly shrapnel. They'd probably bottle-neck at first and he'd have a chance to pick them off before they could clear the entrance. Yeah, let 'em back away, call for a chopper. Jason imagined shooting it down, the blades bisecting pigeons and finally meth-heads and whores on the sidewalk and street below. More fun than he'd had in the whole of the Gulf War, that would be for sure.

He came onto the roof, closed the door behind him, and looked up. Clouds were merging from the right and left, the north and south. It had been only slightly cloudy as he'd entered Garth's house but now a storm was about to erupt. There was still one patch of high space in-between. Jason saw in it the Prince of Dark Bodies. Melanicus!

"Take me with you," he whispered, feeling foolish, feeling elated. He'd searched the night skies so often, to never see the vast black vampire.

But Melanicus couldn't help him. The clouds clashed together and swirled. It began to rain, hard pellets stinging like stones. A bolt of lightning struck near Jason, hitting the roof only a couple feet from him, so bright he saw it even when he squeezed his eyes closed and turned away, so hot he felt the hair on his head and in his eyebrows and eyelashes singe and curl. So hot at least a hundred little capillaries on his bare arms and forehead burst from boiling.

And then he heard crying.

"Garth?" he asked. But knew Garth would never cry.

It was a kid somewhere. Hidden there on the roof? Maybe some new project B.G. hadn't told him about who might have been locked up in a pigeon coop?

No, I've heard this before, a long time ago.

"Hello? You there, No Man?" Jason asked again, looking around, trying to gauge which direction the voice was coming from so he could find the gateway. (The gateway!) But the sharp crack of lightning, it's deep crackle and shriek had left his ears ringing. He was lucky it hadn't completely deaf-ened him.

"Yeah," came a reply, wrapped in muffled sob.

"So is the gate open right now?" Jason wanted to know, his own voice sly.

There was the eyeball, floating toward him. But where was the opening to the place without horizons?

"Take me to the land beyond the gate," Jason told it, growling.

A disembodied wail answered. "I can't. It's not for you."

Jason grabbed it and crushed it in his fist. It plopped wetly like a ripe grape. He'd tried to rescue this kid (this fragment of a kid) once, when he'd been only a boy himself. A split second in his past when he might have taken another road, possessed by an avatar spirit which decided to move on. He heard a scream, compressed into the narrowest of nanoseconds. He tasted the smear on his palm. Yes, it did indeed taste like ocular stickum. Somehow he'd expected meringue, or a mystic version of gummi bears, or the kind of Elmer's glue school children fastened glitter to construction paper with.

Jason chuckled. "Sorry, No Man. Guess my patience didn't get past the gate."

Then he wondered if this had been real or if he'd ingested anything hallucinatory in that *muzan-e*. Some herbs used to be employed for creating ink and some of them had strange properties. One formerly common in older inks was the pokeberry which was also a poison. It failed to frighten Jason, who had done so many drugs and poisons in his life for recreation and enlightenment, that his system had quite a tolerance. He might visualize some, but he probably wouldn't die.

The door to the house below opened. Cops came out, swinging around with weapons ready. The rain was sheets of black and silver. It began to hail: frozen ice the size of oranges and apples. Then oranges and apples really were falling from the clouds. And then jasmine flowers. Then origami fashioned to look like dolls' heads. Then swords of varying sizes. Then entrails and eels.

Jason had all he could do to keep from laughing out loud. The cops couldn't see him. They were going back in, back down, descending the stairs like trolls headed for hellish mines.

++++++++++

And then there is the story taking place in the 11th Century B.C. about the Philistines ripping off the Ark of the Covenant from the Hebrews. They were struck with a mighty plague that, according to The First Book Of Samuel, caused them to be smitten with *emerods* "in their secret parts."

The Philistines had attempted to get rid of the toxic ark by sending it to somebody else, but people would shudder, squat, and grunt "No thank you." As a matter of fact, everyplace they took the Ark to try to unload it—Ashdod, Gath, and finally Ekron—the population became immediately afflicted. So they started making overtures to the Hebrews to get it back.

The Hebrews smirked at one another and said, "Okay, but we want a trespass offering. It's ours all right but we expect you to pay us for the trouble. You'll give us five golden *emerods* and five golden mice."

(Five golden mice! Four latrines, three ritual baths, two soothing balms, and a roll of papyrus in an *emrod* tree!)

Now, here's the hotly contested part. There are varying theories about what *emerods* were. Some learned folk have said the mice and *emerods* were rats and the buboes which erupt during bubonic plague. Not bothering to mention that mice seldom act as plague carriers. But another school of thought insists the *emerods* were actually hemorrhoids. Severe dyssentery can cause very painful rhoids. A couple of these scientists point to the mice as being another thing entirely. Perhaps the rodents had destroyed someone's crops and the two pestilences got mistakenly linked.

And here's the weirdest of the learned notions. That the Philistines were into sodomy. (And some of those wicked buggerers have been known to use live mice in rites not likely to produce a better mousetrap.) The plague God smote them with produced dyssentery which inflamed the rhoids common to those who are frequently plunged. Oh, those funny Hebrews, expecting these thieves to not only return the stolen ark but to memorialize their embarrassing suffering in gold. Wink wink, nudge, nudge.

—Sacred Sepsis
Dr. Louis Godard and Dr. James Singer

CHAPTER
28

Myrtle watched Dr. Singer as he thrashed on the bed in the ER. They were going to do X-rays. They had sent for a nurse to fix him on an IV, keeping him on fluids and supplying a pain killer.

He'd become quite delirious. He was screaming and emitting the strangest farts anyone there had ever heard. She really felt very sorry for him. It had been bound to happen eventually. She'd known this all along. It had only been done for his own good. He'd been kind to her, as no one had ever been. Selfless. And Myrtle had just decided to give him a present. That was, oh, 1994?

Couldn't last forever though.

The ER was backed up. A new strain of flu produced downright ghastly cases of dyssentery. It was running through (you'll excuse the expression) the local grade schools which had just opened again. And food handlers, who were too low-rung on the professional totem pole to have sick pay, were passing the germs on down through undercooked hamburger patties and ice cream cones, the latter particularly popular as it was late August. There had been a run-amuck shooter in the park nearby and the doctors on the trauma team were looking at five vics with shotgun wounds—as well as the perp himself leaking from four police 38's. A lightweight plane had crashed onto a highway; that was another eleven injured. And a postman had been badly mangled by a jaguar some exotic dancer had just introduced into her act at a strip club. The sad thing was that he'd only entered the club to deliver the mail.

"It's okay, boss," Myrtle said to him, getting close enough her voice would not carry beyond the cloth screens which hung between the separate beds. "Most people survive. You will survive."

He probably couldn't hear her. His head shook back and forth, sweat big as coins on his face. He thrust the sheet off him and struggled onto his side and groaned, moaned as noises liquid and slippery sang from his insides.

They had taken off his clothes and put him in a gown. One of those backless things. Myrtle could clearly see his pale, perspiring, clenching butt. She wanted to reach out and pat it affectionately.

There at the anus, she saw the tiny head. It was already emerging. Maybe this wouldn't take him several days of agony. But, of course, it still had to completely come out. *Aureum Incretum*, having reached maturity, needed to leave its host to reproduce.

She'd come by this one when it was only a baby. Down in the tunnels, its parent having crawled out of a grubby immigrant goat-fucker from somewhere in the Gobi Desert. She'd understood it would make Dr. Singer thin. He wanted to be thin. She knew that.

Who didn't want to be thin? It made him seem so much younger, losing all that weight. As if he'd found the little boy who'd been hiding inside him.

"You'll be okay in just a little while. A dog that swallows a fuzzy curler hurts a lot worse when it's passing the bristles. But after it's come out, the relief is so great it's like you just met God."

Myrtle smiled sweetly and left.

+++++++++++

Down in the tunnels. Myrtle didn't know what she was doing there. She thought it was because she'd seen that woman riding upon the crest of sewage spewing out of the Science Building where the floor had cracked open. And this happening so soon after the document came. It had been a few weeks in-between, that was all.

She'd never sent it to the lab. She'd always done every job Dr. Singer gave her, but Myrtle couldn't bring herself to let go of that document. She'd hidden it in her apartment. And every time Jim asked if the lab had called yet, she'd lied.

She'd eavesdropped on the conversation between that priest and her employer. They used an old intercom system in his office; it had been no big deal years ago for her to rig it so she could listen in on anything she wanted. And after she was satisfied that Singer was where she'd hoped he would be in the stages of passing the goldworm, she'd left the ER and gone home to fetch the document.

She'd read it on the cab ride to the subway entrance on Myrtle Avenue. She'd felt strange, both frightened and energized. And once she'd taken the steps down, she'd gone to the ladies room and burned it, flushing the manuscript cinders. There was no way she was going to let the rest of the world see that. They would only know the story from the epistle Aureola's followers had written, that which the professor had published in *Sacred Sepsis*.

And as for what she'd tell him about the ancient Vatican dossier on Aureola? She'd think of something. Maybe she'd say that the lab decreed it a fake. It was what he wanted to hear anyway. Or she could tell him the courier responsible for delivering it had lost it. No, no, couldn't do that. He was waiting on word from the lab. She'd told him the lab had it.

It was better to leave it as a fake. Then he wouldn't care what happened to it.

Perhaps Myrtle would never have to explain it at all.

The tunnel was as horrible as she remembered. Vagrants and druggies turned in their filth to stare at her, well-dressed as she was now. She expected to be assaulted at any moment. Robbed, stripped and plucked, sodomized and fucked.

Let 'em try. She'd learned martial arts at a night course given at the college. She was a black belt. And what were they but pathetic throwaways with more stink than brains?

A couple of piggish guys were weaving back and forth on the balls of their feet, eyeing her, trying to get themselves up for it. One had puke in his beard, and the other had a large yellow stain on his fly and down one pant's leg. She felt a smile spread across her face like a curl in hot butter. She told them, "Try it. I'll kill you. And that's no bullshit."

They sneered but shuffled a few paces backward, maintaining their distance.

Myrtle found the wall she'd done her art work on before Dr. Singer rescued her and brought her into the light. But could it be the same place? Where were her pictures?

It had all been painted over with dull cement paint. Some snotty art critics were responsible, no doubt, with the Guggenheim up their asses. It hurt to find them destroyed.

Myrtle had never been one to have dreams. She'd heard others talk about or rave during theirs when she'd lived down here. She'd since read books and seen movies where dreams seemed so important to the human psyche in particular and to the designs of hopes/fears/fate and myths in general. Yet Myrtle was dreamless. Nothing in nightmares to give her a clue as to her origins.

So her drawings had, for her, taken the place of those missing dreams. Here were the symbols she saw in her mind, not that she understood them but at least this way they were categorized in a kind of cartoonish journal that she could review, telling herself, "Well, there's this and this and that and that. Now what does it mean?"

Gone. Each perplexing bit of ego and id. The jumble which had confused her until she got it out upon the wall where somehow it then soothed.

There were a lot of weird images in her head right now. *How's about one more, for old time's sake*? For whatever it might be worth. Or for zero.

Snapping open her purse, Myrtle dug down through the tissues and dry cleaning stubs and cosmetic flotsam to find a pen. She began to draw.

++++++++++

Ring!

"Hello?"

"Is this Father Malvezzi?"

"It is."

"Hi, I'm Dr. Singer's secretary, Myrtle Ave? We met earlier today…"

"Ah, yes! How is he doing?"

"Not so good right now. But he asked me to call you. It seems he's come across some information on that cult. Something really astonishing he thinks you should see as soon as possible. Can you come?"

"Actually tonight and most of tomorrow I will be at the city's archdiocese. But tomorrow night…?"

"That would be fine."

And Myrtle gave him directions.

The only truth we
make ourselves
                inside,
homegrown and
            our own
where the worms abide

The rest are the lies
bantered forth and back
from god to devil:
Miss Howl and Miss Crack.

CHAPTER
29

She had to be someplace. It was essential she hurry. Why didn't she simply manifest there? Maybe twitch her nose like some sixties TV witch and transport herself. She'd been doing stuff like this, hadn't she? Ending up places without the usual journey, finding herself moved and changed.

Folks with multiple personalities did that. *thought* they had skipped the standard rules of mass and location, when it was really just that another of their selves was responsible.

Was this Dorien's problem? Was this goddess of shit a matter of alternate ego? And what did it say for deep seated dysfunctions that some part of her would claim *that* as an alternate ego?

She almost wished this were true. Then she could check herself into a mental facility and get treatment. Get placed into a nice cotton batting compartment with somebody to bathe her and feed her cookies with sprinkles and sparkly drugs. But this wasn't to be so easy.

She'd found herself away from the college where the sewer had erupted. Hours had passed. It might not even be the same day anymore. Dorien was in her car and driving very fast, to the limits of an old Volkswagen. She was near the East River. As a matter of fact, she was on a dock. Wasn't there a bridge around here someplace? A helpful, big bridge which assisted many travelers across?

Yes, it was out that way, a quarter of a mile maybe. But she wasn't going to end up on it.

She was going into the drink.

Too late Dorien hit the brake. The car took a header off the end of the pier. It seemed to sail down gracefully, seconds like epochs in which she'd been a transmigrating soul. Her life—her lives—flashed before her etched in surreal sepia colors.

When it hit the water, she expected to submerge right away. The dark, vile water would be her grave.

But, no. The car landed upright and bobbed like some kid's toy.

Yeah, a Volkswagen. And it struck her funny that the only piece-of-shit car the goddess of shit would be in would be the kind that floated.

Dorien crawled out of the window and swam to shore. She realized she might actually be able to walk to land, since what was the East River but sewage and swill? It might bear her regally as the mess from the Science Building had. But for some reason, she struck out with arms and legs working. Clinging to this as a last act of her human self.

From then on Dorien might be gone forever.

As if Dorien Warmer had always been only the split from the ego, the false personality. Now the real one would take over for good.

++++++++++

She'd walked for an hour or so after climbing out of the river. It was night now but still hot. Her clothes and hair had dried. She didn't stink from the water and nothing nasty clung to her. Being the goddess of shit, she might have thought things would be otherwise, that she would be gowned in a satiny sheathe of all that she represented.

(Venus is the goddess of love and sex but she's never shown covered in cum, is she?)

Dorien saw the Myrtle Avenue entrance to the subway and descended. She didn't plan to take a train. She could smell where she was going.

She entered a ladies room. This was not her final destination. And she had no reason to go there, so why had she?

To look into a mirror. Because Dorien was still in there, even if she'd thought she'd be gone, erased. The goddess persona must not have quite kicked her out yet.

258

Or maybe she couldn't kick Dorien out. Because it wasn't that the goddess was a separate entity. No multiple personalities, remember? In this time, she was Dorien Warmer. She'd been born as Dorien and, even when she changed and realized her eternal self, she would still be Dorien as long as she was in this incarnation.

Dorien recalled the dreams she had, of other women in other times who had turned out to be the goddess. They felt they were no longer themselves. But obviously they'd had the wherewithal at the backs of their minds to think this, so they had to be themselves, after all. Simply expanded, purpose understood, shattering as that was. Mind-bending. Scary. All of a sudden your body doesn't need food anymore and it doesn't shit, doesn't get sick. You've walked away from your family, your life. You're doing these freaky supernatural things, holding the key to a gateway to the beyond and punishing sinners. You don't feel anything like the girl you were or the woman you had become and every impulse felt totally alien. Sure, why wouldn't you think you were gone and another had replaced you?

In the mirror, she opened her mouth. No more teeth. In their place tiny little orchids had grown. Interesting that this didn't muffle or distort her speech. Did make her breath quite nice, she supposed.

Sunglasses up, afraid to take them down to see the eyes. That was another thing... A big thing. A very major change. Not human.

(And orchids for teeth was?)

She'd always been a bit chubby. But now? It all looked solid, strong. It had to be, to walk a path between worlds. And what a path!

"I'm me," she said to her reflection. "For whatever that's worth. Dorien Warmer, shit goddess."

Wasting time. She turned around and left, hunting beyond the platform for the trains. There were tunnels and there were tunnels. She climbed down where no one who would give a rat's ass might see her. Walked not far, turned. No tracks that way. Piles of rubbish, cardboard boxes which smelled like homeless homes. But currently empty. The inhabitants had scurried.

Down farther, people.

Most of them had dog in their bowels.

The Shit Detail had a captive. They had made a sort of cross with pieces of lumber and nailed a naked man to it. Propped him up against a wall. He was praying feverishly as the black-clad, dark-masked freaks shoved a drugstore pre-packaged enema up his rectum and gave him a good dousing.

"Look! It's Aureola," one of them cried with elation when they spotted Dorien approaching them.

They immediately hit the ground on their knees, faces groveling the filthy floor where they deserved to be.

"Welcome, Saint Aureola. I saw you at a college yesterday. Bless us!"

"We still do your work. See?"

"We've kept ourselves purged as you have preached. We are your empty vessels."

"Please," their victim said hoarsely, "call the police…"

He could barely raise his head. He couldn't look at her because they had caked fecal matter across both of his eyes, thick as mud plasters.

"She won't help you, you bastard. She's Saint Aureola."

His head jerked up at the sound of this name. He wriggled and whimpered, trying to get free. The nails in his wrists and ankles tore, blood spraying.

"No, she isn't," someone else murmured, coming from the other direction, the tunnel's opposite end.

The Shit Detail raised their heads a few inches to see who this was. Dorien did not, for she felt the identity. If she'd been the old Dorien, her skin would have crawled. But she was the new, so she only waited for this creature to join them.

Myrtle grinned. Ah, someone else who'd transformed, who'd discovered her secret self. Why, what pals they would be, reading each other's diaries and painting each other's nails. Yeah, sure.

"We know she's Aureola. She was seen performing miracles at the university," one of the Detail argued.

All of them stood up defiantly from their kneeling positions.

Myrtle threw her head back and let out a howl matching in decibels and vibration a train which thundered down a nearby track. Then she gestured to the cement wall where one rather inept cartoon had been scribbed. More began to rise to the surface from underneath a coat of paint. She gestured again and a skeletal female in one of the drawings poured forth a stream of vomit from its mouth, out of the wall. Pinky curds splashed down.

Myrtle folded her arms and stared at Dorien, as if expecting her to show some proof of divinity. Dorien just gazed at her through those sunglasses.

"Hmmph," Myrtle scoffed. Then she strolled up to the man on the cross. "Father Malvezzi, thanks for keeping our appointment. I guess you're pretty impressed with what I said you might want to see."

He shivered, mumbled in Latin, reacted loosely some more to the forced enema.

"You ought to be grateful you've been made a martyr. Isn't that the highest occupation to which you could aspire? Why, you might even end up being given sainthood. You'll love the perks that come with that," Myrtle teased. But then she grew tired of the joke and grew more serious. "You should have stayed in Rome, old man. Shouldn't have tried to interfere with that document of lies. The world doesn't care anyway, not anymore. The Catholic Church is the butt of so many half-assed secular comedians and is losing faithful so fast, not even a computer could keep count. What did you hope to accomplish?"

260

He worked his mouth as if it hurt too much to answer. But he was determined to reply. "Nothing solidifies faith in God like proof of evil's existence."

"You don't have proof of shit," Myrtle snapped.

"Yes, I do. You're here right now, aren't you?"

Myrtle snarled, ran up to him, and dug her claws into Malvezzi's belly. She practically climbed in, strong as a tigress, ripping through flesh and muscle and into the abdomen. She jerked out quivering loops of entrails and dragged them to Dorien, looping them around her throat. They turned into necklaces of poisonous watersnakes, hissing and snapping. They bit Dorien in the face and scalp and breasts.

The Shit Detail cried in unison, "Ahhh!"

Someone added, "Saints be praised!"

A tiny part of Dorien wanted to scream. She'd always hated snakes. She felt each nauseating sting, smelled venom, but only reached up with a simple caress. The snakes turned into pretty scarab beetles which fell to the ground and crawled away. The snakebites blazed, bruised and swelled, then faded to nothing.

"How did she do that?" she heard the Detail asking each other in subdued voices.

"Kisses don't leave scars," she told them.

Myrtle laughed. "Goddess of shit or Saint of Crapulence—who is the stronger?"

Why even bother going by the old name? She had never been reincarnated. She'd come out of the catacombs after centuries of waiting. She'd sucked up Louis Godard's lifeforce as he died and she sailed over. Flesh again, she found herself in a new Rome far away—one with as much diversity and corruption as the Rome from the empire. But the transformation was a shock (what transformation worth a damn wasn't?) and she'd forgotten who she was for a while.

"Get her!" one of The Shit Detail goaded. "Get the pretender!"

They howled their support, except for one who shuffled to the side and pressed a back to the wall.

Aureola, named for gold—now, wasn't that better than Myrtle, named for a street?—bent forward and pulled up her skirt. She took a deep breath and then ejected a foul black acidic sea of fecal chum. It spattered the walls and pocked them, sizzling into one of the Detail, melting his mask and black T-shirt, burning him horribly. He fell, screaming, trying to roll the burn away into the filth on the ground. No one tried to help him, standing very still to witness these miracles, frozen at attention.

The stuff struck the priest but he'd died already. It hit Dorien full force but then just absorbed into her body like rainwater slipping into the grass.

Aureola glowered. "Don't you want to counter with something? Show your powers?"

"I'll get my turn," Dorien replied softly.

"We'll see," Aureola retorted. She spun around toward the pictures on the wall.

"Like my artwork?" she asked the goddess.

"I'd be impressed if you were a monkey," Dorien said.

Aureola howled again and the Detail clapped their hands over their ears in pain. Blood trickled from the ears of one of them, blooming like red roses through the stocking mask on either side of the head. Surprisingly, this person didn't fall down.

"Oh, thank you, Lady. Thank you for this stigmata," the injured one babbled.

Aureola shouted at the pictures, "Out! Out! Out!"

The horrors so crudely drawn began to creep from the wall, thickening as they dropped to the floor, horned Babylons and skeleton bitches and torsos and shit-imps and monster dogs. A couple limped toward Malvezzi's corpse and the burned Detail member, bending to tear off cooked or dark-marinated pieces to eat. The burned man shrieked unintelligible prayers, kicked his legs, gurgled and gargled as his windpipe was severed. But most attacked Dorien. The Shit Detail howled and applauded, Aureola looking smug as Dorien now resembled a victim out of Hieronymous Bosch. They scratched and bit, tearing out clumps of her hair, mouthfuls of skin, scraping down to bone. A creature part dog/part man with a dick practically to its knees rammed into her from behind. She bent forward from their combined weight, not even trying to shake them off.

I want to scream. It hurts. Why can't I fight? Dignity was fine for the other incarnations; they never had to deal with anything like this.

But there was a stoic calmness overriding the torment, keeping her cool and strong. Goddesses did not cry out. Even deities working their will through physical shape never forgot who they were. Immutably eternal, beyond the comprehension of hagiolaters and their upstarts hags.

Then suddenly she brought up her hand and removed her glasses. Some of the Detail heard her croon, "Gateway...threshold...Aralu calls you home."

A shaft of crooked darkness appeared. The things looked up, startled, then grinned. They scampered toward it, delight on their half-formed faces.

"No, get back here!" Aureola commanded.

But they didn't listen. Each leapt through the gateway, black static snapping when they vanished. Even the two feeding on the priest and the burned man raced for the opening.

"Damn you...you're supposed to be mine. You ungrateful shitters," the saint cursed. The part dog, part man monster loped toward the threshold, enormous wet cock swinging like a censor, and she cried to it piteously, "Frater! Frater, not you, too..."

It never looked back.

She faced Dorien grimly, furious but out of ideas. Her features contorted with hatred.

"My turn," Dorien stated simply, the wounds she'd received starting to close and heal, but not nearly as fast as the snakebites had.

"Hey, I've been dead before. Didn't stop me," Aureola spat.

"Everything that is or ever was grew out of death. Doesn't make you special, child," Dorien told her sadly. "I won't destroy you. Instead, be as you have always been, a scavenger, the servant to the wasteland."

Aureola screamed, fell, and tried to curl up in a fetal position, drawing her knees to her chest. Her followers watched and started to cry as she grew very soft, shape twisting, the scrawny form puffing out, bloating.

"Is she becoming an angel?" somebody asked.

Wings were unfurling from the back but the feathers were matted with filth and overrun with vermin. What she really resembled was a cross between the old harpy of mythology and a common, meaty-headed buzzard. This staggered up on bloody, taloned feet, squawked at the assembled faithful, then flew off down the tunnel.

Dorien turned to The Shit Detail. They could see her eyes now, how these spun inward, turning, turning like watery drains. They couldn't look away.

"I am the gateway. The threshold to Aralu," she said.

The shaft of darkness began revolving, too, like a black tornado. It sucked them in, its gravity so strong it pulled blood right through their skin, eyes out of sockets, and organs out of every unraveling orifice.

Dorien felt the wetness on her face. Touched it and found it was red. Not tears, after all. No, she didn't shed tears for those she sent to Aralu.

She put her sunglasses back on. The gateway closed, leaving the tunnel too humid, close. She turned to the only member of The Shit Detail not to enter Aralu.

"Please, don't," this one chattered as she pulled off her stocking mask. "It's me, Dorie."

Something in Dorien remembered her sister. She'd thought she hated Annet after finding out she'd been feeding dog meat to their dying father. Not because Dorien had loved the rotten old man but because it was a horrible thing to do. And because Annet had tried to drag her into this disgusting cult. She'd done unspeakable things to helpless men, women and children.

What did Dorien feel now?

Nothing.

"No, you are not meant for Aralu," she said to Annet. "You...you're a virgin, aren't you?"

How did she know this? She smelled it. If she'd been told a few months ago that Annet still hadn't slept with a man, she wouldn't have believed it. It had been pretty funny that Dorien was a virgin leaving her teens—before

Gavin, that is—and Annet was five years older than she was. (Well, Gavin managed to find quite a few. Maybe he'd been able to smell them, too.)

Annet brightened as if this gave her hope. "Oh, yeah. I've been good, Dorie. I've kept myself pure..."

The goddess shook her head. "Pure...virginity doesn't necessarily denote purity. But there are other levels. So many other levels."

Dorien pointed down the tunnel and Annet stumbled off, glad not to be sucked apart and away like the others.

++++++++++

The graveyards and morgues were being guarded now. It was harder for Rose to find a meal. But she'd taken to scouring the parks, the places under overpasses, and the docks for some desperate homeless person who had died of the August heat, or from starvation, or from a drug overdose. Maybe they'd been murdered. Didn't matter to her.

Tonight she searched the subway tunnels. Jason went with her, not willing to see her attacked. She might have been a match for Michael in Cairo, but if she were beset by a gang of twenty skinheads? He might hate her but she was still a valuable commodity, and until he found a way to cash in—and soon—he'd have to protect her. He also wanted to make sure she didn't run off with somebody offering to take her to California.

Off to Hollywood. Now *there* was a city of the dead.

Right now, Rose had been shit out of luck. It made Jason think of a guy walking a bitch dog that wasn't happy with any of the places she sniffed out and refused to do her business. Until a guy wanted to pick the dog up and squeeze until the business came out and they were done.

"I could make this real easy," he told her. "Just pick one for chrissakes. I'll kill it for you. You won't have to get your pristine little hands dirty."

She stared at him for a moment and then walked on, nose in the air—yeah to find the odor of death, but also to show how much she detested him.

He pictured in his mind picking her up, squeezing her like a toothpaste tube with brittle bones, the business coming out smelling of corruption all minty fresh.

He hunched as Rose checked out a bundle of rotten rags. There was a little stink of carrion there. But it turned out the fellow had about nine or ten dead rats in a bag. Jason cracked his knuckles and muttered, "Nietzsche said, 'To upset—that meaneth with him to prove. To drive mad—that meaneth with him to convince. And blood is counted by him as the best of all arguments.'"

There was a young woman walking down the tunnel, her very slender frame silhouetted by the scant light. Jason began to smile. He felt it stretch across his face like a waking lion. She was all alone, running as if she'd just had a bad fright.

She was about to have another.

Yum.

++++++++++

Annet didn't even see the big man until he grabbed her. She swung her body in defensive manuevers, The Shit Detail having made sure their people knew martial arts. But he just twisted her foot when she tried to kick him and snapped her wrist when she attempted to strike out. He then tore off her black T-shirt and flung her to the ground, hard enough it knocked out every ounce of her breath.

And then this woman was getting between them. Strange woman, freckled as if she'd been caught in a dust storm. When what light there was struck these just right, they turned a dark orange, as of some medieval red plague.

It made her think of her late father, with his burn spots turning him into a leopard.

++++++++++

"Rose! What are you doing? Get out of the fuckin' way," Jason demanded.

The ghoul sniffed the air as she ignored him. "You are a houri," she murmured, then helped the young woman to stand.

Rose flicked her hand, almost an imperceptible gesture. A patch of air shimmered, changed slightly. Then suddenly Jason realized he was seeing the infernal paradise the dead Iraqi's third eye had shown him. Where virgins were deflowered, then mutilated to suit the master male.

His jaw dropped. Rose was the one he'd seen there! She'd been his djinn all along! Or had he been wrong and it was ghouls who served in that place?

He also happened to notice that there were horizons. This wasn't the location he'd seen as a child, through the closet wall, eyeball of No Man speaking to him from the other side.

Rose took the woman by the arm, firmly yet not unkindly. They stepped into the infernal paradise, and sight of it—and them—disappeared.

"Damn you!" Jason cursed. "You had it all along and you wouldn't show me? Wouldn't take me?"

But if it wasn't the same place with no-horizons, how many such could there be? Was there one for every **Superman**, every true Beast? Charles Fort spoke of the dark spaces; they might be endless realms.

Jason had seen Melanicus only last night. Did this mean he would soon find his own dark space where he might "do as he wilt" forever?

++++++++++

Waste is a word derived from *vastus*, the Latin for "unoccupied" or "desolate." A similar root word in Sanskrit means "wanting" or "deficient."

—Sacred Sepsis
Dr. Louis Godard and Dr. James Singer

CHAPTER

30

Jim wasn't feeling great but he had been released from the hospital.

God! Talk about undergoing the primitive. As soon as a nurse saw what he was trying to pass, they had him in surgery. Used to be such a worm came out under its own power and according to its own timetable. But they drugged it, zapped it, and pulled it out of his intestines and rectum as if he'd only swallowed a thread.

"Positively amazing," the doctor had told him after it was over. "By the way, you might find your insides a bit loose for a while. At least we didn't see too much damage."

Jim sighed, feeling very weak and sore. He shifted his sitting position, wishing they'd just let him stand. "I feel like I just survived one of my students' most popular curses."

The doctor cocked his head. "Oh? What would that be?"

"May you reap the full benefits of the e-coli burger at Fussy's Grill," Jim replied with only half a smile.

The doctor chuckled. "By which I take it *eat shit and die*?"

"You take it right."

"And you, sir, take it easy. And thank you for the article I will now write for the medical journals."

Jim didn't go home. He went straight to his office. He'd been trying to reach Myrtle since yesterday afternoon. Where was she? It wasn't like her not to have been back to check on him or to have at least paged him. Now more than ever he wanted to know about that document the priest had sent him.

He walked through the building. Several of the other profs' secretaries waved.

"You seen Myrtle?" he asked them.

"Not today. How are you feeling? We saw the paramedics take you away yesterday."

"Fine. The worm turned." He managed not to scowl. Although he did wince every time he was asked. All he wanted to do was put it behind him. Ouch.

The office was dark. He switched on the light, sat down at Myrtle's desk, went through the Rolodex to find the lab's telephone number.

"Document? We never received any document, Dr. Singer," he was told.

He argued with them a while. They checked and double-checked. Nope.

He saw a notation on her blotter. sewersybil

It made his skin scrawl. He hadn't seen that for a while, not since he'd taken her out of the subway tunnels a decade ago.

He called her apartment. The message she usually had on her answering machine was a friendly enough *can't come to the phone right now, leave your name and number and I promise...*

Now all he heard was a darkly whispered, "Sewersybil." S's stressed until sibilant. It made his butt cheeks clench, thinking of the worm snaking in his colon.

Had his feral child reverted?

++++++++++

Jim went to the tunnel where he'd found Myrtle years ago. It hadn't been easy climbing down from a proper platform, going away from the tracks toward darkness and stench, pretending he hadn't just had fifty feet of thin, living ribbon unraveled from his ass.

Something dove at his head before he'd even gone ten feet. He ducked and threw his arms up to protect himself. He saw this really weird bird—or was it a bird? It screeched and swooped at him again, flapping very close, staring at him.

For a moment Jim thought he'd gone insane. The face was too human, nothing like a bird or a bat or any other bug-chewed flying creature with more flea-shit than down in the feathers.

He thought the face reminded him of Myrtle. Thing from a nightmare, from some Baudelaire-esque delirium rash found in an opium pipe or green Absinthe bottle or malaria-tainted pussy.

"Myrtle?" he whispered, hardly able to form the words, as if his lips had suddenly frozen. No, bullshit. (Yeah, it *looks* like her...!)

It screeched loud enough to feel like a very long needle in both ears, skreed mournfully and long, beating its wings together until a cloud of greasy dust and ricey lice-sheddings plumed. As he started sneezing, it flew off down the tunnel.

He stood there a moment, watching it go, wondering if he ought to have stayed in the hospital for another day or two. Wonders and prodigies: this was what he'd seen lately. Visions which belonged in cave paintings or upon the scruffy murals in plebeian catacombs.

"I'm a sick, sick man," he told himself.

Where was everybody? The last time he'd been down here there were vagrants everywhere, sleeping or shooting up or rushing from an assortment of things, a few staring at terrible things he was glad he couldn't see. Nobody now.

Last time there had been folks from the world above-ground, from the light, traipsing past Myrtle's pictures, sipping bottled water or imported beer, making sure they didn't touch anything.

Where were they? The pictures, that is. He couldn't recall exactly where they'd been. He hoped he was in the right tunnel. Jim walked slowly in the dark, hand following the wall.

Then he found the beginning of where Myrtle had started drawing. Hey, her cartoons were gone, sort of. Only vague outlines remained, as if an attempt had been made to erase them. The things she'd written on them were still there. So were squiggles representing water, tracks, anything inanimate.

He almost stepped on the first body before he even realized there were two corpses. He jumped back from the burned one on the ground. It looked like the hungry homeless had been at it. He'd heard stories of cannibalism down here. He'd always just assumed it was an urban myth. Actually, the teeth marks didn't look like they came from a human bite. Maybe stray dogs then.

He'd also heard about kids dousing some poor guy with gasoline and then setting him alight. That one wasn't just urban legend.

The second body hung from the crude cross.

"Malvezzi," Jim said, not even realizing he was practically shouting it in surprise. "What the hell."

The Shit Detail. Yes, there was the ubiquitous quote written on the wall behind him in blood and shit. From Nietzsche, "Exhausted I see thee, by poisonous flies; bleeding I see thee, and torn at a hundred spots..."

Had Jim used it in the book? Yes. Not that it had anything to do with

269

sewage, but not everything in the book had a scatalogical term or meaning. Some merely dealt with death or darkness, a connection he'd been trying to make with waste. Now he wasn't sure he even knew what that connection was.

He hung his head, feeling responsible. How could he fail to feel this way? There were idiots out there who were treating *Sacred Sepsis* as if it were The Book Of Genesis. As if everything he'd added around the Epistle Of Saint Aureola were just that—an adjunct and servant-word to her message, auxiliary and subordinate in meaning and function to her story.

The priest had been disembowelled. Jim felt a flashback again to the time at historical Gettysburg, as a child, wanting to help the soldiers by putting their insides back where they belonged. And of the time the catacombs caved in and he'd wanted to save Louis.

Movement caught his eye, down the tunnel. A blonde wearing sunglasses, even though it was dark down there.

The woman from the flood in the Science Building!

Jim straightened up, took a deep breath. She was here. Maybe she was Aureola. Did she have anything to do with Malvezzi's murder?

Jim was sure she had. But, if she was Aureola, then she also had something to do with Louis' death.

He knew he couldn't just let her go on and on. He'd been partly responsible for letting her out and for drumming up business for her. She'd died before. Maybe she could die again.

Maybe Jim could kill her.

++++++++++

Jason was unafraid as he strutted down a street in Sheol's Ditch, feeling relieved now that Rose was gone. He hadn't realized what a stone she'd become around his neck. He flashed a grin into the windows of tawdry storefronts he passed, the muscles in his bare arms rippling even more in sun-warped glass, the barrel of his chest and the monster bulge in the crotch of his jeans creating an almost scarily-deformed silhouette. No one in their right mind would fuck with him. No one in their right mind ever had.

That gang of cranked-up losers who'd mocked him last week, then tried to take him on, hardly qualified as of-sound-minds. He'd made scarlet- and bowel-brown smears of them across the gray cement and soot walls of The Ditch. He'd dragged each one, bones shattered and pert near dead, to a different block of the two centuries old neighborhood. Then he wiped them creamin', bleedin', and shittin' across the local landmarks. Not erudite, no, but anything else would have been mere sophistry. His thoughts may have been raw existentialism but his actions more clearly cut a path for the pragmatic provocateur.

270

At any rate, it was done so everyone would know about it and so none could harbor a doubt. That to fuck with Jason Cave was to suffer a severe breach in good judgement and to have few prospects for a decent life expectancy. They had forgotten for a while, when he was off fighting in the war. Then as he'd traveled through Southeast Asia, South America, the entire of Africa, head-tripping on the varying cultural opinions of life and death, groin-tripping on exotic toys which caused out-of-body reactions based upon reflex and auto-suggestion. Making the most of the learning experience which was this—and every—incarnation. When he'd returned with his wife a year ago, he'd had to teach the home crowd all over. It was a lesson he meted out at regular intervals, to make certain no one forgot again.

A month ago, there had been that one undercover cop who'd owned a couple black belts himself. The narc had been as hard-muscled and swift as some Vin Diesel cum The Rock and Stone Cold Steve Austin cum 3D Incredible Hulk. But Jason had hung that pretty dude...bound and turkey-trussed...by his testicles from a lampost on the corner of Rilke and Buber Streets. Of course, the tender sacs weren't really designed to take all the weight of a couple hundred pounds. No more cum for the narc. With screams that were audible all the way to the dog races, the narc slowly tore free of his hefty pair, pieces of mottled scrotum flapping down like the tatters of an exploded zeppelin's balloon shell.

("Oh the humanity!" croaked some sarcastic kid, who'd been observing this from his mother's stoop. Until she started slapping the crap out of him and pulled him inside.)

(She'd spat at her son. "That's Jason Cave's handiwork, you stupid li'l bastard! For chrissakes, you want somebody to know you saw and say you're a witness? Get us both reamed, you retard?")

Six months ago there had been this girl, about thirteen or fourteen...

He was glad Rose hadn't been with him then—or she might have taken her for a houri—damn it. Still pissed him off when he thought about it.

...but stacked like Christmas. Cinnamon nipples and sharp cider twang cunt, the flesh of her belly soft as a butter pie crust. Some uptown lawyer decided to sue Jason on her comatose behalf when the D.A. said there wasn't enough evidence to prosecute. Mr. Acker's rectum had been tight before the cock but not after both upwardly mobile numchucks. His pale lips had evidentally never known the flavor of blood, excrement and sour sebacious gland seepings.

But all this was irrelevant. Jason had lately been thinking of good old days. When the streets had belonged to him and his colleagues. So many had vanished lately. And at first there had been rumors about the various mobs deciding to eliminate these basically unaffiliated, self-employed entrepreneur "rogues" from the shark pool. Some had suggested a secret government sting with a license to practice extreme prejudice. Others had even thought these radicals were being taken out by The Shit Detail. Hell, a few months ago, it had been theorized that Jason and his extremist cronies *were* The Shit Detail. Even he'd wondered if some of the more enlightened ones might be involved, considering the sayings which were left with the victims.

But he'd heard a woman had been nearby where several had been seen last. And this excited him. He hoped he would run into her. And if he did, would he recognize her?

Now being blonde didn't seem to fit in with the woman he'd followed into Cairo's cemetery. Yet she'd been heavily veiled, so he didn't know.

Most of them—Simone; Boreolo; Everson, the Vigilante of Love; even Big Garth—had believed in that place that Jason had actually seen. (They had all heard his story. From anybody else, they might have jeered.) The subject invariably arose whenever enough of them were assembled and drunk, drugged, sexed up. And wistful for the mythical place where they would be undisputed masters over souls and atoms in the fabled hematoma circus. Where they could on a whim recycle their slaves down to the rictus-pokers and rice worm-lickers and decomp-sop bucket wallowers until liquid was all that remained. Then they would ferment *that*.

She must be the djinn or ghoul or angel of such a place. Perhaps he'd called her up once, while messing around with paraphernalia from his earlier self: Crowley. He'd summoned her and not put her back properly. Maybe she'd been waiting for him, seeking him all this time. Maybe the stars had to be right again and had just become so.

Now here she was and it was the others who were benefiting from his magick, being led to the gate he'd longed to find open again.

This was what happened to Garth; Jason believed it. Garth had prepared to leave the house ahead of the police. Naturally he wanted to eliminate any witnesses against him, so he'd killed the geishas first. Trailed blood down the hallway, entered the gate while dropping the *netsuke*, vanished.

She must still be around. Surely she wouldn't go without finding Jason first. Her ultimate goal was to find him and take him to his world, where he would be God. Crowley had summoned her but she'd not taken him then. No, in that incarnation he hadn't been ready.

Jason knew the people on the street were watching him, trying to pretend they weren't. They wondered if he'd be next. Actually he was the last one left, out of the **Supermen**. They couldn't wait to get rid of him. And they must be curious as to whether or not he was shaking in his shoes. Because, of course, all their pea brains could conceive of was some mundane, mortal hit squad. At the most, the religious ones might think Satan was claiming his own.

So Jason Cave had to be scared, right? Waiting for IT to get him.

But these fools didn't get *it*. Just as they had never understood him. What he symbolized, what he *meant*.

Most regular people couldn't understand the obsession with violence.

Couldn't relate to simple adrenalin rush and complex emotional need. This was from a different realm indeed, the drive to be immersed in every level of a disparate biology, especially in its decline. Artificial or not, personal or not, it represented a release for the extra nth of emotion which such entities were bursting with—even if they might appear cold or without feeling or believe themselves to be empty.

No, this wasn't emptiness. It was surplus.

There was nothing vacant about a person with so much spleen and too many vividly visceral dreams to hold in. This was the ultra survivor, not necessarily of corporeal self but of ego. The super poet of bones, juggling with inexhaustible concepts of mortal philisophy that most "normal" citizens were too cowardly to consider.

Be afraid? Of *it*? Idiots. He'd seen Melanicus. He'd stood not ten feet from the police in the driving rain on the roof and they hadn't seen him, protected by that cloak of invisibility provided by magickal Nature for her **Superman**.

Now Jason flashed a meat-chomping smile at his image and said out loud to himself, "One does not find dread in the beast."

People overheard and, smelling the rank cow-innard iron on his breath, cringed away.

In a sudden fit of expounding, he quoted from *Thus Spake Zarathustra*, shouting at them, "Would that there came preachers of *quick* death!"

He bowed comically, first to the cowering rubes on the sidewalk and then to his rippled reflection in a thrift shop window, his head mirrored above a solemn, headless mannikin sporting a used, cheap black suit. It made him look like a preacher. Or an undertaker.

Jason chuckled. Yeah, if it could be possible to be an existential thug, then he guessed he was that. He'd contemplated for years the perverse nature of himself and others, even as he was in the act of committing outrage. Questioning his ephemeral motives for it as he felt someone's ribcage compress beneath the sole of a really supernal kick. Analyzing his feelings as he rammed a part of his anatomy (or a symbol for it: i.e. a bottle, broom handle, length of PVC pipe or rusty rebar) into a fleshy receptacle for his tormented euphoria. One had to question in order to learn. Jung had said, "I for my part prefer the precious gift of doubt, for the reason that it does not violate the virginity of things beyond our ken."

Jason's mantra was simpler. "Too full?"

Share the overflow.

Fill others.

The normals all thought, "Go away, mutant. This earth isn't for you."

Yet it was. In each raped increment of savage human history it was *his*. It had proved itself in every iota of man-unkind's brutal carnality to precisely belong to individuals just such as he. Man was indeed a mutation of the genus which had preceded it: increased cunning and dexterity providing the impetus to form it into a superbeast, a planetary dominant species.

The trouble with those regular folk was that they forgot they were animals, *super* animals but of a predatory mammality just the same. Jason didn't forget it, not for one second. Never.

He leered sideways at people going the other direction down the walk. Spotted several who filled him to brimming with impulses. An old lady he wanted to hang from a hook in the ceiling back at his apartment. To measure how long it would take gravity and pain to cascade those wrinkles to the floor. A young mother with milk-swollen mammaries he wanted to fuck between the breasts until cream gouted from both of them, until he could catch hers in the lips of his downturned face and her upturned one would drown in his. A too-handsome man of blue-black hair and beard so groomed and oiled it resembled a female pube. Jason wanted to gorge himself on pages from a Mapplethorpe portrait book, then crouch over the man's staked out body, shitting onto the wired-open jaws, listening to the dandy's wail of eating art.

Full! So full! Jason enjoyed his passion drooling from the corners of his mouth, sweating from his armpits, straining at the crotch of his jeans like a dog on a chain.

Damn, *this* was not emptiness. That feral carnivorous grin ogling back at him from his window reflections possessed nothing of the void. There was no tabula rasa there pleading to be written with redemption.

Nature deplored a vacuum and this was why She created beings like him. Like Big Garth, Boreolo, Everson, Simone.

He would show these vomit curds a thing or two. He was buzzin', out to prove something. Hot-wired. In preparation to walking The Ditch today to teach a few **Supermanic** lessons and to search for his mystery woman, Jason had himself a bong party. He'd first smoked some hashish, partly to honor Rose...even if she had betrayed him...and because it was through a mainly Mohammedan city that he'd first seen 'she' whom he believed to be the opener of the gate. (The Moslem troups of centuries past had faith after using hashish that they were invincible in battle. But this wasn't why Jason had used it. There was no dread in his Beast.)

Secondly, he'd smoked some crack, since he was looking for the crack in reality, where he'd step through to exchange his status as **Superman** for one as Superpower.

And, lastly, thinking of she who had dissolved into black, rich matter there in the dead's city, Jason had smoked some real shit, excreted by his ghoul or djinn or angel wife under the dark of the moon. Which, at that phase, resembled nothing less than a fecal pearl in a sky some demon or lord (Melanicus?) had defecated broken glass into. Such night had erupted in the smoke he'd drawn inside himself.

It hadn't been long since he'd consumed the *muzan-e*. He was so wired he knew folks probably saw blue teeth and sparks when he grinned. They were the real empty ones, without an honest erection or juicily lubed-up pud among them. Blank groins, hollow hammers, dreamless impotent nadas.

Big Garth, Boreolo, Everson, Simone had vanished. But a few bodies had been found. In such abominable condition that at first the fact that they *were* bodies had nearly been missed. For flesh, features, the proper arrangement of limbs (bonsai not being a consideration here)...the reality that they *were* or *had been* arms and legs...were so distorted, these might have been organic but alien lumps of tissue, fallen from the sky in the identical manner in which torrents of frogs, stones and twisted ganglia had been recorded by Charles Fort as dropping from heaven.

One man's manna...

These dead didn't drop from heaven. And whatever had been done to them to put them in such a state wasn't from any celestial program/pogrom: sin-punishing or otherwise.

Jason envied the raw ferocity in the damage he'd seen while using sharp elbows to force his way through any crowd gathered around one of these chunks. Even the teeth—dislodged and jumbled within pulp, many crushed to enamel powder—provided no clues save for the occasional inscribed signet ring—badly scratched from shards of bone, the steel balljoint some surgeon recognized as his own work, the part of a wallet sieved through a gloop of rotting stew that made it possible to guess that these gumbo delecti had been:

Thomas the pedantic pervert and glue-gun pederast;

Mae the chloroform-toting vampire wannabee, gourmet of the menstrual cocktail;

Rondi of the custom-made forceps—tonsils, tongues and peach-rind clitorises in his pockets, harvested from drunks and drug addicts unconscious on dung heaps. Not anyone he'd actually have to overpower.

If they'd not been ID'd as murder victims (or some kind of victims), Jason would've figured they had gone where the others had. To the fuck-pandemic paradise. But he guessed that they had not survived because they couldn't make the cut. To be *almost* **Supermen** wasn't sufficient. Such a place—and the woman who guarded it—would have no patience with weakness. It would do precisely as the corpses appeared to have suffered; it would masticate every inch and then hawk them out.

So Jason was unafraid. What did he have to fear? He was no mere child-snatching or drunk-rolling freak, only able to prey upon the helpless. Although he didn't turn aside practice opportunities when they availed themselves.

What was it Sartre said?

"The man who confesses that he is evil has exchanged his disturbing 'freedom from evil' for an inanimate character of evil; he *is* evil...he is what he is."

275

Jason felt sorry for those illiterate, uncultured punks. To not have read the philosophies was to never know the comfort of the buzz words for a violent *cogito*.

"I am evil," he confessed aloud to the old lady he wanted to impale upon the carcass hook. In his eruptive baritone to the young mother wheeling her pram. In hot spittle flecked with lunch's kidney tarts at the man of the pussy facial hair.

"I have also chosen to be terrifying," he added with a phlegm sputter and a steel bridgework rattle in his jaws, forehead popping a throbbing vein. It was a paraphrase of Sartre, putting the third person in a more emotive first.

"De-fuckin'-mentia, buddy," the bearded man guffawed. Obviously not a local.

Jason threw a hard left into the middle of the man's face. He felt the nose bone split like a line of walnut shells, knuckles sinking in with a satisfying squelch.

"Thank you very much," Jason replied as the fellow crumpled to the sidewalk, the jug-teratoid mommie and the shar-pei granny both pissing their bloomers.

Through the window of the dry cleaners next door Jason could see a clerk grabbing a phone to dial 911. The owner hastily snatched it away, saying, "My God, no! I've been in business here fourteen years. You wanna get me burned out?"

Jason smiled, passed by, then stopped in his tracks. He'd seen someone enter a bar, wearing swinging raven fringe. There was a red-headed man leering from a hardware store, red not only in his hair but comprising his entire head. A kid peddled past on a bike, his boombox playing, "I am the god of hellfire...!" Then he saw the sleep place, beds of all kinds. A mattress in the window had two dead hippies on its tie-dyed sheets; they were nothing more than swill and sump.

Jason held his breath and looked around. There, up on the corner where the street folded through a short alley which ran behind a beat poetry/coffee club cum soul food restaurant. Blank verse, caffeine jitters, greasy gestalt, no more cum for animas in aspic. It was the blonde with the sunglasses.

At least, it was some blonde wearing sunglasses. It was August. There were millions of those.

But this one drew his stare as he panted, wanting to scratch an itch spreading down to that chained dog in his jeans. He didn't need to see her in severe Moslem garb. He didn't need the fragrance of patchouli. He didn't need to be pursuing her through ancient crypts which smelled of thousands of years of corruption.

Damn, but she had a beautiful mouth. He moved closer, a venal Icarus, wax wings melting because he flew too close to the perfect orifice. Words slipped out of it, spoken to him? He hadn't heard them clearly, only the purr of a cat, the metallic thrumble of golden gongs, the gurgle-music of a slowly spinning waterspout.

Her skin glistened as if there had been a thundershower when he wasn't looking. Her face was pale—obviously she wasn't the outdoor type, nor was she into tanning salons. Her cheekbones were high, tapering plains to a bone china teacup of a chin. Her long blonde hair clung to her body like wet rainforest leaves and vines.

Jason really wanted to see those eyes. A woman like that—her eyes could suck you in. Even more than the maelstrom mouth or simoon sump of vortex vagina.

He'd actually gouged a chick's eye out once. Then tried to fuck the socket. Couldn't get more than his tip in. An exercise in hot frustration and bone-limited ecstasy.

But this wasn't somebody he would be fucking. This was an *entity*. His previous self, Crowley, had summoned her. He believed this.

"Show me the place," he demanded as he came close to her.

She didn't even ask him, "what place?" That would be a waste of time and fate. This meeting had been pre-arranged. He felt an enormous rush, every second of each preceding incarnation leading up to this moment. Fuck you, Rose. Didn't need you after all. Keep your cored-out, strung-up, licey/crabby/sand flea-bitten houris.

She nodded and whispered, "Aralu."

And there it was! In front of him, rising up from the sidewalk in a shaft of haze no more than four-foot square. And yet he could see deep into it. It had no horizons, just rocks/cliffs/slabs and steeples of stone. No point in perspective where land and sky drew a line in eternity's sand, each daring the other to cross.

He saw Simone, Boreolo, Everson. He even saw Big Garth. But they weren't masters. They were sufferers, crawling on their bellies, being put through their own paces. There was the red-headed man; everywhere were red-headed men. (Others must have seen this place in the past—without entering. It must have been where the idea came from that devils were red.) One of them trotted up to the porthole, smiling and waving at Jason. Then he spun around, bent over, and wiggled his ass. There, plugging the anus was the tip and about four inches of an enormous black penis. The demon reached back and yanked it out, showing veins and shreds dangling from the base of it. A gout of dark blood shot out behind it. And then other things began to rush out as well. A torrid river of matter that made Jason step back, pressing against a dingy wall behind a Chinese herb shop, the Dumpster nearby reeking of ripe ginger root and bull testicles. He leaned away, even though none of it overflowed the boundaries of the threshold.

Streaming out of the red-headed torturer came lumps of tissue. Things with pumping arteries and outside giblets of sudsy pink organs. Little animals so twisted they might have been any or all of a dozen different species. Miniature malformed people, blind, inside-out in part, membranous pasty flesh in sticky goldfish fins making them appear to be liquifying as they swam out of him. Shadowy horrors of living disembodied heads gargling piss and monster turds with opal eyes. Terra cotta statues and bronze bracelets, a Renaissance tapestry unfurling in unspeakable filth, a Raggedy Ann doll with so many holes stabbed into it that black water hissed through, crucifixes bent into swirls like Celtic knotwork, Boreolo's specialized tattoo needles, the highly rococo skeleton key from Everson's cage of bones. A scalp with a samurai's tightly oiled queue hanging from it and a severed hand with the tattoo of a Willendorf Venus on it, headless, limbless. Part of a boot of curiously wrinkled leather, like scrotum skin or fetal tissue. But it was no longer red. The feculent waters had stained it ebon.

Jason's beast actually felt dread. But not for his friends. Only for the illusion he might have dragged around with him all his life. He dreaded having wasted himself on a lie. Damn that No Man kid. He was glad he'd crushed him when he had the chance.

"This isn't right..." he stammered. "This place, I'm supposed to be a god there."

"God is dead," she told him. "Or haven't you heard?"

Jason breathed hard, feeling light-headed. Was there no special El Dorado for fuckers like him? Or were there just places where the shit got flushed? He hated it but he was almost whimpering as he insisted, "Then this isn't my gate. There has to be another. *Mine*."

She nodded. "Yes, there is another place where you have been and shall again be the tormentor of the weak."

He gusted a sigh of relief. He knew it!

Jason grabbed her and lifted her into the air. "Then show me it," he told her, tired of being played with. "Take me there or I'll shake you apart."

And he did begin shaking her, raging, desperate. Her body felt loose as if it had no skeleton, as if it were full of wet sand or wilted flowers.

A man came from the other end of the alley and tackled him. Some skinny old guy.

++++++++++

Jim had seen everything in the gateway. Enough to know she was not Aureola. She'd been who he'd first thought she was, having felt her presence on Mt. Koshtan and in San Inmundo and even in the catacombs. She was real. The goddess of shit. He was thrilled and terrified.

But then this monster of a guy attacked her. Not that he could really hurt her, could he?

Jim wouldn't wait to find out. He rushed to defend her. Too bad he wasn't much of a fighter.

The man dropped the woman as Jim knocked him to the ground. Then he stood up and started kicking the professor. Jim couldn't even get two seconds to try to protect himself, to go fetal with his arms over his head. He felt a size thirteen boot crash through his ribs. Then the man fell onto his knees and grabbed him by the hair, seething into his face, spitting foam and mucous at him. "If thus spake Zarathustra were spoken thusly, what thus would be the Zarathustrian speak?"

Huh? The man was killing him *and* asking him a riddle? Jim tried to move his arms and legs, to swim away from this guy. The woman must surely have escaped by now. Or had gone wherever such a goddess would go—not to the nearest phone to get help but to the past or the future or a crack in distant rocks.

The man growled, "Well, thusly I'll tell thee of a spike of Zarathustrian speak as it was spoken to me!"

Jim felt as he had after the cave-in, when the force of it had blown him right out into the field. He knew he had some broken bones but he couldn't tell exactly where because every neuron in his body screamed at once. And it did no good to try to wriggle away or cry for help or try to assess his injuries. His chances of survival were nil as he read the murder—no, the *annihilation*—in this man's eyes.

The guy continued mouthing at him, spouting nonsense. No! Spouting Nietzsche (so Jim knew he must be hallucinating this), "And this was what was spoken to me. 'Many die too late and a few die too early. The doctrine still sounds strange: *die at the right time!*'"

And then the beast laughed like this was the wittiest remark ever to punctuate a senseless killing with. He brought his fist down square into Jim's chest, right over the heart. It sounded like a hammer on a cheap anvil.

++++++++++

Jason nodded, satisfied, feeling the tremors pass through the old guy's body. The fool was not quite dead but it wouldn't be long. He'd have seconds—maybe even a couple minutes—to reflect on having interrupted an amazing event.

He looked up. The blonde was still there. She'd stood back up and was watching him.

"I want my place," he told her, bugging out his eyes, flexing his fingers. "You say I have been and shall be. Give it to me."

She shrugged one shoulder. "Yes. Mine isn't the only reincarnation from the sewer."

She slipped down her glasses. No whites or pupils or tiny inside corner tear ducts. Only. Spinning. Dark. Water.

++++++++++

Dread in the Beast

Dorien opened the lost place.

The beast looked in and cried in delight, "My own procession of the damned!"

He eagerly plunged through the steaming gateway. His entrance created a pull. Dorien didn't try to fight it too much. She knew she would have to enter. But before she did, she grabbed the dying professor's hand and squeezed it hard.

+++++++++++

"The sleek Brazilian jaguar
Does not in its arboreal gloom
Distil so rank a feline smell
As Grishkin in a drawing room.
And even the Abstract Entities
Circumambulate her charm;
But our lot crawls between dry ribs
To keep our metaphysics warm."

—T.S. Eliot
quoted in *Sacred Sepsis*
Dr. Louis Godard and Dr. James Singer

CHAPTER
31

Lights flashed on, motion-detection triggered, like tall contact-seeking lightning.

Dorien was in the underground where the lost cluttered the walkways, going out and down for miles, for light years maybe.

(Dark Years.)

They moved a little, like children turning within wombs inside comatose mothers. They moved like very old people, those with Alzheimers who awake in wheelchairs or beds in homes for throwaways, not knowing who they are and too frail to do more than shudder.

She'd managed to pull the professor with her. He wasn't far away. But he wasn't moving, even a little. He lay there very still, face down. He must have died anyway. Maybe no one could get there unless they died first—unless they were killed. Dorien couldn't really tell if he might be only alive and badly hurt, because down here she had no special power.

Tears on her face. Yes, she always wept in this place. For

the lost. And she cried, too, because this man had tried to help her—even if she hadn't needed it—and he'd been murdered for it.

Dorien knew she was also crying because she'd thought somehow that he was going to be able to help. It was why she'd grabbed his hand. She couldn't help these poor children of hers, so she'd hoped he would. Not that she had any basis for thinking it. Goddesses apparently weren't without their faults. Not omniscient, that much was certain.

She heard the rumbling of the drain auger, ratchety echo ricocheting off the feculent graffiti that stained the walls.

"Give thy place to me, O Jesus; thine aeon is passed."

"Not the height, it is the declivity that is terrible! The declivity, where the gaze shooteth *downwards*, and the hand graspeth *upwards*."

> "some like it shot
> and some like it hung
> and some like it in the twat
> nine months young."

> "Self-executioner!
> crammed between two nothings."

"'existence' is a rhythm of heavens and hells: that the damned won't stay damned...salvation only precedes damnation."

When Dorien saw the plumber coming and could see who he was now, even beneath the unspeakable filth, even swaddled in his stench-mask and rain poncho...she understood who had written the things on the walls. Words from Aleister Crowley, Frederich Neitzsche, e.e.cummings, Charles Fort. Nothing ever of his own, only quotes from others. He went by the name of Jason in his most recent life.

When had he done these? He'd only just come in ahead of her, hadn't he? Or was time totally fucked up here and he'd been in this place for a long while already?

She saw "the snake" in his pants, emerging from the fly, metal jerking savage whirligig as he approached some teenaged kid who was lying next to Dr. Singer. The kid groaned and tried to sidewind herself away but couldn't move more than an inch or two.

Jason giggled beneath his mask, bloodshot eyes ogling the girl as he knelt and reached down to roll her over, then to pull up her skirt. He kept repeating, "Do what I wilt...do what I wilt...oh fuck it, do what *I will*."

This was when the professor suddenly came up on his side, threw his arms around the plumber's legs, and pushed him off the walkway. There was a nasty splash and a cry of outrage. Jason had submerged but quickly bobbed back up. His mask had come off and he sputtered waste material.

"Old man, I'm gonna grind you out next."

He swam to the edge of the walk and began to climb up.

"Oh, no you don't," Jim growled, jumping to his feet, kicking out to strike the plumber under the chin, actually lifting him another half a foot before the man went back into the sewage. "I've already had one worm up my ass."

Jason began to swim powerfully down the conduit, trying to reach a ladder at the intersection of two tunnels. Singer saw where he was going and began running that direction, sprinting over the bodies of the lost upon the walk. He mumbled and muttered apologies every time he stepped on a hand or accidentally kicked somebody as he stumbled trying to hurry. And as he passed them, they called out plaintively, "Don't leave us!"

+++++++++++

Jim wasn't even taking time to ponder what place this might be. He'd seen that monstrous excuse for a dick, heard its jarring vibration. It dripped blood and flesh and other things he didn't even want to think about. And he wasn't going to let this freak out of the water to demonstrate its uses. He made for that intersection where he saw an enormous wheel, like some kind of metal gate valve. Surely what it was, a control for a valve. Would he be strong enough to turn it? He wasn't in that great a shape anymore, was he? (Was he, in fact, dead? That would really be pretty lousy shape.) He was an old guy, no longer fit from working at sites anymore. (Actually, he'd been fat for so long, he wasn't sure he'd ever been fit. And when he'd thought he'd finally been in great condition, it turned out he'd only lost weight because Myrtle had slipped some kind of tapeworm into him.) He had carpal tunnel syndrome from doing the teaching and writing stint for so long.

He made it to the wheel before the freak with the auger cock reached the ladder. Damn, there was so much water and muck, he found it hard to believe the guy didn't dissolve outright. Didn't gag and go down strangling.

"Give me the strength," Jim said to himself—no, to *someone*, any power at all. "Please, let me do this."

He grunted and leaned into the wheel, grabbing it with both hands, straining his arms and shoulders. He wiped the repulsive slime on his hands off on his trousers and shirt, then grasped the wheel again, moaned and squealed and croaked with the effort. Felt it jerk in his fingers as the veins in his wrists and forearms and forehead popped. It occured to him he had no idea what this wheel even controlled. *Please, don't let it be only the air conditioning.*

The freak had come alongside the ladder. He was reaching out for it...

And then the wheel turned, practically spinning, screeching until Jim winced from the pain in his ears. He turned it again. Again.

Water at the intersecting tunnels began to swirl, lots of it, being sucked into what Jim guessed to be a big drain beneath. He positioned himself at the top of the ladder, ready to kick again if the man managed to climb up. But the freak was being pulled back with the black, brown and yellow vortex.

++++++++++

Jason heard the roar as the huge drain swallowed the funnel of water. He felt three years old again, messed up on acid his folks had given him, tripping out as he stood over the toilet, flushing it over and over. *Whoosh!* Scream. *Whooshsh!* Scream.

They had pinched him black and blue, slapped him, tweaked his little dinger, yanked out some of his hair by bloody babysoft roots, getting nothing out of him but *Whwhooooshsh!* Scream. Unable to look at them, seeing only the swirl of the awful water.

"What did you see in there?" Mom and Dad had eventually asked him. But he'd never said.

He hadn't thought of it in thirty years—or had he always kept it in the back of his mind? Not the flushing and the couple of gallons vanishing. What he'd seen.

A beast bigger than he would ever be, bigger than the black moon, bigger than the Prince of Dark Bodies. It rendered everything else into nothing, into whimpering/puling/puking nightmares of absolute zero. If it scratched off all that was outside and peeled and flayed until it reached original identity, what did it have to play with? Faceless fears and all the refuse it could eat.

He tried to shriek now, hearing the granddaddy of all thunderous *Whwhwhwhooooooooooooshshshshsh!*-es! But the impure waters filled him up, bursting through his seams from a forceful gravity acting on it through him. He went down, sucked through the drain, squandered and jettisoned.

++++++++++

Would he reincarnate again as he had so many times before?
Dorien didn't think so.

She watched as the professor turned the wheel the other way, grumbling that it was harder to close the thing than it had been to open it.

Then he paused as if listening.

"Waterfalls?" she heard him whisper. "Goes so far, infinity's own underground."

He crouched down. Some of the lost were sobbing near where he'd manhandled the wheel. He told them gently, "Hey, it's okay. Don't be afraid. Freak's gone."

"Are you alive?" the goddess asked him.

He looked up at her. He stood and patted himself down. "I'm no longer injured. I was dying, I remember that—oh, so very clearly. There was a whole lot broken inside me. I'll admit I must have been a bag of glass. If this is all healed, then I must be dead, right?"

He glanced around at the slightly moving bodies. He blinked, overwhelmed. "What do I do now?" he wondered.

She gestured to the lost and to the uncountable tunnels and conduits. "Tend to the works, help the children. You're the new plumber."

She turned to go, becoming smoky at her edges.

"What about you?" Jim wanted to know.

She might have sounded tired if she'd been human. But she wasn't, so her voice was simply worn-away stone. "I have to go back. I'm always going back. The shit never stops."

Charlee Jacob has published some sixteen years in the horror and fantasy genres. Her publishing credits include more than 700 poems and around 240 stories. Her novels include THIS SYMBIOTIC FASCINATION, HAUNTER, VESTAL, and her novel DREAD IN THE BEAST won the Bram Stoker award for best novel of 2005. Now fully disabled, she has taken up painting as one of her forms of physical therapy.

"THE PRESERVE MAY VERY WELL BE ONE OF THE BEST DEBUT NOVELS I'VE EVER HAD THE PLEASURE OF READING. THERE ARE NO ROUGH SPOTS, NO FUMBLES, NO MISSTEPS. LESTEWKA DEFTLY GUIDES BOTH HIS CHARACTERS AND THE READER, WEAVING A PLOT PACKED WITH CRISP DIALOGUE, PAGE-TURNING ACTION, AND SURPRISES AND TWISTS WITH EVERY CHAPTER."
—BRIAN KEENE REVIEWING FOR HELLNOTES, BRAM STOKER AWARD WINNING AUTHOR OF THE RISING AND TERMINAL

In the summer of 1967, seven men, members of an elite combat unit, embarked on a covert operation in the jungles of Vietnam. Two died. The survivors were forever changed.

Twenty years later, the remaining unit members receive a letter from an anonymous benefactor, along with a check for $50,000 and a promise of more to follow—if they agree to one final mission. Their task is simple: journey to the wilds of northern Canada to track down and kill three escaped convicts. The convicts are starving and unarmed. Easy money. A cakewalk.

But they have no idea what lays in wait on the snow-topped tundras and in the dark forests of the frozen north. Waiting with sharp teeth and slitted eyes and an old score to settle.

They have no idea.
But they will.
Soon.
They have entered...

THE PRESERVE

"UNRELENTING, EROTIC, AND
THRILLINGLY PERVERSE."

—DOUGLAS CLEGG
AUTHOR OF *GOAT DANCE*,
NIGHTMARE CHRONICLES,
BREEDER AND *NAOMI*

THE CLASSIC EDWARD LEE EROTIC HORROR NOVEL
IS NOW AVAILABLE IN A SIGNED TRADE PAPERBACK
FOR $19.95 + $5 S&H
FROM NECRO PUBLICATIONS
CREDIT CARD ORDERS CALL: 407-443-6494
OR ORDER ONLINE AT WWW.NECROPUBLICATIONS.COM

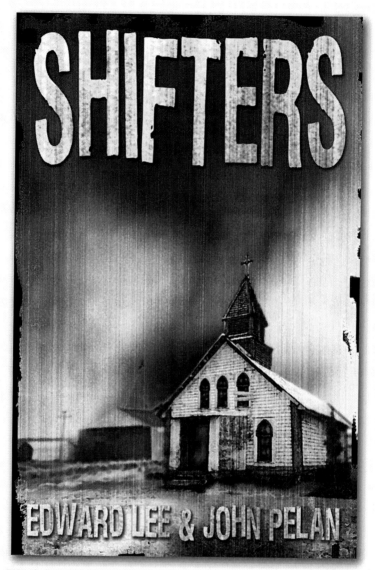